W9-BSK-373

THE BEST LEGAL MINDS . . .

Philip Friedman in "Roads" tells a harrowing tale of murder in the first degree . . . and mercy.

Grif Stockley sends his series lawyer Gideon Page into a messy "Divorce," where passion and violence skew the final judgment.

Lisa Scottoline uses her tale "Carrying Concealed" to remind us that lawyers are also human beings . . . more or less.

Michael A. Kahn enters a Chicago judge's chambers for a revealing deliberation—and revenge in "Cook County Redemption."

Jay Brandon reminds us in "Stairwell Justice" of Lenny Bruce's observation that "the only justice in the halls of justice is in the halls."

Phillip M. Margolin puts an attorney on talk radio in "The Jailhouse Lawyer" to tell about the most brilliant lawyering he ever saw . . . by a defendant.

And **William Bernhardt**, with pithy commentary and even a lawyer joke or two, puts it all together and adds "What We're Here For," a tale that sends lawyer Ben Kincaid into civil court after justice, his way. . . .

THE BEST . . .
LEGAL BRIEFS

THE BEST LEGAL FICTION.
DON'T MISS IT.

LEGAL BRIEFS

STORIES BY TODAY'S BEST
LEGAL THRILLER WRITERS

Edited by William Bernhardt

A DELL BOOK

Published by
Dell Publishing
a division of
Random House, Inc.
1540 Broadway
New York, New York 10036

The stories in this book are works of fiction. Names, characters, places,
and incidents are the products of the authors' imaginations or are used
fictitiously. Any resemblance to actual persons, living or dead, events,
or locales is entirely coincidental.

If you purchased this book without a cover you should be aware that this
book is stolen property. It was reported as "unsold and destroyed" to the
publisher and neither the author nor the publisher has received any
payment for this "stripped book."

Copyright © 1998 by William Bernhardt

All rights reserved. No part of this book may be reproduced or transmitted in
any form or by any means, electronic or mechanical, including photocopying,
recording, or by any information storage and retrieval system, without the
written permission of the Publisher, except where permitted by law. For
information address: Doubleday, 1540 Broadway, New York, New York.

The trademark Dell® is registered in the U.S. Patent and Trademark Office.

ISBN: 0-440-22571-X

Reprinted by arrangement with Doubleday

Printed in the United States of America

Published simultaneously in Canada

June 1999

10 9 8 7 6 5 4 3 2 1

OPM

CONTENTS

Introduction

IF EVERYONE HATES LAWYERS SO MUCH, WHY ARE THEY BUYING OUR BOOKS?

Hey, know why lab techs have started using lawyers instead of rats in their experiments?

Chances are you do. Lawyer jokes are everywhere—they're even more pervasive than lawyer books. Lawyers have replaced ethnic groups and rival sports teams as the principal basis for juvenile humor. People who would never dream of telling ethnic jokes heartily tell and retell "lawyer jokes" without feeling the least remorse about classifying thousands of people as "bad" just because they are members of a group.

How can they get away with this?

Well, they get away with it because everyone hates lawyers, at least if you believe the media—the comedians looking for an easy laugh or the politicians looking for a quick round of applause. The reasons for this negative public sentiment are not hard to understand. Journalistic coverage of legal matters is atrocious. Court TV gives America a preposterously skewed vision of the justice system; it consistently chooses the most atypical, sensationalistic cases for presentation. Supreme Court decisions are usually reported in the most conclusory fashion—a result with no explanation of the deliberation or precedent that led to it. As a result, the decisions often seem illogical and inexplicable.

Although most people understand that in an adversary system, defendants are entitled to legal counsel, many are outraged if the lawyer representing a defendant is successful. And of course, it is an inherent truth of any adversary system that if one side wins, the other loses. That means in every civil lawsuit there will be at least one litigant who walks away grumbling that the system doesn't work and lawyers are all crooks. In fact, since most lawsuits are settled before trial—meaning both sides compromise and neither gets everything it wanted—it is not unusual for both sides to leave the courthouse grumbling.

The American public has come to perceive the courtroom not as a place where truth emerges but where disputes are resolved, usually according to the talents of the lawyers. It is this sense of grayness, this absence of clear-cut lines of right and wrong, that has made many legal novels, such as those by Jay Brandon and Richard North Patterson, so popular. And it is also what has made the public opinion of lawyers so dismal.

As the author of several legal-themed novels, this concerns me. After all, if no one can stand lawyers, you wouldn't expect people to be too keen to read about them. And yet, time and again, the bestseller lists have been filled by the contributors to this book—John Grisham and Phillip Margolin and Steve Martini, just to name a few—all lawyers writing about lawyers. I initially wrote about the law and lawyers, not because of any market trend (which didn't exist yet), but because my wife said I should write about what I know, and that was all I could come up with. I never imagined people would be as intrigued by legal drama as the bestseller lists and Court TV and O. J. Simpson have demonstrated they are.

So if everyone hates lawyers so much, why are they reading our books?

I believe there are several reasons. Our society has become increasingly complex, and as a result, each of us is increasingly dependent on others for survival. As recently as fifty years ago, it was possible to live with very little contact with others; today it is a near impossibility. We all interact more, and the nature of humanity being what it is, interaction breeds disputes. In past generations, these disputes were usually resolved by other institutions—churches, families, community groups. Today people invariably turn to lawyers; the universal, seemingly automatic response to any perceived wrong is "Let's sue!"

This cannot be blamed only on lawyers. I have to laugh when I hear people talk about how "lawyers" are always filing lawsuits. They seem to forget that, in most instances, it is a "civilian," a client, who has approached a lawyer about filing a lawsuit. The lawyer is doing only what he has been asked to do. Lawyers themselves, knowing what they do about how the system works, are typically reluctant to file suits on their own behalf.

Courtrooms have also, in the last fifty years or so, become a cauldron for the shaping of national values. Courts have been called on to resolve disputes of moral or even religious significance—abortion rights, sexual harassment, discrimination based upon race or gender or sexual preference. Previous generations would have said such issues were inappropriate for judicial treatment; today the courts have the final word. As the influence of other social institutions has faded, courtrooms have filled the gap. Is it any wonder people are curious about the inner workings of the judiciary, when so many critical questions are decided there?

Another reason for the increased interest in legal matters stems from the growth of government—which has intensified the public interaction with lawyers and lawsuits. Modern government is increasingly meddlesome; private citizens are either restrained by lawyers or forced to hire lawyers to hold off (or circumvent) a barrage of government regulation. The fact that most politicians are lawyers has not done any good for their reputation, either. Since people are forced to interact with lawyers, it is only natural that they should want to know more about them, that they should want to understand better how the system works.

In the years since my first novel was published, it has become apparent to me that many people have a genuine desire to better comprehend the legal process. The truth is, most people are not the see-it/hear-it/believe-it drones television believes them to be. They want to get beyond the superficial media clichés and learn what it is lawyers and judges do, what really goes on in courtrooms, what's happening behind the scenes at sidebars and in chambers.

Enter the eleven authors who have contributed to the anthology you now hold in your hands. Each of them has explored the world of law and lawyers, bringing his or her own viewpoint and unique insight to what seems an almost boundless arena. What should initially strike readers of this anthology is the enormous variety of theme, style, and content. Lawyer books may seem to all have the same cover art, but between the covers there are worlds of difference. Although each is brilliant in its own way, the dark, almost noirish world of Grif Stockley's Gideon Page is far distant from the brighter, friendlier world of Michael A. Kahn's Judge Harry

Stubbs. Phillip Margolin's avuncular Monte Bethune, spinning his war stories on talk radio, seems worlds apart from Jay Brandon's scrappy "stairwell lawyer," Helen Myers. And the dark highways of Philip Friedman's haunted protagonist must be in a different universe altogether than that inhabited by Lisa Scottoline's lawyer and family man, Tom Moran.

Not that these tales are restricted to federal judges and powerhouse lawyers. Jeremiah Healy's story features John Francis Cuddy, a private investigator, but one who has much to do with lawyers—as did the author, a former trial lawyer and law professor. My story features Ben Kincaid, the idealistic, barely-scraping-by lawyer of my seven-and-counting *Justice* novels. Since the novels have typically focused on criminal cases, I took this opportunity to write about a civil trial—but one that turns out to be not all that civil.

One advantage of an anthology like this is the opportunity it provides novelists to do something other than what they do in their novels. In Steve Martini's tale, we discover the author's talent for humor—all too rarely evidenced in his novels. Richard North Patterson displays a gift for evocation of character and incident in the short form—without the novelist's luxury of unlimited pages—in his tale of a young lawyer's coming-of-age. And John Grisham, freed from the plot constraints of the thriller, reveals a gift for character delineation and crystalline prose in "The Birthday," a story that could easily have been published in any literary journal in this country.

Have these authors' legal novels influenced public opinion of the judicial system? I know they have. I sat on an airplane with a woman who held one of Philip Friedman's novels gripped tightly in her hands, flipping one page after another, underlining the legal terms she didn't know so she could look them up later. I know a judge who keeps Richard North Patterson's novels in his chambers, to help him "keep things in perspective." I chatted at a book-signing with a disillusioned couple who cited John Grisham's novels as "proof" of how corrupt the legal system has become.

I could just as easily mention a dozen other examples. The connecting thread is this: those readers became better informed, more knowledgeable, and perhaps even more understanding about the American justice system as a result of what they read in these novels.

I also can't help but note the frequency with which the word "justice" appears in the titles and text of the stories in this volume. Although I initially took this as a personal tribute (my seven Ben Kincaid novels have all been titled *Something-or-Other Justice*), I now think it may indicate something greater. Crime fiction has always been concerned with right and wrong; when the detective apprehends the murderer, there is a sense that the world has been reclaimed from chaos, that order has been reestablished. These tales may take that idea even further, as the characters struggle to understand not simply right and wrong, but *justice*—a far more difficult, elusive concept. This desire for justice in a world that often seems unjust in the extreme is shared not only by lawyers but by most contemporary Americans—and that may be yet another reason for the current popularity of legal fiction.

Having been a trial lawyer for ten years, I would be the first to admit the system is not perfect. But I don't believe generic condemnations ("The system doesn't work" or "Lawyers are all crooks") do anyone any good. Cynicism is easy, and totally unproductive. If we are to reform the system, we must take a hard look at what actually happens so we can conceive useful, meaningful proposals for change. Obviously, the "teaching" quotient is not the only, or even necessarily the most important, aspect of these novels. But the truth is, most readers are very intelligent people, and often the books they favor most are those that enlighten as well as entertain.

People ask me whether I think legal novels will remain popular. Well, nothing retains "fad" status forever, but I don't see the public interest in law and lawyers passing away any time soon. Our world is more complex than it has ever been, and people are still looking for answers, for solutions. There will always be some who seek to understand the machinery of our society, the wheels and cogs that turn behind the scenes, and who believe that lawyers have the inside scoop on these secrets. Indeed, many believe that lawyers are the ones cranking the gears, and thus are the only ones who can make the wheels turn for them, who can set things right. As long as this is true, people will be interested in novels that, at least for the welcome respite of a few hours, make them believe that justice is still possible.

And for those of you who are scanning for the punch line, here it is: lab techs have replaced rats with lawyers because they don't get so attached to lawyers. And after all, there are some things a rat just won't do.

—WILLIAM BERNHARDT

The recent surge in lawyer fiction has given us many memorable protagonists, but few have been rendered with as much heartfelt emotion and bald-faced honesty as Grif Stockley's Gideon Page, the lawyer featured in several Stockley novels and this short story. Get ready to enter the murky world of Gideon Page—where "truth" is an abstract concept and nothing is precisely what it seems.

The Divorce

GRIF STOCKLEY

"Have you gone to the courthouse and gotten an order of protection?" I ask the woman sitting across from me after she takes off her sunglasses. Lydia Kennerly has a black eye that almost seems painted on her face by a makeup artist. Purple, blue, green. Women. I'm surprised more men aren't killed by them.

"I don't know what that is, Mr. Page," she says, her voice weepy. According to our receptionist, Julia, she has been crying since she showed up in the waiting room an hour ago. Primarily a criminal defense attorney, I'm not a big fan of domestic relations cases, but like urine trying unsuccessfully to ease past a swollen prostate, my cash flow has been reduced to a trickle this past month, and so I've brought her on back to my office instead of pawning her off onto my best friend, Dan Bailey, who seems to specialize more and more these days in spouse abuse.

I explain that a woman (or theoretically a man, for that matter) can get the personnel in the chancery clerk's office to help her fill out a petition alleging domestic abuse, and a judge will sometimes sign an ex parte order kicking the abuser out of the house without even initially seeing her. A hearing where the defendant gets to tell his side of the story will be set, but she can represent herself, and, if successful, get everything from child support to a restraining order that will last for months.

"I want a divorce, and I can pay you," she says firmly, her jaw clenching beneath her makeup. "Besides,

I'm afraid of Al, Mr. Page. He's very manipulative. He can wrap a cop around his finger in five seconds. You have to see him to believe it."

Now that she's brought up the subject of money, I'm quick to tell her, "This can be an expensive proposition if I have to represent you in a contested proceeding."

For an answer she reaches into a purse beside her and extracts five $100 bills. "Will this get me started?" she asks, her brown eyes fluttering out of control, as if I am going to reach across the desk and slap her.

"Sure," I say, and take her money. In most of the cases that come across my desk, this kind of work is a crap shoot. I may never see another penny, but I haven't seen that kind of cash in over a week, since I represented a nickel-and-dime drug dealer who got busted for possession of marijuana. Besides, she is not badly dressed and may be loaded, for all I know. In probably only her early thirties. She is wearing one of those little summer matching outfits that I see advertised in Julia's catalogs up front. The blue dress hugs her figure, which, now that I let my eyes stray from her face, is exquisite. She must be a size five.

America is becoming a nation of polar bears, and I include myself in the population. I promise myself each summer I will lose weight and keep it off, but my good intentions have a shelf life of about a quart of milk. I weighed myself this morning and got the bad news that I am up to 190. Tiger Woods, the only topic of conversation these days on our end of the sixteenth floor of the Layman Building where I share space and expenses with five other lawyers, weighs thirty pounds less and, at six-two, is three inches taller. Of course, I console myself with the knowledge that he is thirty years younger (if that is a consolation). Lydia Kennerly, on the other hand, looks as if she could practically fit in one of those scales they weigh tomatoes on in supermarkets. I haven't seen spouse abuse in any diet books, but it could have a chapter all its own.

I spend the next forty-five minutes getting all the basic information I need, and have her sign my retainer agreement. Lydia Kennerly has no kids, which is a plus. If this guy is as big an asshole as she claims, she could divorce him but never get rid of him if they'd had children. In Arkansas only four months (we have a sixty-day residency requirement for divorce), she claims to like us and wants to stay. She had originally moved from North Carolina to help nurse a diabetic aunt who lives out in the county, but who has gotten better. I suspect it was to get away from her husband, Al, who followed her out two months ago. A bookkeeper, she is now looking for work. Her husband sells cars but isn't working now, which comes as no shock. Apparently the money is coming from the aunt, who is rewarding my client for her services. She and Al have signed a six-month lease on a house in the southwest part of the city. "Can you go stay with your aunt until he calms down?" I ask, having learned from experience that abusive husbands are rarely happy the day they are served with orders of protection or divorce papers.

"I can't bother her with this," Ms. Kennerly says emphatically. "I can stay at a motel for a couple of days."

I suggest the battered women's shelter, but she wrinkles up her nose. Frankly, I don't blame her. As necessary as they are, those places can't be a lot of fun. It is also another sign my client can pay me the five thousand dollars we have agreed upon if he fights it tooth and nail, and I'm not going to discourage her. Several of the details she gives me are vague, but that is not all that unusual. If all you can focus on is whether you can escape having your face rearranged or worse, it is hard to make a list of the furniture.

"How violent is he going to get?" I ask, after I have an inventory of the property and the debts. They don't own much, but they don't owe much either. We are basically a community property state, but it isn't going to help much in her case. This guy doesn't seem to have worked much in the five years they have been married. Alimony would be a wasted effort.

"He's broken my nose in the last year," she admits, touching the side of her face. "It's getting worse."

When her eye heals, this woman will be a looker. She is a little made-up for my tastes but still extremely attractive, with blonde hair, an even tan, and a wide, luscious mouth. Since my daughter, Sarah, has been working for me as a paralegal this summer, Dan and I are continually instructed on how sexist our behavior is. Sarah is quick to point out how much I stare at my female clients (the attractive ones) and how much we comment on their appearances. She is right, but old habits die hard. "Your nose looks fine," I cannot resist saying. It does, proving the medical profession is good for something other than lawyer jokes.

"He's a big guy," Ms. Kennerly volunteers, "and when he goes into one of his rages, he's like a wild animal."

I nod as if I've heard it all before, and I have, but the truth is that one of my secret nightmares is being shot by an out-of-control spouse. Lawyers get killed more often than is absolutely necessary, and I have been threatened more than once. "Have you tried to leave him before but ended up going back to him?" I ask, starting to doodle on my pad.

Ms. Kennerly fiddles with her sunglasses. "I won't

this time," she says, her voice husky from crying but sounding determined. "I've never gotten this far."

She means, I take it, that she has never filed for divorce before. I've taken one bite at the matrimonial apple, but it was a good one. Married to a South American woman after a stint in the Peace Corps thirty years ago, I had a twenty-one-year run until breast cancer got the better of it. Part Indian, Negro, and Spanish, Rosa was gorgeous but stubborn as a Colombian mule. She lived life more passionately in one day than I've managed in the nine years since her death. Since then my love life has probably been as chaotic as Lydia Kennerly's, but without the violence. I've never hit a woman, though I could name several who probably would have felt much better if they had taken a punch at me on occasion. "Does your husband carry a gun?" I ask, drawing a rudimentary .38 on my pad.

"Sometimes," she says, and takes a deep breath. "He wants one of those permits that will allow him to carry a concealed weapon. Not that he needs one. He nearly beat a guy to death with his bare hands who he thought was hitting on me."

Great. If this country gets any more violent, we'll have to change the national bird to a gamecock. I don't have a gun. "Let's go over to the courthouse," I say, and stand up. "I'm not much of a fighter." Actually, I was kind of winning the last one I had, about four or five years ago, before a tooth got knocked out. The trouble with fights is that they are seldom fair. I had gone to a redneck bar in Saline County to talk to a witness, and his friends didn't take kindly to my presence. I picked asphalt from my face for a week afterward. I had to settle for my revenge on cross-examination.

After I get a receipt for her from Julia—who reminds me there is no initial charge for an order of protection, so I don't need a check for court costs—we walk side by side in the August heat to the Blackwell County courthouse. Though I could let her go by herself, she will feel better if I help her. Beside me, she seems so uneasy that I wonder if this guy could be following us. My clients have a way of making me as paranoid as they are. I fired my last bullet forty years ago after my mother confiscated my father's .22 pistol, rifle, and shotgun when he began to go seriously mentally ill. "How did you pick me out?" I ask as we cross against a light. It's too hot to obey the law.

"I did a little research," she says, bumping me slightly as we step onto the curb at Third Street. "I know you've made your reputation as a criminal defense attorney. I thought it wouldn't hurt to have a lawyer who knows a few policemen or detectives."

I look over my shoulder but see only the familiar figure of one of Blackwell County's harmless, mentally ill street persons in the filthy jacket she never seems to shed. How do women stand living in fear? I feel anxious and angry and haven't even seen the guy. Maybe I should get a gun. I'd feel better if Sarah, who is living downtown this summer, would get one. "I've won a few cases," I say, pleased she has heard of me. I've only been in practice seven years, having taken about an eighteen-year detour as a social worker before Rosa pushed me into night law school. Two decades of investigating child abuse was long enough, and I knew I could do as good a job as the attorneys I saw in juvenile court. But it was my wife who, after becoming this country's proudest registered nurse and citizen, insisted I could work and go to school and maintain a marriage. She did.

"So I've heard," Lydia says, as we enter the Blackwell County courthouse, which has been recently remodeled instead of scrapped for one of those hideous low-ceiling boxes you see on TV. I'll feel better once we get past the metal detector, though I suspect they are hardly foolproof. I've read more than one story recently about judges being murdered in their courtrooms. In the elevator to the third floor she is pressed up against me. It is not a disagreeable sensation. "Flattery will get you everywhere," I say, knowing I will be overheard, and our fellow passengers will wonder what she said. Despite the black eye, Lydia is about 99 percent more attractive than any woman I've been around lately. I can smell the faint, musky scent of a roselike fragrance coming from her neck. Why do women get involved with men who would beat them? If Sarah got involved with a man who beat her, I don't know what I would do.

Inside the clerk's office, after we get the paperwork done and have landed in Fifth Division, I ask Barbara Simmons, one of my favorites in the office, if she has seen Judge Ryder this morning. I'd like to do something to make it look as if I'm earning my fee. I've always liked Murry Ryder, who always goes out of his way to treat everyone in his court courteously and fairly, a habit not all his colleagues share. Barbara, who has a daughter Sarah's age, tells me she thinks he has just had a trial settle and is back in his chambers after a stint in the coffee shop. I lead Lydia down the hall and around the corner to the office of Sandra Denny, his case coordinator. Women rule the courthouses, just as they do the law offices. The day will come when women will demand to be the bailiffs too, and the takeover will be complete. Already half the chancery judges are women in Blackwell County.

Judge Ryder has an eye for women, and when Sandra leads us into his office, he is livelier than usual, greeting me as if I were one of his fishing buddies instead of an occasional practitioner in his court. "Gideon, when are you gonna call off this hot weather?" he says, sitting up in his chair to get a better look at my client. The judge is a genuinely handsome man and resembles the late Supreme Court Chief Justice Warren Burger, who, with a bale of cotton for hair, looked the perfect judicial model. Though Burger's opinions never seemed dumb to me, more scholarly types have sneered that there was just as much cotton beneath as on top.

Ever the gentleman, the judge stands up when I introduce Lydia and lets me put on a little testimony, as if this weren't a done deal without him even seeing her. I have instructed her to take off her sunglasses, and in his darkened chambers her eye does look black, instead of the colors of the rainbow. "At least he didn't cut you," the judge says, squinting at her over his reading glasses. "I had a woman in here yesterday whose husband had slashed her cheek with her wedding ring. For some reason it started bleeding during the hearing and was a mess. I had to call Sandra to get a bandage."

Lydia, who doesn't know how to respond to this bit of gossip, simply stares at Murry, and I fill the silence by telling him that the defendant sometimes carries a gun. "If he shows up for the hearing," I advise, "maybe you should have Ralph search him when he comes in. It'd be easy to sneak a gun past the metal detectors downstairs. I just read about another judge in Ohio being shot."

Murry visibly winces, and opens his desk drawer and pulls out a pearl-handled .45 pistol. "I saw that," he says, and, frowning, draws a bead on the door. "If the time ever comes to use this, I'll probably miss and hit Ralph and Sandra." He lays the pistol back in the drawer and makes a note on his pad.

Depending on the judge, ex parte proceedings can get unjudicial in a hurry, and Murry is a character. On the other hand, perhaps he has displayed his famed pistol hoping word will get back to Al Kennerly that the judge intends to die with his boots on. I look over at Lydia, whose expression is hidden behind her sunglasses. God only knows what she is thinking. "I was in Conway last week," I tell Murry. "They have no security. It was about four-thirty, and I walked right into a judge's office. He was the only one there. I could have shot him between the eyes and walked out."

"Who was it?" Murry asks, glancing at Lydia, whose perfect posture makes my back hurt.

I give him a name, and Murry laughs. "You'd never be convicted, even if you shot him during Toad Suck days."

I snicker appreciatively. A gossip, Murry will tell this story himself. But just then, as if she were a wife breaking up her husband's party, Sandra comes in through the door with her book, without knocking. "Are you going to set this?" she asks Murry, her voice coolly professional.

"Sure," Murry says, and gives me a boyish grin. "I'm supposed to be getting a decision out on a case I heard a year ago." As if he were signing the Declaration of Independence, he writes his name with a flourish on the preprinted form and hands it to me.

I stand up and smile appreciatively, as if we are in the presence of a badly overworked jurist instead of a trial judge who is being treated like a schoolboy by a none-too-pleased teacher. "Thank you, Your Honor," I say, and follow my client out into Sandra's office. She smirks at me as she gives me a date for the hearing. "You shouldn't be telling stories like that. It makes them all nervous, and we have enough trouble with disgruntled litigants as it is."

"But they're true," I protest. "It's dangerous being a judge."

Sandra nods gravely at my client, who is inspecting a photograph on her wall. "It's dangerous being a woman, too."

After a trip to the basement to have the order served at the sheriff's office, I follow Lydia Kennerly out the automatic door to the sidewalk and ask, "What did you think of the judge?"

She leans toward me and whispers, "I think he was showing off a bit."

Is that what was going on? I know that my daughter would probably agree. As we trudge back to my office, the oppressive humidity visibly wilts Lydia, and I have to slow my pace beside her. "He's actually a pretty good judge," I say, taking her arm, since she seems to wobble as we step off the curb, still four blocks from the Layman Building. "Are you okay?"

Her thin top clings to her chest, and she stops to pull her blouse away from her skin, as if this gesture will cool her off. "This is harder than I thought it would be. I feel kind of dazed by everything all of a sudden."

I nod, forgetting as usual how terrible women must feel, even as they go through the easiest part of the process. I'm glad now that I came over with her. Unless someone helps you, it can be a cold kind of business. And it never hurts to schmooze a bit with the judge. "It's okay," I say. "I'm going to be there for you every step of the way."

She places her hand on my arm and says fervently, "Believe me, Mr. Page, I'm counting on that."

In my office that afternoon, I hand Lydia's file to my daughter to draft the divorce complaint. Sarah will be a senior at the university in Fayetteville. "I would have interviewed her," she says, frowning at my handwriting.

"She must have been pretty. You realize that you tend to see the good-looking ones yourself."

I swivel my chair and prop my feet up on the bottom right-hand desk drawer. Is that sexist too, I wonder, a little weary of my daughter's never-ending litany. It has long been my dream that someday we will be Page & Page, Attorneys at Law, but in truth we are off to a rocky start. A history major at Fayetteville, Sarah is quick to judge me, and so far I haven't gotten passing grades. "You weren't here," I remind her. As part of our arrangement, Sarah volunteers at the battered women's shelter one morning a week. My daughter, a carbon copy physically of her late mother, is a continual work-in-progress: since junior high, at various times she has been a fundamentalist Christian, cheerleader on the pom-pom squad for the Razorbacks, member of a feminist group called WAR (Women Against Rape), AIDS volunteer, and now, apparently, my self-appointed conscience.

"Did you tell her to come to the shelter?" Sarah says, looking at a snapshot of Lydia's bruise. "She's pretty."

"That's not a crime," I remind my daughter, who even has her mother's exotic coloring and thick ebony hair. "She's going to a motel for a couple of days, until we can get him served and out of the house. I went over with her to get an order of protection."

Sarah rolls her eyes. Getting an order of protection for clients is usually her job. "She must have some money."

"That's not a crime either," I say. Sarah hasn't quite gotten the hang of the free enterprise system yet, believing that no client, especially a battered woman, should be turned away. It's an admirable sentiment, but so far none of my creditors have taken it in lieu of a check. "By the way, this guy could be dangerous. She says he carries a gun sometimes and has really gotten out of control."

Sarah makes a face. "Dad, did you know that over 40 percent of all murdered women are killed by their intimate male partners?"

"No," I say, eyeing a bag of hard candy in the drawer, but resisting getting it out. I've already had six pieces, and it's not even two. At twenty calories apiece, they add up. "Is that unexpected?" Since she began volunteering at the shelter, Sarah is forever quoting some statistic about domestic violence. Yesterday it was that a woman is beaten every nine seconds in this country. The day before it was that at least 25 percent of women in domestic violence situations are pregnant.

"Think what that means!" Sarah says urgently. "A woman is safer on the street than in her own home. In fact, domestic violence is the leading cause of serious injury to women, more common than muggings and car crashes combined."

"We're a violent species," I agree, wondering how accurate Sarah's information is. She's become a walking *USA Today.* "I know that I've read somewhere that it is women who usually initiate violence. Some guy was supposed to have done a study."

"That's ridiculous!" Sarah says predictably. "If I brought you some of the shelter's literature, would you at least read some of it?"

What I love about my daughter, as I did her mother, is her passion. But Sarah has more of a sense of humor, or maybe is simply more sarcastic. She knows I will skim it and say I read it, only to be tripped up when I am quizzed on the material. Dan says I should be flattered that Sarah feels I'm worth saving. "Sure," I say. "Rent a truck and ship it on over."

She laughs. "It's not that much. What would really

be good is if you and Dan would go through the domestic violence training. It's strictly about power and control."

I reach into the desk and pull out my least favorite —purple. "That's not what Ann Landers says," I bait her. "This guy did a survey and said that 60 percent of the women he talked to admitted they hit first."

My daughter slides her hands up and down her jeans, a familiar sign that she is trying to control her irritation. "Ann Landers is four hundred years old. She wouldn't know a reliable researcher if one bit her on the leg. She's not going to alienate half her readership by giving the straight poop on the subject of domestic violence. According to the FBI, in 1989, 98 percent of all assaults by spouses were perpetrated by men against women."

My phone rings, and I have an excuse to end this useless debate. I doubt if Sarah's shelter houses an objective, world-class think tank on the premises for the study of domestic violence. As I talk to one of my clients, who complains endlessly about a parole revocation hearing that is set for tomorrow, my mind defaults to my conversation with Sarah. My own experience as a lawyer tells me she is right. It is women who seek the orders of protection, women who come to our office with bruises, women who call me at home with the most god-awful stories of bullying and intimidation by their mates. Give me a drug dealer to represent over a batterer anytime. These guys, who never admit what jerks they are, are my least favorite clients.

"Sit, Jessie!" I command for the tenth time, but it is no use. My dog, a five-year-old greyhound, whimpers in protest. As I have been shown to do in her dog obedience class, I try to collapse her legs and press down at the same time on her hips, but she shrieks as if I'm killing her. Greyhounds were not made for sitting, her baleful expression tells me.

"You've really got a knack for animal training," my friend Dan says, and laughs through the screen of the gazebo I've had built in my backyard. "We could market a video of you and Jessie and make a killing." He picks up his beer and salutes me.

I wipe the sweat from my forehead. "That's okay, girl," I say, and give her a dog biscuit. "Let's go rest." I open the door of the gazebo and, holding her leash, stand aside so she can go in. As usual, she hesitates before climbing the steps. A genius she is not. "You can do it!" I encourage her.

Dan chuckles and grabs a potato chip from the bowl on the table. "How much did you waste on those lessons?" he asks, delighted by this spectacle of dog-over-human.

"A hundred dollars," I grumble, and toss him a biscuit. "Call her," I order him.

"Come on, sweetie," Dan coos, and suddenly takes a bite of the biscuit.

Seeing her treat disappear into Dan's mouth apparently motivates Jessie into leaping over the two steps onto the wooden boards of the floor, pulling her leash from my hand. She hits the plastic table with her head with enough force to knock the bowl of chips and Dan's beer onto the floor. Her huge jaws snap up the chips while we scramble for them as if we were rival competitors in the food chain. "Damn it, Jessie," I complain, "I should have left you in the house."

"No way," Dan says, having rescued most of his beer. "I wouldn't have missed this for the world. Your two best friends doing what we do best, even if it's hotter out here than a two-peckered billy goat."

I collapse in the chair across from Dan. Eating, he means. "How does it taste?" Dan is huge. Two-fifty and climbing. I don't know what makes him eat so much. Neither does he. Human behavior, he likes to pontificate on these lazy occasions on the weekends, is the last great mystery. Despite all the scientific advances, the mind/body problem reigns supreme.

"I could get used to them," my friend says, chewing thoughtfully. Already finished, Jessie settles her long, sleek body across the boards, which aren't quite flush. Jessie is by far the most attractive of the three of us. Her body is as perfect as genetics can make her. When I take her through the neighborhood on her walk, I never even get a glance, but invariably someone comments on her. And why not? She is incredibly classy-looking, while her owner is not quite in the same category as his retired racer from Southland Park in West Memphis.

"See, our big mistake," Dan says, leaning back in his chair and propping his feet up on the inside beam, "is we think there is some fundamental difference between us and Jessie. If we could just accept there's not, the human race would be a hell of a lot happier."

I brush my hands off and take a deep breath. It must be bred into me to love this humid, unbearable air of an Arkansas summer. "Is that what they taught you in philosophy?" I scoff, ridiculing Dan's major in college. Raised a Catholic, some days I believe there must be a purpose to life, but that is about as religious as I get these days. Dan talks as if he is some tough-minded cynic, but inside he is a pile of goo. He's just come through a messy divorce. He should be happily married with five children, but after twenty years of slogging it out in a loveless duet, he has nothing to show for it. I think he does so many divorces because he likes the kids.

"Science has killed everything," he says. "It's just hard as hell for everybody to admit it."

Through the screen we can hear my phone faintly ringing inside the house, and I almost decide not to get it, but I get up because it may be my girlfriend, Angela, calling from my hometown of Bear Creek in eastern Arkansas. After a tumultuous July, I am trying to negotiate a reconciliation. There is so much water under our respective bridges, we are both afraid to cross. Jessie, having gained the gazebo, does not follow me into the house. Dan hollers, "Bring me another beer, counselor!"

I enter my kitchen, thinking how few problems, in the grand scheme of things, I really have. I have that pleasant, relaxed feeling that warm weather, talk, food, and beer combine to bring. On a Saturday afternoon in August the world doesn't seem a bad place. Dan, after a couple of beers, enjoys woolgathering on the problematical nature of existence. In contrast, I am increasingly content to simply enjoy it, if I could just get the relationship with Angela under control. If I can't understand how my telephone works, there is no need to worry about my brain. "Hello," I say, enunciating carefully. I've finished my second beer and unlike Dan haven't gone overboard on the chips. I don't want her to think I'm sitting home alone getting drunk every weekend. Angela and I go back a long way, maybe too long.

"Mr. Page, this is Lydia Kennerly. I'm sorry to disturb you on the weekend, but I'm really frightened. Do you have a moment?"

Something in her voice raises the hair on the back of my neck. Her husband must have gotten served with her complaint for divorce. I had assumed everything was going relatively well, having gotten him out of their house last week with the order of protection. He had hollered and screamed, but hadn't done anything violent, and on Wednesday she had called to give me the address of a motel he was renting by the week. Sarah filed the complaint for me on Thursday and had taken it and the summons down to the sheriff's office afterward. "What's wrong?" I ask.

"I know Al's been in here," she says. "I knew he'd start this."

I look out the window at Dan and suppress a sigh. He would have taken this case in a second. "Did you get the locks changed like we talked about?"

"Not yet," she says, her voice tremulous. "I should have."

What does she expect, I think, as the air conditioning in my house clicks on. It is ninety outside, but it doesn't feel that hot to me. "Did he take anything?"

"Not that I can tell," she says. "Listen, would it be impossible for you to come over while I get some things? I can't stay here tonight."

More patiently than I feel, I explain that is out of the question and suggest that she call the police. "Tell them you have an order of protection."

"I did," she says, her voice growing more out of control by the second. "They said that if I didn't have proof it was him, they couldn't do anything."

"Don't you have a neighbor who can help?" I ask, watching Dan bending down to feed Jessie a handful of chips.

"No," she says, beginning to cry. "Nobody wants to get involved. He's called and hung up twice. I think he's watching the house."

She knew this would happen to her. She should have moved out of state and not told him where she was going. "I'll make a call to a friend on the police force," I say, trying to resist the guilt I shouldn't have to feel. "I don't know if he can do anything, but I'll call you back."

I call the station and ask for Wayne Hunter, a detective I've known for years, but am told he is off duty tonight. I try to get him at his house, but there is no answer. My call isn't even picked up by an answering machine. I try a couple of other cops but no luck. I get Dan a beer and go back out to the gazebo and tell him what is going on. "You think I should go over there," I ask, "while she gets her stuff?"

Dan, who encounters more of these situations than I do, puts his feet down and rests his arms on his huge thighs. Wearing a pair of shorts that come down to his knees and a pair of flip-flops, he is no more ready than I am to take on an irate husband. "You think she's in danger?"

"Hell, I don't know," I say irritably. "What could I do, anyway? The son of a bitch would probably just come in and shoot me."

"Think how she's feeling," Dan says, getting up. "If we both go and he's watching the house, he probably won't do anything. See, she could be doing some guy, and he's jealous. You know as well as I do how little of the truth we get."

Jessie hears something in our voices and stands up. I wish she were a fighter. I realize I am basically a physical coward. I didn't fight that redneck and his friends in the parking lot because I wanted to. I had no choice. I'll call her back to say we'll come over this time, but I'm not going to make a habit of this.

Ms. Kennerly answers on the first ring, but says there is no need for us to come. She asks me to stay on the phone while she packs a bag, which is easy enough to do. I tell Dan, and he nods gratefully. He wasn't looking forward to getting in the middle either. Ten minutes later, she says she is leaving and will call me later to let me know she hasn't been followed. "I'd tell you the name, but he's probably listening," she says, her voice sounding like a forlorn child's.

I think to myself that this guy has got her number big-time, and again suggest the shelter, but she says that she will be all right in a motel. I suspect she wants to go someplace where she can take a drink. I can't blame her. I'd want a drink, too.

After I hang up the phone, Dan and I, happy as cops who've been told they don't have to work a riot, settle back down in the gazebo, and I tell him what little I know on Lydia Kennerly.

"The good-looking ones can be the most trouble," he responds, the boards under his feet creaking with his weight. "A lot of times in these situations I find the woman is the only thing in the guy's life that he's got going for him. He's an asshole at work and nobody likes him. He can't get promoted or can't hold a job, but he can sure as hell make his wife jump. It really shouldn't be a surprise they go nuts when the woman tries to take off. He doesn't have anything if he doesn't have her."

I look across my yard into the park across the street. Hell, Mrs. Kennerly's husband could be over there watching me. Dan knows from his own experience what Sarah is preaching to me about. It is easier to take from him. And unlike with Sarah these days, our conversation works it way around to other topics, mainly whether Kenneth Starr, the lawyer investigating the Whitewater scandal, will ever leave Arkansas. "Down deep we hate him so much because he reminds us of the carpetbaggers after the Civil War."

I pick up my beer and take a swallow, beginning to feel hungry. It is after six. "Nobody thinks about that stuff anymore."

Dan wags his head. "See, it's part of our unconscious. First, Reconstruction, then the '57 integration mess with federal troops at Central High all year. Now, Kenneth Starr is in our shit again. I'm surprised someone hasn't taken a shot at him."

I take a chip and run it over my tongue to taste the salt. Dan has a way of putting together things that almost make sense. For all I know, he's writing a book on the subject that will make him a million bucks. I ask him if he wants to go get some Chinese takeout at the bottom of the hill, but he looks at his watch and says he has to go home and get ready for a date. "Are you still doing that computer matchup business?" I ask, still dumbfounded that he would pay good money to get hooked up with a woman through a dating service.

He gives me a sheepish grin. "I still have a couple of dates coming to me," he says. "You never know when you'll meet the right one."

I keep my mouth shut, having teased him enough. At one point back in the early part of the summer, the attorney general's office had sent one of its lawyers over to talk to him as a part of an investigation to check out whether these services were scams. The women Dan had gone out with had complained that Dan had lied repeatedly on his personal information sheet. Naturally, he developed a crush on the attorney, a miniskirted girl half his age. "Good luck," I tell him as I walk him to his little Honda Prelude. The older he gets, the younger he tries to act. Though he has a heart of gold, Dan is prone to disaster: over the years, he has been arrested for shoplifting a Twinkie and, more seriously, had an affair with a prostitute he represented.

After he leaves, instead of going out to eat, I hang around the house hoping Angela will call from Bear Creek. I give Jessie her dinner and open a bag of Pasta

Secrets, which has only about six hundred calories even if I eat all of the servings. As I wait in the kitchen for the vegetables to simmer, I think about Dan and realize that his love life isn't that much weirder than my own. Though I am almost indecently attracted to Angela, trouble seems inevitable if we get together. Her recent disclosure of an affair with a man I hated still grates. The fact that he is now in the penitentiary serving a life sentence for murder doesn't make it any easier. I drain the water off my meatless dinner and take it outside to the gazebo with a glass of boxed Chablis. How can I carp about Angela's affair? Two weeks after Rosa's death I spent a couple of hours in a motel with one of her best friends, who was married at the time. I remember there was more grief than lust that rainy afternoon. We both cried. Since then, I have been involved with several other women, not always in the best of circumstances. The good ones I've let get away, or they had the good sense to move on. Angela, who is still trying to sell her house in Bear Creek after her husband's suicide, hasn't made up her mind.

Ten minutes later I go back inside the house for another glass of wine and a book whose main character is dead. Inconsequential in life and now reduced to ashes in a bottle, his memory dominates his friends' lives, at least for twenty-four hours. I wonder how many of the women I've known would show up for my memorial service and what they would say. Maybe it is better not to know. At eight the phone rings, and I race in to get it and wake up Jessie, who is dozing on her pad in the kitchen. It is not Angela, but Lydia Kennerly again, who apologizes needlessly for having bothered me on the weekend. "I overreacted," she says, her voice much calmer than it was a couple of hours ago. "I'll go back to the house Monday and get the locks changed. I'm an idiot for not having done it."

"Don't say that," I tell her, feeling a little guilty for not having gone over to her house when she called. This woman does not need to be beating up on herself right now. Doubtless, she was trying not to provoke her husband any further. Bad reasoning but understandable under the circumstances. "What you're going through is a nightmare. I admire you for having the guts to bring this all to a head."

Instead of cheering her up, my words produce tears. "You have no idea!" she moans into my ear. "My parents would die if they knew what kind of man I married. They would have been so disappointed."

I find myself nodding. It is easy to reduce my clients to irritating phone calls that disturb a nice weekend. My own mother, who lived nine tenths of her life in a segregated era, was horrified by my choice of a wife, who, though beautiful, obviously had Negro blood coursing through her veins. It shocks me to realize how long it has taken me to admit how much her rejection of Rosa hurt me. What did I expect? Spoiled as a child, I obviously thought I could have blown up the town and she would have said, What a wonderful son I've raised. "How long have they been dead?" I ask, spotting a beer can I've left in the gazebo. It looks tacky, and I remind myself to get it before I go to bed. If this woman had a support network, her efforts to leave this guy would be made a lot easier.

"They were killed in a head-on collision ten years ago this month," Lydia says, her voice still shaky. "Are yours still alive?"

I have a knack for saying the wrong thing to this woman, but in the back of my mind I wonder if her decision to finally act has anything to do with this anniversary of their death. It is not a question I will ask, however. It dawns on me that this woman wants desperately to talk, and I oblige and tell her a little about myself. It is the least I can do. After telling her that my father was mentally ill and died in the state hospital, I explain, "But for the schizophrenia and alcoholism, he was a sweet man, if you can believe it."

"I do," she says eagerly and tells me about her own father, who was a civil engineer for the highway department in Ohio. "After he died, I found out from one of his coworkers after his funeral that he'd had a coke habit for years. It was the single most devastating moment of my life."

I watch as Jessie squats beneath the dog door and realize that our species is needlessly cruel. I could have opened the door for her, but I like to watch her squeeze through because she is so comical-looking. "People don't know what to say to the survivors," I say lamely.

"Oh, he knew all right," Lydia says. "I found out later my father had been promoted over him."

As she talks, I watch as my dog urinates in the yard, crouching in a familiar humorous way. It is the only time she seems to lose her dignity. Knowing she has a pretty good life with just an occasional humiliation or two, she returns immediately to the house. "Men probably aren't too high on your list, are they?" I ask, wondering why some women ever get married.

"You'd think that," Lydia says, but then tells me about an earlier marriage, one that worked until he died of a blood clot in his leg at the age of thirty.

I am amazed by the similarity between us and tell her about Rosa dying of breast cancer. She sounds genuinely moved and asks if we had any children, and I bore her to tears, bragging about Sarah. "The sign outside my office will read Page & Page some day, unless we kill each other first."

She laughs for the first time since I've met her, and asks, "So you've never remarried?"

"Maybe," I answer, glancing down at Jessie, who is reminding me that it is time for our nightly walk, "there really is only one person per lifetime." As I say this, I realize I'm beginning to believe it.

"I'm beginning to think I'm living proof of that," Lydia says huskily into the phone. "Listen, would you like to come and sit out by the pool and talk? I'm at the Delta Inn on the way to Benton. I'm just going kind of nuts in this room."

In the background I can hear classical music playing, undoubtedly KUAR, the public radio station. I know she's lonely, but that's not a good idea. "I can't make it tonight," I say, "but thanks."

She says quickly, "I understand."

By her tone, I know I have hurt her feelings. "We go back to court next week," I remind her, trying to put things back on a more professional footing, "to make the order of protection permanent. Are you sure he'll show up?"

"I think so," she says, sounding distracted. She must be changing stations, because now I hear the distinctive voice of Buddy Holly. She's not old enough to remember him.

"Call me back if you have any problems, okay? But, in any event, call me Monday at the office so we can prepare your testimony."

She says that she will, and I hang up, wondering what Lydia Kennerly is wearing tonight.

It is still light out, and Jessie and I have a leisurely walk through the park across the street. We run into at least three couples, which makes me increasingly frustrated with my relationship with Angela.

She should have called me this week. Damned if I am going to call her. Instead of acting our ages (fifty-one), we might as well be in high school. Cat and mouse. But I don't know which I am. Angela somehow trips a switch in me that defies explanation. The first girl I ever made love to (in time-honored fashion by the dashboard lights of my mother's '58 Ford Fairlane the summer after our senior year in high school), and maybe the last, but not at this rate. Jessie, on her leash because of the presence of several stray dogs yesterday, stops every few feet to try to nose through the brush, which is so dense in the middle of summer that it is impossible to see more than a few feet in either direction if we get off one of the dirt paths that crisscross the park. "Come on, girl!" I say sharply, and jerk her leash when she digs her claws in the tall grass. Patience is not one of my virtues.

I drag Jessie home, feeling lonely and sorry for myself. I fill up Jessie's water dish, grateful for her company. I thought by the time I was fifty, I wouldn't feel such turmoil. Maybe I'm the victim of too many Hallmark commercials with nostalgic scenes of aging but serene adults trimming the Christmas tree when some wonderful event happens that hopefully reduces the viewer to tears. I pick up the phone and angrily dial Angela's number, but as I let it ring, I know there will be no answer. I try to read my book but bog down because I can't keep the characters straight. With Jessie's head resting comfortably on my lap in the living room, I click through channels and watch a program about the late singer Marvin Gaye. Drugs destroyed him. Maybe there are people who are aging gracefully, but I'm not one of them. I go to bed at ten and dream, not, as I expected, of

Angela, but of Lydia Kennerly's husband. All I remember when I wake up is that he is huge, Sumo-wrestler size.

Al Kennerly has no attorney but has represented himself about as well as he can, wisely choosing not to cross-examine his wife, who has cried her way through her testimony. He is smaller than I expected, but his shoulders are impressive under a knit shirt. Remembering my comment, Murry had him searched when he came into the courtroom. Actually, the guy doesn't seem like a wife beater at all, but even the mildest-looking men no longer surprise me. I remember Lydia's words about Al Kennerly being a charmer, but it is not so much charm the guy displays as self-possession. He takes the witness stand and coolly denies her every allegation. "Were you not in the courtroom," I ask sarcastically, after he sits in the witness box and tells Murry he didn't beat his wife, "when these pictures of your wife's black eye were introduced into evidence?" I walk over to the bench, and Murry wordlessly hands them down to me, as if he were my assistant instead of the judge.

"Yes, sir," he says blandly, "but I didn't do that to her. She did that to herself."

Although I've shown him the pictures once when Lydia was testifying, I ask the judge if I can approach the witness and hand them to him again. "Are you saying your wife drew this on?"

"I'm saying, Mr. Page," Mr. Kennerly says quietly, turning his head to speak directly to Murry, "my wife is a pathological liar. I don't think she can help it."

"She's a pretty good artist," I say, taking the pictures back from him. He has barely glanced at them.

He says, without expression, "Lydia ran into the

door at night in the bathroom when she was drunk two days before she told me she wanted a divorce."

What a piece of work is this guy! I walk back over to Lydia, who won't look at him. "Is it your testimony these are fake tears, Mr. Kennerly?"

Kennerly turns to Murry and says, "She can cry at the drop of a hat, Your Honor. As God is my witness, I've never touched her in anger. I still love her."

I can feel the hair on my neck begin to prickle. Kennerly is so eerily calm that I realize he is the pathological liar of the two. If she hadn't prepared me for him, I might be tempted to believe him. "So you would like her to get down on her knees," I say, my hand on Lydia's shoulder, trying to provoke him, "and beg your forgiveness for making up this nasty little story and come on home, and everything will be forgiven?" I am laying it on a little thick, but since he has no lawyer, I can get away with it. Murry has seen plenty of defendants who lie as well as this man.

"If Lydia wants a divorce," Mr. Kennerly says, "I'm not going to get in her way. I made a vow before God, and I would like anything to be able to keep it, but if she insists, I understand there is nothing I can do."

I look back at Lydia, who is shaking her bowed head. By the way Murry sits back in his chair, I can tell he wants me to wrap this up. Sometimes witnesses like Kennerly can be entertaining, but this man is not. In the face he looks a little like Frank Gifford. These two litigants are quite attractive. Lydia's eye has healed completely, and until she began to cry, she looked stunning in a simple blue dress with a high neckline. I wonder what the real story is. It's always somewhere in between. Knowing the answer, I ask if he has a permit to carry a concealed weapon, which he denies. He also refuses to admit that he has used his key to come into the house except to get his clothes and some personal items. I shrug and sit down, knowing what this judge will do.

Murry nods, and lectures my client's husband. "I've listened to your testimony, Mr. Kennerly, and I don't believe it. I want you to stay away from your wife. I don't want you to call her; I don't want you to go near the house, and I don't want you stalking her. If you do, I'll see that you regret it. I advise you to get an attorney. Do you understand me?"

Far from looking like an enraged husband, Kennerly responds meekly. "I have no intention of violating the court's order."

"See that you don't," Murry says sternly. He raises his eyes at me as if he is wondering what all the fuss is about. This guy may have popped his wife, but he sees a lot worse on a daily basis. I do, too.

As I walk Lydia to her car, I comment that her husband didn't seem so bad. "I thought he'd be bigger." I realize now that I was prepared to see Mike Tyson walk into the courtroom.

Lydia slaps her thighs like my mother used to do when she was exasperated. "I knew he would come off like a martyr," she says bitterly. "He has an incredible ability to get sympathy for himself."

"He may not even fight the divorce," I point out. "He's only got a few more days to respond to the complaint, and he's got his clothes. Surely you can divide the furniture without any problems?"

"Probably," Lydia says, and then adds fervently, "I'm just so glad this is over! I can't tell you how much I've been dreading it. Thank you," she adds and squeezes my arm. I can feel the pressure of her hand through my suit coat.

I don't point out that she would have accomplished the same thing if I hadn't been present. Murry would have believed her if we'd had nothing more than the black eye. Women don't usually walk into doors. "Sometimes these things don't come off as bad as you think they will."

"Maybe not," she says, sighing. "I'm ready to get on with my life."

I don't want to tell her that she has been overreacting. For all I know, she hasn't. Yet my mind has begun to move on to a criminal trial I have tomorrow in Saline County. I am defending a client on a rape charge that will turn on credibility. I wish my client had been here to watch Al Kennerly.

I explain that Arkansas law will permit her to get an uncontested divorce in only thirty days from the date the complaint is filed. "You can be a free woman in just a few weeks. If he doesn't file an answer, I'll get this set down immediately."

For the first time, I see Lydia Kennerly smile, and it is a pleasure. She has lovely wide teeth, and her eyes positively shine at the prospect of a quick divorce. "Please do."

I leave her at the parking lot a block down from the courthouse, wondering how long she will be able to leave men alone. I suspect not long.

After lunch, Sarah drops by my office to ask how the Kennerly hearing went. "Piece of cake," I tell her. "The guy was meek as a lamb. A perfect gentleman. His story was that she ran into a door when she was drunk, but he won't fight the divorce if she insists."

My daughter visibly relaxes. "I'm so glad. I was worried about you."

Instantly, I feel guilty that I told her that Al Kennerly occasionally carries a gun. Sarah worries enough. She is too serious, but in fact I'm so proud of her that sometimes I can feel tears welling up behind my eyelids. If she knew how important she is to me, it might run her off. I give her back the file and tell her the case might settle fairly quickly. "He's a nice-looking guy. He'll probably want to get back on the meat market pretty quick."

My daughter, learning the ways of the world, sniffs, "If he's not already."

Wednesday night after a successful rape trial (my client was only convicted of assault and will be out in a few months), I celebrate by stopping in for a drink at Kings & Queens, an oldies meat market I stop by occasionally. I tell myself that I am simply here to celebrate and not pick up a woman, but I find myself looking after all. While my client and I waited for the jury to come back, I wrote a letter to Angela telling her that it was time for me to move on. As I stand at the bar watching one of those couples who look as if they've spent every waking moment the last decade at a dance studio (the guy does everything but flip her over his back), I pull the letter out of my pocket and reread it. I have written that it is crazy to think we could have picked up thirty years later and worked things out. I'm like one of those men who goes to a class reunion and meets his old flame. Those relationships surely are built on wishful thinking and memories of souped-up hormones. They didn't work out then, so why should they work out now, I think sourly, as I down a second bourbon and Coke.

The music blaring from the sound system is, appropriately, "Kodachrome" by Paul Simon. The reality is never as good as the memory. A liberal from New Jersey whose father moved to Bear Creek to run our one factory our senior year (I had been shipped off to a boarding school in western Arkansas), Angela rightfully pointed out to everybody how thoroughly racist we were. She was infuriating, and though it was like shooting ducks in a barrel, she won every argument we had on the subject that summer before college. My best friend in junior high, John Upton, attending my mother's funeral a few years later in Bear Creek, nudged me at the cemetery and said wistfully that Angela, who was over talking to my sister, still had the same perfectly rounded ass she'd had in high school. Though I pretended to be shocked by John's typically irreverent comment, it was the first thought I had when I showed up on her doorstep a few months ago while I was in town to try a case that turned out to involve her former lover.

I crumple the letter and thrust it back into my suit pocket, knowing I won't send it. I look up and think I see Lydia Kennerly, but it is another woman with blonde hair who is not nearly as attractive. The bourbon has begun to kick in, but suddenly I feel exhausted. The guy I represented probably did rape his girlfriend, but he was a good liar, too, probably as good as Al Kennerly yesterday. Knowing I have nothing to celebrate and am here feeling sorry for myself, I pay up and drive home, determined to get a good night's sleep. Jessie, who is wild to go on her walk, jumps up at me like an angry wife, and I tell her we will take a short one as soon as I change into a pair of shorts.

As soon as I see the blinking light on the phone, like the idiot I am, I get my hopes up, but it is Lydia Kennerly reporting that she is back at the Delta Inn and asking that I contact her as soon as I get in. Wondering what has happened, I call her and get her on the first ring. "Al followed me home yesterday," she says, her words rushed. "When I came out of the house this morning, he was parked across the street. I just can't stand it anymore."

"Did he hit you or talk to you?" I ask, thinking that Murry might put him in jail, but probably will just lecture the guy again if he hasn't done anything else. I slip off my tie, anxious to get out of my clothes. It has been a long day.

"He's trying to get on my nerves," she says. "I'm moving out of the state as soon as the divorce is final and not telling him where I'm going."

I can even smell cigarette smoke on my tie. Why do I go to places like Kings & Queens? The last time I went there, a schoolteacher told me in nicer words that I was too much of a sad sack to go home with. "That's probably a good idea," I reply, feeling Jessie nudge me from behind. Damn, dogs are loyal, I think, still a little drunk from the second bourbon. I need to eat something. "Did he follow you to where you are now?"

"No," she says flatly. "I went out the back around four and walked around the block and couldn't see his car anywhere. Listen, I'd really appreciate it if you'd just come out for a little while and talk. Is it too late?"

Petting Jessie with my right hand, I hold the phone away from me and see it is not even ten. I'm too angry at Angela to go to bed right now. "If you can somehow get me a turkey sandwich and a Coke, I'll meet you out by the pool," I say, not letting myself think whether I should go. The Delta Inn has a restaurant but no bar. This late there shouldn't be anyone I know. "Are you sure he didn't follow you?"

"I know he didn't," she insists. "I pulled off into a parking lot at Kroger's after I went through a red light and he never came by. I haven't seen his car since noon."

Knowing Jessie will forgive me, I tell Lydia that I will be there in fifteen minutes.

·   ·   ·

As I turn into the parking lot of the Delta Inn, I look carefully for her husband's 1988 Chrysler LeBaron but don't see it. Located on the highway to Benton but still in Blackwell County, the Delta Inn, obviously by design, is configured in such a way that its guests have to drive by a window to check in. If Al Kennerly is lurking about, he's probably at the 7-Eleven a hundred yards up the road. I actually had another client stay at the Delta Inn once. A murder suspect, she was as good-looking as Lydia, whom I can see waiting for me inside the railing of the small pool. Her '94 Nissan Sentra is parked in front of room number 7 just about thirty yards away. I get out of the Blazer, promising myself that I will stay long enough to eat a sandwich and make sure she is okay. With less of a buzz, I'm feeling a little sheepish about coming out here. Yet it feels good in the parking lot. The temperature must be down to seventy, and there is a nice breeze out here I couldn't feel in town.

"Hi!" she says, smiling at me as I come through the iron gate to the pool area. She takes a sandwich from a paper sack and holds up a beer. I had asked for a Coke, but I'm not going to complain.

Two kids are splashing noisily at the far end of the pool, and I wonder where their parents are. I sit down across from her in one of the flimsy deck chairs that are scattered around the pool, and look around. "Those kids are too young to be left alone out here," I say disapprovingly. I remember once taking Sarah, who could barely dog-paddle, to Lake Nixon and losing sight of her. I had brought a paper to read and had looked up, and couldn't find her. If she had drowned, I would have killed myself.

"I'm watching them," Lydia says, handing me a sandwich. "They're doing fine. I never learned to swim when I was a kid. I took classes at our Y when I was an adult."

Though she is stressed out, this woman is starved for a normal conversation, I realize, and we sit talking for the next hour. I sip on the beer and hope I don't have a headache tomorrow. She is steadily drinking little bottles of red wine. The children, unbidden, go in after a half hour, and Lydia and I have the pool area to ourselves. I find myself truly relaxing for the first time today. "I was one of those kids whose parents made her enter every beauty contest there was from the time I was three years old," she says after I ask about her childhood. "From the moment I was born, my looks were everything. I gradually realized how shallow I was, but it was a great way to get attention, and I got the wrong kind for too many years. I'm pretty, though," she adds flippantly, "and look how I've ended up—a punching bag."

There is no evidence of abuse externally, and in fact she looks great in shorts and a cotton blouse so thin that even in the dim pool lighting I can see the outline of her bra. The damage is inside her head. "Don't even think that," I say. "You're out of that kind of relationship for good."

From a cooler beside her chair she hands me another beer, her hair almost brushing me. "It's true though," she says, her voice suddenly close to tears. "I've been dominated my entire life by someone's opinion of my physical appearance. You're the first man who hasn't treated me like that." She reaches over and touches my arm and squeezes it.

I snap open the Budweiser and think I am glad that she can't read my thoughts. I should get up and go home, but at the moment I can't make myself do it. "Some of us are trying to do better," I say, and tell her about Sarah's efforts to reform me. "If she had her way," I conclude, "I'd be neutered."

She laughs, sending the sound of tinkling glass over the water, and I can smell her perfume in the night air.

"You must be very proud of her," Lydia says, patting a lock of her hair and raising her breasts in the process.

"I am," I say, and gush on again about my plans for Sarah someday to join me in private practice. "She's as beautiful as you are," I say, momentarily forgetting her earlier comments.

"Do you have a snapshot of her?" Lydia asks, putting down her wine bottle.

"I think I have an old high-school picture," I say, and tug my wallet from my pants. "You can't really see it in this light."

She leans over again before I hand it to her, and this time I can't resist kissing her. I can't believe the softness of her mouth. She responds, and I almost fall out of my chair trying to keep my balance. This is a terrible idea, I think, but the thought disappears as I feel her hand on my thigh. "Let's go inside my room," she whispers against my ear. "I'm getting a little cool."

I'm not, but I do as the lady says, and cooler in hand, she leads me to the door in front of number 7. Though slightly drunk, I look around and am gratified by how few customers have chosen the Delta Inn this night. Inside, the room is almost laughably small, and the rug by the bed is badly scarred from cigarette butts, but I'm not here to lay carpet. Quickly, we undress and my thoughts of wanting to take a shower are dispelled by the softness of her hands. "You're in good shape," she says, drawing me to her on the bed, which she doesn't bother to turn down.

"I wish," I murmur, glad that she hasn't turned the

light off. In my alcoholic state and as tired as I am, I'm going to need all the help I can get. However, nude, she is magnificent, and I have no trouble becoming aroused.

"Go slow," she pleads, and I wonder briefly about birth control, but reading my thoughts, she says that she has been taking pills. Still, I wish I had a condom. No telling where Al Kennerly has been if he is crazy enough to beat this woman. She is in no hurry and gets on top of me and pins my arms as if we were two boys wrestling. Without any warning, the door flies open, and there is Al Kennerly with a camera snapping pictures as fast as he can. Lydia turns and cries "Al!" but seems in shock, and I have to push her off of me.

I grab for the bedspread, but can't get hold of anything but the edge since we are lying on top of it. I can't believe I've been so stupid. "Get the hell out of here!" I yelp, but my voice is hoarse with fear and panic. My heart in my throat, I try to see if he has a gun, but I am too blinded by the flashes. I finally jump off the bed and grab my pants, but just as quickly he is out the door, slamming it behind him. I run to the window, but he is already backing out of the lot. I turn to Lydia, who is pulling up her panties. She is crying, her head bowed. I turn away and we dress in silence like a couple who've had a fight. When I look up again, she is slipping into her sandals. "I should have known he was watching. I'm sorry," she says, her voice almost too low to hear.

Miserable, I hang my head, knowing I've done the worst thing to a client (besides steal her money) I can do as a lawyer. Yet it isn't the first time I've let my personal life spill over into the professional. I've gone to bed with two potential witnesses in murder cases, including Angela, although fortunately neither came to trial. "I'm the one who's sorry," I say, feeling a hundred years old. "I should never have come over to the motel. I know better. I wonder how he got a key."

Now dressed, Lydia briskly combs her hair in front of the small mirror over the one dresser in the room. "Al can do anything when he tries."

She sounds resigned. I ask, "Aren't you staying here?"

"No," she says, firmly. "He's gotten what he wanted."

I tuck my shirt into my pants. "You can't just go back to him. He'll beat you again."

She shrugs helplessly. "Would you just leave, please?"

Her tone is polite, but there is a warning in it. I've done enough damage for one night, and she wants me out of here. Not knowing what else to do, I walk out, after telling her to call me in the morning. I drive home, feeling wave after wave of self-hatred surge through me. My head has begun to pound, and I feel about to throw up. The traffic is light, and I have to force myself to drive the speed limit. All I need is to be arrested for drunk driving to make it a perfect evening. What was I thinking? I pound my steering wheel in the humid darkness. God knows what will happen tomorrow. Unless I can get those pictures back, Al Kennerly has put a noose around our necks for the rest of our lives. For an instant, I consider driving to their house, but as I get closer to town, I tell myself I will get myself killed if I go over there. Ten minutes later, I turn into my driveway, realizing not only am I unethical but a coward as well. I drag myself into the house and make it no farther than the kitchen before I vomit into the sink. Standing beside me, Jessie whimpers and ambles off into the utility room to sleep. I fall into bed, thinking that even my own dog is disgusted by me.

• • •

"You look like road kill," Dan says cheerfully when I walk into his office the next morning. "Big night, huh?"

I shut the door behind me and collapse into a chair across from his desk. A big night, all right. On Dan's walls are cartoons from the funny papers: Judge Parker, Mary Worth. I feel like turning them to the wall, so they won't hear. "I've committed the mother of all fuck-ups," I begin and tell Dan the whole story. He listens sympathetically, as I knew he would. I've always thought of Dan as more screwed-up than I am, but now I'm not so sure.

"Was she even remotely worth it?" he asks crudely when I finish. "You must have been completely snorkled."

Instead of giving me a moment's pleasure, the thought of Lydia for some reason makes my skin crawl. "We didn't even do it," I say, remembering now that we never got beyond foreplay. Behind his head, a couple of the cartoons seem crooked. I've had worse hangovers, but I've never felt as bad.

Dan shifts his large frame, making his chair, more like a throne than ordinary office furniture, creak beneath him. "I'm not so sure they haven't set you up. Have you thought of that?"

I rub my head. "Last night about three it occurred to me that it was a possibility."

"How'd he get in if she hadn't given him a key?" he asks rhetorically. "I've had clients who could get into a house with a butter knife, but could you or I do it?"

I stare at the floor. "Why would she pick me?" I ask. "I don't have any money."

Dan spreads his hands as if he were a magician after having made a pigeon disappear. "But you've had some high-profile cases recently. You've gotten acquittals from one end of the state to the other in the last year, and they did the piece on you in the *Arkansas Times* just a month ago."

I was supposed to have been on the cover, but it was killed, and made into an inside story. The editors must have decided I was smaller potatoes than the writer who first sold them on the idea. All they had to do is drive by the defendants' homes to figure out how little I got paid. Still, the issue will be a nice keepsake for Sarah. "I don't think Lydia was in on this," I say, trying to remember any clues in her behavior that I should have picked up. "She seems like a typically battered woman to me."

Dan places his hands behind his head and yawns, unimpressed by my testimonial. "Well, you'll start finding out soon enough."

At eleven Julia buzzes me that Ms. Kennerly is here to see me. I go down the hall and find Lydia on her feet, gazing absently at one of our prints in the waiting room. She is wearing a shapeless turquoise dress that hides her figure as if last night's events can be erased by a hot shower and a change of clothes. I wish it were that easy. She doesn't appear to have gotten much sleep either, but I see no bruises. "How are you?" I ask, trying to read her face.

"I need to talk to you in private," she mutters, not even looking at me.

"Come on back," I say, hoping Julia, who has a mouth on her, is busy on the phone and isn't going to be too curious about this appearance. Usually, but not this time, Julia functions as an early-warning system and can spot trouble a mile away. A niece of the owner of the building, who routinely comes to work dressed like a cheap call girl, she normally takes out the frustrations of her job on the lawyers she serves. Today she is wearing a dress that is as sexless as the one Lydia has on. As I lead the way back to my office, I realize I will blame everybody I see this morning for last night.

Back in my office, Lydia faces me across my desk. "He wants ten thousand for the pictures and the negatives," she says immediately. "If he doesn't get the money by five this afternoon, he'll fight the divorce in court and file an ethics violation against you. He said to tell you that if he doesn't get the money, he'll spend the rest of his life getting you disbarred."

I feel my face go clammy, as my worst fears have been confirmed. "Believe it or not, blackmail is a crime," I say, doing my best to keep my voice calm. Idiot that I am, I still don't know whether she is merely the messenger or the bad news. "I can't be a party to anything like that."

"How can you sit there," she says, anger pumping into her voice with each word, "and just think of yourself? Besides showing the pictures to anyone on the street who cares to see them, he says that he'll go see my aunt this afternoon if he hasn't heard from me. It'll absolutely kill her! You took advantage of me last night, Gideon."

I look down at my calendar, trying to remember how much money I've got. I know I have three thousand in an account that is supposed to go to pay my quarterly estimated taxes, and maybe five in an IRA that I took out when I worked for the county, but I couldn't get that out by five. I have some money in a separate account for Sarah's tuition and room and board her senior year, but I can't touch that. "What's the hurry?" I say, pretending glibness I don't feel. "Has he got a plane to catch?"

Lydia's face becomes an angry mask. "He's not kidding!" she cries. "He'll do it! We're not dealing with somebody who's rational. I know you think that, but he's not."

I can see genuine panic in her eyes, but maybe I am projecting mine onto her. I can feel myself beginning to sweat through my undershirt. "I don't know if I can get my hands on that much money by five."

Like a bookie who is running out of patience, she snaps, "He's not going to bargain with you, and I don't have a dime!"

I was afraid of that. To give myself time to think, I take from my drawer a pocket calculator and mash around on it. My credit is stretched to the limit at my bank. What would I tell Sarah if I took her money? *Your old man's worse than you thought. I don't just stare at my clients* . . . I feel as sick as I did last night. "Yeah, I can do it."

Her face, so soft last night, looks like granite. "Bring the money to the house this afternoon, and he'll sign whatever you want him to and give us the pictures and negatives."

My voice is so tight I can hardly speak. As she stands up, I ask, "Have you seen them?"

She sighs wearily. "They're us, all right. I don't think you want your daughter to see them."

The mention of Sarah's name makes me clench my fists, but she is right, of course. I walk her to the front in a daze. It is as if she were a doctor making a house call to tell a patient he has only a few days to live. Neither of us says a word as the elevator closes in my face. I do my best to compose my features, but Julia cannot be fooled. "You look as if that woman told you in a few months she is going to present you with Gideonette," she says maliciously, her old self now that it is too late.

I don't trust myself to speak, and walk hurriedly past her down the hall and barge into Dan's office. He is on the phone, and I sit down and lean over and put my head between my legs. Dan doesn't even have the money to pay his taxes this year, or I would ask him for help. My brain spins helplessly as I try to think of who could help me pay Sarah's expenses. We're all jacklegs on this floor, I think bitterly. The public thinks that lawyers are rich; everyone I know has complained recently of having a tight quarter. John Upton's name comes to me, and I jump up and run to my office and look for his name in my Rolodex, but when I call, the secretary of his insurance business tells me that John and his wife are on a rafting trip on the Colorado River. I hang up and am flipping through the Rolodex when Dan comes in and demands, "What the hell has happened?"

I look down at the floor and say, hearing my voice as if it were coming from a well, "He wants ten thousand dollars by five o'clock this afternoon, or the shit begins to hit the fan."

Dan sits down so hard in the chair across from my table that I think he has broken it. He whistles. "Do you have that kind of money?"

I feel my eyes redden, and I croak, "If I count Sarah's tuition this fall."

Dan says nothing for a moment, then comments, "He's trying to stampede you."

I wipe my eyes. I've been through some tough times with Dan, but I've never cried in his presence before. I must look like as big a fool as I feel. I look out the window past his head. "He's doing a good job," I say, my voice weak.

Dan grips the sides of the chair, making it groan. "Who are these people? Where did they come from? You've got to find this out. This guy may be wanted in ten states. Her, too. I'll call Renny. Give me the file. He can check these people out."

Renny O'Connor is a cop we both trust, and, unlike half the city, he won't spill his guts. "He's not going to find out anything before five," I say, but hand Dan Lydia's folder from my desk.

As Dan stands up, there is a knock on the door. "Who is it?" I ask, trying to keep the irritation out of my voice. Besides dealing with this horror show, I have a brief due at the court of appeals tomorrow that I've hardly started.

Sarah opens the door and asks, "Dad, have you forgotten about today?"

I look down at my watch. I had promised Sarah I would treat her to a nice lunch her last afternoon before she goes back to Fayetteville to register for classes. "No," I say, forcing a smile. "I'm ready. Let's go."

Dan excuses himself, saying he is too busy to eat with us when I pretend to invite him. Concealing Lydia's file label with his right hand, he heads out the door managing not to attract Sarah's attention. I start to get up but sink like a rock back into my seat and tell her to close the door.

"Dad, what's wrong?" she asks. "You look terrible. Julia said something had blown up on the Kennerly case, but she didn't know what."

"Sit down," I tell her, my voice trembling. There is too little time to hide this fiasco from her. "I've done something awful."

"What is it?" she asks, sitting where Dan had been. She begins to twist her thick, curly hair with her fingers, a trademark sign of internal distress. She reminds me so much of her mother right now that it takes my breath away.

I can't look at her, and pick up a pen and begin to doodle on the pad in front of me.

"Dad, what?" Sarah demands, raising her voice. "What did you do?"

I draw a rudimentary camera. How do I rationalize this? Do I tell her that I was getting back at Angela? Do I say that I was lonely and half drunk? That I am a weak and shitty person who doesn't deserve a law license? "Last night I went out to a motel where Lydia Kennerly was staying and ended up in bed with her when her husband busted in and began taking pictures of us."

Sarah cries, "Oh, Dad, no!"

"I didn't go out there with that intention," I say, unable to resist trying to defend myself. "She was frightened and wanted to talk."

Sarah's eyes fill with tears. "How could you, Daddy?"

For the second time in the last few minutes, I begin to cry. "I don't know," I gasp. "I'm so sorry."

Sarah slumps in the chair and ducks her head. She will never feel the same way about me again. "What happened after that?" she asks. "Can you get the pictures back?"

I draw a dollar sign on the pad over the camera. "If I pay ten thousand dollars by five o'clock this afternoon."

"You don't have that kind of money! Besides, that's blackmail!" my daughter gasps, her face flushed a dark red. "That's wrong!"

"It's horribly wrong," I agree, feeling a sense of depression that I haven't experienced since her mother died. "But if I don't, Ms. Kennerly said her husband would spend the rest of his life trying to take my law license. And it's not just that. She has an aunt who's ill that he'll show the pictures to. He'll paste them up all over town."

Sarah puts her hands to her face, and I notice she has painted her fingernails fire-engine red, a favorite

color of her mother's. When we would go out, in typically Latin fashion Rosa would bring out her four-inch
heels, earrings, and jewelry and transform herself into a
high-priced fashion model instead of a nurse who typically came home exhausted at the end of a shift. She
would have killed me if I had pulled a stunt like this.
"Did she call you?" Sarah asks, reaching for a tissue
from the box on my desk.

"Yeah," I say, "but I knew better than to go. I had
already turned her down once."

Sarah blows her nose, an indelicate sound that another time would make us both giggle. "Daddy, don't
you see?" she says, emphatically. "She's set you up!"

"That's what Dan thinks," I admit. "I'm not so
sure." Is it my ego that won't let me agree with them?
They don't know this woman at all, but what makes me
think I do? Why can't I just admit that I am the biggest
fool who ever lived? I've certainly acted like one. Ego.
Mine will be the last part of me to die. I can hear the
undertaker now: Sarah, it won't fit in the coffin. We'll
have to bury him in two sections.

"Of course she has!" Sarah insists. "They've probably done this before to some other poor schmuck."

"You don't know that," I say, lamely, thinking of
Dan's comment. I've never heard her sound cynical. Al-
ways before she has been almost unbearably idealistic.
Maybe I don't know her as well as I think I do.

"She's not offering to pay any of this, is she?" Sarah
guesses.

I shake my head. "She says she doesn't have any
money."

Sarah bows her head and after a long moment says,
her voice strong, "Why don't you take my college
money, Dad? It won't kill me to lay out a year if I have

to. I've got a job again, and I can probably get a student loan, anyway."

I start crying again, but I can't help it. I get up and go around my desk, and we meet in the middle of the room and she hugs me, patting me on the back as if I were a small child. I don't know what I've done to deserve a kid like this. Nothing, obviously. "Thank you, babe," I say, feeling better by the second. "If I can get through this," I say, earnestly, "it'll be a lesson I won't forget."

Sarah, instead of agreeing, nods absently, as if it isn't a promise she expects me to keep.

Instead of having lunch to celebrate my daughter's senior year in college, I go to my bank and withdraw from two accounts $10,000 in one-hundred-dollar bills. Walking back from the elevator with my briefcase packed with cash, I feel like a drug dealer. Dan meets me at the door and motions me back to his office. "Renny couldn't find anything on them, but he said he would be suspicious," he says before I sit down. "He said scams like this are not unusual. You've heard the old joke: when God took the seventh day off, the Devil appeared out of nowhere and tried to blackmail Him. It's the world's second-oldest crime."

I laugh, but the presupposition that I'm a chump is beginning to rub. Dan adds, "Renny felt compelled to add that he'd like to get involved in an official capacity. He'd love to sting this couple."

Duel of the Hidden Cameras. I don't think I want to see the movie. I check my money even though I just looked at it five minutes ago. It makes me nervous. "I think I'll pass this time," I say. "I'll call him later and tell him what happens."

Dan looks down at a pad on his desk. "I called the

clerk's office in North Carolina. They were married, all right."

I want to say that it is not entirely out of the realm of possibility that this woman was attracted to me, but I know the kind of look I will get from Dan. I tell him about my conversation with Sarah, and he comments, "You're lucky. Not every kid would be so understanding."

"You're right," I say and bite my tongue, wanting to remind Dan of the many times he has shown his ass. "I appreciate your help." It wasn't that long ago that I stood by him in municipal court while he pleaded guilty to his Twinkie episode. Assuming I get through this afternoon, it is going to be a long rehabilitation.

I pull up in front of Lydia's rented house in the southwest part of town, a working-class area without trees and traffic, at three-thirty, unable to wait any longer. Her grass needs cutting, and the outside of the modest wooden structure could stand a coat of paint. Somehow, though, I don't think the ten thousand dollars I have in my briefcase will be going to spruce it up. I assume Al Kennerly will be arriving shortly, since I don't see his LeBaron. Yet for all I really know, she is throwing an early surprise birthday party for me with Al, Sarah, and Dan waiting behind a couch to jump out at me. To his credit, Dan offered to come with me, and I would have let him, but Lydia let me know right away that Al, not surprisingly, has decreed no guests. I have a hastily prepared property settlement and divorce decree for their signatures. For a couple who has so little assets, it is quite an expensive divorce.

Lydia, still wearing the shapeless dress she showed up at the office in, opens the door and looks past me into the street as if she half-expects my own photographer to record this happy event. "You've got the money?" she asks, her face hazy through the mesh of the screen door.

I swing my briefcase against the screen, and she unhooks the door and lets me in. "I have to count it," she says, her voice businesslike and brisk.

I walk in past her and am immediately struck by the unlived-in look of this room, whose furniture consists of a monstrous green couch, a coffee table, and a lamp. There are curtains on the walls but no art, mementos, books, or artifacts of any kind. It is the look of a house whose occupants are in transition. I wonder if Lydia Kennerly has been living here at all. I ask, "When is he coming?"

"He'll be here," Lydia says, taking the briefcase from me and sitting down on the couch.

"Where's the rest of this room?" I ask, watching her face closely as she begins to count the money.

"He took some furniture this morning," she says, not looking at me.

Suddenly I have the sense her husband is in the house, and a chill runs down my neck. Since he apparently had no gun last night, and roared out of the parking lot as if he was scared of me instead of the other way around, I haven't worried about my physical safety, but now I am suddenly on edge. I wander around the room looking out the windows, and when I turn around to ask her where he is, he is standing in the door leading to the back of the house, staring at me. Dressed in jeans and a black T-shirt and Dockers, he has his hands in his back pockets. I think to myself that it wouldn't make a lot of sense to kill me, but based on my performance recently, I'm not going to be asked to be an honorary member of Mensa anytime soon.

"Is it all there, Lydia?" he asks, coming over to the couch but still watching me.

"I'm still counting," she says, her voice brittle. "Please just relax for a minute."

"If you lie to me, Lydia," Al says, "you know what I'll do."

Sickened by this asshole and wanting this to be over, I hand him the divorce decree and attached property settlement I've had in my hand since I gave Lydia the briefcase. "You're going to have to sign this."

Instead of reading it, he merely scans it, and it is clear as day that they are in this together. It was makeup, I think, my mind defaulting to the first time I saw her. This is all an act. I'm the biggest sucker ever born.

Growing more pissed by the second, I watch as Al takes a pen from his pocket and carelessly scrawls his signature on the last page, on the line where Julia has typed "Approved." He probably has signed ten of these in the last year. Finished counting, Lydia asks, her voice stagy, "Now, give us the camera, pictures, and negatives, Al."

I walk over to my briefcase and jerk it out of Lydia's hands and begin stuffing my money into it. "Forget it," I say. "I don't give a damn what you cheap little hustlers do."

Lydia grabs futilely at the bag, further convincing me she is part of the deal. "You must be out of your mind! He'll do everything he says."

"You're damn right I will," Al snarls, curling his right hand into a ball. I stand my ground, doubting he will try to hit me, but ready to take a punch or give one. It's not that he's scared of me. It's just not in their script.

Like a kid who's gotten mad and picked up his marbles out of the dirt, I head for the door without another word. Al, as I figured, doesn't make a move to follow.

These people don't want any trouble with the law. As I slam the door behind me, I hear Al yell, "You'll see your ass on the street this afternoon, counselor!"

Out on the sidewalk and temporarily exhilarated before I begin to worry, I say under my breath, "I've seen it every day for the last week, you son of a bitch, so give me your best shot!"

Slowed by the afternoon traffic, I meander back to the office, running into one construction area after another. Pausing at a light, in the Buick next to me I see a man my own age who is obviously on his way home after a frustrating day, judging by the clenched expression on his face. I look in the mirror and see the same expression. I am tempting Fate. Why didn't I give them the money, get the signatures, pictures, and be done with it? A self-destructive streak, ego, outrage, cheapness? I realize I'm not sure. I begin to relax, knowing I've done the right thing. If ignorance is bliss, I ought to be the happiest man in the universe. I drive on, wondering how Bill Clinton gets out of bed every morning.

Afterword

The first person to read "The Divorce," a career legal services attorney who practices with me at the Center for Arkansas Legal Services, was dismayed by the ending. It was her feeling that the twist I gave the story will possibly lead readers to minimize the pervasiveness of domestic violence in our society. It is certainly not my intention that anyone do so. In fact, after twenty-five years of representing women who have been battered physically and psychologically by their male partners, and receiving some of the training that Sarah in my story would like her father to undergo, I am convinced that most of us are in denial about the nature and proportions of the harm done to women and children throughout the world. Certainly, as a male raised in the South during segregation and general white-male domination, I have had to make my own journey.

—GRIF STOCKLEY

Our parents used to tell us that "cheaters never prosper," but we never believed it, did we? In this story, Steve Martini explains why, as he introduces us to Harvey, the uber-cheat. Is it possible that someone with Harvey's consummate skill for deception could ever meet his match?

Poetic Justice

STEVE MARTINI

Harvey was a lazy lawyer,
a cynic, and an ethics destroyer.
He learned his vices at an early age,
practicing to be the devil's sage.
In school he copied homework before class,
and peeked over shoulders on tests to pass.

He wondered where he'd gotten his scruples,
for after all, he was not a bad pupil.

But somewhere in his distant gene pool,
Harvey found a miraculous tool.
He'd inherited a knack to cheat,
a phenomenal gift he couldn't beat.
Way down in that murky depth,
a serious streak of dishonesty crept.
It didn't come from his father or mother,
his aunt or uncle, or any other.
His relatives were working drones,
civil servants worn to the bone.
They worried about bills and had
low-paying jobs.
To Harvey they were just working slobs.
He was different. He was no fool.
He knew how the world worked,
he'd learn to be cool.

THE CLIMB

By the time he was twelve, Harvey had taken on the primal good looks of a predator—tall and handsome with chiseled features—so that by high school the girls were waiting for him. When it came to the fairer sex, Harvey always went for brains. A good body and a beautiful face were consolations if they could be found. But a good mind allowed Harvey to copy a girl's assignments, and look over her shoulder on exams with no complaint. Like a sailor in every port, Harvey had a girl in every class.

He followed the pattern through college and into law school, where it became more difficult. Now the exams were not simple true-false or multiple choice questions. Now they required the originality of an essay, something in Harvey's own words and sufficiently different from others so that he would not be caught.

But Harvey didn't panic. Harvey never panicked. He relied on old talents and an innate genius for deception that seemed to come so naturally, from somewhere deep down inside.

Harvey struck up a relationship with the dean's secretary. She was Harvey's age, but without the prospects of a law school education. The girl became quite fond of him, and Harvey of her. After all, she possessed the combination to the dean's safe. The safe possessed the questions to every exam, along with the model answers prepared by the professors. With no need to study, Harvey loaded up on units. Why waste time? In less than three years he graduated with honors, said good-bye to the secretary, and was on his way.

Now Harvey had to hurdle the bar examination. This was no mean feat for someone who had never studied in school or earned an honest grade. He had considered the problem for a long time, long before he ever left law school. What good was a law degree if he couldn't use it to make money? Only 50 percent of the applicants who took the bar usually passed it on the first shot. Harvey had no intention of wasting time by taking the exam more than once. Besides, bar review courses were long and tedious. They cost money and offered no guarantees of a passing score. Harvey wanted a sure thing.

To this end he hired a private investigator, a slime-bucket named Jersey Joe Janis. Jersey Joe had skinny legs, a beer belly, and triple jowls. It was a physique that amused Harvey, something on the order of Ichabod Crane, only with a spotted tie and a tidy gut that hung over his belt.

Jersey Joe's specialty was following married men to sleazy motels and taking pictures for anxious wives. His services cost Harvey only a small part of the price for a bar review course, and it guaranteed him a lock on the exam.

Janis posed as a gas company employee, uniform and all. He visited a small printing plant in the center of town and told the owner that the gas company had reports of a dangerous leak. The printer and his employees would have to vacate the building, but just for a few minutes. The leak was probably down the street. But still, to be safe . . .

It took Jersey Joe just ten minutes to collect a complete set of the bar exam questions, along with the model answers to each one. Harvey had discovered the state bar's soft underbelly. They used the same printer every year, a relative of one of their executives. After all, isn't that how everybody got ahead?

Harvey maxed the bar exam on his first shot. He set

up practice in the city center, and specialized in a field for which he seemed to have a natural aptitude—the criminal law. Harvey never really understood why, but for some strange reason he seemed to empathize with, and gravitate toward, those accused of crimes. He grasped perfectly their perverse motivations and skewed logic, even as he scoffed at the slipshod practices that got them caught. Of course, that was why they hired Harvey.

Jersey Joe had stood him well, and so Harvey found other areas in which to employ the man's talents. To be specific, in the offices of the county district attorney.

The law provided Harvey with what it called formal "discovery." This required the state to disclose all of the documents and evidence they intended to use against Harvey's clients in any criminal case. But Harvey wanted more. He wanted an edge, something that his competitors in the criminal bar didn't get. He wanted access to the prosecutor's theory of the case, privileged information that was the product of the other side's work. He wanted copies of their notes and confidential correspondence, and the names of their witnesses before their recollection of events became locked in stone, while Harvey could still *reach them,* so to speak.

Jersey Joe played janitor at night. He planted listening devices in the offices of the deputy prosecutors and used good-looking young men to seduce secretaries in the D.A.'s office. With husky voices on overheated couches and steaming shag carpets, they plumbed the depths for office secrets, and compromised the D.A.'s staff to obtain confidential information.

Within a short time, Harvey knew what prosecutors were thinking before they did. He quickly developed an uncanny record of courtroom victories, outflanking the state on points of evidence, and slamming its witnesses with earlier inconsistent statements.

Prosecutors who could not beat him started dealing with him, giving up cases, rolling over like trained dogs on a stage. Harvey became a principal player in the criminal courts, and soon branched out. He began taking high-dollar civil cases. Other lawyers took heed of him. Some took his measure, but didn't like the odds. Using Jersey Joe, and unknown to his adversaries, Harvey was plucking their files and tapping their phones.

Aware of Harvey's talents but mostly of his amazing intuition at trials, judges began to cut him more slack in the courtroom, as if he needed a further edge. Harvey learned that in the practice of law, a reputation for winning goes a long way. That and a little bluster, which he had in abundance, drove most of his opponents to their knees early. Harvey became known as a man who did his homework. What others didn't know is that it was being done by Jersey Joe.

Harvey joined the silk-sock set. Invited to become a partner in a major downtown law firm, he found a whole new set of clients, upper-crust, waiting for him in the tony skyscraper on K Street. Suddenly he was surrounded by powerful lobbyists and corporate high-rollers. Harvey had made it to Gucci Gulch.

> *He met with Jersey Joe out on the sly,*
> *out of the office and out of the eye.*
> *The man didn't fit with Harvey's new digs,*
> *among high-tone clients and partners*
> *who were prigs.*

> *Janis wondered why Harvey had*
> *become so distant.*

*Though his feelings were hurt
he wasn't persistent.
Jersey Joe was a man who bided his time,
smart as a whip though he looked nickel-dime.*

For seven years Harvey led a charmed life, vacation-ing in the best resorts, running with the chic crowd. He counted among his friends the powerful and wealthy, an elite cadre of celebrities and a growing number of influ-ential politicians. He was courted on television talk shows, where he boosted Harvey-authored books tout-ing his legal prowess, never revealing that the words be-tween the covers were ghostwritten by others.

Harvey was appointed to corporate boards, and joined the best clubs. The law school from which he graduated *magnum cum cheatum* named Harvey as an honorary regent. He received an offer, an appointment to the bench, a tribute that he magnanimously declined. After all, what good would Jersey Joe be there?

In any gathering, Harvey's repute as a top-gun law-yer preceded him, until one evening he climbed the highest peak.

After shaking loose with some coin come election time, Harvey met the top couple, and one night found himself sawing wood in the Lincoln Bedroom—*a friend of the family*.

Now he numbered among his patrons the most powerful man in the land. Harvey was appointed to high commissions and became an advisor to the mighty. Such was his celebrity that he was asked to add his name to the list of partners in an even more powerful law firm, where retired cabinet members hung their spurs of state to turn a profit in the practice of law. He had arrived, and on the door it read:

Harvey of Counsel

He appeared in only important cases
where the stakes were high and the clients aces.
These were all people of the high repute,
corporate high-rollers with golden parachute.
Yet in all of the cases that Harvey tried,
it was Jersey Joe on whose skills he relied.

THE CRIME

The world came crashing down because of a missing tag
from a Chinese laundry.

It was early on a Sunday afternoon when Harvey received the call. There was an urgent problem. It was the
White House. It seemed the President needed Harvey's
help.

They met beyond the black iron fence with its
spear-tipped points, over the manicured lawn long dead
beneath a blanket of snow. In that great white house
they stood toe to toe, Harvey and the great man. He was
ushered to the inner sanctum and offered a seat on a
couch before a crackling fire in that grand elliptical
room.

"Some coffee or tea?"

Harvey politely declined.

"Perhaps something stronger?" asked the President.

Harvey shook his head. He wanted to cut to the
chase.

The presidential problems were no mystery to any
who followed the national scene. The man's troubles
had begun not with a single act but a series of events.
Any one of these taken alone might be almost laughable,
but together they eroded Presidential credibility in the
way that glacial grinding carves canyons.

By the time Harvey was called, there were those in Congress who were talking of "high crimes and misdemeanors," the language of impeachment.

Some claimed he used the IRS
to pursue political ends,
specifically to audit
those who were not his friends.

Others claimed he was snooping
through stacks of personal files,
and wondered what their own were doing
on the White House floor in piles.

There were rumors of campaign abuses,
and the laundering of money,
such an incredible list of scandals
the President dismissed them as funny.

But as months turned into years
it didn't take a sleuth
to figure out the President
had a problem with the truth

But now he had another scandal.
This latest was a whopper.
And what he wanted most of all
was a good lawyer to be the stopper.

All things considered, the man was in deep trouble. Still there were compensating advantages. The President was the repository of power in the mightiest nation on earth. Not a bad friend to have, thought Harvey. No doubt he would have been in jail, except for the fact that he deftly controlled all the levers of power.

He had an attorney general who provided cover by the hour. Whenever scandal got too close, and there was fear he might be nailed, a friendly government lawyer popped up, and some other goat would be unveiled.

> *They offered up business kings*
> *and megabucks tycoons,*
> *and had the gall to tell us all*
> *they were saving children from these goons.*

> *They announced programs every hour*
> *and stories for the press.*
> *They would serve up anything*
> *to distract the people from this mess.*

To Harvey, if the ability to thwart the law wasn't enough, the President had personal strengths to boot. He was the very soul of affability. He possessed the hail bluster of a fellow well met, a disarming smile and the wily mind of one who had weathered many a political storm. Harvey had always been struck by the man's uncanny ability to wiggle away from scandal, usually over the bodies of others, and always with moves befitting a belly dancer.

Harvey admired him greatly! In fact they looked a lot alike, same size and build, brothers under the skin. An affinity that had been planted in their very first meeting, a crowded reception at which the President seemed to notice only Harvey. It was as if there were no one else in the room.

Harvey assumed it must have been his natural magnetism.

The President was tall and handsome, with the generous motions of practiced greatness about him. He

possessed the fluid animation of a pope, except that
when he committed sin, he offered absolution to others.

No matter the accusation, his poll numbers kept
rising. Public sympathy for the man flowed like a bab-
bling spring.

Standing in that great house, Harvey incisively ap-
praised the man's situation.

> *A lifetime in office develops good spin,*
> *variations on the truth like a violin.*
>
> *He could deal with scandal, whether*
> *fact or fiction,*
> *and even when dissembling never*
> *tripped on his diction.*
>
> *When cornered he could slip into*
> *the passive tense:*
> *"Nothing going on here, just some negligence."*
>
> *"Mistakes were made, but no laws were broken."*
> *Even if it wasn't credible, it was*
> *very well-spoken.*
>
> *"We cleared it with our lawyers, they said*
> *it was fine.*
> *We may have come close, but we didn't*
> *cross the line."*

Invented by his spin doctors, these evasions had become the mottoes of his administration, like *E Pluribus
Unum* and *In God We Trust*. What was even more mysti-
fying to Harvey was that the public bought it. As he listened to the chief of state, excuses flowed like silken
mercury from the man's tongue. Harvey realized why it

was that the people ate from his hands like pigeons in a park.

The President's face could assume the full flush of humor as if even the most serious charge was a matter of mere amusement. When things heated up and necessity required, he could work up a healthy head of righteous indignation, a variation on the theme:

> *"Mistakes were made, but*
> *no laws were violated."*
> *Those responsible would be annihilated.*

> *Lawyers and staffers wore sackcloth and ashes,*
> *and were regularly featured in*
> *"Breaking News Flashes."*

> *There wasn't any question;*
> *Harvey had his doubts.*
> *Still the President swore*
> *'twas the truth—or thereabouts.*

"How about a cigar?" The President opened a humidor and offered one to Harvey.

"Cuban made and rolled. I get 'em from Guantánamo. Under the fence, as they say."

"Wouldn't mind," said Harvey as he reached into the box and took one.

"Take a few. They're small."

Harvey helped himself. The President already had one; he lit up and blew. This was the man who had only recently stood on the stump and eviscerated the tobacco industry. He looked at Harvey as if he could read minds.

"Cigars don't count," he said.

They laughed to one another, the way great men do. Just a couple of power people.

Two smoke rings settled like halos over the President's head before they slowly dissipated. This might have been a premonition of things to come, had Harvey been paying attention.

They settled down to business. The President puffed and blew.

"With all of my current problems, I don't need any more. By the way, do we have attorney-client privilege?" He said it as if it were an afterthought, before cleansing his soul.

Harvey assured him that they did.

"Fine. That's fine. I just wanted to be sure. I didn't want to use government lawyers. I didn't know who to trust. It's a serious matter, national security and all."

Harvey's eyebrows arched as he lit up.

"It will require a great deal of discretion. Total secrecy," said the President.

"I understand," said Harvey.

After a long pause and some serious puffs of dense blue smoke, evidence of considerable distress, the President spoke.

"I suspect that one of my cabinet members is selling state secrets. Which one, I can't be sure. I need somebody on the outside who can be my eyes and ears. Someone I can trust to get to the bottom of this thing quickly. I don't know if you've heard, but the FBI is a mess."

"I know." If the agency were up to snuff, the man talking to Harvey probably would have been in jail.

"Why me?" asked Harvey.

"You seem to have a knack at trials to get the evidence you need to win your case. That's the kind of thing I need now. You know. Someone who can fill in all the blanks with the right information."

Harvey couldn't be sure, but he thought for a second that the President had actually winked at him. Perhaps it was some mythic secret sign used by the powerful, like the Masonic handshake or rapper talk. Then again, maybe it was just a nervous twitch. Still, Harvey didn't want to be thought of as a hick. He did the natural thing. He winked back, and then quickly rubbed his eye, as if he had an itch.

Immediately the President smiled. It was a sign. Harvey had been initiated into the fold.

"Then you'll help me."

As a lawyer Harvey'd spent a lifetime building up his name. How could he refuse without diminishing his fame?

"I'm glad to find a man who understands duty." The President rose from his chair and put his left hand firmly on Harvey's shoulder. Then, with his right, he pumped Harvey's hand three or four times with enthusiasm, like he was trying to bring up water out on the prairie.

"Together you and I, we'll find this spy. And if you are successful," said the President, "you can write your own ticket."

That word seemed to bring the great man back down to earth, to the crisis at hand. It was what had caused the predicament in the first place—a missing Chinese laundry ticket.

It all started on a summer day, the kind of day that made the capital famous, hot and humid. It began in the commercial laundry of Too Fu Waun.

A thousand-dollar suit, pinstripes and worsted wool, had somehow become separated from its laundry ticket. The man doing the pressing saw one on the floor and assumed the obvious, pinning it on the coat's lapel.

The suit in turn was shipped to its owner in accordance with the ticket, and received by a sergeant-at-arms at the Capitol, where it was promptly hung on a hook in the senate cloakroom. At the end of the day it was collected without question by one Senator Smooch. He took it home and hung it in his closet. It wasn't until two weeks later when he tried it on that he discovered the suit didn't fit. The pants were too tight and the arms too long. What troubled him most was what he found in the suit coat pocket; a signed check, made out for two million dollars, drawn against a bank in Hong Kong. It was stapled to a note:

> MAKE THE DEPOSIT, AFTER FILLING
> IN THE RIGHT NAME.
> I DECIDED TO LEAVE IT BLANK SO
> YOU COULD AVOID BLAME.

Senator Smooch tried on the coat again, but no matter how hard he tried, he couldn't make it fit.

> *He pulled so hard that he ripped one sleeve,*
> *buttoned the pants but found*
> *he couldn't breathe.*
> *He pulled and grunted and made funny faces.*
> *It just wouldn't fit, even with corset and laces.*

> *But what Smooch found next was*
> *the real bombshell,*
> *a shiny gold pin under the coat's left lapel.*
> *He fingered the check and tried not to fall.*
> *Then rushed to the phone and*
> *promptly placed a call.*

> *He buckled up his dignity,*
> *refused to be the pawn.*
> *Smooch had found a spy nest at Too Fu Waun.*

They were selling out the country in
a sleazy deal,
for there on the pin was the Presidential Seal.

The President indeed had a Teflon coating, for Smooch as it turned out was a friend. The call he placed was to the White House. After getting agreement from the President not to veto the senator's heartfelt bill for a deepwater port in Smooch's home state—Nebraska— the senator turned the pants, the coat, the lapel pin, and the check over to the White House.

Now the President and his people were going to get to the bottom of it. Harvey was assured that he would get full cooperation.

"I don't understand one thing," said Harvey. "How did the pin get there?"

"Presidential pins are given out as favors to friends and supporters. But those particular pins," said the President, "they were only given to members of my cabinet."

"Ahh." Suddenly Harvey understood.

"Too Fu Waun is an agent for a foreign government," said the President.

"How do you know that?"

"Trust me," said the chief, and winked at him again.

This time Harvey got it. It was national security. Details were being parceled out on a need-to-know basis. The President figured Harvey didn't need to know. In fact he said he didn't know himself. It was better that way. Then, if he was called before a federal grand jury, said the President, he couldn't be expected to remember what he never knew. To Harvey it all seemed very confusing. Still, he really didn't care.

What Harvey had in mind was
a pivotal maneuver
to find out where the bodies were,
like J. Edgar Hoover.
While some might believe this was
highly reprehensible,
one thing Harvey knew: it would
make him indispensable.

"We know that the suit belongs to one of my cabinet members. The problem is, we don't know which one. You can see my problem," said the President. "I can't exactly go around the table and ask which one of them's been committing treason."

"It would be a start," said Harvey.

"They'd lie to me."

"All of them?"

The President ignored the question and played his trump card. "If the press finds out, they'll have a field day."

"There you've got a point," said Harvey.

"What I need is for you to use your skills, your discretion, to find out who that suit belongs to." He pointed to a chair in the corner behind Harvey. There on a hanger covered in dark plastic hung the dreaded garment.

He shook Harvey's hand one final time, and led him to the door.

"This should be no problem for a top-notch lawyer like you. Like a walk in the park," said the President. "All in a day's work."

The man was very smooth, thought Harvey. He used your own pride like a crowbar for leverage.

As Harvey left the mansion, he realized too late
he didn't have a thing to prove
he'd met the chief of state.
Still, upon leaving he wasted no time.
He called Jersey Joe to help solve the crime.

THE SLIME

As Harvey assessed it, the matter was plain.
He'd turn it over to Jersey and avoid all the pain.
Joe was nimble and quick of mind;
why should Harvey waste his time?

In this case Jersey was up and running so fast that even Harvey was surprised. Within hours he had a plan, and was ready to go. It was almost as if he'd been waiting for Harvey to show up. But then this was no surprise. Jersey had a deceitful mind, the kind that always seemed to work overtime.

The plan was ingenious in its simplicity, artfully thought out and filled with duplicity. In short, it was a gem.

Jersey pretended to be a photographer doing a layout for *Gentlemen's Quarterly*. It was a piece on "The People of Power," something politicians couldn't resist. Dropping the names of a few movie stars who were also going to be in the piece as bait (Jersey found this opened doors), he began to work his way through the cabinet, visiting their homes and offices with cameras slung about his neck.

Of course he came armed with the ultimate "power suit." Every major world leader was wearing it. Hadn't they heard? The ripped sleeve was the latest thing from Italy.

Even if it didn't fit he wanted to see if the colors

worked on them. As soon as it became a stretch to get on the coat, Jersey would move out, claiming he'd left his film behind, or needed better light. He would call another day, and bring his crew next time.

Two weeks went by and Harvey didn't hear a word from Jersey Joe. He was getting a little nervous, so he called. There was no answer from the man, so he left a message on his tape. Jersey had never failed him. Why would he start now?

Days went by and no call came back. Now he was getting worried. Harvey continued to pursue him for days, leaving messages and trying all of Jersey's haunts. He was becoming increasingly anxious. After all, the President was expecting results. It wouldn't do to keep him waiting.

> Finally on a Friday night, he reached
> the man at home.
> Jersey was busy stretching his mind,
> working on a poem.
> Harvey peppered him with questions,
> and probed to get the news.
> Jersey put him off; he still had
> cabinet members to schmooze.
> Two of them were women, attractive
> and quite slinky.
> Maybe they wore men's suits sometimes,
> thinking it was kinky.

Harvey had learned never to question Jersey Joe's tactics. The man was a master of deceit, well trained in the various forms of low ethics. Besides, he had a good point. It could indeed be a member of the fairer sex. After all, espionage was one of those crimes more in keeping with the female mind, not something manly and aboveboard—like embezzlement.

Even though he trusted Jersey, something prompted Harvey to poke around a little on his own. In later years he would often wonder what caused him to go to the laundry of Too Fu Waun. Maybe it was a sudden flash of mental telepathy. Harvey himself wasn't sure. Perhaps it was just that little nagging voice inside that told him something was wrong, not ethically wrong, but some detail out of place.

Waun's laundry was a dark place, and real steamy. It reminded Harvey of his last date at a drive-in as a teenager. As with the face of the girl he'd taken out, he could make out only faint images of the person on the other side of the counter. It was that hazy.

Harvey introduced himself and said he was checking on a missing piece of laundry. Then he described the pinstriped suit to a tee. He did everything but produce a picture.

"I get boss," said the man across the counter. He was obviously not the owner.

A moment later the steam evaporated as someone turned off a noisy piece of equipment in the back of the shop. Harvey was surprised. The man who approached did not appear to be Asian. Harvey wanted to see the man Waun himself. This guy was tall, a big man, and light-skinned like Harvey. He propped himself against the other side of the counter, looked over at Harvey, and smiled.

"Hi. I'm Harry Tool. Maybe I can help you."

Harvey looked him up and down, and refused to play the fool. "I'm looking for a missing suit. I'd like to talk to Mr. Waun."

The man smiled. "There is no Mr. Waun."

"If he's out, I can come back," said Harvey.

The guy looked at him. Now he was getting a little mean around the eyes. "I told you, there's no Mr. Waun."

"Right," said Harvey. "That's why his name is all over your window. And the plastic clothing covers." He picked one up off the counter, as if to make his point.

"I told you there's no Mr. Waun. Now if you got clothes to clean, fine. If not, there's the door."

Harvey'd spent a lifetime in court. He knew when someone was lying.

"Listen. All I'm looking for is a little information. Get rid of your help here and I can make it worth your while." Harvey nodded toward the Asian standing behind Tool.

Tool looked at his helper, but made no move to dismiss him.

Harvey lifted his wallet from his inside coat pocket and slid three twenty-dollar bills across the counter as a show of good faith.

Tool seemed mystified, but he still didn't dismiss the Asian. "I don't know what you want. What do you think I can tell you?"

"I simply want a couple of minutes with Mr. Waun."

Tool took the three bills and just like that slid them into his shirt pocket. All of this was done brazenly, right in front of the Asian help.

"Now what do you want to know?"

Harvey didn't want to talk in front of the help. After all, blood was thicker than water. Tool might sell out his boss. Harvey wasn't so sure about the Asian.

Tool didn't give him a choice. "You got two minutes of my time."

"You're telling me you're Mr. Waun?"

"No. But for sixty bucks I'll pretend."

"I paid you good money to see Mr. Waun."

"And I told you there is no Mr. Waun."

"Then what's his name doing . . . ?"

"It's a sales gimmick. Don't you get it?" said the man. "Too Fu Waun."

Harvey still didn't understand.

"Two for one," said the man. "You get two suits cleaned and pressed for the price of one."

Harvey forced a smile, but there was a sinking feeling in his stomach, like there was something sick deep down inside. For a second he thought Tool might be lying. But "two for one"? That was too lame to be made up. He swallowed hard, and tried to look cool. Then he did the only thing he could think of. He described the pinstriped suit one more time in hopes that Tool would remember it.

"We get a lot of pinstriped suits," said Tool. "You'd have to be more specific."

Suddenly there was a glow of recognition, not from the man Tool, but instead from his assistant:

> *"Ah, yes belong to President you know,*
> *Secret Service come looking for it,*
> *the day after it go."*

Harvey's eyes got wide and his throat got dry. An electric charge flashed through him like the confusion of a deer when the lights hit him, in that instant before the bumper arrives.

Without another word, he left the shop of Too Fu Waun and in a panic started running down the street toward his car. Harvey had to get away. He had to find Jersey Joe.

Before he could get to his car, two men stepped out

of a side alley. One of them flashed credentials in a wallet.

"FBI. You're under arrest. You have a right to remain silent. Anything you say can be used against you . . ."

While the one man read Harvey his rights, the other cuffed Harvey's hands behind his back. Instantly a dark car pulled up at the curb, and the two men pushed him roughly into the backseat.

Harvey's brain struggled to take it all in. He sat in the back of the car in a daze, and stared out the window at the crowd that was assembling to gawk at the caged criminal the FBI had just arrested.

It was like an out-of-body experience, as if he were floating somewhere in space over the dark unmarked car. Harvey couldn't believe that this was happening to him.

In Harvey's case, justice was swift and the trial very quick. Because it involved espionage and national security, it was closed to the public and the press.

In deference to his high office, the President was allowed to testify on a special closed-circuit television hookup. He was a very busy man. The fate of the nation was in his hands.

His cross-examination was televised from Camp David and lasted only twenty-five minutes. On the big screen, as Harvey watched, the President explained that he had a pressing engagement.

To Harvey it seemed that he emitted an almost sinister smile as he said the word *pressing*. He was meeting with the Premiere of China and some Asian business leaders for an important round of golf. And afterward they were going to discuss a number of important foreign-trade issues.

Harvey knew what kind of "trading" was going on. He had everything but the evidence.

The government's case against Harvey was straightforward and clear. The FBI claimed they caught him in the act, exiting the forbidden Chinese laundry where the infamous suit with the check in the pocket had been laundered. According to the government, he was trying to cover his tracks. Harvey, they said, was the leader of an infamous spy ring.

The President filled in the last missing piece of this puzzle: the notorious lapel pin bearing the Presidential Seal. Yes, he did recall it. It was truly a collector's item. You see, there were only four of them in this style that had ever been made, at the President's own personal expense, of course.

They'd been given only to generous campaign contributors, people who had slept in the Lincoln Bedroom. The other three were all accounted for. The only one that was missing was the pin given to Harvey.

Of course this was a lie. Harvey knew the truth, but how could he prove it? The President had carefully laid the trap and covered all the tracks. It was the reason he'd seized on Harvey in that very first reception. It wasn't because of Harvey's generosity, or the fact that they were spirits of a kind. It was because of Harvey's size and build. The President realized that his suit, the one his valet had stupidly delivered to the laundry with the check still in the pocket, and which had mistakenly been returned to the senate cloakroom, would fit Harvey perfectly.

The President had found his pigeon—and just like the public, he had Harvey eating out of his hands. Now Harvey would pay the price.

The final insult came when the defense put on its case. Harvey called Jersey Joe to the stand. It was his only chance. After all, Jersey was the one person who knew the truth—that Harvey had been framed by the President.

Jersey took the stand, put his hand on the Bible, and swore he'd tell the truth.

"Have you ever seen this suit before?" The lawyer held it up in a clear plastic bag.

"Nope." Just like that. Without hesitation.

Harvey's lawyer was flabbergasted. Harvey was stunned.

"You do know this man?" The lawyer pointed to Harvey sitting at the counsel table.

Jersey squinted from the stand, lifted his glasses to look closely at Harvey.

"He looks like somebody who might have invited me to his office once a long time ago, but I can't be sure."

Jersey hesitated for a moment.

"No. On second thought, I don't think I've ever seen him before. In fact I'm sure of it."

Harvey's head fell into his hands at the table. He was lost.

It wouldn't be until months later, long after Harvey was sentenced, that he finally discovered what happened. Jersey Joe had been named Commissioner of the Internal Revenue Service.

It was a new twist on an old story—"The Emperor's New Clothes." Only in this case it was Harvey who'd been caught in his BVD's.

> Espionage carries a lifetime term,
> so Harvey had time to sit and squirm.
> The cell was cold and the other cons were scary.
> Harvey wasn't getting out until
> the 30th of February.

The President had gotten to Jersey Joe.
Harvey'd been betrayed; a very low blow.
He had many years to think about ethics.
The age-old question: was it social or genetics?

Harvey and the President were the same size.
They shared a lot of other things,
the same color eyes.
If Harvey knew the truth,
he wouldn't be so bitter.
He was made of sterner stuff. He was no quitter.

He and the President both had been adopted.
It wasn't through bad friends that
they'd been co-opted.
They shared one feature that neither
man could know;
they'd inherited their morals from
their dad, Jersey Joe.

Afterword

I am somewhat dubious about saying anything, for fear there might be those readers who would go so far as to suppose that the story is something more than fiction. At one point I toyed with the utterly ridiculous concept of having confidential information in the hands of the FBI regarding illicit political deeds that the FBI fails to pass on to the Justice Department. Then I thought— "Nah. No one would ever believe it." Actually the character for Harvey came from the darker side of a large mythical rabbit I once heard about. It's what happens when things of the mind take on an aspect that is larger than life. Of course it is all fiction. After all, in the end Harvey reaps *poetic justice*. When was the last time you heard of that happening?

—STEVE MARTINI

In addition to having one of the most memorable opening lines in this collection, Jay Brandon's "Stairwell Justice" probably comes closest to showing how law is really practiced in today's criminal courts, where the enormous caseload mandates that over 97 percent of all cases be plea-bargained. In other words, not nearly so many cases are decided in Perry Mason's courtroom as in Jay Brandon's stairwell.

◆

Stairwell Justice

JAY BRANDON

◆

"Motion to have the jury killed, Your Honor."

"Come now, counsel," said kindly old Judge Burr, leaning down from the bench. "That seems a little radical, doesn't it?"

Helen acquiesced to reason. "All right, then, I'll amend the motion. Motion to have that fat bitch in the back who held out for probation killed."

The judge looked thoughtful. "Now that's a reasonable request. I'll grant that."

While the defense lawyer sputtered out an objection, the prosecutor, Helen Myers, turned and glided toward the jurors, smiling. When she smiled she looked guileless as a child, and lawyers who knew her flinched.

The jury hadn't heard the exchange at the bench. The jurors, who had been sequestered together for a week, looked grumpy and unshaven—even the women—and did not smile back at the prosecutor.

"Just for my own information," Helen asked gently, "there's only one of you still voting for probation, isn't that right? Which one is it?"

The other jurors turned and glared at one woman in the middle of the back row, who looked nervous but raised her chin.

"Thank you. Fran?"

The bailiff approached. Helen reached for the bailiff's gun, drew it out of its holster, and cocked the heavy instrument, pointing it at the ceiling. The jurors gasped and leaned as she lowered it. The holdout juror in the back row opened her mouth and glared, but Helen cut her off.

"You have the right to die," she said, and pulled the trigger. The gun made a satisfying explosion in the close confines of the front of the courtroom, and the juror whooshed out of the jury box like a punctured balloon and splatted against the back wall. She still had that ugly look on her face, so Helen blasted her again. All the jurors stared, and some of them began to applaud as the prosecutor carefully handed the gun back to the bailiff, who checked it matter-of-factly and holstered it.

Turning to the judge, the prosecutor said, "I believe we can continue with deliberations satisfactorily now, Your Honor."

She actually murmured that line aloud in her bedroom. Helen Myers rose slowly out of sleep, smiling. It had been a variation on her most satisfying dream. The one that made it worthwhile to get out of bed in the morning, on the ever-so-slim chance it might come true. Helen clung to it as she realized she was waking up, stretching luxuriously in the fluffy cave of the bedclothes.

She tried to hang on to the satisfaction of the dream, before reality reminded her she would be in that courtroom later this morning, and at this point would be very lucky even to get to a punishment phase.

Some lawyers are great trial lawyers. Some are great book lawyers. Some are great at negotiations, at finding the good clients, at collecting fees. Elmer Shemway was the finest stairwell lawyer in the history of the Bexar County Courthouse.

Now, every lawyer is a stairwell lawyer now and again. "Look, step over here for a minute," a criminal lawyer will say to his client, or a civil lawyer to his opposing number. A few ethically challenged attorneys have even been known to stop a judge in the relative privacy of a stairwell for a minute's ex parte conversation. But no one conducted these impromptu conferences as consistently or as well as Elmer. He was in his fifties, tall and slightly stooped from years of huddled conversations, with the gleam of a working mind behind his black-framed specs. The oldest lawyers in the courthouse in San Antonio said Elmer had been a hell of a trial lawyer in his youth, but no one had seen him try a case to conclusion in more than a decade. His great talent was for resolving cases short of trial. Like all lawyers, Elmer feared and mistrusted juries. No matter how good the case looked, something could always go wrong in trial, while a negotiated settlement was certain. Furthermore, trial was a nervewracking pain in the wallet, wasted time that could be better spent acquiring new clients or settling cases: earning money, in other words.

So Elmer Shemway had become the master of the two-minute coercion. He would disappear into the stairwell with a stiff-necked defendant who adamantly refused even to listen to a plea-bargain offer, and emerge with a seemingly different person, one meekly willing to talk turkey. Divorce negotiations might have reached such a pitch that the parties screamed that by God they would stay *married* to each other rather than budge another inch. Elmer's client would be standing in the courthouse hallway with that raised-chin, long-necked, untouchable attitude when suddenly an arm would emerge from the stairwell and the client would vanish with a sort of squeak, only to reappear moments later to say begrudgingly that oh, hell, she'd never really liked that old china of Great-grandmother's anyway.

More than a few prosecutors had cockily followed Elmer down half a flight of stairs and there improved their plea-bargain offers significantly or even agreed to dismiss cases. What did he have on these people? No one knew. The survivors of these sessions in what was universally referred to as "Elmer's office" would never discuss details. This shamefaced brotherhood, which numbered in the dozens, would occasionally glance at each other and shrug or even grin, but they wouldn't talk.

Now Elmer faced his greatest challenge, because his client, a mild but strangely adamant customer named John Willow, might be a con man but steadfastly maintained his innocence in spite of numerous sessions in both Elmer's real and makeshift offices—and prosecuting the case was Helen Myers, who hated shifty defendants and would pursue a case like this, through strong evidence or weak, to the bitter end like she was working on commission. They were in the third day of trial, after hard-fought jury selection, and though Elmer maintained a pleasant quizzical expression, he was beginning to hate everybody in the building, including his client. Helen shared his emotion.

Helen asked her witness, "When did you first notice these discrepancies in the accounts, Mr. Garza?"

"Objection, Your Honor," Elmer interrupted. "Relevance?"

"I will connect this to the defendant, Your Honor," Helen said. She stood tall and straight, one leg cocked slightly forward. Her light brown hair fell to her shoulders; she turned clear blue eyes on Judge Burr. Helen had learned to appear feminine, never hard, before a jury, but could switch in a moment to an expression that defied anyone to cross her. Judge Burr wasn't afraid of her face. He liked Helen, and was letting her get away with perhaps more than she should.

"You keep promising that, counsel," he said idly, but concluded, "Overruled."

"It was about April of last year," the brokerage manager testified.

"And how many people had access to those accounts?"

"Objection," Elmer said, rising quickly. "There's no evidence that this man knows *every*one who might have been able to get into those account records, every potential hacker, intruder, after-hours electronic entrepreneur—"

"Now I object to defense counsel testifying," Helen snapped.

"Perhaps you could rephrase the question," the judge suggested. Elmer sat down with satisfaction. Part of greatness at avoiding trial is the skill of making trial as hard for one's opponent as slogging through wet Play-Doh. The prosecutor had hardly gotten a question out without drawing a long objection from Elmer. If she was going to keep him in this damned courtroom, he was going to make her equally miserable.

"To your knowledge," Helen said forcefully, "how many people could have transferred money out of those accounts, Mr. Garza?"

The smoothly dressed manager raised his chins and said, "Only at the absolute most, four people."

"And was one of those people Jeannine Powers, the financial adviser on several—"

"Objection, leading."

"Sustained."

"Who were those people who had access, Mr. Garza?"

"Well, primarily Jeannine, because she was the financial adviser in charge of several of the accounts."

"So did you suspect Ms. Powers of some sort of misconduct?"

"No. I thought of Jeannine as one of the most scrupulous, strictly honest people I had ever known. I absolutely crossed her off the list of suspects. At least at first."

Elmer said lazily, "Object to speculation, Your Honor."

"This isn't speculation, this is my case!" Helen snapped, throwing down a pencil that bounced off the table with a spectacular snap and roll. "Mr. Shemway is doing his damnedest to prevent my presenting my evidence, but I have a right—"

"Let's take a short recess," Judge Burr said, in the tone of a grade-school teacher. Helen took a deep breath and glanced at the jurors to see the effect of her outburst. The six in the front row were looking at her nervously or sympathetically, but in the middle of the back row the plump, self-satisfied-looking woman smirked at her. Then this juror, the one Helen was becoming sure she would never win over, turned toward the defendant, and smiled.

Damn her.

Standing together by the clerk's desk, under the unoccupied bench, the prosecutor and defense lawyer looked more like weary soldiers of the same army than like opponents. "Look, just make me an offer," Elmer said. "Don't worry, he won't take it. Just give me something to talk over with him."

"Twenty years," Helen said.

"Hel-ennn," the defense lawyer said reprovingly.

"El-mer," she snapped back. "Let's just try it to the end, okay?"

"Look. I don't know what bug's gotten into you,

but could you just back off for a minute and look at this reasonably? There is an air of unreason about this case that if we can all work through—"

"Tell me your client's innocent," Helen said sarcastically.

"Tell me you can prove he's guilty. Look, you've got the account manager dead to rights, why don't you be content with her?"

"Because she didn't do it alone. Your guy conned her into it. He's the one who ended up with more money in his account than he put into it."

"Gee, Helen, isn't that what's supposed to happen with an investment account? Would you only be happy if his balance had gone down every month?"

They stood in grumpy silence. The clerk, Belinda, who always maintained an unflappable calm even when courtroom chaos was at its height, looked back and forth between them and said, "You two need to go on a quiet vacation together."

Helen and Elmer glanced at each other, rolled their eyes, and let their gazes fall on the defendant, who sat as he had throughout trial, in quiet contemplation at the defense table.

"Look at him," Elmer said. "Does he look to you like the great seducer?"

The defendant, John Willow—if that was his real name—was of medium height, medium age, and medium appearance. Not remarkably handsome, certainly, but he had a good chin, an attractive forehead, and a quiet, appealing demeanor. He always kept his eyes down or averted around the prosecutor, so Helen felt she hadn't gotten the full effect of his personality.

"I'll bet he's got hidden reserves," she said. "Real handsome guys don't have to learn to be charming. It's guys like this who can get to a woman."

"Really? Has that been your experience?"

"Stuff it, Elmer. Look at that—woman"—Helen gritted her teeth as she said the word—"on the back row of the jury. She sees something in him."

"You've noticed that, have you? You know you're going to have a holdout there no matter who else you convince."

"We'll see."

The clerk, Belinda, had wide thighs and wise eyes and often seemed to be thinking about something other than the apparent topic of conversation. She seemed like someone who in her private life had ready access to sex or drugs or unconditional love. The continuing crises of the courthouse didn't bother her, because somewhere else she had a real life. She didn't hesitate to advise others to acquire the same. After Elmer walked away, Belinda said to Helen, "You been on a real mean streak lately, girl. How long since you had a date?"

"Date?"

"That's what I thought, you've forgotten what one is."

Helen tried to change the subject. Nodding toward the defendant, she asked, "What do you think of this guy?"

"I don't think as much of him as your pal on the back row seems to. Or as much as your prime witness does. But then, I haven't had her experience with him."

Belinda had had her way with the topic after all. Helen went to put in a call to the witness in question, who was on Helen's team only because she was under indictment herself.

But as trial progressed that afternoon, Helen watched the defendant more closely. John Willow was as formless as oil on water, and sometimes he seemed to be changing before her eyes. Usually he looked mild as a movie cliché of a harmless bank teller or old pharmacist, but occasionally there was sudden decisiveness in the tilt of his head, and strength in the sure movements of his long fingers.

Observing him much more closely was that woman on the back row of the jury, the one Helen had dreamed of killing because the jerk was so obviously smitten with the defendant. Helen began to watch her as well, and an idea took shape. Was John Willow the great seducer? his lawyer had asked. Here was the answer. The juror was silent witness to the defendant's subtle charm, if only people would watch what was going on. How could Helen display that charm to the rest of the jury?

She fantasized throwing the defendant and the juror together for a brief session, under secret scrutiny. Maybe she could get him for jury tampering as well. But where?

During a midafternoon recess, the prosecutor watched where the jurors went. Some of them huddled together, two or three went out on the balcony to smoke, a few down to the coffee shop in the basement. Helen didn't see the woman from the back row.

The defendant was with his lawyer, conferring at the stairs. Helen took the elevator down to the basement, and so missed the sight of her most important witness, Jeannine Powers, coming up the stairs, where Elmer Shemway intercepted her.

When trial resumed that afternoon the defense lawyer had a strange ease, not observed in his courtroom demeanor in many years. Elmer even slacked off on his objections. With another lawyer Helen would have wondered if he'd already spotted some error in the trial, but not Elmer. What happened in the courtroom would be final. Appeal was something neither he nor Helen cared about. Elmer's objections hadn't been designed to create reversible error, they'd just been to harass Helen. Now he no longer cared.

What was wrong with her case? Where had she screwed up? Or was it— She glanced quickly at the rotten juror, who was demurely lowering her eyes. Helen hadn't found the woman in the coffee shop during the afternoon break. When she'd come back up to the courtroom floor she'd seen the defendant emerging from the stairwell.

My God, had she missed their meeting?

Judge Burr was known for the promptness of his five o'clock recesses. When trial adjourned for the day, Helen was across the few feet to the defense table in a heartbeat. As Elmer stood, she was in his face, saying, "I'm going to have your license."

"Gee, Helen, don't you have one of your own?"

"You're gonna think it's funny when you're looking for another way to make a living at your age!" Helen was almost spitting in fury. The defense lawyer saw that she was serious, but his face betrayed no other knowledge. Helen had to spell it out. "You put those two together. You contrived—"

"Who?"

She controlled herself. "Your client and that juror. Now you're sure of her, aren't you? He talked to her. I saw him coming out of the stairwell—"

Elmer turned to his client. "John?"

The defendant spread his hands, with that damned innocent look on his face. Even when he looked at Helen his eyes were somehow hooded. "But Mr. Shemway, you told me not to speak to the jurors. I haven't, I swear. I don't even know which one she's talking about."

Helen thrust a finger toward his nose. "*Do* swear to it. Come on, right now, before the clerk. Then I'll have you for perjury, too!"

"Helen—" Elmer took her arm very gently and led her aside. "This is fantasy, Helen," he said in an undertone.

"Oh yeah?" She stood up to him. That gleam of intelligence in Elmer Shemway's eye went suspicious. Helen dropped her clincher. "Then why have you been so relaxed the last couple of hours, Elmer? Why have you just been sitting there like the case is already in the bag?"

The defense lawyer hesitated, then decided to answer. "Because you've got a worse problem than a juror making lovey eyes at my client, dear. You don't have a case anymore. Why don't you talk to your main witness, the one you've been saving for last?"

Helen felt coldness on the backs of her arms, creeping across her back, making her shoulders stiff. "You mean his lover?" She nodded her chin toward the defendant.

Elmer shook his head reasonably. "His codefendant. That's all they've even been, to everybody except you."

Helen looked past Elmer and saw Jeannine Powers entering the courtroom. The woman was about Helen's age, early thirties, and had Helen's same air of professionalism, though that had been crunched lately by her legal problems. Now Powers, in her business suit and glasses, had a look of resolve Helen didn't like.

Elmer graciously gave them some privacy. "You can even use my office," he said as he drew aside.

But Helen used the empty courtroom instead. "You'll be on first thing tomorrow," she said to Jeannine Powers. "You remember what we've discussed?"

"Yes, but I'm sorry, Ms. Myers. I'm not going to testify to that."

Helen felt suddenly hollow. She held the feeling at bay with a stern tone. "And why not?"

Powers's lips were clenched in a crooked line. She opened them to say, "Because it's not true. John never put me up to shifting any money around in the accounts. Anything I did was my own idea."

"The extra money just happened to end up in his account."

The broker spoke carefully. "I think—whoever did that—did it because John didn't seem like the kind of man to make a fuss about numbers. He wouldn't have involved the authorities, he would have—just kept quiet for a while."

"Or maybe it was supposed to be a little present for him. Was that it? Were you courting him?"

Powers lowered her watery eyes and didn't answer.

Helen clenched her fist, driving down the hollowness. Her face was hot. She still had the weapon she'd had all along. "You know what it means if you go back on our deal. Your getting probation was contingent on your testifying truthfully in this trial. You can forget that now. If he's innocent then you're guilty as sin. I will ruin you. You won't like prison, I guarantee."

Helen had just let the hammer fall, but oddly, Powers didn't crumble. She had an expression of satisfaction, in fact, as she looked up again. "I don't think that will happen. Part of our deal was for me to make restitution. The judge can only order me to pay back those other accounts as a condition of probation. If you send me to prison, nobody gets their money back and everybody will be very unhappy with you."

Helen's mouth opened but she had nothing to fill it for a moment. Jeannine Powers smiled slightly as the prosecutor's hesitation confirmed what Powers had just said.

Helen recovered herself. "So you've gotten legal advice."

As if in answer, Elmer Shemway stuck his head in the courtroom door. "You ladies done?" he asked cheerfully.

Jeannine Powers's face softened. "I'm sorry, Ms. Myers. For everything. I screwed up, but I can make it right. I won't drag John down with me."

"It was you in the stairwell with him," Helen suddenly realized. "Not the juror, you."

Powers blushed. She turned away, murmuring another apology. In a moment, the defense lawyer took her place. Elmer shrugged apologetically too, but couldn't keep his happiness from showing. "So are we done? Do I have to come back here in the morning, or will you do the gracious thing and fill out the dismissal form now?"

"*You* put them together," Helen said. She was glaring. Mention of dismissal made her fingers tremble.

Elmer didn't deny anything. "There's no legal reason why they can't talk to each other. They're friends."

"They're on opposite sides of a case in progress. They—"

"Not anymore," Elmer said. Then he added kindly, "It doesn't reflect on you, Helen. It was a weak case to begin with. All you had was the word of an admitted thief. The jury probably wouldn't have believed her anyway. I don't know why you did."

Because Helen had understood, in a way Elmer never could, how a woman like Jeannine Powers could be susceptible to a con: a woman of professional acumen and forceful personality, but one whose nights were too long and too quiet. Helen had seen through

John Willow. From his initial court appearance she had discounted his mild expression, had seen the quiet, insistent charm of a seducer.

The courthouse was draining of people, clerks and lawyers and judges swirling down the stairs and elevators as Helen swam against the tide upstairs to her office. The hollow feeling still threatened her, made her want to just sit down and put her head in her hands. She fought the feeling. This case wasn't over. She wouldn't let it be.

Upstairs she automatically picked up her messages off the secretary's vacated desk and took them into her own tiny office, which was decorated with boxes of files and stacks of paper. The lone bright spot on her bulletin board was a postcard sent to her from the Caribbean two years ago, when her parents had taken an anniversary cruise.

Helen slumped at her desk. More evidence. She needed more evidence. Maybe in the morning she could turn Jeannine Powers again, but if not, she needed other evidence to replace her testimony. Helen's evidence was thin enough: she had the stolen money ending up in John Willow's investment account. She needed something to show his hand in that theft, some act, some guilty knowledge. But she had already interviewed everyone at the brokerage, everyone with money missing from their accounts. None of them could put John Willow's fingerprints on the stolen funds.

Idly, she sifted through her mail. Official stuff, nothing personal. At first she skipped over the one with the Seattle postmark, because she didn't know anyone in Seattle. But then she noticed it was from the District Attorney's Office in Seattle.

The computer system had shown no criminal record for a John Willow with this defendant's birthday.

But that hadn't been good enough for Helen in the intensity with which she had prepared this case. She had sent his prints and pictures to a dozen big cities across the country, particularly those with a significant computer industry, because that was the defendant's occupation.

Fingers beginning to tremble again, she opened the envelope from Seattle. Enclosed documents fell in her lap. One was a reproduction of a photograph, a picture of an unhappy man with police lights in his face. Helen stared, then her heart beat faster. She picked up the picture and planted a big kiss on it.

At home, she had a glass of wine to celebrate. Later, when she noticed how dark it was outside, instead of doing anything about dinner she had another glass of wine and put on a CD. The smooth voice of the singer, doing a great impression of a woman in love, wrapped itself around Helen. The hollowness in the pit of her stomach had turned to warmth. Or maybe that was the wine. Helen hugged herself, warding off a slight chill that made her skin tingle.

She had the picture propped up on her coffee table under a candle. She studied it again, raised her glass to him, and smiled broadly. Her hands turned from warming to caressing. For the first time in months, she wanted a cigarette. But she didn't indulge that urge. She stayed in the big easy chair, drifting into fantasy, anticipating the morning.

"Uh-oh," Elmer Shemway said to his client. He had just seen Helen Myers's smile.

Half an hour earlier, when the courtroom was almost empty, Belinda had noticed it too. "Girl, you dragged out of here yesterday and bounced in this morning. What happened?"

"I had a good night," Helen had said, blushing.

Belinda brightened. "Met somebody?"

"No. Something to do with the case."

Belinda snorted. "Unless you are really twisted, a 'case' doesn't make you blush like that."

"Well, I—I had a pleasant evening after that, too."

Belinda had lowered her voice after that. "Really? Something—sensual?"

Helen had laughed, nervously as a schoolgirl. "Well, it was self-inflicted, but—"

Belinda had smiled at her proudly. "Still, that's a big step for you, isn't it? Tell me, were you thinking about—him?"

"Him who?"

Belinda had laughed as if Helen had said something coy.

And now Elmer Shemway approached her apprehensively. "Good morning, Helen. Has Ms. Powers changed her mind again? You know, I'll be able to impeach her with what she said—"

Helen smiled at him. "That's not it. I'm sure this will be a shock for you, Elmer. Did your guy tell you he's on probation?"

Elmer grunted as if she'd punched him. Helen enjoyed the sound. They both turned and looked at John Willow in the doorway. Innocence must have been a permanent feature of his face, because he still looked it, even with what Helen knew about him.

"For theft," Helen added with satisfaction. "He stole from the company where he worked in Seattle."

Across the room, John Willow looked at her quizzically. Not at his lawyer, at Helen. Then his expression turned remorseful. He seemed to know what was happening.

Elmer was thinking quickly. "Probation means it's not a final conviction. It's inadmissible evidence. And if I don't put him on the stand—"

"I don't need to prove the conviction, Elmer, just the theft itself. I'll prove the theft in Seattle to show pattern, motive . . . It's admissible for that."

Elmer sighed. "Let's go talk to him."

Helen was delighted to do so. She felt the stir of triumph as she glided toward the defendant. She wasn't even apprehensive about following the men into the privacy of Elmer's "office," down half a flight of stairs. When the three of them were alone on the landing Elmer quickly briefed his client. Willow nodded. He put his strong hands together and ran the tips of both index fingers along his lips.

"Why didn't you tell me, John?" Elmer asked.

The defendant had the voice of a penitent down pat. You had to admire his technique. "Because I thought I'd put it behind me. It was a terrible mistake. I pled guilty because I was protecting someone else."

"Yeah, right," Helen sneered. "A woman, right? You're famous for your gallantry."

Elmer intervened. "Now what, Helen? Do you want to make an offer? I'm sure John will be more receptive now."

Helen still felt the fierceness of victory, like the warmth of last night's wine. "You don't get it," she said. "I'm going to get him sent to prison here, then I'm going to Seattle to see his probation gets revoked there. He can do a comparative study of Texas and Washington state prisons."

"I don't think you can do either of those things, Helen. You still can't prove this one, and if you can't prove he committed another crime you can't get him revoked in Seattle. Let's be reasonable. Probation . . ."

Still studying the defendant, Helen thought. It was true her evidence was still very thin. Even assuming Judge Burr allowed her to prove the theft in Seattle, she might not have enough to convince the jury. Especially with that bitch on the back row as a wild card.

Elmer saw that he wasn't getting through. The stairwell was a narrow space. He had counted on that confined feeling many times over the years, but now he felt it himself. He saw Helen staring at John Willow, trying to penetrate him. Elmer looked at the client, who was standing there downcast, and saw Willow's fingers twitch slightly.

Elmer's gaze returned to Helen. The woman was taut as barbed wire. "What is it about him, Helen?" Elmer asked softly. "What makes you think you know him better than any of the rest of us do?"

Helen didn't answer quickly. For a moment she pondered her own motives. She looked John Willow over closely. What was it about him that made her so sure of his guilt? She noticed for the first time that he was compactly built but well-proportioned. His suit didn't emphasize his shoulders, but she would bet they were nicely wide.

"John?" Elmer's voice was disembodied. The defense lawyer could have been fading out of the stairwell, leaving only his deep, smooth voice; the voice of reason. "Don't you have anything to say to Ms. Myers?"

Willow felt the prosecutor's eyes on him. His gaze traveled up Helen, starting at her feet. She felt it. His scrutiny made her stand straighter. Finally his eyes lifted to hers. For the first time, he gave her a direct stare. His eyes came unhooded.

• • •

Elmer Shemway emerged from the stairwell alone. When Judge Burr took the bench and the jury was in place, two conspicuous seats at the counsel tables were empty. The defense lawyer said simply, "We were conferring in the stairwell when Mr. Willow and Ms. Myers suddenly left together."

"Together?" Judge Burr stared. "Where were they going?"

"They didn't tell me, Your Honor. But there was a certain—intensity in the air. I think they were eloping."

"Mr. Shemway, I am a retired, visiting judge, but I still have contempt powers. If you won't give this court a straight answer—"

Elmer did his best, but convinced no one. Trial was recessed, bailiffs sent through the halls and the stairwells. The judge himself called the D.A.'s office, where prosecutors and secretaries were soon scouring their offices and making calls, to no avail. Late in the morning the judge extended the search citywide by issuing an arrest warrant for the defendant, but that didn't help either. The prosecutor and the defendant were gone.

But not forgotten. Judge Burr recessed the trial indefinitely, but that didn't end the search. Elmer Shemway was held briefly under arrest on the theory that, driven to fury by the refusal of the prosecutor and his client to negotiate, he had killed them both. The stairwell was sprayed for traces of fresh blood. Elmer's suit was analyzed while he stood furiously in a raincoat in a detective's office. He was finally released when investigation turned up no evidence of foul play.

The search slowed, but the theorizing heated up, even going science fictional. A prosecutor came up with the idea that Elmer Shemway had sort of absorbed them both, absorbed their contradictory natures, made them part of himself: a triumphant culmination of what he normally did in stairwells.

That prosecutor was reassigned to the juvenile section, miles away, but people continued to stare very curiously at Elmer Shemway as he made his cheerful rounds through the courts. He couldn't drag another lawyer into a stairwell for weeks.

The beach at Isla de las Mujeres. That's where people told Helen she was. She took their word for it. A narrow beach, but of pure white sand, and it was barely populated. She walked out under the bright sun, feeling the ever-so-gradually-deepening water rise up her legs. She plunged into the clear blue, almost evaporating into it, losing her own outlines, until she walked out again, droplets forming on her skin, the sun desiring them. She was turning brown, setting off the bright blue bikini to advantage.

Helen plopped down full-length on the comfortable pads of a lounge chair and sighed. She felt like the heroine of a movie, fled from legal complications to a remote beach.

But that was an illusion. Helen was still on the case.

She turned toward the adjacent lounge chair and looked at John Willow. She had been right about how he was built—not large, hardly taller than Helen herself, but well-proportioned. Blond crinkly hair on his chest, freckles beginning to appear on his wide shoulders. He smiled at her. She could see his eyes, deep green like the Caribbean farther out from shore.

She had him now. Flight was evidence of a guilty conscience, and no one could deny that John Willow had fled from his trial. Helen could no longer prosecute the case, of course, but she could be the prosecution's star witness when trial resumed—whenever that might be. She could testify to his flight to avoid prosecution.

She would also be able to testify to his seductive ways. That was her plan, anyway. In the stairwell back in San Antonio she'd been so sure, but my God he was slow. He hadn't even touched her yet. She watched surreptitiously for the charm he must have exercised on his partners in crime. On that subject Helen hoped soon to be an expert witness—if John would show more response than he had so far.

She lay back on the lounge, dropping sunglasses over her closed eyes. She warded off thoughts. Too much of her life had been spent thinking. For a lovely tranquil moment she just existed, under the sun.

So slowly it could have been in her imagination, she became aware of a warm hand on her leg. It was John's hands she had noticed in court as much as his eyes: his long fingers with their rounded, gentle tips. Those fingers stroked her thigh, drifting unhurriedly higher.

She slitted her eyes and saw him leaning toward her, coming closer. Helen's lips parted in a wide smile.

"Mmmm," she murmured. Ah yes. Oh, good.

More evidence.

Afterword

This story is dedicated to the clerks of the Bexar County judicial system . . .

. . . most of whom know more about legal procedure than the lawyers they watch pass through their courtrooms every day.

When I was in law school, my friend Robert Morrow—already a lawyer then—pointed out to me a man he said was known as a great stairwell lawyer. Ever since then, I've wanted to write a piece of fiction pointing out that legal skills come in a great variety, few of them courtroom-related.

Fictional lawyers always seem eager to go to trial, to get into the courtroom and display themselves. What all lawyers know and few of these fictions acknowledge is that the great majority of lawyers never go to trial, and even among "trial lawyers," trial is usually the least desirable outcome of a case. So I also wanted to write a story about a damned good lawyer who hates to go to trial—believe me, a very true-to-life character.

I'd also like to note that a small segment of readers will recognize that this story takes place in the century-old Bexar County Courthouse, rather than in the much newer Justice Center next door. The Justice Center is new and spacious and clean, but its stairwells are pitifully unworkable as conference spaces.

Finally, the title of this story, of course, is a tribute to our esteemed editor. Other tributes are scattered throughout. I want to thank you for your service today, ladies and gentlemen. I've been watching you and I've noticed that you were paying very close attention to the evidence . . .

—JAY BRANDON

A young man's first adventure in the "real" world is a favorite subject for writers, but through the eyes of young Charles Morris, Richard North Patterson tells the story with such honesty and heart that it is fresh in approach and universal in impact. Charles's tutelage under senior lawyer Sam Goldman is a distinguished work of fiction you will not soon forget.

The Client

RICHARD NORTH PATTERSON

I liked Sam Goldman from the first.

He stuck out his hand. "Well, Charles Morris, tell me about it."

I was thrown off for a moment. "The long version, or the condensed one?" I managed.

Goldman's eyes brightened. "The condensed, to start. If it catches my interest, I'll ask for the whole thing."

"All right. I need a job."

An hour later, I had one.

After a month or so, Goldman asked what I had thought, while I waited in his reception room. "After all, I'm not one of those gilt-edged firms who were courting you."

I took inventory of my first impressions. His office was on the sixth floor of an old bank building. It had one door, wooden, with an opaque glass square which was actually a grid of small pentagons, lettered in black: SAM GOLDMAN, ATTORNEY-AT-LAW. I had entered to a sixtyish receptionist who looked like someone's nice aunt. "You must be Mr. Morris." She smiled, and then buzzed Goldman to announce my presence, her voice suggesting that he would be pleased. The room was small but light, with several bright prints and some green potted plants in the corners. I sat in a leather chair on one side of which was an ornate standing gold ashtray with a couple of nicks to confirm its age. The table on the other side was dark mahogany, and there was no

Wall Street Journal on it. Instead, there were two back issues of *Natural History* and a copy of *Variety*.

"I thought," I told him, "that you were the first place I'd seen in Mobile that didn't have a receptionist with a voice like buried secrets, or portraits of dead partners on the wall. Also that the place was too small to represent a bank, so you must have clients you could really see."

Goldman smiled and I recalled also that I had thought he resembled Jack Benny, whom I remembered from the time my parents first acquired a television set and we would watch Jack Benny being outquipped by the gravel-voiced black man. Benny and Goldman had the same aspect of bemused kindness. "He's an old man," I had thought of Goldman. He was seventy, in fact, and had a fringe of gray hair, liver marks on his hands, and the halting movement old people have as if the movement is from memory and their memory is failing. He was short and thick-waisted; his voice was a rich, ancient rumble, like smoke and bourbon. But his grip was strong and his speech quick and colorful.

"I'll tell you the reason the large firms represent banks," he answered, with the solemnity of a man revealing a great truth. "It's the idiot nephew principle. If you check into it, it always started about three generations before, when a founding partner's idiot nephew married a banker's daughter, thereby spawning seventy-five years of overbilling and a couple of interlocking directorates. Unfortunately, my grandfather's idiot nephews hadn't immigrated yet, and therefore were no good to me at all."

I grinned back, cheerful with the knowledge that I had chosen well. I had been up in the Northeast for seven years, at college and law school, and had pondered staying on. But Mobile meant continuity, an adding up of things, and I couldn't cut off my youth as if it were a dead stump. I savored the feeling of home now; the absence of rush and unexpectedness, the green and moss, the slow, sleepy timelessness of it. And Goldman was an honest lawyer, as I wished to be, who gave value and billed his poorer clients just enough, as he put it, "so they don't go somewhere else." I learned that after his wife's death he had grown lonely, and especially so since his son left for Washington and his old partner, Kraus, retired to Key West "to make a profession out of old age." Goldman's clients were still his profession and his pride—protecting their interests, advising, being valuable. So he had work to do, and I was needed.

At first, I depended on him totally. I would sit in front of his walnut desk, picking up the faint, pleasant odor of leather and good cigars, while he peered intently at my work through half-glasses, marking in pencil with crabbed strokes of a blue-veined hand. Then, patiently, he would teach me, concluding with a pointed story. For Goldman, law wasn't casebooks, but vectors of life—anthropology, sociology—and people, causing it all. Some of those people were old now. "Half the time my office looks like God's waiting room," Goldman would say. "I feel like a damned undertaker. It's a hell of a thing, watching your friends die, or getting ready to." So I learned wills and trusts for Goldman's friends, learned as well to love the law—its quirks and arcane points—and to feel its growth, its tracing of human relations, as they twisted, changed, evolved through time, like gnarled branches. Goldman's praise grew frequent. So I began to do the Bensons' work.

Case Benson had been Goldman's breakthrough client, his prize, and forty years later the Bensons were still special, with their tangle of small corporations and tax shelters which Goldman had nurtured, like an exotic plant. Benson was over seventy now, with sharp, Southern eyes, steel-blue, which crinkled when he smiled; eyes that seemed made to take in a field of crops, or spot a deer, as if a rural past were stamped on his genetic code. He would visit in the morning, around ten. "Morning, Sam," he would say, and sit in the chair to the left of Goldman's desk, stretching his legs in front of him. After a while he would strike a match, and they would talk through the thin blue haze of Benson's cigar, shrewdly, with the economy of men who had not merely time to kill but affairs to tend.

The visits had an almost ritual quality, as if each man were a pillar of the other's reality, which required periodic checking. And there was warmth there. At first, I was a stranger to the warmth, but slowly, I became a part of it. The two men repeated stories for my benefit, explained, amplified, and I knew the meetings were better for my presence. I came to anticipate the visits, savor the feeling of them. I never overstepped, said too much, or told stories of my own. But I learned: of Benson's beginnings, of his politics, and most important, of his business. Gradually, I took over the nuts and bolts of Benson's work: the taxes, the contracts, the acquisitions. Goldman reviewed it all minutely.

Late one afternoon, I asked the reason for that. Goldman stared thoughtfully at some middle distance. "I suppose," he finally said, "that it's very hard to let go. It's admitting that you aren't essential, which is like admitting that you're going to die." He waved away my answer before I could make it. "All that's foolish, I know, and your work is fine. But Case Benson's my oldest client and he came to me when I was quite young, very eager, and with no money. Benson had some capital but he needed loans. I helped him get some during the Depression, when leverage was a dirty word and he didn't have much security. He bought into a paper mill and then into this and that, and I grew with him. I could have been his partner, but it's foolish to be partners with your client—you lose your freedom. I never wanted Case Benson to make a tycoon out of me.

"The important thing was that he was my first big gentile client. This was a traditional place, and people were slow to change. But a Jewish lawyer could get gentile business if he was in the right spot. I know some of these people still talk about having this good Jewish lawyer." Goldman was smiling now. "They think that sounds very sophisticated, like having been to Europe. Anyhow, Case Benson helped me get new business, by example as much as anything, and it made things easier for me. Case is a good man, even if his sons aren't worth a damn." Goldman stopped abruptly and looked at his watch. "It's five-thirty, Charles. Would you like a drink?"

So Sam Goldman and I took to having a bourbon or two, after the work was done and Mrs. Selfridge, the receptionist, had gone home. Some days, one of us might be too busy, or tied up with clients. But if work had wound down and the phone stopped jangling, I would drift into Goldman's office about five-thirty. Goldman would reach for the decanter in his credenza and I would go for ice from the refrigerator jammed in the corner of the filing room. And then Goldman would pour the bourbon in two glasses, carefully, sealing an act of hospitality.

While he poured, I would look around the office, at the sculpted head of the black man on Goldman's desk, or the ancient lawbooks on the shelves, or the picture of Robert Kennedy on the wall behind Goldman's high-backed chair. It bore a personal inscription and finally I asked about that. Goldman pondered as he snipped the end off his cigar with a small gold penknife. He lit the cigar, and took a reflective puff. "He was a decent boy, that one, even if folks didn't like him. I helped him down here a little, gave his people an office to work from when they had those troubles with Wallace and the big firms were keeping their heads down. That was a shameful time, but our people have grown since then. People change, but sometimes you have to kick them in the butt, and that's what the Kennedys did, after the blacks started kicking them a little. Back then it was bad, though, and Sarah and I used to get calls from the Ku Klux Klan at night—they were going to kill me or castrate me because I was a 'nigger lover,' they said. I finally got a dog whistle and put it by my bed, and when one of those ignorant SOBs called, I'd blow it in his ear. I understand that hurts considerably, and after a while they stopped calling. They were always better at hurting people who couldn't hurt back—bombing schoolchildren or beating people in packs."

The stories fascinated me. My own family had always implied that blacks would have evolved through the natural gentility of the better whites, without all this marching and disruption, which had just upset people, put their teeth on edge. I explained this once and Goldman smiled. "They'd still be waiting to use the john marked 'Coloreds Only' if they hadn't raised some hell. It's funny, though, what I learned about myself after things got better. I'd tried to help blacks for years and then we won, and I was half surprised and missed the fight a little. The damnedest thing is I go to Birmingham now and the Hyatt House is filled with blacks having a convention or something, and I can't get used to it. You see, I'd had a piece of the system too." And Goldman shook his head at his own foolishness.

So I poured a second drink and told about when I was a sophomore at Columbia, and had gone out with a black girl from Barnard. We had smoked a little marijuana and spent the night together, and I'd expected some great revelation, but it had been like anything else, two people, that was all. "I had this idea I was going to understand Ray Charles better or something. Finally, the girl admitted that she had thought the same thing, in reverse. I owned up about Ray Charles and she said maybe I could try being blind, too. I was feeling pretty foolish, but she laughed—at both of us—and we wound up friends. But I can't say I learned much about black people from it. Just about myself." Goldman nodded and smiled, and the conversation went on, through politics and recollection, and the day's work.

Sometimes I would mention Case Benson's sons. Goldman had seen to it that I did their work, hoping that we would become friends, as he and Case Benson had been. But whereas the old man was a businessman, the boys were plungers, impatient men looking for the big kill. They bought land and influence feverishly, and were friends with the governor, to whom they gave money and condescended behind his back. I sensed that they saw Goldman as a family relic and me as a cub lawyer, of no account. It worried me, even then: it was the one thing that Goldman could not correct, perhaps did not fully know.

One morning they came to my office to discuss a case. Carter Benson was a dark man around thirty-five, handsome in a reckless way, with a hard, closed-off face and gambler's eyes. Case Jr. was thirtyish, a sullen, taffy lump of resentments which I didn't fully fathom. They had sprawled in their chairs with ostentatious boredom while I explained the suit. "The question is whether you knew the stairwell in your building was dangerous *before* she took that fall. As to that, there's only one document in your files that bothers me." I pushed a photocopied page across the desk at Carter Benson. "It's this memo from the property manager to you, one week before the accident. You'll note that he says the stairs are badly lit and shaky in two places. Did you read that?"

Carter Benson tossed the memo back on my desk. "And if I did?"

"Then it probably would be smart to settle."

Benson pointed at the memo. "Does the other side know about that?"

"Not yet. But they've subpoenaed us for all relevant documents."

"Why don't you just lose it?" Benson said casually.

I shook my head. "I can't do that."

"You're our lawyer," he snapped, "not our spiritual leader."

"Look, Carter, I won't be unethical—for you or anyone."

"There are other lawyers, Charles."

I fell back upon Goldman. "If you're not satisfied," I dodged, "why don't we get together with your father. Sam Goldman's ethics have been good enough for him." And Carter Benson backed down, knowing that his father would disapprove. But after that, the Benson boys made it clear that I was of no use in practical things. And I saw in them the breakdown in people's relations: the cheating, the corner-cutting, the shoddy products. "I don't like them worth a damn," I admitted to Goldman.

Goldman's face was furrowed with concern. "Case has never asked me to do anything dishonest. He believes as I do—that if you're honest, you'll last—and be able to stomach yourself at the end of it. So stand up to them, Charles, and they'll respect you. But remember," he pointed a stubby finger, "as long as they're within the law, you're their champion—that's the basis for our profession. The client must believe that whatever you know—or whatever you think of him—will stay within this office. If you don't remember anything else, remember that." Goldman caught himself in mid-lecture and tried to make light of it. "Anyhow, Case and Julie didn't have children until they were past thirty-five, so those boys aren't as smart as they could be. If they'd waited much longer, we'd probably have to lead the boys around on a leash."

I felt the tug of misgivings through my amusement. "You know, they're getting thick with a couple of politicians over in Baldwin County, campaign money and the rest. Any notion why?"

Goldman shrugged. "No, but I suppose we'll find out, sooner or later. Anyhow, as long as Case is alive, we'll keep the boys on the reservation." I knew that was what he believed. So I let it go, and Goldman began puzzling over the neutron bomb. "Imagine that, it kills the people and saves the buildings." He shook his head, then brightened. "They could drop it on Germany. They have miserable people, but fine cathedrals."

I nodded agreeably. "You could turn Germany into a nice museum, like Williamsburg." We both laughed, because Goldman wouldn't harm anyone. And the conversation went on, and the days and months, turning like pages in a book. I learned, not just law, but people. I learned to doubt coincidence, to read motive, to negotiate when money or passion was at stake. "You're a fine young man, Charles," Goldman said, "and a fine lawyer." His words meant more to me than money or prestige. I was growing, and I felt that, and my debt to Goldman. I grew to understand that he was giving me his practice, his ideals, and all the things he knew. I had been admitted to his world, as rare and special as a daguerreotype.

His window looked on the soothing blue sameness of Mobile Bay, and summer evenings it filtered the fading sunlight in golden shafts, lending the gauzy richness of an ancient colored photograph in which the tints have blurred. I would feel the leather grain of the old lawbooks, taste the ashy glow of bourbon, its biting warm coldness over ice. The grace of Mobile enveloped me, the spell of a particular place and time, the easy expectedness of things. And at the center was Goldman in his high-backed chair, his wit and opinion strained through decency, softened by a deep, quiet drawl.

I thought that the change began when Case Benson died. We had been in Bienville Square after lunch, dodging the pigeons. I was wearing a white linen suit. Goldman had complimented me, and we strolled along, Goldman gesturing while I walked beside him, half a foot taller. We turned through the marble entrance into the old bank building and took the elevator up to the office. Mrs. Selfridge sat behind her desk, wearing a tight, queer expression. "Mr. Benson is dead," she said. "Heart attack." And Goldman walked to his office and closed the door.

It was his memory I noticed first. The change was subtle: Goldman wouldn't forget the things themselves, but whether he had mentioned them before. "Have I given you the Peterson will?" he would ask, having asked the day before. Or he would meet with a client, then describe the meeting twice. At first, Goldman would do such things, then cock his head, as if he had heard a false note in his brain. And then slowly, perceptibly, his doubts vanished, and the forgetfulness grew.

He began losing things, keys, files. One afternoon, I found him standing behind his desk, staring as if utterly lost. "I've lost my damned penknife," he said. "Can't find it." I spotted the gold penknife at Goldman's feet. "Got it," I said brightly. "Can't find things," Goldman had grumped. "Sarah could always find things." And I felt a sadness, as if I had begun to lose him.

Goldman became slower, more tired. Sometimes he would go home early, or his hands would tremble slightly in the late afternoon, when he poured our drinks. So I began to dictate letters for his signature, explaining to him that he couldn't advise me if he was tied up with details. I scrambled to use what he had taught, to hold the confidence of clients, not in me, but in Goldman. And after dinner, I would return, alone, to review Goldman's work.

The Bensons received my special attention. The sons had taken over, with new ideas and the casual disdain of the young for the old. Goldman held no magic for them: they treated him with a bored courtesy as painful as a slap in the face. Or so it seemed to me, but Goldman didn't notice. To him, their meetings were suffused with his service to Case Benson, and I thought that the sound of his own voice must recall the easy confidence of the relationship between the two men. The boys, with their quicksilver greed, were to Goldman not real in themselves, but rather a touchstone to memory. It was as though some primal part of Goldman grasped at them as at a talisman from which he could wrench wasted powers, renew faded skills. I marked their impatience, feared that Goldman would lose them, feared more what that would do. The office—Mrs. Selfridge, his clients—was his world now. I covered my distaste for the Bensons with renewed concern for their affairs.

· · ·

One gray morning in the fall, Goldman called me to his office. The Bensons were there, unexpectedly. They lounged silently in front of his desk, their posture oddly impersonal, as if Goldman were an overstuffed chair they were about to give to the Salvation Army. The silence had a tautness to it. "For God's sake, Sam," I thought, "be sharp today."

Goldman reclined in his chair, expansive. "I'm glad you boys are investing in land; it's something that doesn't dissolve. I remember when your father asked me about the parcel on which is now located the Merchants Bank Tower . . ."

I began doodling, the random scrawls and slashes of an idiot. Goldman puffed at his cigar with a quick, shallow rasp. "It had some old dry-goods store on it and looked worthless. So your daddy came to me and I said—"

"'This land is the only gold mine in Mobile,'" Carter Benson finished.

My head snapped up. Goldman was looking puzzled, as on the day he had lost his penknife.

Benson spoke in a bored monotone. "You told us all about that, Mr. Sam. Last week." He paused. The insult ripened until it filled the room. Goldman's face crumbled slowly into ruins of itself. I felt a numb humiliation, as physical as shock. Benson's voice sliced through it. "What we want are the contracts for those parcels we're buying in Baldwin County."

"The files are on my desk," I said. "I'll have the contracts tomorrow."

Benson turned to me with blank, bored eyes. "I wanted them last week."

I stretched my hands in entreaty. "I've been so pushed I just didn't get to it. I'm sorry."

Goldman was staring, as if a spectator at some new

game for which he didn't know the rules. "All right," Benson said. "Tomorrow at ten." His voice seeped the polite disgust of a man who had borne incompetence until it had overwhelmed him. "Mr. Sam," he nodded, and left abruptly, his brother trailing after.

Goldman turned to me, trying to remember when he had given me the files. He saw my face, and the confusion turned to kindness. "Don't worry, Charles. Just finish those contracts. They seemed fairly impatient." I began to leave, then turned in the doorway. Goldman was staring out the window, at nothing.

I stopped at Mrs. Selfridge's desk on the way to my office. "We have some new Benson files, on land in Baldwin County. I'd like you to find them—while Mr. Goldman's at lunch."

She nodded. "The Bensons are in your office." She hesitated, then spoke in a ragged voice. "If they leave, it will kill him. I mean, he would know then—"

I nodded. Her eyes held sudden guilt, as if she felt her fears were knives, aimed at Goldman. She looked quickly away, to straighten the papers on her desk.

The Bensons were seated in my office. "When you finish those contracts," Carter Benson said, "I want you to ship our files to Mike Ritchie at the Mead, Carlton firm."

Benson's eyes were empty. My face felt like an open wound. "Look, about the contracts—" I tried.

"We'd just be more comfortable with another lawyer. Sam Goldman's old. We don't have time for things like this morning."

"He's senile," Case Jr. said, with brutal finality.

I was too shocked to answer. Carter said, "Have the files ready tomorrow." They left.

The moment hung in the room, like stale air. Once,

I started to Goldman's office, but I couldn't tell him he had been fired by Case Benson's sons. I sat there as the walls soaked up my thoughts. Then Mrs. Selfridge brought in two manila folders. "They were in Mr. Goldman's credenza," she said.

I found myself playing with my pen set, stabbing the pen into its holder. Finally, I willed myself to start the work. I thumbed the files mindlessly, checking the location of the parcels by rote. Then I caught myself staring at a page, and awoke to the nagging of a half-framed thought. "People do things for a reason," Goldman had told me, "even children and idiots, and even if the reason is absurd. Don't blame something on coincidence unless you've nothing else to blame it on." I asked Mrs. Selfridge for all files on land purchases in Baldwin County. There were several. I reviewed them intently, scribbling notes on a yellow legal pad.

At two-thirty I asked for the Benson correspondence files. I riffled through an inch of onionskin copies, then stopped at one letter toward the end. Carter Benson was proud and privileged, it said, to help in the campaign of a representative who shared his interests. I took out a map of Baldwin County, tracing the highways which split the map like red arteries. Then I worked back through the land files and made one X on the map, in pencil.

The thought had grown slowly, unbidden. I had refused the meaning of it, treated it as an abstract thing, a puzzle. But the X on the map gave it life; what it was, what I might do, if the last piece fit. I stared at the X, as if to see my future in it. But what I saw was Goldman's face when Carter Benson had finished his sentence. I reached for the telephone and called the state house of representatives.

That evening, Goldman and I had our drinks. He

seemed tired, asked me to pour the second drinks. "Have you finished with the Bensons?" he finally asked. "I'm working on it," I said, and excused myself to go home.

The next morning the rain slapped fitfully against my office window, making the room seem a dismal cocoon. I waited, not drinking my coffee, but breathing it in, as if inhaling calm.

At ten, Carter Benson came. I held out the contracts. "I've proofed them," I said. "They're fine."

Benson sat and gave them a cursory glance. "Are the files ready?" he asked, still looking down.

"No," I answered.

Benson stared at me. "Why not?"

"Because I know what this land is really worth to you. You're going to build a racetrack," I told him. "If it was just land, you'd get a hundred acres anywhere, but you need location—land near the highways." I pointed at the contracts. "These are next to the Interstate near Route 59—right in the middle of your racetrack."

Benson's face was tight with self-control, his eyes slightly narrow. "Bullshit, Charles. Horse racing isn't legal here."

A wave of rain pelted the window, then stopped, leaving a greater silence. I spoke into it. "There's a new bill to legalize it, introduced by the guy you just gave five thousand dollars to." Benson started to speak and I cut him off. "I know, contributions are legal. But suppose some reporter starts looking at the land purchases. You've bought them through different companies, but with some informed help, he'd find you, the big contributor.

"Two things could happen. Your bill would almost surely fail, leaving you with empty land and a bad reputation. Absent that, the sellers on the land you need would ask a painful lot of money."

"None of this is against the law."

I nodded. "Just shady enough so it can't be known."

Benson fumbled in his pocket for a cigarette, found one, and lit it. The smoke rose in sinuous wisps, thrusting, turning, diffusing in an acrid haze. "What do you want?" he asked.

A sweet, strong anger was constricting my chest. "We keep your business, and I do the work. When Sam's gone, I'll ship your files to Ritchie because, quite frankly, I can't stand either one of you bastards. But while Sam's here, you'll treat him with respect. Starting today. At four-thirty you're to come to his office, pick up the contracts, and thank him for his work. And bring your brother."

Benson listened with unnatural calm. He sat mute for a moment, face strained with unspoken anger. Then he spoke, voice seething with the heat of betrayal. "You sit here dribbling virtue out the corners of your mouth and you're nothing but a goddamned blackmailer. You'd sell your clients' secrets to humor one senile old man."

"Life is choices, Carter. Ethics, or let you ruin Sam —and you're not worth his spit the best day you ever lived. So if I seek absolution, it won't be from you. All I want from you is an answer."

Benson gazed slowly around the room, as if he saw it for the first time. He spoke to the wall. "This isn't much like Goldman and the old man, is it?"

"Not much at all."

Benson looked back at me. "I can put this deal through without you," he said with sudden firmness.

"Four-thirty. Sam's office," I repeated. Benson inspected me with cold deliberation; then he rose and stalked out.

I went to lunch alone, and bolted a double bourbon, as if I were with Goldman. But when I returned, I felt strange to myself. I shook it off and took Goldman the contracts.

He sat at his desk, picking at a cellophane cigar wrapper which defied his fingers. He put it down, smiling sheepishly. "Need a damned can opener," he complained, and took the contracts. "When are they expecting these?"

"I think they'll be here about four-thirty."

"I'm sure these will satisfy them," he said appreciatively, and put them down. He returned to the matter of the cigar, pushing his glasses back along his nose as if to see it better. I debated whether to help. Then I thanked him and returned to my office.

The day was sluggish. I fidgeted with some files, wasting time, then called an old girlfriend in New York to talk about nothing. At four-thirty I went to Goldman's office. The Bensons did not come. I felt suddenly drained by sadness as profound as mourning, though I wasn't sure for whom. I tried asking about the contracts, but my words and Goldman's passed each other, as if I were chatting with the radio. "The Merchants Bank Tower was a gold mine," Goldman was saying. "I told Case, 'Maybe you get a construction loan, build an office there—' "

"The Bensons are here," Mrs. Selfridge said through the door.

"Send them in," Goldman answered, pleased. The Bensons entered and stood in front of Goldman's desk.

"We have the contracts," Goldman said.

Carter Benson took them. He looked quickly to me,

then shuffled silently through the contracts. The metallic clack of Mrs. Selfridge's typewriter punctuated time.

Benson looked back to Goldman. "Thank you, Mr. Sam," he said in a low voice.

Goldman smiled. "No trouble. Have time to visit?"

Carter Benson glanced at me with a sour half-smile. "For a while," he said to Goldman, and our bargain was made.

Goldman motioned them to the chairs. "Been meaning to ask you all how you'd feel about buying an interest in a bank. Your father used to talk about that, but we could never find the right opportunity . . ."

When they had left, Goldman turned to me. "They seem to have calmed down. I'm sure they remember we've been their champions." He glanced at me with sudden sharpness, then the glance hazed over. "Anyhow, I'm going to check some smaller banks and see if I can turn up an investment."

"Good idea," I agreed. I looked at my watch. "Five-thirty, Sam. Care for a drink?"

Goldman grew older, slower. He came to work later, and often left early, to rest. Some days were better, and on those days I sought his advice. But he was quieter when we had our drinks. And sometimes I would find him looking about his office, as if he were a boarder in a strange room.

He seemed to enjoy the Bensons' visits. He reminisced while they sat quietly in front of his desk, not so restless that he noticed. After a time, Carter Benson would come to my office and we would talk, cool and wary, long enough to do our business. I can't say what decision Goldman would have made. It doesn't matter, really.

Carter Benson built his racetrack. And one summer afternoon—at five-thirty—I found Sam resting at his desk, as if asleep. I sent the Benson files to Mike Ritchie. But the light through Goldman's window seems harsher to me now.

Afterword

I was revising the manuscript of what became my first novel, *The Lasko Tangent,* and was studying creative writing with Jesse Hill Ford at the University of Alabama at Birmingham. Resolved to try my hand at short fiction, I handed Jesse the first draft of this story. Jesse pronounced it "the work of an instinctive novelist trying to wedge himself into the short story form." (More recently, the occasional unkind critic has suggested that I'm now struggling to wedge myself within the novel form.) But with Jesse's encouragement I persisted—an early lesson—and three rewrites later sold it to *The Atlantic Monthly.* Wisely, I retired on the spot.

Still, "The Client" remains special to me for yet another reason. As a young lawyer in Alabama I practiced law with Abe Berkowitz, a wonderful trial lawyer, a considerable raconteur, and one of the few great men I have ever known—a philanthropist, a visionary, and a forthright advocate of civil rights in a time and place where that required considerable courage. The character of Sam Goldman captures a bit of Abe, and for me, that will always be enough.

—RICHARD NORTH PATTERSON

Ben Kincaid debuted in Primary Justice *as a young, idealistic, and somewhat naive attorney with negligible trial skills. By his seventh appearance, in* Extreme Justice, *he's older, wiser, better in the courtroom—but struggling to maintain some semblance of those early ideals, and still keep his law practice afloat. In this story he makes a rare excursion into civil law, where he has to use all his creative powers to extract some measure of "justice."*

What We're Here For

WILLIAM BERNHARDT

Ben Kincaid squared himself behind the podium. Every direct examination had its challenges, but this one was proving more challenging than most. He had to treat his client gently, to lead her through her story without pushing her over the brink. He had to pay close attention, ensuring that no important detail was omitted from her testimony.

And he had to try not to look away from his client's face.

"About what time did you leave the fund-raiser, Tess?"

The woman in the witness box cast her eyes downward as she spoke, looking more toward the hardwood floor than toward her counsel. "It was very early in the morning," she said. Her voice was barely audible; the jurors had to lean forward to hear her words. "Just after 1 A.M., I think."

"Please tell the jury what you did after you left."

"I got in my car—it's a Honda Civic, about five years old—and started driving home."

Ben watched carefully as she spoke, detecting a tiny but discernible trembling. "What route did you take?"

"I was following Seventy-first crosstown. I live in the Richmond Hills development, and that seemed like the best route home, even with all the construction."

"And what if anything happened during your drive home?"

Tess Corrigan hesitated. "I was on Seventy-first facing east." She stopped, swallowed, inhaled. "I had to turn left onto Harvard. The light turned green, and . . . and I didn't see any oncoming traffic—"

"So what did you do?"

"I— I—" Even with her face partly masked, Ben—and the jury—could see her hesitation, her unwillingness to proceed. She was dreading the retelling, almost as she might dread revisiting the actual event. "I began making my left turn . . . and out the corner of my eye, I saw a car coming toward me—"

"Would you describe the car, please?"

"It was a dark color. Green, I think. A big car—one of those Ford Expeditions."

"And what happened?"

"I saw the car racing toward me—" Her voice broke off.

"Yes?"

"I tried to get out of the way, but I was already halfway through my turn, and there was nowhere I could go, no time to get away. I saw the car careening toward me, but there was nothing I could do—" Her wide eyes reflected the horror she must have experienced when it happened. For a moment, Ben felt as if he was with her, trapped in that tiny car, watching certain disaster speeding closer but unable to do anything about it.

Ben cleared his throat. "And . . . what happened next, Tess?"

"That's all I remember," she said, exhaling, and it seemed as if all fourteen faces in the jury box released their breath at the same moment. "When I woke up, I was in the hospital. And I was like . . . this."

Her hand went up to her face, barely touching the bandage that was still in place, six months after the incident. Her face was a scarred and bloody nightmare. Her nose had been flattened; her eyes were so swollen they were barely visible—tiny pinpricks of blue peering out from the bruised flesh. A deep laceration cut across the center of her face, stretching from her left ear to the middle of the opposite cheek. It had been sutured; the distinctive patchwork scarring was readily visible. A white bandage covered the center of her face, concealing part of her forehead and the place where her nose used to be.

Ben cleared his throat, fighting back the catch in his own voice. He tried to keep his emotions at bay, but it was all but impossible. He had known Tess for years; they had worked together on countless charitable and civic projects—at the hospice, the library, the women's shelter. She had given so much of herself to others; it tore him up inside to see what had happened to her. "Has the accident . . . affected your work?"

Tess laughed abruptly, and it wasn't a happy laugh. "Affected my work? I was a model—a fashion model. I was paid to look good."

"How often did you work?"

"I had regular modeling jobs at Tulsa restaurants and private functions for Renberg's, Aberson's, and some of the other top clothing stores in town. It's how I supported myself—how I've supported myself since I was eighteen."

"Have you . . . been able to continue your work?"

"With this?" Once more, her hand touched her bandage. "With a face that makes me look like—like—an extra from a horror movie? Not hardly. I haven't worked since the accident." Her voice dropped in volume. "I'll never work again."

"Have you investigated the possibility of reconstructive surgery?"

She shook her head slowly. "I talked to some doctors about it, back at the hospital. But the damage to my face is so extensive . . . it would be incredibly expensive. Literally millions of dollars. My health insurance carrier won't cover what they call cosmetic surgery. And I can't begin to afford it."

"What are your plans for the future, Tess?"

"Plans? I don't have any plans." Her head turned, and for the first time, Ben detected tears forming in the wells of those barely visible eyes. She blinked rapidly, fighting them back. "I can't work looking like this, and I can't do anything to change the way I look. I don't have any plans. I don't have any . . . future."

Ben bit down on his lower lip. He needed a break almost as badly as she did. "Thank you, Tess. No more questions, your honor."

Judge Hawkins leaned across the bench. "Thank you, counsel. Why don't we take a break before we begin cross-examination?"

"Your honor." Ben turned and saw opposing counsel, Charlton Colby, rise to his feet, adjusting the jacket of his immaculately tailored suit. "I have a motion I'd like to put before the court. Perhaps while we are in recess . . ."

"That'll be fine." Judge Hawkins excused the jury and the witness, then waved the two lawyers back into his chambers.

The private chambers of Judge Harold H. Hawkins —Hang 'Em High Hawkins, as he was known to the defense attorneys in town—was a hodgepodge of western art and sports memorabilia. OU football mementos draped a reproduction of Remington's famous broncobuster sculpture. Ben wondered if Hawkins actually decorated this room, or just dropped things off and forgot about them.

"What can I do for you gentlemen?" Hawkins asked, settling back in his chair. "I hope this isn't going to delay the trial. I want to get this thing over with."

"No, your honor," Colby answered. "I'm hoping it will have just the opposite effect." Colby was a senior member of Raven, Tucker & Tubb, Tulsa's largest law firm. He was representing Peggy Bennett, the doctor's wife who drove the Ford Expedition that hit Tess Corrigan. "I'm making a motion to dismiss."

"What?" Ben's eyes flew open. "You must be joking."

"Not in the least," Colby said, in a voice that was one part world-weary and two parts dead. "I'm entirely serious. Kincaid hasn't proved his case."

"I haven't finished calling witnesses."

"But you said yourself, at the pretrial, that the plaintiff was your key fact witness. I've heard what she has to say, and it didn't prove anything."

Ben felt his face reddening. "It proved your client rammed into Tess, causing the accident that destroyed her face."

"It did nothing of the sort. True, there was an accident, but as to fault—"

"Your client barreled into her—"

"Your client was blocking the intersection. She had a green light—not a left turn arrow. Which means she was supposed to make sure there was no oncoming traffic before executing a turn. She failed to do so. She has no one to blame for her injuries but herself."

"Tess *did* check for oncoming traffic; she didn't see anything. Your client was speeding. She came up on Tess too quickly. First there was nothing, then there was a Ford Expedition moving so fast there was nothing Tess could do about it!"

Colby cocked his head to one side. "Really? Prove it."

Ben's teeth clenched together. "How can you be so smug? Are you willing to do anything to win a case?

Didn't your mother ever teach you about right and wrong?"

"All right, boys, calm down." Judge Hawkins spread his arms expansively across his desk. "Let's try to be civil. Mr. Colby has made a motion to dismiss. I gather Mr. Kincaid opposes the motion."

"Damn straight," Ben muttered.

"Well," the judge continued, "I will say this, Mr. Kincaid. I don't think this is a frivolous motion. You haven't proved the defendant is at fault."

"The trial isn't over yet," Ben fired back.

"Thank you, counsel, I was aware of that. Which is why I'm going to deny the motion. But consider yourself warned, Mr. Kincaid—if you don't come up with some evidence of liability before you close, I will entertain Mr. Colby's inevitable motion for a directed verdict."

Ben felt a chill race down his spine. It was a plaintiff's lawyer's worst nightmare—to have the verdict directed against his client before the other side so much as called a witness.

"Mr. Colby," Judge Hawkins asked, "are you planning to cross-examine?"

Colby shrugged. "I see no need."

"Good. I think we've all had about enough for one day." Hawkins checked his watch. "Let's call it quits and resume tomorrow morning."

No one objected to that proposition. Ben returned to the courtroom, where he found Tess waiting for him at the plaintiff's table, her eyes wide with anticipation. He knew she was counting on him, hoping against hope that he might find a miracle somewhere in the midst of all the misery. But the truth was—he was failing her. Tess's case was only a short step from dismissal.

Ben's face tightened. *Damn!* Last week he'd managed to help two suspected drug dealers and a bank robber. Why couldn't he help Tess?

"Did I blow it?" she asked.

"Of course not," Ben reassured her. "You were perfect. Colby just had some motions he wanted to sling at the judge. The case will proceed, just as we planned."

"Is it going okay?" she asked. "I mean—are we winning?"

Ben remained silent. The judge's warning was still weighing heavily in his brain. "We're going to be fine," he said at last. "If we tell the jury what happened, tell them the truth, I don't see how they can help but find in your favor." Assuming the case ever gets to the jury, Ben added silently.

"Excuse me."

Ben turned and, to his surprise, saw the defendant, Peggy Bennett, standing beside her husband, Dr. Edgar Bennett. Dr. Bennett was the one who spoke.

"Pardon me for interrupting," Dr. Bennett continued, "but I just wanted to tell Miss Corrigan how sorry we are—"

Ben glared at opposing counsel. "Colby, if this is some ploy to weaken our resolve—"

"No, no," Dr. Bennett said, holding up his hands. "Mr. Colby had nothing to do with this. He didn't want us to have any contact with you at all. But I feel compelled—" He stretched out his hands toward Tess. "I mean—I just want you to know—how sorry we are. We don't believe this was Peggy's fault. But we still regret the consequences."

Ben peered deeply into the man's eyes. What was going on here? Bennett did seem genuinely disturbed—about something. But what?

"Edgar," Peggy Bennett said softly, "perhaps we should go."

"That's for me to decide," Dr. Bennett said curtly. "Please remain quiet and stay out of the way." A beeping sound emerged from the doctor's suit coat. He pulled out a cell phone, punched the Send button, and said, "I'm busy. Call back in ten minutes." He disconnected the line and returned his attention to Tess. "I also wanted you to know, miss, that if there's ever anything I can do—"

"You could accept our settlement proposal," Ben said.

Dr. Bennett drew in his breath. "I can't do that. My insurance carrier is calling the shots, and they don't think your case will hold up in court. Besides, it would be perceived as an admission of guilt. It wouldn't be fair to my wife."

"Then I don't know what more we have to talk about," Ben said. He sidestepped slightly, closing off Bennett's line of sight to Tess.

"I understand," Dr. Bennett said, his head bowed. "Still—you have our sincere regrets."

After the Bennetts left, Ben sat beside his client. "I'm sorry about that," he said, placing his hand gently on Tess's. "The man obviously wants to soothe his conscience—without opening his checkbook. We'll figure out something that—"

"I just don't know what to do," Tess said abruptly. She covered her scarred and ruined face with her hand. "I don't know where I can go. It's as if everything I had —everything that mattered—was taken away from me in the blink of an eye."

"There's more to you than your looks," Ben said gently. "You're a good person. You've put in more time than anyone I know for charity, for the library. You spend ten hours a week working with kids down at the women's shelter—"

"Which I also can't do anymore," Tess said, and all at once, the tears she held back during the trial began to stream out of her eyes. "My face is too scary, they say. I frighten the children. They—" Her voice caught. "They asked me to stop coming."

Ben felt as if someone had drilled a hole in his chest. He hadn't heard that before. Not only was Tess without a career—she was without a purpose. She really had lost everything.

Absolutely everything.

Ben had several other matters at the courthouse that required his attention; he had to file a motion in the Marquez robbery case, then had to get a hearing scheduled in the Mary Mathers solicitation matter. He saw Judge Hart in the hallway and ducked; she was still waiting for his brief in the Cantrell contract dispute and he didn't want to have to explain why he hadn't done it yet. Sometimes he felt like he had so many cases going at once he couldn't keep them all straight. Other times he wondered how he could possibly stay so busy and still not make any money.

Ben made a few more stops after he left the courthouse—a quick detour to his apartment to feed Giselle, then an even quicker sojourn to The Right Wing for takeout. Finally, he headed back toward his office. It was after dark before he arrived.

Thanks to the determined and occasionally less-than-legal efforts of his investigator, Loving, he had secured new office space in the Warren Place complex on the south side of Tulsa. Though budgetary concerns left the space drab and still largely unfurnished, compared to Ben's previous office, this place was the Ritz. Now he just needed some Ritzy clients to go with it.

Ben was surprised to find all three members of his

staff still in the office. His legal assistant and intern, Christina McCall, and his secretary and office manager, Jones, were huddled together at a desk, poring over a ledger. "What are you two up to?"

"Last day of the month," Jones answered, not looking up. "Time to do the accounting."

"So how's it look? Grim?"

"And then some." Christina brushed her ample mane of strawberry-red hair behind her head. "We've barely made enough to cover the essential bottom-line item."

"Meaning—?"

"My salary."

Jones nodded. "And mine. But after that, there's not much."

"What about our accounts receivable? Any likelihood of collecting anything in the near future?"

"I'd like to think we might collect on Lauren Grimes's bill, but she informs me that you agreed to waive your fee."

Ben redirected his eyes toward the ceiling. "Her baby's sick, and she really doesn't have anything to spare . . ."

"And, of course, Madame Martel owes us a fortune for that libel suit. But I understand you told her she could pay her bill off in tea-leaf readings."

"She's a very nice woman," Ben explained, "but her business has been falling off since that article in the *World* . . ."

"What were you thinking, Boss? We need cash! Cold hard cash!"

"I for one am enjoying the tea-leaf readings," Christina said. "I had one this afternoon. Madame Martel says I will go far."

"We can hope," Jones muttered under his breath.

"She says I have an effervescent spirit."

"I think you can take pills for that." Jones closed the ledger with a thump. "Any chance of collecting our contingency fee on Tess Corrigan's case anytime soon? One third of a personal injury judgment would be most welcome."

Ben shrugged. "We're still putting on our case . . ."

"Any way to put some settlement pressure on? Convince them to make a compromise payment before it goes to the jury? Get a little something to tide us through the month?"

"Sort of twist the case around to make ourselves a quick profit?"

"Isn't that what we're here for?"

Ben frowned. "Doesn't matter—prospects for early settlement are pretty dim at the moment."

"I'm sorry to hear that. I'm not even sure we're going to be able to pay the office rent."

"So you're telling me this isn't the month we're going to buy that fancy new photocopier?"

"That would be one way of putting it, yes."

"Why would you want a fancy photocopier, anyway?" Christina asked. "If you ever get any extra cash, you need to invest it in decor. This place looks more like a monastery than a law office."

"Women," Jones sniffed. "Always decorating."

"Don't give me that sexist crap. You think I don't know why you little boys want a new photocopier? You think I haven't seen what you do? Doctoring photos and copying them so they look real. Making goony faces and pressing them into the machine. Mooning the photoelectric lens."

Ben began to feel a bit warm. "I have never mooned anyone in my entire life. Much less a photocopier."

"Yeah, right. Next time remember to take the copies out of the collator."

Loving, Ben's bulky, two-hundred-and-then-some pound investigator, stepped out of his office into the hallway. "How goes the war, Skipper?"

"Not as well as I'd like. I've got a job for you."

Loving came to attention. "That's why I'm here."

"I'd like you to keep an eye on the defendant's husband, the doctor. Edgar Bennett. Follow him around, see what you can learn."

"You got it. What am I lookin' for?"

"I wish I knew. But something's going on with him. When I looked into his eyes today, I got the strongest feeling that . . . I don't know. That something was bothering him. I'd be a lot happier if I knew what it was."

Loving gave Ben a little salute. "I'm on it, Skipper."

"Thanks."

Ben pivoted just in time to see his client, Tess Corrigan, coming through the front door. Once again, he faced the monumental challenge of looking at her face without reacting.

"I brought the pictures," Tess said quietly.

Ben took the photos and escorted Tess to his office. The photos were all black and white glossies—professional shots taken from her modeling portfolio. Ben hoped to get them in front of the jury, to emphasize the profound difference between Tess-then and Tess-now.

"Will I . . . have to testify again?" Tess asked. Ben could see she was trying to be brave, but more than anything on earth wanted to be spared a return to the witness stand.

"No," Ben said. "Colby said he doesn't plan to cross-examine you. It wouldn't get him anywhere. He could conceivably call you when he's putting on the defense case, but I think that's unlikely."

"Oh thank God," she said. The relief surging through her body was evident. "Thank God. So what do we do next?"

"Well, first thing tomorrow morning, I need to call the defendant to the stand. She'll be a hostile witness; she won't want to give me anything. But I have to try. It's critical that we establish that she was at fault."

"I don't think she's a stupid woman," Tess said. "She won't be tricked."

"It's not a matter of tricking her," Ben replied. "It's a matter of eliciting the truth. If I can do some damage to Mrs. Bennett on the stand, her attorney may be willing to talk settlement."

"And then?"

"Then we start negotiating. To get what we want."

"Which is?"

Ben caught her eye. "What do you want most?"

Tess didn't answer, but her eyes drifted unmistakably to the top photo on Ben's desk, the glamour shot of Tess-before, Tess with the unblemished face, Tess with the perfect smile.

What she wanted most was, of course, the one thing she couldn't have.

The next morning, Ben called Peggy Bennett to the stand and had her declared a hostile witness, which allowed him to conduct his direct examination as if it were a cross-examination. He could lead, he could badger, he could interrupt. And hope that it did Tess some good.

"Could you please explain why you were driving the Expedition at one in the morning, Mrs. Bennett?"

"I was driving my husband to the hospital. He'd

gotten an emergency call." Peggy Bennett remained prim and composed. She was thin and quite attractive, especially given her age. To Ben, it felt as if he was drilling Nancy Reagan.

"Couldn't he drive himself?"

"He could, but if I drove, that meant he could continue to sleep during the drive."

"During the drive to the hospital? That couldn't be more than—what? Ten minutes?"

"Ten minutes of sleep can make all the difference between a surgeon who's sluggish and tired and a surgeon who's at the top of his form."

"But surely you can't always drive your husband to the hospital."

"No, not always."

"So are you suggesting that sometimes when he operates he's sluggish and tired?"

"Objection!" Colby said, bouncing to his feet. "Offensive and irrelevant."

"I'll sustain the objection on the latter grounds," Hawkins said, batting his eyelids. Ben wasn't sure if the judge was being coy or just trying to stay awake.

"Mrs. Bennett, you said you got an *emergency* call from the hospital," Ben continued. "Presumably that meant they wanted your husband as soon as possible. Were you driving very fast?"

"Not at all. Every call from the hospital is an emergency call. I'm used to it."

"But you were speeding."

"I most certainly was not. I was driving at the limit, no more."

"When did you first see my client's Honda Civic?"

"Only an instant before I hit it."

"Why didn't you see it sooner?"

"Perhaps I misspoke myself." She smoothed one of

the folds in her skirt. "I saw her car—but it was in the opposite lane. I had no reason to believe she would attempt to turn left directly in my path."

"Why didn't you see her sooner? Were you paying attention to the road?"

"Of course I was. It would be irresponsible not to."

"Are you sure you weren't distracted? Perhaps you were having an animated conversation with your husband?"

"I told you, he was asleep."

Damn. Ben was well outside the scope of the pretrial deposition he had taken from Mrs. Bennett—which was always dangerous. But he had to try to find something useful. "Maybe you were talking on your car phone?"

"I don't have a car phone." She looked at Ben as if he was surely one of the stupidest persons who ever lived. "My husband has a cellular phone, like most doctors, but he didn't have it with him that night. I was fully attentive, with my eyes on the road. Which didn't help me a bit when your client swerved directly in front of me."

Ben sighed. He was beating his head against a brick wall and he knew it. Time to change the subject. "What did you do after the accident?"

"I was stunned, initially. And quite injured." She paused, glancing, if only for a moment, at Tess. "But not nearly so badly as the woman in the other car. Edgar, of course, was awakened by the crash. He hobbled over to the nearest house and called for ambulances. The first to arrive took Miss Corrigan to the hospital. We rode in the second."

"Was that the same hospital where your husband works?"

"Of course. St. Francis. I was treated for minor head

injuries and a scrape on my arm. My husband had a gash on his right leg. They performed an MRI on both of us to make sure we hadn't suffered a serious head injury. Then they sent us home."

"But they didn't send Tess Corrigan home that night, did they?"

Peggy Bennett's eyes adjusted themselves slightly lower. "No," she murmured. "I believe she had to remain some weeks after. Her injuries were, of course, much more severe."

Having nothing left to try, Ben reluctantly dismissed Mrs. Bennett. Reluctant—because he knew perfectly well he had failed to prove she was at fault for the accident.

Ben's next witness was Maria Verluna. She was much younger than Mrs. Bennett—early thirties, Ben guessed. She had dark hair and a dark complexion; Ben guessed she was probably of Latin American descent.

"Please tell the jury what you do for a living."

"I work in the emergency room at St. Francis Hospital," Maria said. "I'm a nurse." She was nervous; Ben could see it in the way she fidgeted with her hands. But everyone was nervous when they were called to the witness stand.

"And were you working during the early morning of March 15?"

"I was. I drew the night shift that week." If Maria did hail from another country, there was hardly a trace of it in her very American-sounding voice.

"Were you on duty when Tess Corrigan arrived at the hospital?"

"No. She arrived shortly before I did and was treated by other people. I came on about 1:40 A.M."

"Were you there when Dr. and Mrs. Bennett arrived?"

"Yes, I was."

"I assume you recognized Dr. Bennett. Since you both work at the same hospital."

"Yes," she said, after only the slightest hesitation. "I—knew him."

"Did you assist in the Bennetts' treatment?"

"Of course. Dr. Ferguson was in charge, but I helped clean and bandage the wounds."

"Let me ask you about what you saw," Ben said, folding his arms. Once again, he was preparing to go outside the scope of Maria's pretrial deposition, thus violating one of the cardinal rules of trial practice—don't ask a question unless you know the answer. But at the moment, he was desperate. "Did the Bennetts' behavior seem . . . odd in any way?"

Maria's brow creased. "I don't know what you mean."

Well, that makes two of us, Ben thought, but did not say. "Did they do or say anything out of the ordinary? Given the circumstances."

"I—don't think so."

"Did you see any evidence that they had been drinking?"

"Certainly not."

"Did you smell their breath?"

"No—but I think I would have—if they'd been drinking."

"But you can't be sure."

"Yes, I can." She looked up quickly, glanced at Dr. Bennett, then looked back at Ben. Now that was interesting, Ben thought. Why would she be checking Dr. Bennett? "We took blood samples from both of the Bennetts, and at the request of the police department, we had Mrs. Bennett's sample tested. There was no trace of alcohol. None at all."

"You're certain of that?"

"We ran the tests twice—standard procedure where a contested automotive accident occurs. She had not been drinking."

"Did the Bennetts say anything about the accident?"

"No. I don't believe Mrs. Bennett spoke all night, except in answer to direct questions."

"And her husband?"

Maria shook her head. "Edgar never said a word, either."

Edgar, Ben thought, making a mental note. Not Dr. Bennett. *Edgar.*

He continued questioning her for another ten minutes, hoping to turn up something that might be of use. But she seemed defensive and extremely unwilling to incriminate anyone. In the end, he got nothing. Which was unfortunate. He needed a home run, but all he got was another strikeout.

During the afternoon break, after a quick trip to the men's room, Ben saw the Bennetts in the hallway outside the courtroom. Mrs. Bennett was walking hurriedly toward her husband, carrying a large briefcase in her hands.

"Is that mine?" Dr. Bennett asked.

"Yes," his wife replied. "The hospital sent it over. They thought—"

He snatched it from her hands. "I'll take it."

Peggy Bennett frowned. "I'm perfectly capable of carrying your briefcase."

"I don't need you to carry my briefcase. You might hurt yourself." Bennett's eyes scanned the hallway, finally lighting on Ben. Ben looked away.

A moment later, Ben felt a sharp tug on his arm. It

was Colby. "Could I speak to you in private for a moment?"

"If you must." Ben followed him to a quiet corner of the hallway.

"We're still willing to reach a fair settlement," Colby said. "Like I told you before trial."

"Twenty thousand dollars? You must be joking."

"It's a generous offer."

"It won't even pay her existing hospital bills!"

"Kincaid—when are you going to get it through your head? You don't have a case! I'm sure what happened to your client is terrible, but the fact is, it's not my client's fault. And even if it was—you can't prove it."

"I won't accept that," Ben said firmly. "There has to be a way."

"Get real, Kincaid. I'm trying to do you a favor here."

"No you're not. You're trying to get your rich client off the hook."

"If you don't take my offer, your client is going to end up with nothing!"

Ben bit back the words he was desperate to fling. He hadn't forgotten the judge's warning. The frightening fact was, Colby could be right.

"Why are you doing this?" Ben asked. "Why are you so determined to play hardball on this one?"

Colby stiffened slightly. "I always try to represent my clients to the best of my ability."

"This isn't one of your usual corporate battles we're talking about, Colby. Tess Corrigan is a real live human being."

"You're being insipid."

"Why are you handling this case anyway, Colby?"

"I'm not sure what you mean."

"You're one of the top litigators in your firm. You

probably bill—what? Two hundred bucks an hour? I understand your firm represents the insurance carrier—but this case seems like junior associate material. Don't you have bigger fish to fry?"

Colby smiled thinly. "Dr. Bennett is the president of the Yale Medical Arts Consortium."

"I see. So you're out here wading in the muddy waters of personal injury court so you can impress Dr. Bennett and grab some of the big corporate bucks."

"I wouldn't have put it quite that way."

"If you'd been reasonable, we could've settled this before it came to trial and before everyone spent a bundle on discovery. But of course, that wasn't what you wanted. That wouldn't have pleased your fellow partners at Raven, Tucker & Tubb. That wouldn't have allowed you to run up a lot of billable hours magnifying simple disputes."

"Sour grapes, Kincaid? I know you used to be at Raven—till you were drummed out." His face twisted into a smirk. "I hear now that you're on your own, you don't eat quite as well."

"True," Ben said. "But I sleep a lot better."

Ben did his best with the remaining witnesses—the police officer who first arrived at the scene, an after-the-fact eyewitness from the house closest to the accident—but by the end of the trial day, he was no better off than he had been before. He was not an inch closer to proving the liability element of Tess's case, and without that, he knew all too well she didn't have a prayer of recovering anything. No matter what he did, the omnipresent motion for directed verdict loomed just over his shoulder.

Ben drummed his fingers on the dash of Loving's pickup. "So . . . is every night this exciting?"

Loving removed one of the headphones from his ears and smiled. " 'Bout the same, yeah."

"Jeez." Ben shifted uncomfortably in his seat. "If I'd known how tedious a stakeout was, I might have thought twice about asking you to tail someone."

"Aww, it ain't so bad." The big man stretched, then punched the Stop button on his Walkman. "It's peaceful, really. Gives a guy some time to think. And to catch up on my books-on-tape."

Ben arched an eyebrow. "Books-on-tape?"

Loving shifted around his massive frame. "Yeah. So?"

"You mean—you're listening to—"

"What? You think you're the only one in the office who knows how to read?"

"Well, no, but—"

"What'd'ya think these headphones are for? Decoration?"

"I thought you were probably listening to music."

"Oh I see. 'Cause I'm a big guy who didn't go to college, you think I spend all my spare time getting drunk and listening to country-western tunes."

"I didn't say that."

Loving folded his arms across his chest. "I'm hurt, Skipper. Truly hurt."

Ben pressed his hand against his forehead. How had he gotten himself into this? "Look, Loving, I didn't mean to impugn your intellectual integrity—"

"Shh." Loving's eyes were riveted front and forward. "He's moving."

Even from their distant vantage point, Ben could see Dr. Edgar Bennett leave the front door of his home, walk to the driveway, and slide behind the wheel of his repaired Ford Expedition. An instant later, they were on the move.

"Lights are out in the house," Ben murmured. "Wife must be asleep. So where's the good doctor going?"

Loving followed Bennett as he turned onto Riverside Drive, keeping his headlights dim and staying a safe distance behind. "Probably goin' to the hospital," Loving commented.

"Maybe. But let's see."

They continued to creep along behind him, cruising down Riverside, then turning left onto Seventy-first. Just a minute or two before the doctor would've arrived at the hospital, he took a sharp right.

"If he's going to the hospital," Ben commented, "he's taking the scenic route."

A few moments later, Dr. Bennett pulled into the driveway of a small one-story house. Loving eased past, then quietly parked on the opposite side of the street.

Bennett walked to the front door, and a moment later, someone let him inside.

"It's the middle of the night, his wife has gone to bed, and he goes out to see someone," Ben murmured. "Loving, we have to find out who lives in that house."

"Already on it." Loving punched a number into his cell phone. "Hey, Maggie? Yeah, I knew you'd be up. Can you do me a favor?" A brief spate of sweet-talking ensued. It seemed pretty strained to Ben, but apparently it got Loving what he wanted. "Yeah. Take a look in the cross-index directory and tell me who lives at 1245 South Bridgewater."

Loving waited barely a minute for his answer. "Thanks, Maggie." He punched the End button and disconnected the call.

"Well?" Ben said anxiously.

Loving grinned. "You're gonna love this." He drew in his breath. "Maria Verluna."

• • •

The first thing next morning, Ben surprised everyone in the courtroom, including his client, by calling ER nurse Maria Verluna back to the witness box.

"Ms. Verluna, I'll get straight to the point. You're having an affair with Dr. Edgar Bennett, aren't you?"

The reaction from the jury box was only a reflection of the reaction from the witness stand. "*What?* What are you—"

"Ma'am, let me spare you a lot of heartache. I've had you followed. I know Dr. Bennett's been coming over to your house late at night. In fact, he was there last night, right? Showed up around midnight and didn't leave till just before sunrise." Ben paused. "I assume you weren't playing pachisi all night."

Maria stuttered, groping for words. "I still don't—I don't know—"

"Ma'am, I have a witness. A private investigator. I can call him to the stand if you like, and he can fill the jury in on all the dirty little details. He's even got pictures."

Maria stuttered for several more moments before giving in. "There—there's nothing dirty about it. Edgar and I are in love."

"I'm sure. But that's not really the point. Why didn't you tell the jury you were having an affair with the defendant's husband?"

"I—I—" She looked down at her hands. "I suppose I thought they might not believe me. If they knew the truth."

"Well," Ben said, "you might've been right about that. But I think there was more to it. I think you were covering something up."

"Your honor," Colby said, jumping to his feet, "is

this relevant? Counsel is trying to drudge up dirt to disguise the fact that he hasn't got a case."

Judge Hawkins tilted his head to one side. "He's entitled to try to impeach the testimony of adverse witnesses. Overruled."

You mean I finally won one? Ben thought. About time. "Ms. Verluna, please tell the jury the truth. Dr. Bennett was at your house the night of the accident, wasn't he?"

"What? Why would you think—"

"Well, I'll tell you why I think that. I couldn't figure out why Dr. Bennett didn't have his cell phone when the accident occurred. An important doctor like him—surely he normally takes it to work with him. He's certainly had it every day in this courtroom. Why didn't he have it then? And then the answer came to me—because he wasn't leaving from his house. He was leaving from your house. Isn't that so?"

Maria hesitated. "I don't—I mean, I can't—"

"Isn't it true?" Ben insisted.

"You have to understand—"

"Miss Verluna—*isn't it true?*"

Maria's voice was barely more than a whisper. "It's true."

Colby rose to his feet. "Your honor, I must renew my objection. What does it matter where Dr. Bennett was when he left for the hospital? He wasn't even the driver of the car!"

"I'll make the relevance crystal clear with my next witness, your honor," Ben replied. "Just give me five minutes. That's all I need."

Judge Hawkins pursed his lips together and frowned, but eventually gave Ben the nod. "The objection is overruled."

"Thank you." Ben dismissed Maria and announced his next witness. "I recall Peggy Bennett to the stand."

The rumble in the courtroom as Mrs. Bennett made her way to the front was audible, almost tangible. In a few short minutes, the trial had gone from imminently predictable to totally topsy-turvy. And there was more yet to come.

"Mrs. Bennett, you heard the testimony of the last witness, didn't you?"

Her face remained even, measured, but there was a certain sourness to the turn of her lips that Ben was almost certain had not been there before. "I did."

"Most people in this courtroom were surprised when they heard what she admitted. But you weren't surprised, were you?"

Her lips parted, slow and cool. "I'm . . . not sure what you mean."

"You already knew your husband was having an affair. You've known for some time, haven't you?"

"What makes you think that?"

"I think you misunderstand the procedure here, Mrs. Bennett. See, I get to ask the questions, and you have to answer them. You knew about your husband's affair, didn't you?"

The few seconds before she spoke seemed an eternity. "I did."

"You had to know—because you drove over to Maria's house and picked him up the night of the accident, didn't you?"

This time, the pause before speaking was even more pronounced. "An emergency call came in from the hospital. They needed him, but he didn't have his pager or his cell phone. So I . . . went to collect him."

"At Maria Verluna's house."

Her eyes closed. "That's correct."

"And this whole time, you haven't said a word about his affair, have you? You've stayed quiet. You've protected him."

Her head nodded slightly.

"In fact, you're still protecting him, aren't you?"

Her eyes opened. "I . . . don't know what you mean."

"I think you do. You're not just protecting him from the shame and ignominy that would follow if people knew about the affair. You're protecting him from the civil liability that would result if people knew he was the one driving the car that hit Tess Corrigan."

The reaction in the courtroom could not have been much greater if a rocket had exploded. Heads turned; lips parted. Hushed whispers filled the gallery. Several heads in the jury box leaned forward, eyes wide with interest.

Mrs. Bennett's hands gripped the rail, trembling slightly. "You're just—just desperate to get something for your client. You don't know what you're talking about."

"I think I do. You see—I've had a chance to observe your husband these past few days. I've seen the way he treats you. And as a result, I can tell you something else you already know. He's a major-league male chauvinist. I don't believe for a minute he'd let you drive the car; I don't care how tired he was. He would insist on driving."

"You're crazy. I—I—" She looked up suddenly at the judge. "Do I have to listen to this?"

"I'm afraid you do," Ben said quickly. "Because I haven't even gotten to the worst of it. There's one more ugly detail I haven't even mentioned. When your husband came out of Maria Verluna's house—he'd been drinking."

"*What?*" Slowly but surely, Peggy Bennett's steely facade was dissolving. "It—it isn't true."

"I don't know why he was drinking," Ben said, ignoring her. "Maybe they'd had a late dinner. Maybe it helped him get aroused. I don't know. But I'm absolutely certain he was drunk."

"That's crazy talk. If he'd been drunk, I wouldn't have let him—" She stopped short.

"Let him what? Drive?" Ben nodded. "I thought so. Oh, I'm sure you tried your best to talk him into letting you drive. But he wouldn't hear of it. Not a manly man like that. He shushes you when you try to speak and he wouldn't even let you carry his briefcase yesterday; no way he'd let you drive. He insisted on driving—drunk—which is why he drove too fast and why he didn't see Tess Corrigan until it was too late to do anything about it!"

"No! You can't prove any of this!"

"I think I can." Ben returned to plaintiff's table and withdrew a stack of yellow forms. "As Maria Verluna testified, they tested your blood and found it clean. Why shouldn't it have been—you hadn't been drinking, right? But since Dr. Bennett wasn't the driver, they didn't test his blood. They did, however, set aside a sample of his blood for one year's storage in the deep freeze —standard practice in accident cases. I had it tested this morning." Ben passed the yellow forms to the bailiff, who in turn handed them to Mrs. Bennett. "And guess what? His blood alcohol level was three times the acceptable level. He'd drunk the equivalent of three fourths of a bottle of red wine." Ben turned toward the jury. "Small wonder he couldn't drive worth a damn."

Mrs. Bennett stared at the forms, her face red with blotches. "There—there must be some mistake—"

"There's no mistake, ma'am. We ran the tests twice.

He was drunk." Ben took a step closer to the witness stand—as close as the judge would allow. "And he was driving the car, wasn't he?"

As Peggy Bennett raised her head, a tear spilled down her right cheek. "I tried to talk him out of it. I told him I should drive. But he wouldn't listen to me." Her eyes were wide and pleading. "I tried to. He just wouldn't listen."

"Thank you," Ben said, almost under his breath. "Thank you for telling us the truth." He pressed his hands down on the podium. "I have just one more question for you, Mrs. Bennett. *Why?* Why did you protect him? Why did you lie for him? Why did you take the blame?"

Peggy Bennett stared at Ben blank-faced, as if the answer was so obvious it barely needed speaking. "He's my husband," she said, simply.

"But—he—" Ben struggled to find the kindest possible words. "The way he treated you. The things he did—"

Peggy Bennett stared back at Ben, tears streaming down her cheeks. "He's all I've got."

Ten minutes later, the lawyers were back in Judge Hawkins's chambers. "I'd like to make another motion," Colby announced.

"I thought you might," Hawkins said. "Proceed."

"Move to dismiss," Colby said flatly. "I'll file a brief as soon as I can slap it together."

"Dismiss?" Ben leapt out of his chair. "Are you kidding? She admitted it! I've proven liability—"

"On the part of Edgar Bennett, maybe. But alas, you didn't sue him, did you? You only sued Peggy Bennett. And that woman is blameless."

" 'Fraid I have to agree with him," Judge Hawkins

said, leaning back in his chair. "If you'd sued them both jointly, I'd keep the suit alive. But you didn't. I'm gonna have to dismiss this sucker."

Ben pressed forward. "But there must be some way—"

Hawkins stopped him with a wave of the hand. "Ain't no 'buts' about it, counsel. Fact is—you sued the wrong Bennett. This case is dismissed."

After they returned to the almost empty courtroom, Ben conferred briefly with his client. A moment later, he confronted Colby, who was sitting next to Dr. Bennett.

"I hope you don't think you've seen the end of this," Ben said. "The statute of limitations hasn't come close to running. I'll refile—this time naming Dr. Bennett as the defendant."

"I'm sure you will," Colby said, doing his best to seem bored and unimpressed. "And we'll go through the usual rigmarole. The case might finally get to trial six months from now—if you're lucky. Of course, now that we know what you know, we'll be fighting you every step of the way."

"This isn't just a game," Ben said. "A woman has been injured."

"And even in the event you should win at trial," Colby continued, "we will of course appeal. What's it take to get a case heard by the Court of Appeals these days—two years? And if we lose there, we'll appeal again, this time to the Oklahoma Supreme Court, which will take another two years. So the way I see it, Kincaid, you've got a five-year wait before you have even the slightest chance of seeing any money. And of course, during those entire five years, Dr. Bennett will be putting his property into his wife's name, transferring it to his closely held corporations—making himself positively judgment-proof."

"You can't divest property to avoid paying a judgment. I'll trace the assets."

"You'll try. But that, too, will take years."

Ben's teeth clenched together with rage. He leaned toward Dr. Bennett, meeting him eye-to-eye. "Don't you have any sense of responsibility for what you've done? Don't you understand you've destroyed a woman's life!"

"Dr. Bennett is represented by counsel," Colby said, matching Ben's volume. "If you have something to say, say it to me."

"I'll say something, all right," Ben said, rising to Colby's height. "How can you live with yourself?"

Colby shrugged him away. "Please, Kincaid. No one likes a sore loser."

"This isn't about winning and losing."

"No, this is about representing my client. Which I did. The Rules of Professional Conduct charge us with a duty to zealously defend our clients to the best of our ability."

"I'm sick and tired of hearing people use the ethics code like it was some kind of Get Out of Jail Free card. The Rules were supposed to improve the moral responsibility of practicing attorneys. Instead, they've become an excuse trotted out at opportune moments to justify the most shameless tactics—winning at all costs. That isn't what we're here for!"

Colby tried to brush past him. "This is very tiresome, Kincaid. If you'll excuse me—"

"Not yet. I want to talk to your client. And since your vaunted Rules of Professional Conduct say I can't do that outside your presence, stay put." He crouched over the table so he could meet Bennett eye-to-eye. "I want you to understand two things, Dr. Bennett. I will never let this case rest. I don't care what Colby's high-powered law firm throws at me. I will never give up until you pay for what you did." Ben took a deep breath. "And here's the second thing. From now until the day you finally pay up, I'm going to make your life a living hell!"

Colby looked shocked. "Mr. Kincaid!"

"This will be my holy crusade, Dr. Bennett. I will make sure everyone in town knows you were driving drunk, that you hurt someone, and that you refuse to take responsibility for your actions. I'll make things so hot for you, you won't be able to sleep at night. Every time you take a breath, I'll be lurking right over your shoulder."

Colby pushed himself between them, breaking it up. "Kincaid, your conduct is shocking. I'm going to report you to the ethics committee."

"Do whatever the hell you want, Colby. I'm not afraid of you. Or your law firm." He cast a backward glance at Dr. Bennett. "I meant what I said. Every word of it."

Slowly, almost painfully, Dr. Bennett's lips parted. "What is it you want?"

"Like I've been saying all along," Ben fired back. "Five hundred thousand in damages. Not a penny less."

Bennett shook his head. "I can't do that."

"You're worth ten times that much."

"That's not the point. If I make a financial settlement with you, I've as much as admitted liability. I've admitted I drove drunk and almost killed someone. I'd be drummed out of the hospital. I might even lose my license to practice."

"There would be no admission of liability in the settlement agreement."

"It wouldn't matter. People would know." Bennett drew in his breath. "I'm sorry, but I can't pay your client a dime." Slowly, hesitantly, Bennett pushed himself out of his chair. Colby grabbed his briefcase and followed along behind. Ben watched as they crossed the courtroom together, knowing full well he wouldn't see either of them again for months, and that Tess's only hopes for recovery were remote and years away.

"Wait," Ben said, just before they reached the door. "I have one more proposal."

The entire office staff, Christina, Loving, and Jones, were gathered in the main conference room of the office. "All right, Ben, spill," Christina said. "What's the big secret?"

Ben smiled. "I'll tell you as soon as—" He looked up abruptly. "Tess, please come in."

Tess Corrigan stepped into the conference room. The last bandage had been removed from the center of her face, but otherwise she was unchanged. Her face was still riddled with sutures and scar tissue. "I was told you wanted to see me?"

Ben nodded. "We have a settlement proposal from Dr. Bennett."

Her eyes widened. "We do?"

"Subject to your approval. But let me tell you up front—there's no money involved. Bennett doesn't want to pay you a penny, and he's prepared to stonewall for the next five years to avoid it."

"Oh." The light in Tess's eyes dimmed.

"But here's the deal. I suggested, if he wouldn't pay you in cash—how about arranging reconstructive surgery for your face? He is, after all, a doctor. He knows other doctors. They all do favors for one another, provide services on the cheap. Plastic surgery to fix your face would cost you millions, but Bennett could get it for a lot less—probably even for less than the five hundred thousand we were shooting for."

"And he agreed?"

"He did. If you accept the offer—he'll pay all costs associated with your treatment. Whatever it takes. Till you look the same way you did in those black and white glossies."

Tess's eyes widened. Her lips parted, but no words came out. "I—I don't know what to say—"

"You don't have to take it. I'm willing to fight this thing as long as—"

"He'll fix my face? Really?"

"Really. If that's what you want."

"If that's what I want? That's all I've ever wanted." Tears spilled out of her eyes. "What did I care about the money? It wouldn't have been enough. All I ever wanted was my face—my smile—" All at once, she threw her arms around Ben and hugged him tightly.

"So . . . does this mean I should accept?"

Tess laughed, then planted a kiss on his cheek. "Please. As soon as possible." Her damaged face transformed itself into an ear-to-ear smile. "Thank you so much."

Ben smiled and shrugged. "Just doing my job."

After Tess left, Jones leaned across the conference table. "Well, I have a question."

Ben loosened his tie. "I bet I know what it is."

"How do we take a contingency fee on the promise of medical services?"

Ben suddenly took interest in a spot on the wall somewhere over their heads. "We . . . uh . . . don't."

"So," Christina said, "basically, we're in dire financial straits, we've spent six months on this case, and we're not going to get paid a dime."

"Uh . . . that would be . . . um—" Ben cleared his throat. "That would be more or less accurate, yes."

Christina shook her head. She rose to her feet, moved forward—and planted a kiss on Ben's cheek. The same one that was still moist from Tess's kiss a few moments before. "You old softie, you."

Ben squinted. "Then . . . you're not mad at me?"

Christina smiled. "How could anyone be mad at you?"

"Well—" Jones started.

"Don't answer that question." Christina turned back to Ben. "We'll pay the rent somehow. And we can always wait on your photocopier."

"And my fall wardrobe," Jones grumbled.

"The important thing," Christina said, "is that we got our client exactly what she wanted. Correction—exactly what she *needed*. And that's what we're here for, isn't it?"

All Ben could do was smile. And agree.

Afterword

One problem civil trial attorneys face that is particularly dispiriting—and that creates considerable ill will between lawyers and their clients—is the fact that no litigant ever gets everything he or she wanted. Compromise is commonplace, and even when a money judgment is awarded, the parties are faced with the realization that money—usually the only remedy awarded by a civil court—cannot right all wrongs. As a trial attorney, I found the most valuable resolutions came about when the lawyers got past the pervasive "money-grubbing" aspect of civil litigation and concocted creative solutions that were more helpful in the long term than money judgments could ever hope to be. So in this story, I wanted Ben to challenge himself in a different way, to burn some creative energy concocting a remedy that could give new meaning to the word "justice."

—WILLIAM BERNHARDT

*Well, here's one that will prevent us getting an
endorsement from the National Judges Council. But
it's worth it to enter Michael Kahn's skewed brain
and meet the Honorable Harry L. Stubbs, an
extraordinary federal judge caught in an even more
extraordinary situation.*

Cook County Redemption

MICHAEL A. KAHN

Here's where we are:

High above Dearborn Street in Chicago's Loop, inside the chambers of the Honorable Harry L. Stubbs. It is an imposing room, these chambers. Fit for a pharaoh, adequate for a federal judge. Tall ceilings, dark paneling, large picture window opening east upon a royal view of Lake Michigan. A massive walnut desk. Behind that desk a high-back leather chair that's more throne than seat. And on that throne, U.S. District Judge Harry L. Stubbs, beads of sweat forming on his forehead.

His Honor leans to his right and releases another fart.

Fiber shock. Has to be. Christ Almighty, I'm going into fiber shock.

In the middle of the room, dominating the foreground, is a burled walnut conference table encircled by eight leather chairs. On one wall are floor-to-ceiling bookcases filled with bound law books. On another are portraits of Abraham Lincoln, Ronald Reagan, and Henry Hyde, along with a framed DePaul Law School diploma and a plaque displaying a bronzed Illinois State Highway Patrol badge. On the desk, a standup family portrait of a plump blonde woman and three blonde daughters, all wearing glasses. Hanging from a brass coat rack in the corner: a black robe and a bright plaid sports jacket.

His Honor lifts his haunches and releases another fart.

Married to a fiber zealot, for God's sake.

Yesterday morning Bernice had placed a homemade bran muffin next to his coffee mug. Had the heft of a waterlogged softball, the flavor of drywall. The Muffin from the Black Lagoon.

His Honor's stomach rumbles. Gas pressure builds again in his colon.

This morning she'd kissed him on the forehead and placed a bowl before him. He'd stared down at what looked like a pile of hamster turds.

"What in God's name is this?" he'd finally asked.

"Bran Buds, Father. Just packed with yummy fiber."

They'd tasted even worse than they looked—a moist blend of sawdust and industrial sand. His Honor had forced down half a bowl, all the while imagining what would happen if the president of Kellogg's ever found himself in the courtroom of U.S. District Judge Harry L. Stubbs.

His Honor shakes his head. Who'd have thought that the cute blonde he'd pulled over for speeding thirty-one years ago out on I-55 would become, during the thirtieth year of their marriage, a born-again believer in the divine grace of an ample bowel movement? After twenty-nine years of Wonder Bread, Uncle Ben's, and Rice Krispies. Go figure.

Another wince, another fart.

Then again, he concedes, he isn't exactly the trim highway trooper anymore. When they were newlyweds she called him her John Wayne—although even then it was a reach for a guy five-foot-nine. It is far more of a reach now. Over the past thirty years he's added ten inches to his waistline, lost most of his hair, and padded those square jaws with a set of jowls. Last weekend at the True Value, while selecting a new belt for the sander, he thought he'd spotted former Cubs manager Don Zimmer across the aisle—only to realize with a start that he was looking at his own reflection.

His Honor pulls a handkerchief from his back pocket and wipes the sweat off his forehead.

Definitely fiber shock.

There is a rap at the door.

"Christ," he mumbles, squeezing his butt cheeks together. "It's open."

Into chambers lumbers His Honor's enormous docket clerk, Rahsan Abdullah Ahmed (née Lamar Williams). Six-feet-six inches tall, 285 pounds, big as an ox, black as coal, and—on first impression—dumb as dirt. First impressions can be misleading.

"Good morning, Rahsan."

"Mornin', Yo' Honor."

Their first months together have been tough ones for Judge Stubbs. He enjoyed the pomp and circumstance of the district court, right down to the traditional *Oyez, Oyez, Oyez* to open court each morning. He used to cringe when Rahsan banged the gavel three times and announced to the crowded courtroom, with a hearty *Oh-yeah, Oh-yeah, Oh-yeah,* that the United States *District Coat* was now in session.

But that was then. Although Rahsan would never dub voiceovers for Darth Vader, it hasn't taken Judge Stubbs long to recognize his docket clerk's true value. He's had *law* clerks, of course—those young kids with fancy degrees from snooty law schools. Even though they have all the street smarts of a Lake Forest dowager, those damn kids can research like there's no tomorrow, and that is important to former Highway Trooper Harry L. Stubbs. He isn't looking to blaze new paths in the law, especially after what the Seventh Circuit did to him last year in the *Arnold Bros.* appeal. Judge Easterbrook wrote the opinion for the panel. Made him sound like some yahoo who'd slipped his electronic cuffs, the pompous bastard. So these days, he turns to his law clerks for the law. But when His Honor needs something more important than legal research, he has Rahsan. His law clerks occasionally let him down; they can't always find a precedent. But his docket clerk, God bless him, never lets him down.

"What do we have this morning?" Judge Stubbs asks.

Rahsan shakes his head with weary patience and tugs on the right side of his thick Fu Manchu mustache. "Oh, jes' the usual tattletales and crybabies."

He hands Judge Stubbs the stack of motions that have been set for hearing this morning. His Honor checks his wristwatch and sighs. He could close his eyes and picture them: grim squadrons of lawyers armed with briefcases emerging from skyscrapers along LaSalle Street and marching toward Dearborn, leaning forward with determination. Soon they'll be converging on the elevators below for their ascent to the courtrooms of Judge Stubbs and his fellow judges of the Northern District of Illinois.

Morning motion call.

Judge Stubbs leafs through the all-too-familiar pile of papers, the distaste evident on his face. Motion to Compel Production of Documents. Motion for Extension of Time to File Reply Memorandum. Motion for Sanctions. Motion for Continuance. Motion to Compel Answers to Interrogatories. Motion for Sanctions. Motion for Leave to File Sur-Reply. Motion for Extension of Time to File Amended Complaint. Motion for Leave to File Brief in Excess of Twenty Pages. Motion for Continuance. Motion for Sanctions.

Same old crap.

Like most of his colleagues, Judge Stubbs detests the morning motion call. Sitting up there on the bench, listening to the parade of lawyers accusing each other of picayune violations of the rules, he feels like that old woman who lived in a shoe.

He looks up with a weary sigh. "Anything else?"

"Got ourselves an emergency motion, Judge. They seeking a T.R.O."

"Really? One of ours?"

"No, suh. Belong to Judge Weinstock."

"One of Marvin's cases? Why are they here?"

"He on vacation. This week and next."

"New case?"

"No, suh. Complaint filed six weeks ago."

"Six weeks? Why the sudden rush?"

Rahsan shakes his head. "Don't know, Yo' Honor. Parties want a hearing. Presiding judge sent 'em down here."

"Am I the emergency judge this week?"

"Yes, suh. This week and next."

Judge Stubbs opens his desk calendar and studies it. "Well, looks like we can probably squeeze them in today. I have a pretrial conference at ten. Not much after that."

"I already tole 'em be here by eleven sharp."

Judge Stubbs looks up and smiles. "You have their motion papers?"

"Yes, suh. Right here." Rahsan Ahmed hands Judge Stubbs the court papers and stands up. "Motion call be startin' in ten minutes, Judge. I'll rap on the door when it's time."

And here's how we got there:

Five weeks back. Inside the men's room at the Union League Club. Marble sinks, polished brass fixtures, neat stacks of crisp hand towels, a sumptuous row of porcelain urinals fit for the gods. It is an elegant room, exactly what one would expect to find in one of the most exclusive downtown men's clubs in Chicago. And thus the last place in Chicago one would expect to find Jimmy Torrado.

Jimmy combed his thick black hair in the large mirror over the marble sinks, trying to maintain his cool. He ran his finger under his collar and then straightened his tie, checking his reflection. He wasn't used to wearing a coat and tie, but you do what you gotta do. Trailed the son of a bitch for a week, trying to figure out how to get close enough to do it, to get past his driver and his secretary and the rest of the damn entourage. And then it hit him, like one of those bulbs flashing on in a cartoon: serve the guy in the crapper. Grinning, Jimmy leaned forward and stared in the mirror. There was a little blackhead on the bridge of his nose. Yes, sir, he said to himself as he pinched out the blackhead between his thumbnail and fingernail, you got to get up pretty early in the A.M. to get the drop on Jimmy Torrado.

He heard a rustle of newspaper from one of the toilet stalls. Then the sound of toilet paper unrolling. Jimmy Torrado took the documents out of his blue plastic briefcase and waited. The toilet flushed, the stall door opened. A silver-haired guy stepped out with a *Sun-Times* folded under his arm, moved past Jimmy toward one of the sinks like he wasn't even there.

Yep, that was him.

Jimmy waited until the guy started washing his hands. Big green gems on his cuff links, manicured fingernails, gold Rolex watch. Guy was loaded, no question.

"You Lester Fleming?"

The silver-haired guy turned his head toward him

as he lathered his hands. Didn't say a thing—just stared at Jimmy with those cold blue eyes. Sub-zero eyes. He rinsed the suds off his hands and reached for a towel, taking his time, drying his hands like he had all day, Jimmy just standing there, shifting his weight from one foot to the other.

Still drying his hands, he looked at Jimmy. "What do you want?" he said in a hoarse voice, more a demand than a question.

Jimmy Torrado held out the court papers. "You are hereby served with the summons and complaint in this lawsuit. You're also served with a motion and some other court papers."

Fleming didn't take them. Didn't even glance at them. Just stared at Jimmy Torrado, who was starting to feel like a real jag-off standing there with the papers in his outstretched hand and this arrogant bastard drying his hands and giving him a look like he was some kind of retard.

"You gonna take 'em or what?"

After a moment, Fleming's lips curled into a smile. A nasty damn smile. He turned away and dropped the towel into the hamper. "Leave the papers by the sink, greaseball, and get the fuck out of here."

Torrado slapped the papers down and grabbed his plastic briefcase. He stopped at the door and looked back. "You just been served, asshole."

After Torrado left, Lester Fleming glanced down at the stack of papers. The top page was the summons in *Mid-Continent Casualty Assurance Co. v. Lester M. Fleming*. He lifted the document. Below it was the complaint. He skimmed through it, expressionless. Then came the motion for T.R.O. and the supporting memorandum of law. Fleming leafed slowly through the motion, stopping at the final page:

Wherefore, this honorable Court should enter a temporary restraining order and preliminary injunction freezing all liquid assets of defendant Fleming by enjoining and prohibiting defendant and any banks, savings and loan associations or other financial institutions with whom defendant Fleming or his firm maintains any accounts from removing, withdrawing or otherwise transferring any money out of any such accounts.

He read the paragraph again, mulling it over. After a moment, he looked up at his reflection in the mirror, his frown slowly fading.

Rahsan Ahmed lumbers out of Judge Stubbs's chambers just as Norman Feigelberg, one of the judge's law clerks, scurries into the reception area. Judge Stubbs's secretary has gone down the hall for another Diet Coke, and that leaves the two of them alone in the room. As usual, it's a bad hair day for Norman Feigelberg. With his kinky black hair (this morning mashed up to the right side) and his horn-rimmed glasses (the bridge repaired with white adhesive tape), Feigelberg could pass for the younger, myopic brother of Kramer on "Seinfeld."

Feigelberg stares up at the docket clerk, squinting at him through thick lenses. "You just see the judge?"

"Yep."

Feigelberg nervously twists the bottom of his necktie around his index finger. "How's he feeling today?"

"It's that damn fiber." Rahsan wrinkles his nose. "Smell like something died in there. Po' mothafuckah fartin' to beat the band."

Feigelberg giggles, his head bobbing.

Rahsan steps back and waves his hand in front of his

nose. "On the subject of odors, Norman, you ain't exactly no rose yo'self."

"What's wrong?"

"Yo' breath is death."

Feigelberg grimaces. "I've got that darn gum infection again. I think it's a wisdom tooth."

"Here's some wisdom for you, baby. Get yo' ass down to Walgreens and bring back a gallon of Listerine, 'cause I don't intend to be smelling that aroma all day."

Inside chambers, Judge Stubbs grins as he re-reads the complaint in *Mid-Continent Casualty Assurance Co. v. Lester M. Fleming*.

He leans back and shakes his head in wonder.

Lester Fleming.

Twenty-one years ago, but he'll never forget that day. Started out as a lovely spring morning—a lot like today. His first trial in the circuit court of Cook County. Oh, sure, he'd tried a few cases out in DuPage by then, but this was the big time. This was Chicago. Better yet, he was going up against the famous Lester Fleming.

More like the infamous. Even then, back all those years, back before mayoral candidate Jane Byrne accused him of being a member of "the cabal of evil men," Lester Fleming already had a reputation. He'd started his career in traffic court on North LaSalle, where he quickly became known as a fixer. From there he moved into plaintiff's personal injury work with Sam "The Watermelon Man" Blumenfeld. When Sam went down on eleven counts of mail fraud thirteen years ago, the partnership of Blumenfeld & Fleming became the Law Offices of Lester Fleming & Associates—the "associates" being an interchangeable group of a half dozen young lawyers and paralegals who worked up the hundreds of fender-benders brought to Fleming by the chasers who prowled the highways of metropolitan Chicago with police radios in their cars. Although his typical client had a claim worth less than twenty grand, Fleming easily made up in volume what he gave up in size. He'd figured out early on that you could make just as much money settling two hundred little claims a year as you could nailing one or two big verdicts.

Lester Fleming, eh? I might finally get a chance to nail the S.O.B.

On that morning twenty-one years ago, Harry Stubbs drove in from Hinsdale nervous but confident. Nervous because he was always nervous before a trial, and especially before this one. Even though he was several years older than Lester Fleming, he was far less experienced—after all, Fleming was already trolling the halls of traffic court when Trooper Stubbs was attending his first class at night law school. But confident, too, because he had reason to be. He had the facts on his side. He had the law on his side. Better yet, he had evidence that Fleming's client had staged the accident. The whole thing was a fake, and he had a witness who could testify that Lester Fleming had helped the plaintiff stage it.

Harry Stubbs fantasized on his drive downtown that morning: he would not only beat the great Lester Fleming, he might even get the man hauled up on charges before the disciplinary commission. Yes, sir, he told himself on that lovely spring morning, the name Harry L. Stubbs would be in all the newspapers.

And it was. As the losing attorney in a $145,000-damage verdict—at the time the largest nonjury damage award in the history of the state of Illinois, and thus worth a front-page story in the *Sun-Times*, complete with a photograph of a beaming Lester Fleming.

The trial had been an outrage from beginning to end. After the first hour—after Judge Madigan overruled every one of Stubbs's objections and granted Fleming's motion to exclude most of Stubbs's evidence —it finally dawned on Harry Stubbs: the fix was in. Worse yet, Madigan was a shrewd Irish fox who knew exactly how to throw a case while protecting his record on appeal. The judge announced the verdict at the end of the second day of trial, immediately after Harry Stubbs finished his increasingly frantic closing argument. He'd sat numb at counsel's table while Fleming postured for the press outside the courtroom. He'd remained at counsel's table while Fleming and the judge met in chambers. He'd finally started packing up his court papers when Fleming emerged from the judge's chambers puffing on a thick cigar.

Fleming had paused near Stubbs. "Tough luck, pal."

Stubbs had glared at him. "That wasn't luck. I know what you did."

Fleming smiled, the cigar clenched between his teeth. "This ain't the boonies, kid." He took the cigar out of his mouth, studied it for a moment, and took another puff. "Welcome to Cook County."

Fleming had strolled out of the courtroom chuckling, trailing a wispy line of cigar smoke.

Welcome to Cook County, eh?

Judge Stubbs flips through the court papers back to the signature block on the last page. Abbott & Windsor. Seven lawyers on the signature block. Typical big-firm wolf-pack litigation. But the real lawyer, the one who will actually do today's hearing, will be one of the top three names on the list: L. Debevoise Fletcher, Gabriel Pollack, or Melvin Needlebaum.

He's heard about Fletcher—or maybe read about him in Kup's column. He's one of the Abbott & Windsor bigwigs, which means he's probably just a name on the court papers. A "show" partner. He's heard about Needlebaum, of course. All the federal judges had. Needlebaum might be the brains of this operation, but he won't be the mouthpiece. That left Pollack. Probably a junior partner—one of those Young Turk hotshots. Which is okay. So long as he knows how to put in the evidence. Seems like half the lawyers who appear before him can't tell hearsay from horseshit.

A knock on the door. "Motion time, Yo' Honor."

A moment later, Rahsan Ahmed lumbers into the courtroom to take up his position below the bench where Judge Stubbs presides. Rahsan stands at attention, eyes on the tall door to the left of the bench, the door that leads directly from Judge Stubbs's chambers into the courtroom. The gavel looks like a toy hammer in his huge hands. Approximately forty lawyers are scattered through the immense courtroom—some at the counsel tables, a few in the jury boxes, the rest on the rows of benches in the gallery. At the appearance of the enormous black docket clerk, the lawyers put away their newspapers and begin gathering their court papers. A few cough or clear their throats.

Rahsan's mere presence in the courtroom commands obedience. The bone structure of his face gives him a natural scowl. Add to that his fierce eyes, and he seems to glower up there in a way that thoroughly intimidates all these lawyers with tassels on their shoes. You can see it in their eyes as they approach the podium during motion call, peeking over at him as if they're about to get clotheslined by the middle linebacker from Hell.

Meanwhile, inside his chambers Judge Harry Stubbs stands by the coatrack, slipping on his black

robe. He snaps it closed as he moves toward the courtroom door. Pausing a moment, he can't help but grin.

Welcome to Cook County, eh?

His Honor turns the doorknob. That's Rahsan's sig-
nal: the doorknob turning. Through the door His
Honor can hear the gavel pound three times. He hears
Rahsan order everyone to rise. The Honorable Harry L.
Stubbs opens the door and steps into the courtroom.

Oh-yeah, Oh-yeah, Oh-yeah.

Forty-five minutes into the hearing Judge Stubbs de-
cides that he likes this Pollack kid. Smooth and professional, nothing flashy. Like DiMaggio coming in on a
fly. He isn't crazy about the beard, but it looks fine on
Pollack.

Judge Stubbs glances beyond Pollack at plaintiff's
counsel table. The geek in glasses scribbling frenetically
on a yellow legal pad has to be Needlebaum. Every few
minutes he looks up with that lunatic grin and then
dives back into his legal pad. Judge Powell warned him
about Needlebaum: *Guy'll bury you in motions and
briefs, Harry.* He'll put a stop to that pronto. He'll tell
the attorneys after the hearing that he doesn't want to
turn this case into a paper war.

"Objection, Judge. He's leading the witness."

Judge Stubbs looks over at Stan Budgah at the defendant's table. *What was the question?* Doesn't matter.

"Rephrase the question, Mr. Pollack."

"Certainly, Your Honor." Pollack turns toward the
witness. "Did Mr. Fleming say anything else, sir?"

Stan Budgah gives a grunt of satisfaction and sits
back down.

Judge Stubbs glances down at his notes and frowns.
Stan Budgah?

He knows Stan back from his days in private practice. This is probably Stan's first appearance in federal court in years. Budgah is strictly a ham-'n-egger who mainly handles collection matters in state court. Probably the fattest collections lawyer in Chicago. Judge Stubbs can hear Budgah's raspy, open-mouthed breathing all the way across the courtroom. Stan certainly dresses the part: shiny green sports jacket with a pair of cellophane-wrapped cigars sticking out of the breast pocket, a fat purple tie splotched with soup stains, a white short-sleeve Dacron shirt stretched over a big gut, gray wrinkled slacks with the crotch starting halfway down his massive thighs, scuffed black shoes, and a good two inches of hairy calf showing above the tops of his blue socks.

Seated next to Stan Budgah at counsel's table is Lester Fleming, looking, as usual, tanned, trim, and immaculate in his gray pinstriped three-piece suit, blue oxford cloth shirt, and red-on-navy club tie. He seems almost bored by the proceedings. Fleming could be Central Casting's answer to a call for an eminent corporate litigator type. Indeed, if someone were to walk into the courtroom cold, they would assume that Fleming was the lawyer and Budgah was the defendant, probably in a criminal prosecution for running a dirty bookstore.

As Judge Stubbs studies him, Fleming looks up. Their eyes meet. Fleming gazes at him calmly, his face devoid of expression, not a hint of concern. It's unnerving. Even though Judge Stubbs is up on the bench, cloaked in judicial black, and vested with the might and authority of Article III of the Constitution, he is the one who breaks the stare. Flustered, he glances down at his notes.

"Your Honor." It's Pollack. "We offer into evidence Plaintiff's Exhibit Six, the closing statement given to Mr. Ortega by Lester Fleming on the date it bears."

Judge Stubbs turns toward Stan Budgah, who is in the process of heaving his bulk out of the chair. "Any objection, counsel?"

Budgah squints and nods his head. "I'll object, Judge. I'll certainly object."

"On what grounds, Mr. Budgah?"

He waves his hand dismissively. "Relevance, materiality, best evidence rule, hearsay."

"Overruled. Exhibit Six is admitted into evidence, Mr. Pollack."

"Thank you, Your Honor. I have no further questions for this witness."

"Any cross-examination, Mr. Budgah?" Judge Stubbs asks.

Budgah starts to rise again when Fleming touches him on the shoulder. He leans toward Fleming, who speaks softly in his ear. Budgah shrugs, and turns back to Judge Stubbs. "Nothing, Judge."

TRANSCRIPT OF PROCEEDINGS BEFORE
THE HONORABLE HARRY L. STUBBS,
JUDGE PRESIDING

[Excerpt from examination of Rudolph Martin, Claims Adjuster for Plaintiff Mid-Continent Casualty Assurance Co.]

Q. (By Mr. Pollack) Did you have any further conversations with Mr. Fleming regarding the claim of his client, Mr. Ortega, against your insured?

A. Another telephone conversation.

Q. When did that conversation take place?

A. Later that same afternoon.

Q. Describe it, please.

MR. BUDGAH: Objection, hearsay.

THE COURT: Overruled.

A. Mr. Fleming called back and said that his client was willing to settle for $15,000. We agreed to that amount.

Q. This was on March 14th?

A. Yes.

Q. Did Mid-Continent Casualty prepare a settlement check in the amount of $15,000?

A. Yes.

Q. Did you send that check to Mr. Fleming?

A. Yes.

Q. Mr. Martin, let me show you a copy of a canceled check that has been marked as Plaintiff's Exhibit 12 for identification. Is this the check you sent to Mr. Fleming on or about March 16th?

A. [Witness examines check.] It is.

Q. Is that the only check Mid-Continent ever issued in settlement of Mr. Ortega's claim against your insured?

A. Yes.

MR. POLLACK: Your Honor, I offer into evidence as Plaintiff's Exhibit 12 this check for $15,000 made payable to the order of Manuel Ortega and his attorneys, Lester M. Fleming & Associates.

THE COURT: Plaintiff's Exhibit 12 is received into evidence.

Q. (By Mr. Pollack) Mr. Martin, you heard Mr. Ortega testify earlier today, correct?

A. Yes.

Q. Did you hear him testify that Lester Fleming told him that he had settled the claim for $13,000?

A. Yes.

Q. Did you, sir, understand that the claim had been settled for $13,000?

A. No. Mr. Fleming and I settled the claim for

$15,000. That's why I had the settlement check prepared for that amount.

Q. Did you also hear Mr. Ortega testify that on March 20th Mr. Fleming handed him a purported check from Mid-Continent for $13,000 and asked him to endorse it on the back?

A. Yes.

Q. Did Mid-Continent ever issue a check for $13,000 to Mr. Fleming's firm during that period?

A. No.

Q. Mr. Martin, do you have Plaintiff's Exhibit 12 before you? The $15,000 check you issued to Mr. Fleming to settle the case?

A. Yes.

Q. Please turn it over. Is there a signature on the back?

A. Yes.

Q. Read what's written on the back.

A. It says, For Deposit Only and then it's signed. After the signature it says, Signed on behalf of Manuel Ortega and his attorneys, Lester M. Fleming & Associates.

Q. Does Mr. Ortega's signature appear anywhere on the back or front of that check?

A. No.

MR. POLLACK: I have no further questions, Your Honor.

THE COURT: Mr. Budgah?

MR. BUDGAH: Yeah, I got a few questions here.

Q. (By Mr. Budgah) This Ortega claim you've been talking about—that wasn't the first case you ever settled in your career, right?

A. No.

Q. You settle hundreds of claims each year, right?

A. Yes.

Q. Thousands in your career, right?

A. I suppose so.

Q. Yeah, I suppose so, too. [Laughs] And you talk on the phone to plaintiffs' lawyers every day of the week, right? Talk to them about settling their claims, right?

A. Yes, sir.

Q. Probably talk to several lawyers each day about settling claims, right?

A. Yes, sir.

Q. And Mr. Fleming here, why you've probably talked to this gentleman at least twice a week every week for the past ten years, right?

A. Probably.

Q. And now you claim you can remember the details of one telephone call more than four years ago, one out of all those thousands of calls?

A. Yes, sir.

Q. Come on, Mr. Martin. How can you possibly expect this court to believe that you can remember the exact details of that conversation?

A. For two reasons, sir. My boss instructed me to always make notes of any conversation I had with Mr. Fleming. He said Mr. Fleming couldn't be trusted because he would sell out his clients. I looked over those notes this morning. The other reason I remember that conversation is because Mr. Fleming told me that Mr. Ortega wouldn't settle for a penny under $15,000 and that if we didn't agree to that amount he would sue us for bad faith. I had never had anyone threaten me that way. That's why I remember that telephone conversation.

MR. BUDGAH: Oh. Okay. Let's see. [Pause] No further questions.

THE COURT: Any re-direct, Mr. Pollack?

MR. POLLACK: None, Your Honor.

THE COURT: (To the Witness) You may step
down, sir.

Judge Stubbs stares at the document. "Something's
screwy here," he finally says, leaning back in his chair
with a puzzled look.

The three of them are in chambers—Judge Stubbs,
Rahsan Ahmed, and Norman Feigelberg. Judge Stubbs
asked them to join him after he adjourned the hearing
for a ninety-minute lunch recess.

Feigelberg pulls at his earlobe nervously. "What do
you mean?"

Judge Stubbs slides one of the trial exhibits across
the desktop toward his law clerk. "Look at Exhibit Six."

Feigelberg squints at it:

LESTER FLEMING & ASSOCIATES
CLOSING STATEMENT

Client: *Manuel Ortega*	
Settlement Payment:	*$13,000.00*
LESS:	
Attorney Fee (40%):	*5,200.00*
Court Costs:	*125.00*
Medical Bills:	*2,225.00*
NET TO CLIENT:	*$5,450.00*

Date: *March 20, 1996*

Accepted: *Manuel Ortega*

"You heard the testimony," Judge Stubbs says.

Feigelberg studies the closing statement and nods
his head as the judge continues. "Ortega went to Fleming's office for his settlement money. They gave him

that closing statement and a check for his portion of the settlement."

When Judge Stubbs pauses, Feigelberg looks up. "Okay," he says uncertainly.

Judge Stubbs glances over at Rahsan, who leans forward and places a giant finger next to the first entry on the closing statement. "Says here the case settled for thirteen grand, right?"

Feigelberg frowns at the entry a moment, and then he pages rapidly through his notes from the morning's testimony. "Wait a minute," he says, his frown deepening as he studies his notes. "The settlement check from the insurance company was for fifteen thousand."

"Exactly," Judge Stubbs says.

Feigelberg looks at the judge, then at Rahsan, and then back at the judge. "I don't get it."

Rahsan grunts impatiently. "Norman, the man stealing from both sides." He gestures toward the check. "He settle with the insurance company for fifteen grand but tell his client he settled for thirteen grand. Client don't know any better, insurance company don't know any better, and ol' Lester pocket the difference."

Judge Stubbs nods. "His clients are easy marks, Norman. Most of them are poor Hispanics and blacks— the folks most likely to be scared by the legal system, and thus the folks most likely to believe a fancy attorney when he tells them that thirteen grand is a great deal."

"Wait a minute," Feigelberg says, studying his notes. "How many cases does he settle with Mid-Continent Casualty?"

"Close to a hundred every year," Judge Stubbs says.

Feigelberg raises his eyebrows in amazement. "And you think he might be skimming two to three thousand dollars per case?"

Judge Stubbs shrugs. "Could be." He looks toward

Rahsan and slowly shakes his head. "It doesn't make sense."

"What doesn't?" Feigelberg asks.

Rahsan turns to Feigelberg. "Stan Budgah."

Judge Stubbs nods. "In this kind of case," he explains to Norman, "Fleming ought to be represented by the best lawyer he can afford, and he can afford the very best."

Rahsan tugs pensively on his mustache. "It like he don't care."

"Maybe he and Budgah are close," Feigelberg suggests.

Rahsan snorts. "An' maybe I'm the chocolate Easter Bunny."

His Honor's stomach rumbles audibly. He casts a furtive glance toward the lunch bag resting on the corner of the couch by the large picture window. Inside will be yet another tomato-and-sprouts sandwich on her homemade high-fiber special—two dense slices of bread bristling with those damn wheat flakes that look and taste like burlap. Suddenly, the vision of a thick, juicy hamburger on a puffy white bun with a side of onion rings covered with ketchup floats before his eyes like a desert mirage. He shakes his head, trying to clear the vision.

Rahsan glances at his judge with compassion. "Come on, Norman," he says, standing up. "We got work to do."

"But what about lunch?" Feigelberg whines.

"Forget about lunch, Norman," Rahsan says. "We don't have *time* for that shit. I'll go downstairs to the clerk's office and check the federal dockets. I can't leave the building 'cause I got to be here when court resumes. That means you going to have to get your ass over to the

Daley Center and sweet-talk one of them clerks to run his name through every docket in the building. Every single one, Norman. Anybody got a suit against Lester Fleming in the Circuit Court of Cook County, I want to know about it. You understand me?"

Feigelberg nods with resignation. "Yeah, yeah."

Rahsan checks his watch. "We be starting up again at one-thirty. I'm guessing they be putting on evidence 'til three. You make sure you back here before then, Norman."

"What's the rush?"

Rahsan's eyes widen. "Where you grow up, son? In Mister Rogers' Neighborhood? This is an *emergency* motion. They want our judge to freeze the man's assets. Every last penny."

"So?"

"I got a feeling our judge gonna wanna to do that." Rahsan pauses. "For some reason our judge got himself a big ol' big hard-on for Mr. Lester M. Fleming, Esquire." Rahsan shakes his head. "Before I let him enjoin the man, I gotta know if there's something out there in the weeds gonna jump up and bite us in the ass. So get a move on, Norman. Time's running out."

Norman Feigelberg's eyes blink rapidly behind the smudged lenses. "He's brilliant," he says as he leafs through his notes. "Even diabolical."

They are seated in Rahsan's tiny office down the hall from Judge Stubbs's chambers. It's 2:45 P.M. Afternoon recess. Five minutes ago the judge left the bench—more like dashed from the bench—in what appeared to be, at least to Rahsan, a lower-intestinal crisis. Rahsan's seat in the courtroom is the closest to the judge, and during the thirty minutes preceding the recess he heard several unmistakable sounds escaping from His Honor's nether regions.

"Let's hear it," Rahsan says.

"Okay," Feigelberg mumbles excitedly, still searching through his notes. "It started with their divorce six years ago. It was a nasty one. They'd been married twenty-one years. Two kids—one's twenty, the other seventeen."

"Damn, is this about the kids?"

"Nope. The house."

"What house?"

"Their house." Feigelberg looks up from his notes, his eyes swimming behind the thick glass. "She got it in the property settlement."

"So?"

"He had to make the monthly payments, you see. There was this big balloon payment—$300,000—due last October."

"Which he didn't pay."

Feigelberg looks up with surprise. "How did you know that?"

"Get on with it, Norman. Recess almost over."

"Okay, okay, okay." He pages through his notes. "So he didn't make the balloon payment. The bank starts foreclosure proceedings. His ex-wife—Evelyn Fleming—she sues him and she sues the bank. Him for money, the bank to stop the foreclosure."

"And?"

"She put up a good fight on the foreclosure. I read her affidavit." Feigelberg finds the place in his notes. "She has her invalid mother living with her in a converted first-floor bedroom, she wants her daughters to get married there, she has an office in the basement where she does calligraphy for wedding invitations, she has the family dog buried in the backyard, that sort of thing." He pauses. "Didn't matter. The court entered judgment January 28th."

"When's the foreclosure sale?"

"In two weeks." Feigelberg shakes his head angrily. "And it's going to go for a whole lot more than $300,000. The house is in Wilmette near the lake. It's shot up in value since they bought it fifteen years ago. There's an appraisal in the file for $3.4 million. And guess what? I called the broker handing the sale. He thinks Lester Fleming is going to bid on it. He'll buy it just for spite."

"No way, baby." Rahsan leans back in his chair, shaking his head, his beefy arms crossed over his chest. "We gonna enjoin his ass."

"That's the problem."

Rahsan frowns. "What's the problem?"

"She still has her right of redemption."

"Her what?"

Feigelberg finds the page of his notes. "Under 735 ILCS Section 5/15, there are these provisions about stopping foreclosures. One establishes reinstatment rights, and another governs redemptions of foreclosures of residential real estate in which the mortgagor—"

"Speak English, Norman, and make it fast."

Feigelberg pauses, organizing his thoughts. "We're talking about a foreclosure, okay? Fleming's ex-wife is called the mortgagor. Under Illinois law, she has a right of redemption, even after the bank starts the foreclosure."

"What's that mean?"

"If she tenders the full amount owed before the deadline, the bank has to give her back her house free and clear."

"Full amount owed," Rahsan repeats. "You talkin' the three-hundred grand?"

"Plus interest and costs and stuff."

Rahsan shakes his head. "Where she gonna get that kind of money?"

"From Lester Fleming."

"How? With a gun?"

"No, with a lawsuit."

Rahsan gives a cynical chuckle. "She better hurry."

"She did hurry. That's my point. Remember I said she filed a lawsuit against Fleming? Well, once the other court entered the foreclosure judgment, her lawyers went into high gear. Last Friday they got the judge to enter a judgment against Lester Fleming for the full amount of the redemption: $323,345.00."

Rahsan leans forward. "Last Friday?"

Feigelberg nods. "I saw the order."

"So what's she doing now?"

"According to the court file, her lawyers served garnishments on all his banks. They should have responses by this Friday. It'll be close, but she ought to be able to collect the money in time."

"What do you mean 'close'?"

"The right of redemption expires three months after entry of the foreclosure judgment."

"When's that?"

"A week from tomorrow. She has until then to tender payment to the bank."

Rahsan tugs at his Fu Manchu. "And if she misses?"

Feigelberg snaps his fingers. "Poof. She loses the house. And meanwhile, everything is hush-hush. Fleming got the circuit judge to file the case under seal four weeks ago. No one in the press knows what's going on."

There is a rap on the door. The court reporter pokes her head in. "The judge is ready, Rahsan."

"Be right there," Rahsan says to her. He stands up and looks down at Feigelberg with a frown. "Let me see if I got this straight, Norman. Fleming's ex-wife got everything set to grab his money and save her house just in the nick of time, right?"

Feigelberg nods. "Exactly."

"And the only thing that can go wrong—only thing standing in the way of a happy ending—is if some federal judge by the name of Harry Stubbs happen to enter an order freezing all Lester Fleming's assets before redemption day. I got that right?"

"Well, I suppose that it's possible that something else—"

"Come on, Norman, spare me the mumbo jumbo and answer my question: I got that right?"

"Yes, you have it right."

Rahsan stares down at him for another moment, his hands on his hips. Then he looks up at the ceiling. "Shee-yit."

Judge Stubbs turns to Stan Budgah. "What about the defendant?"

Budgah turns to Fleming, who shakes his head. Budgah heaves himself out of his chair and faces the bench. "Defendant has nothing further, Judge."

"Very well," Judge Stubbs says, pausing to close his notebook and put down his pen. "Will the defendant rise?"

Down below, Rahsan Ahmed clears his throat.

Lester Fleming stands, his expression almost serene.

"Mr. Fleming," Judge Stubbs begins in a God-of-the-Old-Testament voice, "this court is profoundly disturbed by the evidence presented this afternoon." He pauses.

Fleming gazes at him, unruffled, his eyes distant, as if he is listening to a piano concerto instead of the preamble to a federal injunction.

Rattled, Judge Stubbs frowns and shakes his head. "Yes," he says, aiming for a stern tone, "profoundly disturbed."

Rahsan Ahmed clears his throat louder this time.

Judge Stubbs pauses and glances down at his docket clerk. The two exchange a silent look.

"Ah, yes," Judge Stubbs says, turning toward the lawyers with a slightly perplexed expression. "The court, uh, will be in recess, gentlemen." He checks his watch. "It's three-twenty. We will reconvene shortly."

They are alone in chambers, just the judge and Rahsan. Norman Feigelberg stands at the door, waiting. He isn't trying to eavesdrop, but he can't help but hear.

Judge Stubbs pounds his fist on the desktop. "This is not divorce court, dammit." He shakes his head fiercely. "And I'm not some penny-ante domestic relations judge."

Rahsan nods calmly. "You're absolutely right, Yo' Honor." His tone is soothing, almost a purr. "You're a federal judge."

"You bet."

"With all the constitutional power you need to see justice done."

"Yep, and I know exactly how to see justice done here." He crosses his arms defiantly over his chest. "I'm gonna burn his ass."

Rahsan nods calmly and stands up. He walks slowly, pensively, toward the picture window. Judge Stubbs turns in his chair, following his enormous docket clerk with his eyes. Rahsan tugs at his Fu Manchu as he meditates on the view of Lake Michigan. He knows his judge. He knows enough to let this silence linger a bit longer. When enough time has passed, he turns toward Judge Stubbs.

"The man is using you," he says in a quiet voice.

"Using me?" Judge Stubbs gives him an incredulous stare. "Using *me*?

The docket clerk nods. "Using you to get at her."

"Come on, Rahsan. You expect me to believe he set this whole thing up to screw her out of money in a state court case?"

Rahsan shrugs, keeping his posture nonconfrontational. "The man's an opportunist, Yo' Honor. He didn't set up the lawsuit, but he figured out how to use it. Look what he done so far: got this hearin' delayed, then got it switched to you, and then hired that tub of lard to represent him—all to make sure he gonna lose this motion."

Judge Stubbs scratches his neck, bewildered. "I don't get it. Where's the angle? She's already got a judgment against him, and she'll earn post-judgment interest on it. After all, this is just a *preliminary* injunction. It'll only last until Judge Weinstock gets back and holds the trial on the merits. Once the injunction is lifted she'll be able to collect her money *plus* interest."

"Money won't do her no good then. She want her house back, and that means she need that money now." Rahsan pauses for emphasis. "You enjoin the man, the lady gonna lose that house. When Judge Weinstock finally get around to holdin' the trial on the merits, you ain't gonna see hide nor hair of no Stan Budgah. No, suh. Lester gonna show up with a whole new army of high-priced lawyers, and they gonna be ready to rumble."

Judge Stubbs hesitates for a moment, and then shakes his head angrily. "This is bigger than some gal's house, Rahsan. Don't you see that? Lester Fleming is defrauding that insurance company. He's stealing from his clients. Good God, man, he's violating federal laws.

What am I supposed to do? Look the other way? Let him continue to prey on the public?"

A languid shrug. "The man been preying on the public for twenty-five years. Couple mo' months ain't gonna destroy the country."

"Oh, come on, Rahsan. We can't take that attitude. This is a court of law."

Rahsan walks slowly back across the room and stops in front of the desk. He places his massive fists on the desk and leans forward, towering over Judge Stubbs. Rahsan stares down at his judge, his dark eyes as focused as laser beams. "The man is using you."

"I really don't think—"

"The man is playin' you fo' a fool."

Judge Stubbs pauses, his eyes blinking. "A fool?"

"A fool." Rahsan straightens up and shakes his head slowly, gazing at his judge. "And you ain't no fool. No, suh."

Judge Stubbs frowns and studies the desk blotter. Rahsan moves back and lowers himself into the chair facing the desk. He waits.

Finally, Judge Stubbs looks up. "What can I do?"

Rahsan tugs at his mustache. "I've been thinking 'bout that."

"Tell me."

"Let's get Norman in here first."

Judge Stubbs and Rahsan Ahmed wait. They are both watching Norman Feigelberg, who is frowning, his head tilted back, his eyes squeezed shut. Several seconds pass.

"Ah," he finally says, lowering his head and opening his eyes. "I know just what we could use."

"What?" Judge Stubbs asks anxiously.

Feigelberg looks at them with a sly smile. "A little comity."

"Lord Jesus!" Rahsan says in disgust. "Norman, you got shit for brains? We need law, not jokes."

"No," Feigelberg says nervously, "not comedy. Comity. C-O-M-I-T-Y. It's a basic principle of law."

"Right," Judge Stubbs says, nodding soberly. "Comity. Yes, comity." He pauses. "How, uh, exactly do you see that applying here?"

"Federalism, Your Honor." Feigelberg pauses and glances up at the portraits of President Reagan and Congressman Hyde. "You know, states' rights, federal court deference, honoring the sovereignty of the state courts. That sort of thing."

Judge Stubbs begins to smile. "Ah, yes, I like that." *And,* he thinks, *Judge Easterbrook will, too.* But his smile fades to a look of concern. "Are there any cases out there?"

"Absolutely," Feigelberg answers confidently. "We're talking about an integral tenet at the matrix of constitutional law. I'm sure I could find several excellent precedents down in the library."

"Forget the library," Rahsan says. "We don't got that kind of time. Didn't they teach you 'bout the Constitution at that University of Yale?"

"Sure. I took the course. We had—"

"You got the textbook in your office?"

"Well, actually, I do."

"If this comity thing is such a—what you call it?— an integrated tennis match in constitutional law, some of them fine cases ought to be right there in that textbook. Ain't that right? Maybe even a few opinions from the Supremes themselves."

Feigelberg is grinning. "You're right."

"Well then what you waiting fo', baby? Get over there and bring His Honor back some words of wisdom from our Supreme Court."

• • •

With a flourish, Judge Stubbs signs three copies of the order he's just read aloud. He hands them down to his docket clerk and watches as Rahsan gives one to Stan Budgah and one to Gabe Pollack. Pollack remains at the podium, rereading the last two paragraphs of the order. Budgah returns to the defendant's table, where Fleming snatches the two-page order from him.

"Gentlemen," Judge Stubbs says, "Judge Weinstock will be back from vacation in two weeks. The injunction will remain in effect until his return. If any procedural issues should arise before then, you can contact Judge Weinstock's docket clerk." He pauses, his eyes on Gabe Pollack. "Any questions?"

Gabe looks up with a pleased but slightly puzzled expression. "None, Your Honor."

Judge Stubbs turns toward the defendant's table. "Mr. Budgah?"

Budgah is watching his client, who is seated at the table staring at the last two paragraphs of the order.

"Mr. Budgah?"

Budgah looks at the judge, glances warily at his client, and then back at the judge. "Uh, I think we're okay."

"Very good." Judge Stubbs closes his notebook and stands up. "We'll be in recess."

Rahsan bangs the gavel. "All rise!"

Judge Stubbs pauses at the door, his hand on the knob, and turns back. Fleming is still seated at the defendant's table, the order clenched in his hands. Even from across the courtroom, Judge Stubbs can see the vein throbbing in his temple. Fleming looks up. Their eyes meet, and for that moment there is no one else in the room. All of those intervening years vanish, but this time it is Fleming seated at counsel's table. He glares at

Judge Stubbs, who gazes back serenely. And this time it is Fleming who breaks the stare. He looks down at the order. Judge Stubbs waits a beat, wishing only that he had a cigar, and then he pushes through the door and disappears.

The TV news reports miss it completely, of course, as does the *Sun-Times*. But the late edition of the *Tribune* —which runs the story under the headline CHICAGO LAWYER SUED FOR FRAUD; FEDERAL JUDGE FREEZES ASSETS— flags it toward the end of the article:

> The order carves out an unusual exception to enable the collection of any judgment against Fleming arising out of a foreclosure involving the Wilmette residence of his former wife, Evelyn. As a result, Fleming's assets can be garnished solely to redeem the home from foreclosure even though the assets remain completely outside Fleming's control.
>
> Northwestern Law School Professor Harold Kussell described this exception as "quite unique," but noted that the order cites two Supreme Court cases as precedents. "Judge Stubbs labels the exception 'a comity exclusion,'" Kussell explained. "Frankly, it's a clever extension of existing law and should be immune from attack on appeal."

Oh-yeah, Oh-yeah, Oh-yeah.

Afterword

When I was a young trial lawyer, an appearance before a judge—especially a federal district judge—was as intimidating as an appearance before the Wizard of Oz. Indeed, those first few times in court I felt like the Tin Man trembling before that awful, floating head. But gradually I came to realize that there was an ordinary man behind the curtain. And eventually, as I spent more and more time in particular courts, I discovered that the robed authority figure up on the bench was not necessarily the source of justice in the courtroom. Within the sphere of every busy judge move various officials—law clerks, bailiffs, docket clerks, secretaries—and you ignore them at your peril and your client's peril. Indeed, I have stoically presented a full afternoon of evidence to a federal judge who was not merely asleep but gently snoring throughout my dazzling performance, all the while taking some comfort in the knowledge that the decision in the case would be rendered and written by His Honor's young law clerk, who seemed to be taking careful notes of the proceedings—and who ultimately wrote an excellent opinion (i.e., in my client's favor). And thus, though I have never met Judge Harry Stubbs, I have logged days in courtrooms where the real judge was someone other than the robed figure on the bench.

Finally, a few words on Judge Stubbs and his gastrointestinal predicament. Most of us who were once law students had a professor who introduced the doctrine of legal realism through a favorite adage of that branch of jurisprudence: *Judicial outcomes are influenced less by legal precedent than by what the judge had for breakfast that morning.* I used to wonder whether that adage was to be taken literally. For poor Harry Stubbs, legal realism reaches its epitome through Bernice's lopsided bran muffins.

—MICHAEL A. KAHN

If there is a universal experience shared by all young associates, it is surely the hours spent outside the jury deliberation room or in a cocktail bar listening to senior attorneys spin their war stories, usually at great and unavoidable length. In this tale, Phillip Margolin transplants the storyteller to talk radio and allows him to tell one of the best war stories yet.

The Jailhouse Lawyer

PHILLIP M. MARGOLIN

"I'm Lyle Richmond and you're listening to Talk Radio. My very special guest tonight is six-foot-five, has a full head of wavy gray hair, steely blue eyes, and the squarest chin this side of Mt. Rushmore. If I also said that he is wearing a Stetson hat, a bolo tie and Ostrich-leather cowboy boots, I'd bet that most of you in my listening audience would guess that we're going to be speaking to criminal defense attorney Monte Bethune. He's visiting us just one week after winning a stunning acquittal for Iowa Governor Leona Farris, who shot her husband in front of millions of viewers on national television.

"Welcome to the show, Monte."

"Thanks for having me on."

"Did your lucky outfit win the Farris case for you?"

"I wish it was that easy, Lyle. I give all the credit for the governor's acquittal to the jurors, who were able to see through the government's smoke screen and find the truth."

"I'm sure you had a little part in leading them through that screen of smoke, Monte."

"I try, Lyle."

"Our listeners will be pleased to hear that you're in our fair city on a book tour to promote your autobiography, *The Best Defense*. They can meet you tomorrow afternoon at Benson's Books on Comstock and Vine from three o'clock to five."

"That's right."

"How's the book doing?"

"*The Best Defense* is going to debut at number four on the *New York Times* bestseller list, this Sunday."

"Congratulations. And I can tell our listeners that it deserves to be there. This is some terrific book."

"Thanks, Lyle. I wrote it to try and give my readers an idea of what it takes to try high-profile lawsuits."

"You certainly do that. The chapter describing the way you won that forty-million-dollar verdict against Dental Pro had me on the edge of my seat."

"My clients deserved that verdict. It was only by sheer luck that my investigator was able to prove that Dental Pro was using radioactive materials to make their dental implants."

"You were up against some high-priced legal talent in that case."

"It seems that the other side always puts its best lawyers against me."

"Sort of like those showdowns in the Old West where the young gunslingers would call out the fastest gun. You always beat them to the draw, though."

"Not all the time, Lyle. I've lost my share. I even talk about some of those losses in my book."

"The Chicago Strangler case."

"That's right. There was a case where I was definitely outgunned by a bright, young D.A."

"That was Everett Till, wasn't it?"

"The current governor of Illinois. Every time we meet, Everett thanks me for putting him in the state-house."

"Is Till the best you ever went up against?"

"Whew. That's a tough question to answer, Lyle."

"Is that because you've been up against so many hotshots?"

"No. That's not the problem. Everett is definitely

the lawyer who tried the best case against me, but he's not the best person I ever faced in court."

"I don't get you, Monte."

"The best person I ever tried a case against wasn't a real lawyer. He was a jailhouse lawyer."

"What's a jailhouse lawyer?"

"A con. Someone who learned his law while serving a jail sentence."

"You mean a crook?"

"Exactly. But this fella was one very smart crook."

"I sense a story here, Monte. One that didn't find its way into *The Best Defense.*"

"You've got me there. I guess the problem is that this story is a little embarrassing."

"Spill, Monte. I'm sure all my listeners would love to hear about a convict who could get the best of the best lawyer in the U.S.A."

"Okay, Lyle. I don't mind telling tales on myself, and this case was tried when I was still a little wet behind the ears. Not that I would have seen what was happening even with all my experience."

"Let's hear it, Monte."

"Okay. Now, this happened in 1970. I was two years out of law school and two years into my stint as a deputy district attorney in Portland, Oregon. You're a little young to remember those days. The war in Vietnam dominated everything. Then, there was Black Power. Bobby Kennedy and Martin Luther King had been assassinated, and every day brought more riots and protests. I guess you could say that there was general chaos across the United States, with the exception of the Multnomah County District Court, where I was stuck trying shoplifting cases, drunk drives and other boring misdemeanors.

"I was specializing in traffic cases on the morning I

was assigned *State of Oregon v. Tommy Lee Jones.* It had been a rough week. After a string of victories, I had lost two tough Driving Under the Influence cases, back to back, and I needed a win. A big smile crossed my face when my supervisor told me that Tommy Lee was handling his case Pro Per. That means by himself, without a lawyer. There's an old maxim I'm sure you've heard that holds that a lawyer who represents himself has a fool for a client. That maxim is doubly true for a jailhouse lawyer. Knocking off a top defense attorney was more satisfying than steamrollering a poor fool who thinks that he's Perry Mason, but a notch was still a notch.

"District Court Judge Arlen Hatcher's courtroom was on the third floor of the Multnomah County Courthouse, an intimidating concrete monster of a building that takes up a whole block in the center of Portland. The older courtrooms are stately, with marble columns and polished wood. Hatcher, a career prosecutor before his judicial appointment, had only come on the bench eight months ago. He was stuck in a newer courtroom that had been squeezed into a space previously occupied by an administrative office. Plastic and imitation wood dominated the decor.

"Two long counsel tables stood before the judge's dais. Tommy Lee was sprawled disrespectfully in a chair in front of the table closest to the jury box. His wild Afro, scraggily goatee, and soiled jail clothes made him look fierce. Any lawyer worth his salt would have made certain that Tommy Lee shaved and came to court in a suit, but Tommy Lee could not afford to hire an attorney and he refused to let the court appoint one.

" 'You the pig they sent to pers'cute me?' Tommy Lee snarled when I walked to the other table. His bravado didn't faze me, and I flashed him a patronizing smile.

" 'Simmer down, Tommy Lee,' warned one of the two jail guards who were assigned to watch the prisoner.

"If you're wondering why Tommy Lee was so heavily guarded when the charge was only reckless driving, you might be interested in knowing that two months after the traffic citation was issued in Portland, Tommy was rearrested on a fugitive complaint out of Newark, New Jersey, that charged him with murder. Tommy Lee was also handling his extradition battle by himself.

"The bailiff rapped the gavel and Arlen Hatcher stomped in. The judge was tall and lean and walked with a slight limp. His cheeks were sunken, his eyes narrow, and his thin lips curled into a wolfish grin whenever he overruled a defense objection. Judge Hatcher loved to bedevil defense attorneys, and he was always happiest at a sentencing.

"I jumped to my feet when Hatcher took the bench, but Tommy Lee stayed seated. Old Arlen fixed the defendant with his death stare. Tommy Lee didn't blink.

" 'Please stand when the judge enters,' the bailiff ordered menacingly. Tommy Lee uncoiled slowly, his eyes still locked on the judge. When he was fully upright, I called the case and the judge told the bailiff to call for a jury. That was when Tommy Lee made what I thought was his fatal mistake.

" 'I don't want no jury,' he said.

" 'What?!' Hatcher asked incredulously.

" 'One pig or six fascist sheep, it don't make no difference.'

"Old Arlen turned scarlet. 'You ever hear of contempt?' he growled. 'One more reference to barnyard animals and you'll be an expert on it . . . Mr. Jones.'

"Now, I'm certain that 'Mr. Jones' was originally 'boy,' but Hatcher quit calling Afro-Americans 'boy' on the record after the Oregon Supreme Court reprimanded him. Actually, Hatcher wasn't any more prejudiced against blacks than he was against any other defendant.

"That was another reason why I thought that Tommy Lee was a fool for defending himself. He needed a lawyer who knew the ropes. Hell, with a client like Tommy Lee, any lawyer in the county would have swallowed nails before letting Arlen Hatcher handle the case.

" 'You understand that you have a constitutional right to have your case tried by a jury of your peers?' Hatcher inquired.

" 'Whatcho think? I ain't dumb. I also know I have me a right to not be havin' no jury.'

"A gleam appeared in Hatcher's eye, and his lips twitched from the effort of suppressing his glee at having Tommy Lee's fate thrust into his hands. I could almost hear him calculating the maximum sentence he would be able to impose after he found Tommy Lee guilty.

" 'Very well, Mr. Jones,' Hatcher said, 'I'll be glad to hear your case. Are you ready to proceed, Mr. Bethune?'

"My only witness was Portland Police Officer Marty Singer, a big happy-go-lucky man, who was painfully honest. Marty always told the truth on the stand. Some deputy district attorneys complained that Marty's honesty had cost them cases, but I preferred him as a witness because jurors always believed him.

"As soon as he was sworn, I established that Marty was working as a traffic patrolman on February 8, 1970. Then I asked him if he had made an arrest that night in downtown Portland for reckless driving.

" 'At 9:35 P.M., I was on patrol on Salmon near Third,' Singer said, 'when I saw a vehicle weaving in and out of traffic at a high rate of speed. I put on my lights, but the car continued to drive erratically for a block or so before it pulled over.'

" 'What did you do then?'

" 'When both cars were parked, I exited my vehicle and approached the driver. The first thing I did was ask him for his license. While he was trying to extract the license, I leaned close to him and smelled the odor of an alcoholic beverage on his breath. This, coupled with his erratic driving, made me suspect that the driver was intoxicated, so I asked him to exit his vehicle.'

" 'Did you ask the driver to perform any field sobriety tests?'

" 'I did,' Singer replied.

" 'What did you ask him to do?'

" 'I had the driver walk a straight line, count backward from one hundred, and repeat several words that are difficult for impaired drivers to pronounce.'

" 'How did he do?'

" 'To my surprise, he passed all the tests. That's why I charged him with reckless driving instead of driving under the influence of intoxicants.'

" 'Officer Singer, did you examine the driver's license?' I asked.

" 'Yes, sir.'

" 'Who was named on it?'

" 'Bobby Lee Jones,' Singer answered.

"My heart dropped into the bottom of my brilliantly polished wingtips.

" 'Er, you mean Tommy Lee Jones, don't you, Officer?' I asked, in order to give Singer a chance to cover his gaff.

"Singer looked confused. 'I'm . . . I think it was Bobby Lee,' he said. Then he brightened. 'But, later, he said he was Tommy Lee Jones.'

" 'Later?'

" 'When I said that I was going to arrest him.'

" 'Then the driver said that he was Tommy Lee Jones?'

" 'Right. He told me that he had borrowed his brother's license without his permission.'

"I breathed a sigh of relief and pointed at the defendant.

" 'Is this the man that you arrested?'

"For the first time since Singer had begun his testimony, Tommy Lee came alive. He sat up straight and stared at Singer as if daring him to make the identification. Singer hesitated.

" 'Yes,' he answered shakily, 'I think that's him.'

"If this had been a jury trial, Lyle, I would have been dead after Singer's crappy identification, but old Arlen hadn't heard a word since Tommy Lee called him a pig. Hell, Singer could have testified that the driver was a Caucasian dwarf and it wouldn't have made any difference as far as Tommy Lee's fate was concerned.

" 'Did you arrest the driver and take him to jail?'

" 'No, sir. He was polite and cooperative, so I gave him a citation, told him his court date, and let him go home.'

" 'One last question, Officer,' I asked. 'Did something happen before the defendant's court date that caused him to be taken into custody?'

" 'Yes. He was picked up on this murder case out of New Jersey.'

"Of course, this was all totally improper, mentioning the murder. A real lawyer would have objected and asked for a mistrial. But all's fair in love and war. If Tommy Lee wanted to represent himself, he'd have to live with the consequences of his decision. To my delight, I could see Judge Hatcher writing the word 'murder' on his pad. He circled the word a few times. Then he gave Tommy Lee another dose of the death stare.

" 'No further questions,' I said.

"Now, a good defense lawyer would have made mincemeat out of Singer's I.D. and would have had a good chance to win the case, but Tommy Lee seemed to be his own worst enemy. First, he put on his fiercest face. Next, he stared at Singer menacingly. Then, he began to insult my witness.

" 'Ain't it true that you told the brother you stopped, who ain't me, that you would fix his case for fifty bucks?'

" 'That is not true,' Singer answered, as his ears started to glow. Marty went to church regularly and he took the teachings of the Bible to heart. Accusing him of dishonesty was one of the worst things a person could do.

" 'How much you say you'd charge him, then?'

"I objected, Hatcher whacked his gavel down hard, and the trial continued with Singer and the judge glaring at Tommy Lee.

" 'You say that this so-called arrest was on February 8, 1970?' Tommy Lee asked, his tone heavy with sarcasm.

"Singer nodded.

" 'You drunk or shootin' up, like you usually do on that date?'

"Hatcher smashed his gavel down before I could object.

" 'One more impertinent question like that,' he warned, 'and I'll hold you in contempt. This is an officer of the law up here. Show him some respect.'

"Tommy Lee leaped to his feet.

" 'I got no respect fo' a honkey pig who perjures

hisself and say he be arrestin' me when I wasn't there,'
Tommy Lee screamed.

"The two guards wrestled Tommy Lee back onto his
chair. Singer was seething. Hatcher had begun to drool.
I just sat back and enjoyed the show. With each word he
spoke, Tommy Lee was digging himself a deeper grave
into which I knew I would soon be booting his body.

" 'How come you so sure you arrested me?' Tommy
Lee challenged when all was calm again.

" 'I remember you,' Singer said, a lot firmer in his
identification than he had been when I had questioned
him.

" 'Don't all us niggers look the same to you?' the
defendant asked with a sneer.

Singer was really angry now. " 'I have no problem
distinguishing one black man from another, Mr. Jones,'
he replied firmly.

" 'Ain't it really true that the man you stopped was
my brother, Bobby Lee, who gave you my name to beat
the rap?' Tommy Lee asked, violating a rule that every
first-year law student knows. Every time Tommy Lee
challenged Singer's identification, he was giving the officer an opportunity to restate his opinion that Tommy
Lee was the person that he had arrested.

"Singer looked grim and shook his head. He was
adamant now.

" 'You are the person I arrested, Mr. Jones.'

"Tommy Lee swung around toward the back of the
room and pointed to a black man who was seated there.

" 'Ain't it him you stopped?' he challenged.

"Singer studied the man. His hair was neatly
clipped and he was clean-shaven. He was dressed in a
three-piece business suit, a white silk shirt, and a ma-
roon tie. He was everything that Tommy Lee was not,

and it only took Singer a moment to answer the defendant's question.

" 'That is not the man I arrested.'

" 'You still sticking to your nonsense story that it was me you stopped on February 8, 1970, even after bein' face to face with this man?' Tommy Lee asked incredulously.

" 'It was definitely you that I stopped.'

"The verdict was a foregone conclusion. I never saw anyone bury himself so badly in all my life. I rested and Tommy Lee had no witnesses. At least he'd had the common sense to stay off the stand. At the time, I thought that was the only thing he had done correctly. Hatcher took all of half a minute to find Tommy Lee guilty."

"I'm confused, Monte. I thought you said that this Tommy Lee guy was the best you've ever gone up against in court. It sounds to me like you pounded him into hamburger meat."

"That's the way I saw it, too. I remember laughing my way through lunch as I told the other deputies about my victory. But Tommy Lee had the last laugh.

"I only saw him once more after his conviction. It was three weeks later. I was handling Criminal Presiding when the bailiff called Tommy Lee's extradition case. The man the guard led into the courtroom looked the same and was dressed in the same jail clothes, but his attitude was different. He smiled when he saw me and extended his hand.

" 'You sure got the best of me, Mr. Bethune,' he said, and I noticed that the thick Negro drawl had disappeared.

" 'I was just doing my job, Mr. Jones,' I assured him. 'Nothing personal.'

" 'I'm aware of that,' Tommy Lee responded.

"Judge Cody took the bench and I told him that this

was the time set for Tommy Lee to contest New Jersey's request that he be extradited to its jurisdiction so he could be tried for murder. Based on my experience with him in our court case, I expected Tommy Lee to come out swinging, but he surprised everyone by waiving extradition and agreeing to return to New Jersey voluntarily.

" 'You're certain that's what you want to do?' Judge Cody asked. He was very conscientious about protecting the rights of those who appeared before him.

" 'Yes, Your Honor,' Tommy Lee replied politely.

" 'All right,' the judge said. And that was the last I ever saw of Tommy Lee.

"But it wasn't the last time I thought about him. See, Lyle, I knew, in my gut, that something was wrong. He was just so different in the two court cases. The way he talked, the way he walked. What had caused Tommy Lee's transformation from a wild-eyed radical to a polite and well-mannered citizen? That question really bothered me, but it wasn't until a little before quitting time, two weeks later, that I figured it out.

"Tommy Lee and the well-dressed black man he said was his brother did look alike. It was the wild Afro and the soiled jail clothes and the radical-black histrionics that had thrown me off. Had Officer Singer really arrested Bobby Lee Jones? Was Tommy Lee taking the rap for his brother? That was the logical explanation. Bobby Lee looked successful. Tommy Lee was a bad actor with a long record of arrests and convictions. That was it, I decided. Tommy Lee was taking the fall for brotherly love. It made me think better of him. For a moment, I felt a warm glow.

"Then a warning bell began tinkling in my subconscious, and I suddenly felt an attack of nausea. The extradition file was in a cabinet on the other side of the office. I raced to it and my hand shook as I grabbed the manila folder from the drawer. I prayed that I was wrong, but I was certain that I wasn't. As I read the extradition warrant, I could see Tommy Lee pointing at Bobby Lee Jones as he asked Marty Singer, *You still sticking to your nonsense story that it was me you stopped on February 8, 1970, even after bein' face to face with this man?*

"And I recalled Singer's firm and unequivocal response: *It was definitely you that I stopped.*

"You see, Lyle, that murder. The one that took place clear across the country, three thousand miles away, in New Jersey. According to the extradition papers, it was committed on February 8, 1970."

Afterword

For twenty-five years, I had a full-time criminal defense practice. During that time I handled every type of case imaginable, from bizarre traffic citations like "Television in Front Seat Viewable by Driver" to a dozen death-penalty murder cases. I also came in contact with every type of client. Although they are generally a pain in the neck, I do have a fond place in my heart for jailhouse lawyers. These are criminal defendants who have picked up a smattering of law during their years behind bars. They believe that they know more about the law than their lawyer—and sometimes they are right.

Early on in my career, I was appointed to represent a jailhouse lawyer who was being held in jail on serious charges. I made it clear to him that there was no way in the world that any judge in the courthouse would ever release him on bail. Moments later, he fired me and represented himself in court. The next day, I ran into him in the lobby of the Multnomah County Courthouse in Portland, Oregon, where I tried most of my cases. I was astonished to see that he was out of jail, and he explained to me that he had convinced the judge to release him on his own word to appear in court. That incident convinced me never to take the intelligence or skills of jailhouse lawyers for granted.

The story you have just read is my tribute to these loony lawyer wanna-bes, who, every so often, prove to be a lot sharper than we law school graduates.

—Phillip M. Margolin

Jeremiah Healy's private investigator, John Francis Cuddy, has appeared in a series of mystery novels renowned not only for their intricate plots but for their serious consideration of current social issues. This story is no exception, as Cuddy is enlisted by a lawyer friend to track down that most elusive of quarries—the truth.

Voir Dire

JEREMIAH HEALY

ONE

Bernard Wellington, Esquire, had that mournful look of an old dog betrayed by incontinence.

I watched Bernie ease himself into the high-backed swivel chair behind his desk, a muzzy twilight through the wide bay window silhouetting both man and furniture. An inch taller than my six-two-plus, you'd have pegged him an inch shorter, almost four decades spent bent over legal tomes stooping his shoulders and spoiling his posture. A widow's peak of black hair coexisted peacefully with the fringe of snow at sideburns and temple. Wellington's head and hands were disproportionately large, his voice a baritone burred by the long-term effects of good scotch. Descended from a Boston Brahmin family, he'd betrayed his corporate-law heritage in choosing criminal-defense work coming out of Harvard, lo, those many years ago.

That fine October Monday, though, Bernie had left a message with my answering service around lunchtime, asking me to meet him in his office at 5:00 P.M. Meaning after court.

As I took a client chair, the nail on Wellington's right middle finger began picking at some leather piping on the arm of his high-back. "John Francis Cuddy, it's been a while."

I hadn't seen him since doing the preliminary investigation for one of his armed robbery defendants five months earlier. "What've you got, Bernie?"

"What I've got is Michael Monetti."

The *Globe* and the *Herald* both had run third-page stories when Monetti, a career hood, was indicted some months back for the attempted murder of a "business associate."

I said, "His trial ought to be coming up soon."

"We impaneled the jury last Friday afternoon."

"A little late in the game to be calling for a private investigator."

"Ordinarily, yes. But . . . ." Something was obviously bothering Bernie. "John, indulge me a moment?"

"Sure."

Wellington cleared his throat, the way I'd seen him do in the courtroom to focus attention on himself without having to raise his voice. "As I believe you know, the Commonwealth of Massachusetts has been one of the few states in the Union not permitting attorney voir dire of prospective jurors."

I reached back to my one year of law school for the French phrase meaning *to speak the truth.* "But the judge does ask them preliminary questions, right?"

"Right. However, an attorney who can't confront jurors individually before they're impaneled doesn't get much information or guidance toward exercising peremptory challenges. The typical juror questionnaire provides just generic data such as occupation, marital status, and children's ages. That's the reason for this new experiment."

"Experiment?"

"Our esteemed legislature passed a bill establishing a pilot project in three counties. Under the project, each attorney has a total of thirty minutes to question the entire jury panel on bias, temperament, etcetera, etcetera."

I thought about it. "Not much time, but still fairly

helpful when you're representing somebody as mobbed up as Monetti."

Wellington seemed hurt. "My client is not 'mobbed up,' John."

"I don't recall any 'esteemed' judge letting him out on bail."

"And a travesty, that, especially when his extended family has been clustered in the front row of the audience every minute of the trial. The proud father is a former brick mason, the doting mother a retired schoolteacher. Michael's older sister prospers as a registered beautician, and he once bragged about the career of a second cousin who does standup comedy, like that chap Rich—"

"Bernie?"

A pause before, "What?"

"Maybe you should save the 'he comes from a good family' argument for the sentencing phase of the case."

A stony look. Wellington always had been better in the courtroom than in his office. Finally, though, a grudging "Alright."

"And—no offense, Bern—I still don't see why you want to bring me in now."

The stony look softened, and Wellington leaned back into his chair's headrest, the leather bustle depressed and cracked from the countless times he must have pondered knotty problems of strategy and tactics. "I'm troubled by one of the jurors, John."

"How do you mean?"

"Our case falls under this new pilot project, and I had a truly splendid sequence of questions to include in my voir dire. But, for all the prospective male jurors called to the box from the pool, Michael insisted I use his questions instead."

"His questions?"

"Correct. My client wanted to know if those jurors had ever been in the armed forces, or arrested, or even if they'd worked in a 'strategically sensitive' industry."

Didn't make sense to me. "I can maybe see the 'arrested' part, Bernie, but what would Monetti's other questions have to do with his attempted-murder charge?"

"Nothing, John. And worse, Michael's approach undermined my opportunity to use the individual voir dire as a way of warming up the jury for him."

"So what happened with them?"

"The male jurors, you mean?"

"Yes."

"Two had in fact been arrested, and the prosecution used peremptory challenges on both."

"Meaning Monetti's questions actually helped the other side decide who it should ding?"

"Correct again." Wellington seemed to sour at the memory. "Of the remaining males called from the pool, one had been in the army, another the navy. Michael had me challenge both."

"Why?"

"He didn't say."

And I still didn't see Monetti's strategy. "What about the rest of the jurors?"

Wellington closed his eyes for a moment. "One had worked at a defense think tank on Route 128, and my client wanted him off, too. However, the three males who answered negatively to all of Michael's questions were eventually seated."

"Because neither the prosecutor nor you challenged them."

"That's right," said Wellington. "But believe me, I wanted to knock off one of the trio, a Mr. Arthur Durand."

I thought about it. "I'm guessing he's the juror who's 'troubling' you."

A nod. "I didn't like him from the get-go, John. The juror questionnaire said Mr. Durand was unemployed, never married, no kids. In person, he also wore old clothes and had this tendency of scratching his nose and squirming in his seat." Wellington caricatured both. "Plus, the man's hair and beard were longish and unkempt, and he had rather a dopey cast to his eyes."

"I don't know, Bern. That last part makes this Durand sound like perfect juror material for Monetti."

Another hurt look. "Except for Michael's hundred-dollar razor cut and thousand-dollar suits. In any case, though, while I just didn't like Mr. Durand, my client insisted on keeping him."

"And?"

Wellington sighed. "And we finished impaneling Friday afternoon, Mr. Durand being the last one from the pool to be seated. Then the jury was excused for the weekend and went home."

"No sequestration order?"

"Not for 'just' attempted murder, John." A deeper sigh. "So, we reconvene this morning, and guess what?"

"I'm drawing a blank, Bernie."

"All the jurors show up, including our Mr. Durand. However, it being just the first day of testimony, I didn't really know them very well yet."

"Know them?"

"Yes. After a few days of trial—even without attorney voir dire at the beginning—the jurors become burned into your brain by face and seat number."

"Because you're looking at them while the prosecutor is at bat with a witness?"

"Or while I'm cross-examining. But the first morning of a new case, I probably couldn't pick five of the jurors out of a lineup."

"Except for this Durand."

Wellington came forward in his chair. "Yes and no. I look over at him, and he's both gotten a haircut and shaved off the beard. The clothes are about the same, but when I move around the courtroom, his eyes are following me, like Mr. Durand is now actually paying attention. Oh, he still fidgets in his chair and scratches his nose, but something . . . I don't know, bothers me."

I shook my head. "Bern?"

"Yes?"

"Could there also be something you're not telling me?"

Wellington leaned back again, now swinging his chair in a slow, twenty-degree arc. "I've represented Michael on and off for the better part of two decades, John. Despite my Herculean efforts on those earlier occasions, his past record combined with another felony conviction this time around would carry a life sentence."

"And?"

A nearly glacial sigh now. "And once before—years ago—Michael had two of his loyal employees seek to 'influence' someone in the Commonwealth's witness-protection program."

Christ. "That was bright of him."

"Michael thought a change of testimony might result in at worst a hung jury, with the prosecutor maybe not pursuing a second trial or the second jury coming back 'not guilty.' "

"And did Monetti's ploy work?"

"No, but I'm afraid my client learns a lesson hard, John."

I chewed on that. "Meaning you're afraid he may

have had his muscle pay a visit to the nonsequestered Arthur Durand."

Wellington closed his eyes. "That other time Michael tried it, the whole case nearly blew sky-high. Fortunately, the witness called me instead of the prosecutor."

"Called you?"

"To request a 'cash consolation' for his 'mental anguish.' "

I thought I knew Bernie better than that. "You didn't pony up the money."

A shocked expression. "Of course not. But as a result, we had to take a plea bargain thirty-percent worse than the deal originally offered by the prosecution. I told Michael, 'Never again,' or I was through representing him."

I didn't envy Wellington his ethical stand. "So, what do you want me to do?"

He leaned back into the cracked headrest, his fingernail picking at the leather piping some more. "I don't know, John. Perhaps you could come to court tomorrow, watch Mr. Durand for a while in the jury box, and then follow him afterward. That might give me some sense of whether Michael's stepped over the line again."

"Bernie, you want a private investigator shadowing a current juror?"

"Unless you've got a better plan."

Frankly, I was thinking about turning down the assignment altogether. But the return of the mournful, hangdog look to Bernie's face kind of took that option off the board.

I said, "Would tomorrow after lunch be alright?"

"You can't make it any earlier?"

"There's somebody I want to visit in the morning."

Bernard Wellington, Esquire, started to ask me who, but remembered just in time to catch himself.

TWO

There really aren't any trees on her hillside to turn yellow or orange in the autumn, but the grass does what it can by exchanging summer's green for a salt-bleached brown. And the breeze off the harbor water is bracing enough, the gulls shrieking as they scavenge in that part of South Boston where Beth and I grew up, got married, and still spend time together.

In a manner of speaking.

I drew even with her row, opening the little campstool I carry now to spare my bad knee too much standing. The headstone reads as it always has. ELIZABETH MARY DEVLIN CUDDY. No easier to look at, though.

John, why aren't you working?

Smiling, I squared my butt on the stool. "What, you don't think your enterprising husband could have a cemetery for a client?"

Beth paused. *Something's troubling you.*

"No man could ever fool a good wife."

Never kept you from trying. Want to talk about it?

I found that I did.

As always, she listened patiently. Then, *So what's really the problem for you, the client or the case?*

"A little of both, I guess. Bernie Wellington's just fine. I even admire him for that stubborn way he clings to his ethics. But I don't like working for Michael Monetti, and I really don't like risking my license by following a current juror in a felony case."

But you're working for Wellington, not Monetti, right?

"Technically."

Literally. And whatever you find out might make the system work better, not worse. So, you really aren't doing anything wrong.

I didn't have a counterargument. "Will you represent me should the system disagree?"

Another pause, but this one more like the time it takes to force a smile. *Would that I could, John Cuddy. Would that I could.*

As a gull wheeled overhead, somebody said, "Amen."

Back in my office on Tremont Street across from the Boston Common, I called a friend named Claire who has the computer access of a Microsoft billionaire. She answered on the third ring, and I asked her to run "Durand, Arthur" through what she calls her "databases." Claire said she'd have to get back to me, and I told her to leave a message with my service. Then I locked up, went downstairs, and headed over to the Park Street Under subway.

Michael Monetti had attempted the killing of his associate in Cambridge rather than Boston, so the trial was being held at the relatively modern Middlesex Superior Courthouse across the Charles River rather than our dilapidated Suffolk County one. A Green Line trolley carried me to Lechmere Station in East Cambridge, and I walked three blocks to the tall, gray-stoned building. After clearing metal detectors at the lobby level, I rode an elevator to the sixth floor.

The courtroom itself had hush-colored carpeting, polished oak benches, and a domed ceiling. From earlier experiences, I knew that dome gave the space the acoustics of a concert hall, ostensibly so no one in the audience outside the bar enclosure would have to strain in order to hear testimony from the witness stand. In reality, though, so much as a whisper from anywhere—including counsel tables—could be heard clearly everywhere.

Given the lunch hour, I was able to get an aisle seat in a row on the prosecution side of the audience. On the first bench across the aisle sat the people I took to be the Monetti family. An older man with scarred hands and an older woman with a stern demeanor were sandwiched around a fiftyish woman whose face shared characteristics of each apparent parent. Other people in the second row comforted them by nodding in unison or squeezing a shoulder.

Suddenly, a side door near the front of the bar enclosure opened, and Bernie Wellington came through it. He was followed by a slick, well-dressed guy in his late thirties, two bailiffs—one male, one female—leading him into the courtroom. I recognized Michael Monetti from the media coverage of his indictment. He shared the family features, but whereas the other members looked stalwart, Mikey resembled a killer whale somebody had shoehorned into a double-breasted suit.

As Bernie Wellington made eye contact with me, Monetti turned his chair at the defense table toward his cheering section. Smiling, he told them not to worry. The jail food wasn't so bad, he'd had worse, how was their lunch, and so on. The dome's acoustics carried every syllable back to me.

After the stenographer moved toward her seat and the court clerk toward his kangaroo pouch in front of the bench, the judge appeared from her chambers door, everyone rising. She was African-American and fairly young. When we were all settled again, the female bailiff who'd escorted Michael Monetti into the courtroom went to another side door and knocked. Seconds later, the jurors began filing through and into their rectangular box against the wall. Once they, too, were seated, the bailiff took a chair near the telephone table at our audience end of the jury.

Then Wellington stood and asked the judge if he could have a moment. She granted his request, and he came through the gate of the bar enclosure, walking down the aisle toward me.

Leaning over, Bernie brought his lips to within an inch of my ear, his voice as delicate as a lover's kiss. "Thanks, John. Durand is in seat number twelve, closest to you and that court officer."

I nodded, but waited until Wellington arrived back at the defense table, Monetti writing something on a pad and tugging on Bernie's sleeve. After that decent interval, I looked over to the bailiff seated at our end of the jury box. Just past her in the last chair of the front row was a skinny man scratching his nose with his left index finger. He had dark hair which indeed looked freshly cut, a suit jacket with lapels ten years old, and a collared shirt without benefit of tie. Suddenly, the skinny man shifted a little in his seat before cupping the scratching hand over his mouth and whispering to the young female juror on his right. She rushed one of her own hands toward her teeth, stifling a laugh.

The judge glared at the two of them in a way that told me it wasn't the first time she'd done so. Then the prosecutor—a red-haired and freckled-faced lad who looked all of sixteen—recalled one of his witnesses to the stand.

A police lab tech, she waxed eloquent about various fibers found at the scene of the crime. I tuned her out and glanced occasionally toward the jury. To the naked eye, Arthur Durand was paying attention, alright.

After the lab tech, the prosecutor put on a male ballistics expert, who testified that the three bullets removed from the victim's soft tissue came from the nine-millimeter Sig Sauer carried by Michael Monetti in violation of this statute and that. I left the courtroom just as the ballistics witness stepped down off the stand, because I wanted to be outside the building and in position to follow juror Durand on foot, by cab, or via public transportation.

At a little after five, Durand wended his way through the crowd at the courthouse door, his shoes making the clacking noise of a cheap computer keyboard as he walked to Lechmere Station. Instead of the subway, though, he hopped an Arlington Heights bus, and I climbed on very casually with a bunch of "other" transferring commuters. The bus made stops through East Cambridge and then Somerville, Durand getting off in a decaying neighborhood about half a mile before the Arlington town line.

I followed him down the bus's steps and out the door, crossing the street so as to parallel his route of march. He passed a couple of alley mouths with Dumpsters slightly overflowing. At a wider side street, Durand turned. When I reached the intersection, I saw a block of wooden three-story houses.

I waited until he stopped at a house painted that hardware-sale shade of lavender. If Durand hadn't nodded his head toward the car parked diagonally across and up the street, though, I'm not sure I would have spotted them.

Two men, sitting in the front seat of a beige Ford, the Crown Victoria model with white-walled tires. At that distance, I couldn't make out faces, but the guy at the wheel was sipping through a straw from a big fast-food cup. His partner on the passenger side was motionless except for a single tug on his earlobe, the way Carol Burnett used to end her monologue.

Then Arthur Durand went up the stoop and into the lavender three-decker. I kept walking, but only around the block.

The Crown Vic was now halfway down the street from me. Unfortunately, I couldn't see its rear license plate because of a truck between us. On the other hand, I'd certainly known a lot of vehicles like it over the years.

The favorite unmarked car of plainclothes police everywhere in the state, though usually with only black-walled tires.

I didn't understand why Arthur Durand would be getting special protection as a juror unless Michael Monetti's stupid ploy involving the earlier-case witness had gotten around. However, best to invest some time and be sure.

I moved to the other side of the street, which gave me an unobstructed view of the two men's heads but still not their registration tag. The driver stopped sipping his drink and turned to his partner, saying something. The wheelman had straight sandy hair, the other dark curly hair, which was about the extent of description I could get without becoming obvious enough to be made by them.

I found a quiet doorway and waited.

It was nearly midnight—and me nearly starving—when the driver turned to his partner again, the other nodding and tugging on his ear some more. Then finally the Crown Victoria started up and pulled away.

But not so fast I couldn't get their plate number.

THREE

A groggy "Who the . . . ?"

Into my end of the phone, I said, "Claire, this is John Cuddy."

"What time is it?"

"By my watch, seven A.M."

Her voice grew an edge. "Seven? You call fucking farmers at seven, Cuddy. Cyber-wizards, we like to sleep a little more toward noon."

"Sorry, Claire, but I've got a lot to do today, and I didn't pick up your message until after twelve last night."

"Yeah, well, hold on a minute."

A bonking noise came across the wire along with a distant, muffled "Shit."

Then Claire's voice was closer and clearer again. "Goddam phone. I should get a speaker thing, one of you guys ever paid me half what I'm worth for finding all this stuff for you."

"Your weight in gold, Claire."

"That some kind of crack?"

"No, it—"

"I mean, I lost five pounds in the last month, and I don't take kindly to—"

"A compliment, Claire."

"What?"

"It wasn't a crack, it was a compliment. As in, 'You're worth your weight in gold.' "

"Yeah, well, remember that when you're writing my check." A rustle of paper. "Let's see . . . let's see . . . 'Durand, Arthur,' right?"

"Right."

"Okay, with no middle initial, I wasn't sure how many I'd turn, but I've got three out by Springfield, two

north of Worcester—probably a father-and-son thing—
and just the one in our own Slummerville."

"Unkind, Claire. Give me the Somerville listing."

"That's Durand, Arthur 'G.' as in 'George.' " More
rustling. "Let's see . . . No service record, no arrest
record."

So, Durand had told the truth answering those
questions.

Claire said, "He does have a driver's license, but no
current car registration. Social Security is—you want
the number and all?"

"Not necessary. Has there been any activity on the
account?"

"Nothing from job withholding. Just a . . . yeah.
Yeah, he's been collecting unemployment for about
three months now."

Making the man someone who, as a juror, might be
vulnerable to a bribe offer. "And before that?"

"Worked in a video store."

"Any time in 'sensitive industries'?"

"What, you mean defense contractors, that kind of
thing?"

"Yes."

"Cuddy, I think you overestimate our Durand, Arthur G."

"How about bank records?"

"Simple savings and checking," said Claire. "No
real activity beyond depositing his unemployment and
writing his rent checks."

"You have a payee on those?"

"Yeah. 'Stralick,' that's S-T-R-A-L-I-C-K, Rhonda
M."

"Address?"

"Same as your guy shows in Somerville."

So, maybe a resident landlady. "Any credit cards?"

"Negative."

"Bank loans?"

"Also *nega-tivo*, though I gotta tell you, Cuddy, I can't see how this Durand could qualify to finance anything beyond a tattoo."

"You turn up much else, Claire?"

"No records of marriage, divorce, or birth of child. The guy's your basic loner/loser."

"I can ask if he's available?"

"I'm not that fucking desperate, thank you very much. Let me just total your tab here."

"Hold it."

"Why?"

"I've got a license plate I'd like you to run."

"Jesus, Cuddy, you have any idea how much of an uproar the Registry of Motor Vehicles is in about this new federal law?"

"Which law's that, Claire?"

"The one's supposed to keep 'stalkers' from getting computer access to the home addresses of any sweeties they see driving by. But, if the Commonwealth doesn't pass its own statute, we're—"

"Claire?"

"What?"

"Just this one tag, please? And today, if possible."

A grunt. "Why not? You got me up at the crack of dawn, I'll have plenty of time to fucking *carpe diem* and get the registration for you too."

I waited until after court would resume at nine before leaving my apartment and walking downstairs to my old Honda Prelude behind the building. Going to Arthur Durand's place by car would be a lot more direct than trolley-and-bus, and in seven hours the night before I'd seen all of two cabs cruising the drag at the foot of his street.

I made my way to Somerville using the Western Ave bridge and Central Square in Cambridge. Turning at Durand's corner, I did a drive-by of the lavender three-decker but didn't see any Crown Victoria staking out the block. There was a parking space near the next intersection, though, and I took it.

Walking back to Durand's building, I studied its exterior. If you could forgive the color, the clapboard facade was fairly well maintained, especially when compared to its neighbors. I climbed the stoop; three bells mounted next to the door had just unit numbers rather than names below them.

Figuring that an owner would live on the first floor to enjoy the backyard, I started with "1." After thirty seconds, I tried it again. Same lapse of time, same lack of result.

I was about to press the button once more when the door huffed open, a piece of rubber insulation making for a pretty tight fit against the jamb. The woman on the other side struggled to still look forty. Her platinum-blonde hair was spun around her head like cotton candy, biggish ears not quite hiding under it. The facial features pushed through makeup applied in layers, and even a nice manicure couldn't hide the veins bulging on top of her hands. She wore a sweatsuit the color of the clapboards and fuzzy bedroom slippers.

"And who might you be, luv?"

A slight English accent. "John Cuddy."

"Well, now, John." Hooding her eyes, she canted her head. "You're the cute one, aren't you?"

"Ms. Stralick?"

A wariness now crossed her eyes. "You know my name?"

" 'Stralick, Rhonda M.' " I took out my identification holder.

Reading, she said, "Private investigator?"

"That's right."

"I don't know nothing about anything."

"That's okay." I closed the holder. "I'm just here for an employer who's thinking of hiring one of your tenants."

Wary became surprised. "Arthur?"

"Probably. I have 'Durand, Arthur G.' "

Stralick didn't seem convinced. "Who wants to hire him?"

"I'm afraid that's confidential. But what I have to do won't take very long."

Another change of expression. "Good. That'll give us more time to get acquainted, won't it?"

Said the spider to the fly. "Could I come in?"

Stralick made a sweeping gesture with her right arm.

After closing the front door, she led me along a short corridor to an apartment entrance past the base of a staircase that would serve the upper two floors of her house. "Please excuse the mess, John."

That would take some doing. In the living room, television trays functioned poorly as magazine racks, supermarket tabloids scattered like giant playing cards across one of those sculpted carpets popular twenty years ago. Opposite the flower-print couch was a widescreen Sony, the video on but the audio muted. Three teenaged girls—one white, one black, one Latina —sat awkwardly on a stage, an older man sporting evangelist hair roaming the audience with a handheld mike. The brightly printed caption at the low left of the screen read, STEP-DAUGHTERS PREGNANT BY THEIR STEP-FATHERS.

I thought, And the mothers who love them both.

"What was that, John?" said Stralick, behind me.

Must have thought out-loud. "Nothing."

Next to the TV was an armchair with the bulbous design of a '52 Chevy. I went to it as my hostess took the couch, near enough to me that our knees almost touched.

Then she trotted out the hooded-eyes trick again. "So, what do you want to talk about?"

"Mr. Durand indicated on his job application that he was currently unemployed."

"Three months' worth," said Stralick.

"I'm sorry."

"No need to be sorry, luv." She licked her lips. "What I meant was, Arthur hasn't come up with the rent for the last little while."

"I see. Before that, though, was he prompt in his obligations to you?"

"Moneywise, yes."

"How about 'otherwise'?"

A shrug. "Arthur helps me out with the storm windows, the snow shoveling, that sort of thing." A coy smile. "But for real 'otherwise,' he's not exactly the life of the party."

"Sober, responsible types make better employees."

"You don't understand, John. After I divorced the bloody mound of shit who lured me to your country, I got a little lonely. But Arthur, he's quiet as a church-mouse, he is."

Stralick paused, maybe to give me a chance to jump in. When I didn't, she made a face before saying, "Weeks can go by, and I won't even hear him, much less see him. No taste for fun, Arthur." Another wetting of the lips. "If you get my drift."

"Fine with my client."

Stralick's eyes narrowed to slits. "I hope you're not as dull as your 'client,' luv."

I gave her an ingratiating smile. "Any reason you can think of why Mr. Durand shouldn't be hired?" ·

"Only if it'd mean you'll visit with me longer."

A proper bulldog, Ms. Stralick. "I wonder, then, could I get a look at his apartment?"

Now wary again. "Why?"

"I just like to see the place where a prospective employee lives. Helps me put some flavor into my report, maybe even make it a full-blown recommendation."

"God knows that'd be a help, what with Arthur in arrears on his rent the way he is."

"And it would also be good if my visit today could stay our little secret, okay?"

"I like 'secrets' as much as the next girl, luv, but I do have a question first."

"What's that?"

Back to coy. "If you know Arthur's unemployed, what makes you think he's not up there now?"

"Because Mr. Durand advised my client he'd be on jury duty for a while."

Stralick finally seemed convinced. "Right, then. Only I have to go with you, of course."

"Of course," I said, neutrally.

"Kind of captures him, if you get my drift."

Rhonda Stalick had managed to rub or bump against me three times during our trip up the staircase. Arthur Durand's apartment consisted of a living room with bay window in front, bedroom next, bath and kitchen at the back. The worn, faded furniture seemed to be the only furnishings, and the rooms gave off a spic-'n'-span shine. Which didn't tell me much.

What wasn't there told me something, though. No

knickknacks, keepsakes, or even photos. More like a large, spartan motel room.

At least until you got to the kitchen.

"Damn him!" Stralick went to the sink, using a paper towel from a cylindrical dispenser to crush three or four cockroaches scurrying over a dead pizza box. "Arthur's usually neat as a pin, he is."

There were beer cans and other takeout trash on the flanking counters. "Maybe Mr. Durand had somebody over last night and forgot to clean up."

"Not bloody likely. No family, no visitors, no personality." She began to lift the box by its edges.

"You might want to leave that where it is."

Stralick looked at me. "Why?"

"So Mr. Durand won't know you let somebody in to see his apartment."

"Oh. Right you are, luv." She let the box drop back into the sink, then made a sensual ritual of wiping her hands across the thighs of her sweatsuit. "I hope this business with the bugs doesn't ruin our nice little mood."

Seeing an out, I took it. "Afraid so. Delicate stomach."

"Just my luck." Rhonda Stralick tried to put on a happy face. "Well, then. Next time you're in the neighborhood, you'll stop and visit awhile, won't you?" Now the hooded eyes again. "If you get my drift."

More like her tidal wave.

Outside, I'd just put the key in my Prelude's door-lock when I noticed the beige Crown Vic, parked beyond the intersection this time. I ducked my head a little, but I couldn't do much about having been seen leaving the lavender three-decker.

I executed a three-point turn to avoid driving by

them and glanced in my rearview mirror. Instead of following me, the sandy-haired driver seemed to be squinting in my direction and talking to the dark-haired ear-tugger, who himself was writing something down.

Probably the letters and numbers on the Prelude's license plate, but there wasn't much I could do about that either.

FOUR

Back in the office, I dialed Bernie Wellington's number. His secretary told me that, not surprisingly, he was still in court on the Monetti case. I asked her to have him return my call as soon as possible.

I considered trying Claire again, too, but twice in one day seemed to be skating over the edge of her good will. Paperwork on other cases occupied me until almost three, when the phone rang.

A sound nearly as shrill as her voice.

"John Cuddy."

"You own a pencil?"

"Ready, Claire."

"Alright, let's see . . . let's see . . . Yeah, the tag belongs to a rental agency."

That felt wrong, though it explained the white-walled tires. "You sure?"

"I'm insulted. But not as much as if I was the one actually running the plate."

"Give me that again?"

"I told you about this new federal crackdown on computer access, right?"

"Right."

"Okay, so I had this friend of mine over at the Registry do the search for me. He says the tag's from a Ford Crown Vic—some ridiculous color that amounts to 'beige'—and the car belongs to, and I quote, 'Best-Ride Car Rentals, Inc.,' over by the airport. Here's their address."

The name and location—almost five miles from Arthur Durand's apartment—meant nothing to me. "Claire, you ever hear of this outfit?"

"No, but my friend at the Registry has."

"In what context?"

"The 'connected' context."

Uh-oh. "A mob launderette?"

"Or maybe just a captive business the wiseguys turn to when their own wheels ought not to be involved. Help you any?"

"Maybe, maybe not. But thanks, Claire."

"Hey, Cuddy, do me a favor, huh?"

"What's that?"

"Mail my check before you pay these 'Best-Ride' people a visit, okay?"

Couldn't blame her for asking.

After leaving two more messages for Bernie Wellington and not getting a return call, I decided to postpone the rent-a-car agency till the next morning. Locking up for the night at five-fifteen, I went downstairs to the parking space behind my office's building. In the Prelude, I crawled with the rush-hour traffic over to South Boston and the "Jack O' Lantern" tavern.

That part of Broadway near L Street in Southie is undergoing a general—if not quite gentle—gentrification. A lot of the old blue-collar, shot-and-a-beer joints are being squeezed out, their liquor licenses bought up by fern-and-butcher-block places for the new condo crowd. With orangy lights shining through tooth-gap windows, and an oval bar inside a walking moat before the tables start, "the Jack" is sort of a compromise: a good place for dinner with the wife and kids after work, then a watering hole for serious barflies from nine or so onward.

Maybe the early hour was what lulled me.

I'd been sitting on a stool at the bar, just finishing a steak platter with two Harp lagers, expertly drawn by Eddie Kiernan behind the taps. About five-eight and skinny as a rail, Eddie had played shortstop in the high minor leagues before coming back to the neighborhood and opening the Jack. In fact, I spent most of my dinner that evening listening to him grouse about the competition from his chi-chi new neighbors—"the wormy bastards"—and the skyrocketing rates for liability insurance they'd brought like a plague along with them.

Checking my watch, I saw it was nearly seven-thirty, so I got up to use the men's room and try Bernie Wellington one last time before driving home. As I made my way between the bar and the tables, a guy leaving his own stool slammed into me, then staggered back. A little theatrically, I remember thinking at the time.

Maybe six feet tall and solid, with sandy straight hair and an oft-broken nose, he flared. "The fuck is wrong with you, asshole?"

I took in half a breath. "I believe you're the one who bumped into me."

"The fuck he is," said a different man, standing at the bar.

I turned. Same size and build, but black curly hair and standard nose. He tugged on his left ear once, and I began to get the picture.

Sandy stepped up first, throwing a right cross at the left side of my face as I stayed turned toward his partner. I parried the sucker-punch, looping my left arm over Sandy's right and catching his fist under my armpit. With the heel of my left hand braced under his elbow, I lifted up, hard. I could feel more than hear the joint dislocate, but I heard more than felt Sandy's scream of pain as I released the hold.

Curly had swung his left just as I hunched my right shoulder up to protect my head and neck, but he'd had the time to realize that his first had better count. It rocked me into a table of four, who'd pushed back and stood up as the fighting began. Sandy was on the floor now, cradling a floppy forearm, facial features squinched up, voice down to a keening moan. When Curly stepped in to follow with his right, I used the table to support my own bad left knee. Then I side-kicked out with my right foot aimed at his left shin, all his weight having transferred forward onto that leg.

This time I did hear the cracking sound, Curly toppling like a felled tree with about as much noise. By now, Eddie had come out from behind the bar, a Louisville slugger in his hands. I was about to initiate appropriate inquiries of the two on the deck when instead Eddie jabbed me in the solar plexus with his bat as though he were doing bayonet drill.

I joined the hamburger plates on the party of four's table.

By the time my breath started returning to me, Sandy had struggled to his feet and gotten Curly up as well, the combined three good arms and three good legs carrying both of them through the Jack O' Lantern's door and into the October night.

Eddie was standing near my left thigh, his bat at half-mast.

I said, "Why . . . me?"

"I was scared shitless you were going to maim the wormy bastards. My liability premiums would shoot out of sight."

I forced some air down into the lungs. "Then how come . . . you didn't . . . hit them first?"

He gave me a jaundiced look. "I said I was insured, John, not insane."

As Eddie Kiernan promised the table of four he'd bring them new meals, I decided I couldn't blame him either.

When I was able to breathe in for a count of eight without cramping, I left the tavern and made my way to the Prelude. Nobody had touched it. I got in, drove home, and climbed the stairs slowly, thankful for not having worse wounds to lick.

Once in the apartment, I checked with my answering service for the office. A message from Bernie Wellington, asking that I reach him the next day before court.

I went to the CD player, choosing some soft and soothing soprano sax, courtesy of the late Art Porter. Then I lowered myself onto the couch and stretched out, trying to make sense of a situation that was anything but soft and soothing.

Then I tried some more.

I started awake in the dark, the pain above my gut keeping me from sitting straight up. I'd been having a dream —about Rhonda Stralick, I'm embarrassed to admit— when a throwaway line of hers during my "visit" that day clicked into place. And suddenly something Bernie Wellington had mentioned joined it.

If I was right, Michael Monetti's oddball voir dire questions made perfect sense. I could even understand why the two guys staking out the lavender three-decker had rousted me at the Jack.

But I needed to confirm one more piece of the puzzle to be certain, and I came up with a way of doing it I thought might work.

FIVE

That next Thursday morning, I took considerable care leaving the apartment building for two reasons. First, my solar plexus was still a tad ginger, thanks to Eddie's bat. Second, if Sandy and Curly also had a friend at the Registry to run my plate, then they—or their replacements—could have a home address for me as well.

In the parking lot, I got down on hands and knees, examining the Prelude's undercarriage to be sure no "aftermarket" options had been added to the ignition system. Starting up, I decided to avoid my office, since that was for sure where the muscle boys had been waiting before following me to the Jack O' Lantern.

It could have made for a long day, but our Museum of Fine Arts on Huntington Avenue had a great photographic exhibit by Herb Ritts to go with its other, usual wonders. About 11 A.M.—and knowing Bernie Wellington would be in court—I used a pay phone to call his secretary. I left only a blind message with her for him to try me at the office after lunch.

No sense in risking Bernie's license, too.

Later that same Thursday, I drove from the museum across the Charles to East Cambridge. Parking the Prelude a few blocks west of the Middlesex County Courthouse, I loitered discreetly outside the main entrance. At four-forty, Arthur Durand appeared in a stream of people too randomly dressed to be lawyers and too jaded to be anything but "citizens summoned to serve." That same young woman from the jury box was walking beside Durand, and he seemed to exaggerate some mannerisms of head and hands as he said something to her. She laughed again, this time not covering her mouth as in the courtroom, and they waved a casual good-bye, Durand scratching his nose with his left index finger.

I watched him move off toward Lechmere Station. When the woman turned north, I fell in behind her, half a block away and across the street.

Sometimes you get lucky.

At the corner, she got into the passenger side of an idling station wagon, one of those Subarus you see Australia's Paul Hogan hucking on TV. There was a man about her age behind the wheel and a toddler strapped into a plastic restraint bucket against the rear seat.

The lucky part was that a taxi had just slewed to the curb in front of me, dropping off an elderly couple who'd already given the driver their fare.

The young family's car entered the traffic flow, my cab trailing it.

"Marjorie, come on, huh? You want this family package or that one?"

"Hey, Phil, give me a break, okay? I've been listening to witnesses and lawyers since Monday. It doesn't look like we're anywhere near finished, and this Monetti guy isn't exactly O.J. material, you know?"

Phil wouldn't let go of his bone. "Yeah? Well, try picking up Troy each afternoon from day care."

"Like every other week of our lives I *don't?*"

I eavesdropped on them silently as we all shuffled our way along the cafeteria line of a Boston Market franchise, the operation that was lucky to survive changing from the successful marquee name of "Boston Chicken." The charming Marjorie and Phil couldn't make up their minds on which of the many dinner options—including roasted turkey and baked ham—to choose. Their toddler, Troy, was between them, his head following their argument like a rapt tennis fan watching an important match.

Marjorie finally went for the turkey combo, and Phil paid at the cashier before carrying the trays of food and drink to a nearby booth for four. I took my own ham platter to an empty table across from them.

After we all had settled in, husband wisely said to wife, "Let's change the subject, okay?"

"Okay," replied Marjorie, a relenting tone in her voice as she cut up a side dish of broccoli for Troy-boy.

Phil forked some turkey off his plate. "You still can't talk about the case?"

"Not until the judge says so, like after we vote and everything. But I'll tell you this. If it wasn't for Arthur, I'd be stir-crazy by now."

"He's that other juror you sit next to?"

"Right." Marjorie turned to her own meal. "The judge already had to tell him twice to stop saying things during dead spots in the testimony or whatever, account of how he was, like, breaking me up."

I again thought back to Rhonda Stralick's evaluation of her tenant as Phil said, "Jokes? During a murder trial?"

"Attempted murder." Marjorie took a slug of her cola. "But really, without Arthur and his impressions keeping all us jurors loose, I don't know where we'd be."

Phil pushed more turkey into his mouth. "Impressions of what?"

"Not of 'what.' Of 'who.' Arthur can do Sylvester Stallone and Arnold Schwarzenegger—"

"From the TV, Mommy?" said boy Troy, until now content to while away the meal smearing mashed potatoes across his face.

"That's right, honey. From the movies on TV." Then back to Phil with, "And Arthur has this wicked Johnny Carson, too, even better than that guy used to do."

"What guy?"

"Oh, you know. Rich-somebody-or-other."

"Rich who?"

"The one who did that great President Nixon. C'mon, Phil, you have to know who I mean."

Her husband claimed he didn't, but I was pretty sure I did.

"Wellington."

"Bernie, it's John Cuddy."

"Good Lord, John," came the voice from the other end of the line. "Where have you been?"

"Kind of busy, Bern."

"*You're* busy? The Commonwealth expects to rest tomorrow, which means I'm supposed to open the defense case Monday, and I've been trying to reach—"

"It's a long story, and you might be better off not hearing all of it."

A hesitation. "How bad, John?"

"Let me ask you something first."

"What?"

"When you were impaneling the jury for Michael Monetti, did anything odd happen?"

"Odd? You mean, other than those questions he had me ask?"

"Right. Specifically with Arthur Durand."

"Well, yes." Another hesitation. "Not odd, so much, though. More coincidental."

"Tell me what you mean."

On the other end of the line, Wellington seemed to gather his thoughts. "After I asked Mr. Durand the last of Michael's voir dire questions, I came back to our defense table to confer with my client about challenging him. Just then, one of Michael's family in the audience behind us sneezed rather loudly, and the entire courtroom laughed." Bernie's voice grew weary. "Trust me, John, that's been my only comic relief in the whole process."

"Was that also when Monetti told you to keep Durand on the jury?"

"When Michael said not to challenge him, right. And I don't mind sharing with you that it still feels wrong to have that chap in the box. Defense attorneys are being sued all the time now for 'ineffective assistance of counsel' if they fail to use all their peremptories and the jury returns a verdict of 'guilty,' and here's my own client basically ordering me not to—"

"Bern?"

"What?"

"I'll get back to you."

"John—"

SIX

The next morning, Friday, I got up at 6 A.M., my solar plexus barely twinging anymore. After dressing in old clothes, I drove the Prelude across the Western Ave bridge and through Central Square again, eventually reaching the foot of Arthur Durand's street. No sign of anybody surveilling the lavender three-decker today, but that didn't mean their overall plan wasn't still on.

I left my car and walked into the mouth of the nearest alley. Taking ten more steps, I hunkered down behind its Dumpster.

To wait.

At seven-forty, I heard the distinctive keyboard

clacking of a certain person's dress shoes coming from the direction of Rhonda Stralick's house. I moved back to the mouth of the alley again. When the thin man who scratched his nose and shifted in his chair crossed the opening in front of me, I clotheslined him with my left forearm.

He went down hard, but not quite out.

I grabbed the collar of his jacket and dragged him quickly behind the Dumpster before he was focusing well again. After propping his butt and torso into a sitting position against the brick wall of the alley, I squatted onto my haunches. His eyes slowly registered me in front of him.

"What the . . . the fuck is going on?"

"My friend, we need to have a little chat before court resumes this morning."

He tried to make his hands work, palms pushing at the ground to scrabble back up.

I laid my own hands on his shoulders to calm him down. "You find yourself in deep weeds, boyo. Very deep weeds."

"The fuck are you—"

"First I talk, and then maybe you talk. Understand?"

He didn't say anything to that.

"Michael Monetti's criminal career is going south on him. One more felony conviction, and he never sees the sun again outside of exercise time in a prison yard. However, he's also about to be tried for attempted murder, and so something has to be done. Mikey once had his muscle tap a state-protected witness, but that didn't work out so well for him. Then he has a brainstorm about the current situation."

I looked down into the man's eyes and thought

back to Bernie Wellington's "good family" speech. "Specifically, you. The accused's gifted second cousin."

"I don't know what—"

"Be patient, I'm not done yet. Mikey made it easy for you. Sit with the rest of the family at the front of the courtroom's audience that first afternoon of trial last week, sort of 'hide in plain sight.' Then watch as the jury's selected. If one of the males answered Mikey's voir dire questions the right way, you'd study the guy, see if he was also 'right' in other ways. Your approximate height and weight, hopefully some telltale mannerisms that would be easy to mimic."

I had my subject's undivided attention now.

"A man named 'Arthur Durand' turns out to fit the bill nearly perfectly, especially since his unkempt hair and beard would kind of haze anybody's memory of his facial features. So, when it comes time to maybe knock the guy off the jury, you send Mikey a little 'keep him' signal in the courtroom. A cough, maybe. Or a sneeze?"

The second cousin's eyes jumped.

"Now move on to that night—a week ago today. Your cousin's enforcers follow Durand home to Rhonda Stralick's three-decker around the corner. Meanwhile Mikey's sister the beautician gives you a haircut, so nobody would think it odd that 'Durand' had shaved off his beard, too. Your rough resemblance to the guy and considerable talent can do the rest, particularly for people like the other jurors, who'd never seen Durand before that afternoon."

"I'm . . . I'm Arthur Durand."

"You're not listening, my friend. The enforcers take Durand out of the three-decker, remove any photos of him there, and put you in his place. Bingo. The next day of trial—Monday morning, now—there's a juror among the twelve who's eventually going to create a 'hung' jury by voting his cousin 'not guilty' for sure. Maybe you'd even make a few friends in the box during the course of trial, what with some snappy patter and a knack for impressions of famous people. Like that great comic, Rich Little, used to do. It wasn't the real Durand's personality, but you might get a couple of other votes to swing your way, especially if you paid close attention to the evidence and raised good arguments during deliberation. The district attorney would think twice before pursuing a second trial if there were enough 'not guilty' votes the first time around. Hell, even an acquittal wouldn't be out of the question if most of your fellow jurors took a shine to you."

"I'm telling you. I'm Arthur Durand."

I shook my head. "You're a bit nervous now, right?"

No answer.

"Right?" I repeated.

A grudging "Right."

"Okay. Only problem is, you've been forgetting to scratch your nose the way Durand does. Or—more accurately—did."

A glimmer of something beyond nervous. "What are you talking about?"

"Let me guess. Mikey told you they were just going to snatch Durand for the course of the trial, then put him back into his life and you into yours, right?"

"I'm not saying."

"Fine. Just listen, then. The juror questionnaire covers things like job, family, and so on. Guess what? Durand had nobody. On the surface, great for your cousin's plan, because there'd be no one to miss Durand while he's 'gone' during the trial. Mikey even camped his enforcers each day outside the three-decker, probably as babysitters so your winning personality didn't go off romping at night and maybe piss in the stew somehow. But why would your cousin want you living in Durand's apartment this last week?"

No response.

"Mikey gave you an answer to that one, didn't he? 'Hey, cuz, we need to have somebody moving around up there, make some noise so the landlady hears her tenant.' Again, on the surface it seems plausible. But there's a real risk, too. What if Rhonda Stralick should run into you on the stairs? Or come a-knocking on Durand's door, looking for the rent money? She knows her tenant pretty well, wouldn't be fooled into thinking you were him. And that seems to me a bigger risk than her not hearing 'Durand' walking around up there for a few days."

The second cousin was thinking about it, because his eyes started moving left-right-left, kind of jittery.

I said, "So let's explore things a bit more. Mikey tells you he's just keeping Durand on ice for a while. Only thing is, how could your cousin be sure Durand wouldn't talk later about his little 'interlude'?"

Still no response.

"And if Durand wasn't going to talk—because he'd been handsomely bribed or was just rationally terrified—why bother to substitute you for him in the first place? Why not simply intimidate the real Arthur Durand into being the juror who'll definitely vote 'not guilty' and therefore at worst buy Mikey a second trial?"

Nothing except for those eyes flicking, like lightning bugs caught in a jar.

"Don't feel stupid, my friend. It took me a while to figure it out, too. Start by remembering that your cousin got burned when he approached that witness in the earlier case. Then think about those questions Mikey had his lawyer ask the male jurors for this go-around. Armed forces, arrest, sensitive employment. Durand answered 'no' to all the above. So tell me, what do those experiences carry with them?"

The second cousin shook his head.

"Okay, time's up, anyway. They all require the person involved to be fingerprinted, boyo, meaning Durand never had been. I'm guessing the same is true for you."

He swallowed hard, maybe seeing where I was heading.

"Now, here's the stumper: if Mikey's enforcers have been parked outside the three-decker, and—"

"But they never showed up yesterday."

The first real admission. "I'm not surprised. They spotted me nosing around Wednesday, found out who I was, then set me up for a barroom beating that night."

The second cousin shook his head some more. "But . . . you don't look like—"

"I was able to discourage them."

He just stared at me.

"Now let's get back to my question, okay? If your cousin's enforcers have been babysitting you since they snatched the real Mr. Durand, and the rest of the Monetti clan—including even you—has been sitting dutifully in the courtroom, who does that leave to look after the poor kidnap victim, shut up in a room somewhere?"

The eyes did jumping jacks in the man's head. "Jesus fucking Christ."

"I'm afraid so, my friend. Arthur Durand is dead, probably killed by Mikey's enforcers that first night a week ago. However, when the trial ends—say another week from now—any evident 'disappearance' of a juror who'd just sat on a major case is going to be investigated fairly carefully by the police, something your cousin would not exactly welcome. Especially since Durand's landlady will maintain that her tenant is 'quiet as a churchmouse' while the other jurors would call him more the 'class clown.' So, better if Durand's body itself turns up simply and quickly, the result of some tragic 'accident,' maybe. Only problem? A roughly two-week-old corpse would be a tough sell to any medical examiner told that 'Arthur Durand' was alive and well through the end of jury deliberations. Therefore, I'm thinking Mikey will need a fresher body to stand in for the real Durand."

"But . . . but . . ."

"Which brings us back to why your cousin wanted you in that third-floor apartment this past week. You're probably about Durand's height and weight, but you wouldn't have had his dental work. So—after a disfiguring collision, say—the M.E. will be asked to match up the unlucky corpse with the missing Arthur Durand, and guess what? The fingerprints on the body will match those found in Durand's apartment."

"You're saying . . . you're saying Michael's gonna kill me?"

"Look at it from his standpoint. When the trial is over, you're kind of a loose thread, and potentially very embarrassing. What happens if your career as a standup comic starts to take off, and one of the jurors who sat with 'Arthur Durand' for two weeks recognizes you? Maybe he or she would go to the authorities with this odd piece of information."

"But Michael's . . . I'm his own *blood*."

"I'd bet your cousin sees it more as his own *future*. On the other hand, you know him better than I do. Which way do you think he'll flip on this one?"

Not much doubt from the eyes now, but no reason to leave any in his mind, either.

I said, "On the third hand, let's assume I'm wrong

about Mikey's views regarding the bond of family. Even then, my friend, I blow the whistle on your little masquerade here, and you're up for at least conspiracy in the murder of the real Arthur Durand."

He looked down, eyes flicking left-right-left some more, then back up to me. "The fuck am I gonna do?"

"We go to the courthouse together this morning, and you have a frank talk with the judge and the district attorney."

His eyes got wide enough to see white all around the pupils. "What're you, nuts? If I wanted to fucking die, ratting out Michael would do it."

"You tell the authorities about what he's pulled here, and they'll place you with their witness-protection program."

"Yeah, and how safe am I gonna be in that? Michael's guys already broke the thing once."

"That's not all they broke."

"What?"

"The barroom, night before last. The both of them are in body casts by now."

"So Michael sends two more after me. What're my chances then?"

"Better than they are now."

The second cousin looked down again. "Basically . . ." He coughed twice, tears trickling along that nose he was no longer scratching. "Basically, what you're saying is, I gotta go in and tell the truth."

"The system calls it 'voir dire.' "

His face came back up. "Huh?"

"Never mind," I said.

Afterword

Before both teaching law and writing mysteries, I was a civil litigator in Boston. At that time, Massachusetts did not permit attorney voir dire of prospective jurors. Impaneling the jury for one of my cases, I realized something: at the beginning of even a major trial, the men and women seated in the rectangular box tended to be a relatively faceless mass. In fact, until about the second day of testimony, the dozen deciders of my client's fate were nearly as anonymous to me as people at a Halloween party all wearing the same kind of mask.

I wrote that thought down on a piece of foolscap and filed it in a folder I label STORY IDEAS. Nearly twenty years later, when Bill Bernhardt contacted me about this anthology, I was fortunate to stumble upon that piece of foolscap from my trial long ago. I hope you've enjoyed the spin I put on the ball in "Voir Dire."

—JEREMIAH HEALY

Everyone has a favorite John Grisham book, but among lawyers the preferred novel is almost always A Time to Kill, *because of its brutally realistic characters and spellbinding courtroom action. In "The Birthday," Grisham displays his ability to create an equally gripping narrative in only a few pages, as well as his talent for depicting characters who will remain with you long after this short story has ended.*

The Birthday

JOHN GRISHAM

The good doctor awoke in the darkness just before noon. Somehow, through the black-painted windows, a ray of sunshine bounced and reflected and landed in a faint circle on the carpet. He turned away from it, moaning, and rattling the cheap metal frame under the dirty mattress.

His eyes burned but he did not touch them. He opened and closed them, blinking slowly in a hopeless effort to see without hurting. His brain pounded fiercely against his skull—the aftermath of a fifth and a half of six-dollar vodka.

Today was another birthday. The mail would arrive at two. He cursed the vodka, a morning ritual. This was the eighth birthday. She had found him last year in this battered trailer in this armpit mobile-home ghetto where engineless pickups were parked in the streets like statues people were proud of, and where illegitimate toddlers urinated on the curbs, and where televisions shrieked nonstop through ragged storm doors. She had somehow tracked him here. She always knew where to find him.

He took a job selling medical supplies and moved into a duplex where no one could find him. The sixth birthday was on a Sunday, and he was asleep, dreaming, when someone knocked on the door. He just missed her, but she left another envelope with a picture of the birthday boy, now thinner, shriveled, more grotesque. There was no note. He cried over the photo and went for the narcotics. He woke up three days later without a job.

He served ninety days for shoplifting, and borrowed money for the last time from his mother. He found this trailer. He sold some of his pills to buy food.

He sipped the vodka and read for the hundredth time the newspaper account of a good doctor gone bad. The jury gave Jeffrey four million, and the appellate court affirmed. His ex-wife took what she wanted, and he bankrupted the rest. His malpractice carrier paid its limit of a half a million to little Jeffrey and there was simply no more with the bankruptcy and all. He loved to play tennis, the paper said.

The seventh picture was the worst. Jeffrey's head was much too large for his body, and it was clearly just a matter of time before the birthdays ceased. Last year when he opened the envelope, he sat at the same table and cried over the pictures until he made himself sick and vomited.

Suddenly, he was cold. He pulled the robe tighter around his neck and stuffed his hands deep in the pockets. The folder contained many other things, the divorce papers, letters from lawyers, notices from the state medical board. But he'd read them a thousand times, and the words never changed. He'd looked at the pictures of the little boy a thousand times and prayed hopelessly that the next one would show a healthy kid on a new bike with a big birthday smile. He had grieved over the pictures, gotten drunk over them, moved around like a gypsy because of them, hated them, planned suicide over them. But he wanted to see the next one. Maybe it would be different.

He was drunk now. He drained the plastic cup and threw it on the floor. He collected the photos, wrapped the rubber band back around them, and stood up. His hands were shaking, and he was mumbling to himself when he heard a faint knock on the door. He froze, having no idea what to do. Then, another knock. He held the table for support. A female voice said, "Dr. Green?" She was on the steps.

He made his way to the door and opened it slowly. He peeked around the facing through the storm door. For a moment they studied each other. She seemed to have aged well in the seven years since he had seen her. She was wearing a red dress and a long dark coat. Her eyes were wet. He could hear a car idling not far away. There was nothing in her hands, no envelope, nothing.

"I didn't bring a picture," she said.

He felt himself getting sick. He leaned on the door facing her, but could think of nothing to say. The birthdays were over.

"Jeffrey died two months ago," she said with the resignation of one who was grieving but knew the worst was over. She wiped a tear from her cheek.

"I'm sorry," he said in a voice so weak and shaky that he was inaudible. He tried again, "I'm so sorry."

"Yes, I know," she said. Another tear emerged from her eye and then she actually smiled. She breathed deeply. "I'm tired of hating you, Dr. Green. I've hated you so much for eight years, and now it's over. Jeffrey's gone. He's better off now, and I have the rest of my life to live, don't I?"

He was able to nod slightly. He gripped the doorknob from the inside.

"So, I don't hate you anymore. I'm not going to follow you, and I'm not going to send pictures. And I'm sorry for doing those things." She paused. "I want you to forgive me."

He collapsed and fell to the floor, crying and sobbing pathetically. She knelt on the steps and watched him through the door. He covered his eyes with his hands.

"Please forgive me, Doctor," she said.

"I'm so sorry," he managed to say between hard, loud sobs. "I'm so sorry." He rolled to his side and curled together like a napping child. She stood, watching him. Then she left him there, crying and shaking and groaning to himself.

He awoke on the floor a few hours later. The door was still open, and through it he could hear the sounds of children riding bikes and playing games in the street. He could hear loud TVs through open doors as the heavy housewives had their daily visits with Oprah.

He was too weak and too drunk to stand, so he crawled across the green shag carpet in the den to the dirty tile in the kitchen and back onto the carpet as it led down the hall to the bedroom.

He locked the bedroom door as if someone out there might want to stop him. The pistol was under the mattress. He knew he didn't have the courage to use it, but something forced him closer to it. He felt a strong desire to at least hold the gun in his hands.

The characters in Philip Friedman's novels are surely among the most finely drawn and psychologically insightful in contemporary fiction, popular or literary. One of the most common complaints leveled against short stories is that, because of the relative brevity, plot is emphasized and character is shortchanged. Friedman proves that this is not always the case in this story about a lawyer whose past comes back to haunt him in a way he never could have imagined.

Roads

PHILIP FRIEDMAN

The night before, when they suggested it, it had made sense to him, this madness of driving nearly a thousand miles to stand up in a courtroom and try to save yet another stranger from death. He'd even had plans for accomplishing something on the drive: honing his argument for the morning or doing work on the cases that would be clamoring for his attention when he got back.

But constructive thought had eluded him so far and there was no hope of it now, strung out as he was on the black vitriol that passed for coffee at the last place he'd fueled up. There was no great reason for his being behind schedule, just a series of small miscalculations starting with a bungled predawn departure from a hotel in an unfamiliar town and an unfamiliar state that left him getting rolling an hour later than he'd planned, and then a solid mile of torn-up pavement leaving a single passable lane of stop-and-go past sweating men in orange reflective vests that labeled each of them INMATE, delays that had plunged him into a clog of morning rush hour he'd scheduled himself to avoid.

Now, even if everything went the way it was supposed to from here on, he'd arrive with no time at all for sleep or even a decent nap, just a question of getting out of the car and then maybe time to shower and have something to eat, pickle his gut and buzz his brain with more coffee, and it would be showtime.

And what a show it would be. As a rule the appellate process didn't lend itself to theatrics, but this case had drawn dramatic reaction at every stage—not so much for the lurid crime as for the jury's condemning to death a defendant so young and attractive and previously unblemished—thus assuring that the dour precincts of the courthouse would be enlivened by opposed camps of chanting demonstrators and the full crush of the world press. And as always the State's argument and his own would draw two huddled knots of loved ones: the already bereaved relatives of the victims and the defendant's family, still clinging to the forlorn idea that their own bereavement might be averted by some last-minute legal magic—or chicanery.

Miles ahead of him and off to the right—across an immeasurable expanse of countryside whose featurelessness was interrupted only by scattered farm buildings, an occasional silo and a small, improbable stand of high-tech windmills—he could see towers of black, gray, and silver clouds, laced at irregular intervals with bolts of light. Here and there inky smudges connected their bellies to the ground, the visible manifestation of downpours whose magnitude he could not guess. The day, grown hot and humid enough to drive even mad dogs indoors, promised now the false relief of thunderstorms that would leave the air steaming, their only redeeming feature the intense beauty of nature's great forces unconfined.

He could remember when he'd first seen vistas like these, with spectacular weather rolling across endless skies—on youthful excursions from one side of the country to the other, coming and going from college. And the one time he hadn't made it. Driving across Nevada in the days when there'd genuinely been no speed limit and he'd cranked his British roadster up to one-oh-five and held it there until he'd burned out the valves. Had nursed it over Utah mountain roads and limped, smoking, into a small town in Wyoming, not that far ahead of the season's first snow, hoping someone might be able to fix the car, or if not fix it then get it running well enough for him to make it to Rock Springs or anyway someplace big enough to have a real garage where they could send for parts.

But it hadn't worked out that way. Everybody'd been nice enough on the surface, but he'd known they were all thinking he was some kind of hippie with his foreign car and his hair cut none too short, never mind that among his friends it almost passed for a crew cut. They'd stared at his car, stuck their heads under the hood and clucked their tongues but they sure didn't have parts that fit into one of those things—where'd you say it was from?

He'd ended up swapping it to the owner of the last gas station he'd made it to for a twenty-year-old pickup truck that probably hadn't been on the road in years. The gas-station owner had gotten the truck running as part of the deal, though *running* turned out to be a relative term. *Lurching* might have been more accurate.

So he'd set off again, puttering down the still-new Interstate not a whole day ahead of the bad weather, his macramé saddlebags propped uneasily against the passenger door to keep out the wind that whistled, roared, and chattered in through the rust holes. The snow had caught him in Green River and he'd holed up in not much of a hotel for three days, till the storm had blown off to the east and the roads had been plowed clear.

He'd emerged from the hotel to find that the pickup truck had died. At first he'd thought it might just be the battery, but the best one he could buy hadn't done the trick, the problem apparently being more pervasive than a lack of energy, though a specific diagnosis seemed to be as far beyond the local mechanics as if he'd still been driving the roadster. As a would-be law student, his budget, though larger than that of many of his friends, had not accommodated extensive experiments at resuscitation on a truck he hadn't wanted and had no reason to keep.

The blare of a horn behind him pulled him back to the present. He was doing fifteen miles an hour over the limit but he had no desire to impede the progress of the behemoth threatening to chew up his rear bumper. He'd seen *Duel* three times over the years and enjoyed the way it captured the road paranoia induced by the sight of an eighteen-wheeler so close in your mirror you could count the bugs smeared on its radiator grille. He slid into the slower lane, noted a blue sign offering food at the next exit and felt a gnawing in his stomach. Except for the meager snacks he'd brought along for sustenance, and the acid coffee at the last gas station, he hadn't eaten since before leaving the mountains at first light.

That bright, cold long-ago morning in Wyoming he'd breakfasted well, fortifying himself to dicker with yet another garage owner, this one younger, with the face of an undiscovered movie star, a man who looked like he had a horse hitched out back and preferred it as a means of transportation to any of the noisy and unreliable vehicles whose woes paid the rent and put food on the table.

This time he'd come away with a bus ticket to Denver—more or less in the right direction, though not on the route he'd mapped out for himself. It was where the garage man had been planning to go with his wife, to visit her ailing mother, and cash had never been part of the negotiation, which had announced itself as barter from the first exchange. In the end the garage man had handed over the ticket with evident relief, obviously just as happy to have his wife go alone.

After another night in a room too icy for decent sleep he'd settled into the bus's first available window seat, about halfway from the driver to the rest room in the rear, not even realizing that he fully expected the empty seat next to him would be taken by the garage man's wife—because the tickets had been purchased together, perhaps, and he'd heard something about reserving a place and so mistook the bus for an airplane, or a Broadway theater; or because he thought the ticket he had in his pocket, smudged with thumbprints of old motor oil, had put him for the length of the ride in the garage man's place in some way more powerful and pervasive than merely having acquired his departure point and destination.

So, subconsciously awaiting the arrival of a wife fit to complement the improbably handsome garage man —equally tall and lean but fair and fine-featured where he was dark and craggy, with long blonde hair and ice-blue eyes, legs strengthened by years of clasping the flanks of a spirited horse, eager now to get out and away from her sterile life, with no ailing mother at all but a hankering for the bright lights of Denver, the hundred-foot lobby of the Brown Palace Hotel—he was surprised when the seat next to him was seized by a large woman in a greasy serape who, to judge from his quick look at her, was no less than sixty—slack leathery face dotted with moles, sagging circles of flesh under dull eyes, lank gray hair escaping in wisps from what might have been intended to be braids—though he supposed living out here in the unforgiving weather, working on some ranch or slinging hash in a truck stop or whatever work sustained her, mother to he couldn't guess how many children, she could be any age—fifty, or even forty, or less—a woman who by the smell of her hadn't washed herself any more often or more recently than she had the grimy serape or the stained red shirt whose collar was visible at her dirt-seamed neck.

At the last minute, as the bus had belched its way into motion and begun easing away from the convenience-store depot, bearing no passenger who could remotely be the missing wife, the pickup truck—unmistakably the same one, though he found it incredible to see the thing alive again, driven by the man whose ticket the driver had punched only minutes ago—had pulled athwart the bus's bow. Could it be that the garage man had discovered that the truck worked after all and was here to reclaim his ticket and clamber aboard with his long-legged blonde wife, returning the truck to its rightful owner?

He'd even stirred in his seat, mentally inventorying his possessions and planning his exit. But he noticed that the garage man was unmoving behind the wheel of the pickup, and that in addition to reviving it he'd had time to install a rifle rack against the back window of the cab complete with a rifle and a shotgun both looking— even as seen through the bus window—mellowed with long use and fond care.

A woman had climbed out of the pickup's passenger seat, leaving the rust-holed door hanging askew as she charged to the bus and pounded to be let in. She'd picked her way back along the aisle, nothing like he'd imagined. He'd looked at her first out of curiosity, knowing when he saw her that she had to be the wife and thinking that maybe she did have an ailing mother after all, though in retrospect the defense lawyer in him had long ago seen any number of ways to demolish that assumption, the fact of two people traveling in a pickup truck together hardly being persuasive evidence that those two people were married to each other, not even in Wyoming a quarter century ago.

Having looked, he'd found that he couldn't look away. She was short, with dark hair, plump cheeks, a mouth made for smiling though it was not smiling now. A general sense of roundness about her but he'd been able to see as she moved down the aisle—half sideways, as if reluctant to brush against anyone or anything, her sheepskin jacket pushing open with the motion—a waist so small he'd almost believed he would be able to span it with his hands. And her eyes, dark and deep, the irises so large they left only a hint of white on either side, and as troubled as her downturned mouth, flashing across him and pausing for a single heart-tugging moment.

Those eyes, that impression of a welcoming softness above and below her startlingly narrow waist, had haunted him for many years afterward, not in any steady way but at odd moments when he least expected such a visitation, prompted by what he did not know, until finally she had faded into dimness, and with her the image of infinite possibility he'd had that day—her hair dramatic against a linen pillow, the lushness of her body spiced by a scent of the sea, the glare of sun on whitewashed walls—all a construct of his mind, based on nothing: that one day he had seen her, she had simply continued down the aisle and found a seat somewhere behind him.

His stomach gurgled, hunger intruding its rude claim over thoughts of the past. He checked his watch again though he didn't need to, knew he couldn't afford the time it would take to stop for food. The gas tank was still half full; he was counting on making it the rest of the way with only one more stop. He reached across the seat, grabbed the plastic grocery bag from the floor on the passenger's side and pulled it onto the seat where he could reach into it as he drove. It was mostly garbage by now, banana peels and empty vegetable juice cans, but he pulled out a last small can that still had the heavy weight of not having been tapped, and a foil-wrapped power bar of partly cooked oats and honey and nuts and whatever else, all sintered together like a concrete block and not much tastier.

The food helped, but it didn't quiet his mind enough to keep it from slipping off the case that was the propellant for this ride. At least his bladder was holding out, that was a distraction he didn't need. If it came to it, he'd just keep driving and piss into the empty spring-water bottle rolling around on the floor by the passenger's seat.

A half hour into that remembered bus trip from Green River to Denver, he'd gotten up to use the smelly, soupy-floored chemical toilet at the back of the bus, making his way there slowly, using the seat backs to keep his balance, his eyes mostly on her—sitting by a window in the next-to-last row looking intently out at the blank white landscape, mountains in the distance. She had looked up once as he approached and quickly looked away, not enough to reprise that first, riveting contact, nothing he could reasonably interpret as an invitation or even the slightest willingness to have him join her.

He'd endured the rest of the ride to Denver, aware through every minute of it of the woman six rows behind him, but not moving from his seat because except for the one next to her there were none that looked much better than where he was; and because he thought it was too blatant a rejection of the woman in the serape

just to get up and relocate, having in those days been ex-
quisitely attuned to such slights, both as giver and re-
ceiver.

And he'd endured, too, the humiliation of calling
home from Denver and having his parents arrange for a
plane ticket through the travel agent who booked their
annual excursion to Tuscany. And the further humiliation of his father's silent reproach for the ruined car or
the lost money it represented or simply his incorrigible
unreliability. What kind of lawyer was he going to make
if he couldn't arrange the small details of his life better
than to blow the engine of his car driving from there to
here?

He'd made a decent enough lawyer, it had turned
out, though not the lawyer his father had had in mind:
three-piece-suited, white-shirted, and fit to occupy a
desk at the self-important white-shoe law firm that handled The Company's business. The Company, capital
letters implicit, all his father ever called the agglomera-
tion of buildings and machinery and people over which
he lorded it with calm if neofeudal authority.

Instead he'd gone straight into the prosecutor's office, impelled by the naive idea that the best way to make
the system work was to labor from within its most prob-
lematic element. Although the folly of that notion had
quickly become apparent to him, he'd put in his four
years, soaking up everything he could about how the
place worked, doing his job with zero enthusiasm but
great attention to detail. Then he'd jumped ship and
gone to work as a public defender, as he should have
from the beginning, bearing expertise that was deep but
not very wide in the strengths and vulnerabilities of the
district attorney's office. As a defense attorney he'd been
tireless, quickly becoming not just a winning lawyer but
a sort of roving mentor, until his days had become too

precious for anything except the work that was most pressing and important.

There was always more work for him than he could do, and he couldn't pretend anymore that he didn't hate it. How many cases had he consulted on or argued himself? How many appearances before how many judges?

The tide was turning—*had turned*, if he was to be honest with himself. It wasn't just the doctrinaire legislators, it was the true will of too many of the People. Execution was more common than at any time since he'd started to practice, maybe since he'd been born. Not just death sentences but actual judicial killings. It was a trend that strained even *his* belief in the fundamental rightness and perfectibility of the system of laws, and he knew it would get worse, even though he also knew that the trend carried the seeds of its own reversal: sooner or later there would be one case egregious enough to turn the national stomach, a miscarriage of justice so notable that the pendulum would begin to swing back and his job would get a little easier and a little—he caught himself thinking, not for the first time—a little less thankless.

But that was wrong, or anyway *ought* to be wrong— it stung him to realize that "thankless" was perfectly apposite, that there was too often no real thanks for what he did because he so often was the last on the scene and it was all already hopeless, so the most he got was a moment's gratitude from the bereaved who had loved the man he had not been able to save this time in this place, gratitude that was sincerely voiced but evanescent almost to the point of never having actually been felt.

Despite all that, his foot stayed on the accelerator, hurrying him toward the desperation that awaited, the distant storms for now no more than a decorative part of the landscape. He hoped they would stay there, not add further delay by making him pull to the side of the road, even though he knew it wouldn't hurt him right now to get in a quick nap. Lately he'd come to expect that he'd be tired in the afternoon, for no particular reason except that he hadn't been sleeping well for a while now, and no reason for *that* except that he worked too hard and didn't eat what they said you should and wasn't taking time for exercise the way he once had, telling himself it was because of his knee even though there were things he could do that wouldn't hurt it, even though he knew exercise was important for him. The truth was he begrudged the time, had too much to do, his cases were too important for him to be trundling off to some place where he could swim and then back to the office when he was done. That was why he'd taken a house this summer with its own pool, though he'd managed not to use that either.

Maybe his life would have been more rational, more ordered, if he'd ever married, but his love life had been like that long-ago interrupted cross-country trip—unrealized fantasies, real-life women who obsessed him even as they eluded him completely, and unsuitable women who regularly and aggressively claimed the space next to him and wouldn't make room for anyone else, and whom he was self-destructively slow to reject. He'd read something once that had seemed to encapsulate his experience perfectly: "The fickleness of the women I love is equaled only by the infernal constancy of the women who love me"—George Bernard Shaw quoted as the epigraph to some then brand-new novel, about which he remembered only that it had made him laugh aloud beginning to end. But Shaw had left out— or left implicit—how hard it could be to shake off that hellishly constant love, or to make yourself unlovable enough for it to evaporate on its own.

. . .

A darkening of the sky brought his mind back to the task at hand. The clouds were rapidly becoming part of his immediate world, no longer just a distant image, a piece of the postcard world past which he journeyed. If he was going to have to stop for the storm anyway, better if he could find a place to do it where they could fill up his stomach and his gas tank. Because he definitely was not going to drive through any serious flatland thunderstorm. Stopping might make him even later than he already was, but that had to be acceptable when the alternative was a real chance he wouldn't arrive at all.

Though at this point, try though he might, he couldn't divine what good it was going to do, really, for him to be there in person. The papers had all been filed in a timely way, the appeals team had hassled out the theory of the oral argument on the phone and in e-mail and faxes, the whole arsenal of long-distance collaboration. It shouldn't matter who stood up in the courtroom to make the argument. But at the last minute his cocounsel had decided they'd been wrong to worry about the negative effect on the judges of his being a big-city lawyer, that his skills of persuasion and his experience at making this kind of argument more than outweighed the disability inherent in being a Yankee in a Southern courtroom. A measure, he thought, of their sense of futility, their desire not to be the ones to bear the blame when the decision went against them.

He pulled off the highway at the next exit, reassured by another of the blue signs, this one promising food and fuel. At the end of the off-ramp was a stop sign and a two-lane blacktop road. A green and white road sign named two towns he'd never heard of, one to the right, one to the left. There was no other information, and looking right and left he saw nothing to indicate which way might lead to either food or gas. There were hills here, undulations, really, just enough rise and fall to truncate the limitless vistas he'd been passing through an hour ago, and the light was out of the sky, the air heavy with the moisture that was the advanced guard of the coming storm, making it impossible to see any real distance, to judge which of the two roads that curved off into obscurity might be the more promising.

He was too hungry—and tired, now, too—to have the patience even to flip a coin. He turned right, if only to avoid having to go under the highway.

As he had seen from the intersection, the road curved almost at once, and then it curved again, back the other way, and again. It rose and fell slowly as it swept back and forth, bordered on both sides by scrubby bushes that obscured whatever might lie any distance ahead. He remembered to note the mileage. If for some reason he had to come back to the highway in the rain, he didn't want to miss the on-ramp.

He drove slowly, straining to see ahead and off to the side, anywhere he might catch a glimpse of civilization. He passed fences and occasional barns and ranch buildings some yards from the road. Nothing like a commercial building, no billboards, no sign of a living human being.

As he drove, the sky got darker and the clouds lower, so that even with his headlights on he had the feeling he was driving through an infinite, winding tunnel whose walls weren't always apparent but whose ceiling threatened to crush him. He was on the edge of despair, convinced he'd made the wrong turn at the exit ramp and would have to go back and try the other direction, with little hope of making it to gas or food before the storm, no choice but to pull over and wait it out wherever he was.

Frustrated, infuriated, cursing himself for an idiot, he began to look for a place to turn off so he could get himself going back the way he'd come without risking a U-turn on the twisted, darkening road. Taking deep slow breaths and reminding himself that his agitation had to be partly the result of hunger and fatigue, and that he was where he was and no amount of agonizing about it was going to make it any better. Ahead, just past the next turn, he glimpsed what looked like a turnoff to the right and as he came around the arc of road saw that in fact it was a wide place in the pavement, the beginning of a parking area, and then saw gas pumps and a low, glass-fronted building topped by the large neon sign of a convenience-store chain.

He sighed with relief and slowed down to coast off onto the parking apron just beyond the pumps, by the entrance to the store. His front wheels had just crossed the blacktop seam that divided private from public when a flash of lightning brightened the scene in front of him enough to burn a temporary image onto his retina. Almost simultaneously a loud rolling crash of thunder rocked the car and a torrent of rain eclipsed everything in front of him. He drove as much by the lightning's afterimage as by what he could actually see, grateful that he was already slowed to a near stop.

There was a car parked by one of the pumps, two cars in the spots nearest the door, a motorcycle in the no-parking area between them. He swung wide of the second car and stopped. Sat for a moment as the downpour continued to rock the car. Made sure the windows were all up and the engine and everything electric was turned off, then slid across to the passenger's seat so he wouldn't have to run the extra distance around the front of the car, gathered himself, and pushed the door open. He hit the ground on the run, swinging the door closed behind him without looking, not stopping to lock it. Dashed the ten yards to the entrance door pelted by the rain that was falling in huge, heavy, hard drops, pushed the door open and ducked inside, pausing to catch his breath and let himself drip off. His knee was throbbing and his clothes were soaked through; water streamed from his hair down his face and down his back. He felt he should shake himself like a dog coming out of a swimming hole.

He looked around. It was an average-size convenience store, aisles of packaged and canned food and motor oil and bathroom necessities, refrigerated cabinets full of soft drinks and beer, the bright harsh fluorescents making it jarringly unreal after Mother Nature's brooding darkness. Scanning the aisles, he saw no one. He took a few steps, water still pooling around his feet, realized that the cashier's stand was empty, cleared his throat to say hello, anyone here, but was stopped by movement he caught in his peripheral vision, someone coming around the end of the last aisle.

He looked and for an instant saw the woman from the Denver bus more than twenty years ago, the wife of the garage man, impossible as that was—she'd be twice the age of this woman, who could barely be twenty-five. But if not for the impossibility of it he'd have sworn it was the same woman—bigger hair but the same plump cheeks and soft bow of mouth, jut of chest and lush roundness of hip, the same narrow, narrow waist. And, most astonishingly, the same eyes, deep and dark and huge. The same but not the same, because when his met them, held them, she didn't look away. All she did was move her hand enough to call attention to the gun she was pointing at him.

While he stood there dripping she looked him up and down, assessing him—seeing what? Some old guy? But he wasn't that old—in his prime, really. Still, his hair was thinner and grayer, his natural athletic leanness had begun to soften at the waist and hips, he wore bifocals . . . He resisted the impulse to suck in his gut, to stand up straighter despite the pain in his knee—this was a holdup in progress, not a beauty contest or a singles bar.

With another small movement of the gun she motioned him to the back of the store where four people were lying on the floor on their stomachs, bodies neatly aligned side by side—a display that took away his breath until he saw that they all were breathing: all of them alive, and no evidence they'd been hurt. He noticed that their heads were all turned to the left, presumably so they couldn't see each other's faces and communicate that way, or see what was happening in the store behind them. He was, he reckoned, about to become the fifth body in the row. He didn't mind the discomfort, though he was worried that if she wanted him to assume his prone position too quickly it might aggravate whatever was already bothering his knee, and that would mean standing up tomorrow morning to make his argument in significant pain or, worse, exhausted and with his mind under a stifling blanket of painkillers.

As he neared the horizontal lineup—a cashier, plump and about eighteen, and three customers: a man in dark green workclothes, in his mid-thirties; a teenage girl with mousy brown hair and clothes that looked like thrift-shop specials; and a man in his twenties, burly, wearing jeans and a black leather jacket, the motorcycle owner most likely—he was surprised to see no sign of the woman's partners in crime. Unless she was pulling the job on her own, though that seemed unlikely if not quite impossible, and the air she had of waiting said she was on guard duty for someone else.

She'd been sidling along in front of him, watching him carefully, gun trained on his midsection. She stopped and, as he'd expected, indicated that he should lie down where he'd be the latest addition to the neat row. He nodded, tried to smile, hands held out slightly from his sides, palms up, to make it absolutely clear he posed no threat. He felt ridiculous, even though his heart was beating marathon-fast and fear had paralyzed his chest. He lowered himself as carefully as he dared, thoughts of protecting his knee all but extinguished by the awkwardness that imposed and the danger that his sluggishness might produce an impatient response.

Because not straining her patience had become the central issue in his life for all the future that mattered, not worries about chronic pain, and surely not the absurd notion of preserving his ability to argue a case in a courthouse he would in all likelihood be able to reach only in time to be buffeted by the after-the-fact accounts of the participants—if he ever reached it at all.

Afraid as he was of panic, he knew he had to open his mind to the possibility that this might end badly, the knowledge that people lined up on the floor like this were sometimes shot in the back of the head as a way to unclutter a getaway and complicate a subsequent prosecution.

Lying there with rainwater puddling around him, his cheek pressed to the cold, gritty floor—he doubted it had been washed anytime recently—he tried to marshal his skittering thoughts. How do you deal with a situation like this, trapped and powerless, at the mercy of people whose minds and motives you know nothing of? He'd made his life among people who did things like this, championing them, even one who'd done this very thing—the wheelman in a trio of convenience-store robbers, one of whom, not his client, had cracked one day and left four people with holes in the backs of their heads and not much in the way of foreheads or faces. But in all that contact, all that necessary examination of histories and influences and motives, he could not find any insight into what moved such people that might be useful to him here, any sense of what he could say or do now to increase his chances of surviving this.

Lightning and thunder punctuated the world outside the store. He heard heavy footsteps, a rough male voice.

"Any trouble?"

No answer. He visualized the woman shaking her head: it's okay. Or nodding in his direction, pointing the gun at him for emphasis, to let her partner know there was one more in the row.

Then he heard motion behind him on the floor, and a young woman's voice—the cashier or the girl customer—"Please mister, just let us go. We're not going to tell."

"Where's the money? I didn't find no money." So it must have been the cashier.

There was no response at first, then, "Please mister. The manager must've took it. He came in here before to count—"

"That's all there is, you fat shit?"

"Please mister—"

The voice, thin and high and desperate, was cut off by the echoing blast of a gunshot and a scream that together covered what might have been the sound of impact, then sobbing—the girl customer—and with the sobbing incoherent words of pleading. "Not me, don't kill me, I don't want to die—"

"Shut up!" the gunman roared and there was another shot, and within the reverberation an extra fringe of sound, a horrible sound at once solid and liquid whose exact cause he didn't want to know.

A man's yell, something between a shout and a scream, and then a scuffling noise and someone kicked him going by overhead and the gunman's harsh voice, "Stop!" and he saw the workman run a step and a shot and the man stumbled and another shot that caught him on the way down.

Loud noises now of conflict. He rolled over fast, saw the woman hovering a few feet away, panic in her face as she watched the biker struggling with a man who had to be the gunman, her partner, the two men grappling for a big silver automatic.

He pushed himself upright, ignoring the pain in his knee, and lunged for the woman, falling against her, his hand reaching around for the gun she held as she staggered under his weight and tried to push him away. He was focused on the gun, there was nothing else in his universe, not the biker or the gunman or the horribly gory . . . things . . . on the floor, only that gun and abruptly it was in his hands, the woman backing away as at the same time the gunman broke free of the biker and shot and shot again and again, so the biker's body bucked and slid under the impact of the bullets.

He had the gun in his own hand under control now, pulling the trigger but to no effect, pressing harder as if that would help. The gunman turning toward him—

Desperate he yanked on the slide and it glided back smoothly, slammed forward almost on its own to move a bullet into the chamber the hammer cocked now both hands on the gun butt arms out pointing at the gunman not hearing the woman screaming, squeezing the trigger trying to hold the gun steady against the recoil ignore the pain in his knee, watching the red flowers appear and spread on a soiled T-shirt image of a stock-car race as the gunman danced backward the same steps he'd led the biker through, then crumpled to the floor.

His ears rang. He couldn't hear anything. His knee was all pain, his whole leg, his whole side. He could barely stand. He turned slowly to face the woman, the gun still clenched in his aching, white-knuckled hands, his finger quivering as he held it free of the trigger. She stood motionless, dark eyes blank.

Looking at her he saw the rest of it, every moment inevitable—the trial and conviction, the sentencing for the deaths of cashier and customers, just as the wheel-man he'd once fought for had been called killer though he'd never left the car. Other images crowded in—a drifter executed for killing a man he swore he'd never met, an illiterate janitor whose lawyer had shown up drunk every session of a murder trial that was over in three days . . .

Rain continued to pound against the store's glass facade from a roiling black sky. Along the horizon he could see a bright narrow ribbon of pale blue and shining white. He lowered the gun.

The woman stood there immobile.

He waited, the gun pointed at the bloody floor.

Finally, with excruciating slowness, she took a sideways step. Then another. Not quite looking at him, her shoulders shaking with fear of what he might do.

He let his eyes close a moment, weighted by exhaustion almost great enough to blunt the pain in his leg. Opened them and saw her halfway down the aisle, moving faster now, intent on her goal. Just short of the door she turned and stared at him—as heartstopping a look as he remembered from the woman on the bus—then bolted out the door into the rain.

His knee gave way. He toppled, caught himself against the nearest shelves, scattering aspirin and breakfast cereal. Braced himself and slid down to sitting. He laid the gun on the floor and leaned back to wait for the police.

Tom Moran is a lawyer-hero in the classic mold. He thinks quickly on his feet and can wilt witnesses with devastating cross-examination—even under extremely stressful circumstances. Count on Lisa Scottoline to remind us that lawyers are also human beings, more or less.

Carrying Concealed

LISA SCOTTOLINE

It was almost seven o'clock in the morning and Assistant District Attorney Tom Moran was late for court. He shaved lethally fast, slipped into his suitpants, and pinwheeled into his pinstriped jacket, all the time rehearsing his cross-examination in a continuous loop. If Tom didn't break this witness today, he'd lose for sure. He jumped into his wingtips and sprinted downstairs, his tie flying behind him.

Tom hit the hardwood running and snatched his briefcase from the floor like it was a baton on the final leg. He had perfected his handoff at St. Joe's Prep and could still hear the roar of the crowd cheering him toward the tape. WEEEAAAH! Then Tom realized that it wasn't cheering he heard, it was one of the twins crying in the kitchen. At three months old, the babies cried a lot. *Gastric reflux,* Marie called it, but Tom didn't think these two words should ever appear together.

He stopped in his tracks at the front door, his hand on the brass knob. The crying from the kitchen intensified. Tom checked his watch. 7:12 A.M. A tsunami of guilt washed over him. He had worked all night at the office, and Marie had been alone with the twins. He couldn't leave without checking on her. Tom dropped his briefcase and dashed into the kitchen, where he froze in disbelief. Marie was asleep standing up, rocking the crying infant in sagging arms. "Honey, wake up!" he shouted.

Marie's eyelids fluttered open. "Does it come in navy?" she asked, drowsy.

"Marie, wake up, wake up." Tom rushed across the room and grabbed the wailing baby. It was Ashley, who was his favorite of the twins, even though Marie made him swear not to have a favorite. "You were sleeping."

"No, I was shopping," she said. Marie leaned against the kitchen counter, dark shadows encircling her blue eyes and her strawberry-blonde hair uncombed. She hadn't lost the weight from the babies yet and wore a tentlike chenille robe over her Eagles T-shirt. She wasn't the girl he married, but Tom was too sensitive a guy to expect that. It would be nice to have sex again, however.

"Sit down, you look exhausted," Tom said. "Did you get any sleep last night?"

"I'm fine. Fine, really. I slept a little. Really." Marie sank into a chair, bumping into the kitchen table. Pink pacifiers rocked on its pine surface and an empty plastic bottle rolled onto the floor. In the middle of the table like a human centerpiece was the other twin, Brittany, slumbering through the ruckus in a quilted baby chair. Marie raked her fingers through her hair. "Ashley's cold is worse, she's coughing and wheezing. I had her on the nebulizer three times last night."

"What's a nebulizer?"

"That thing." Marie waved a hand at a grayish machine on the counter. A clear plastic tube snaked from the machine, and at the end of the tube was a small plastic cup like a doll's oxygen mask. "Got it yesterday from the pediatrician, but it didn't help. I have to take her in again, and the pediatrician's in his Cherry Hill office tomorrow. I mean, today."

"Cherry Hill?" Tom felt terrible for her. "How will you get two babies to Cherry Hill? You're beat."

"I'll do it somehow, I have to. Ashley's not really a problem, if I could find someone to sit with Brittany."

"What about your mom? Can't she help?"

"On Tuesday? Her golf day?"

Tom bit his tongue. His bitchy mother-in-law, St. Teresa of the Perpetual Cigarette. "How about your sister?"

"Out of town."

"Again?" His sister-in-law was never around when she wasn't borrowing money. Damn. Tom jiggled Ashley and winced against the racket. The baby was so loud he couldn't hear himself think. "I wish I could help you," Tom said, and suddenly Marie looked up at him, her eyes full of adoration. It was the way she used to look at him. Back when they had sex.

"You can?" Marie asked, with a relieved smile. "But you're on trial."

"What?" Tom said, confused. Brittany was screaming full-throttle, and he still had his mind on the sex part.

"Tom, how can you take Brittany if you're on trial?"

"Take *who?*"

"Brittany." Marie was still giving him the love face, and Tom swallowed hard.

"Me take Brittany?"

"I thought that was what you said." Marie's love face dropped like a mask. "You'd take Brittany for the day so I could take Ashley to the pediatrician. Isn't that what you said?"

What? Was she insane? "Right. Absolutely. Sure." How could Tom say no? He didn't have time to think about it. He'd figure something out. The D.A.'s office had 34,350 secretaries. One of them had to be lactating.

"This is so wonderful of you, Tom. I'm at my wit's end. You sure you can do this?"

"Don't worry about it. It's not a problem. Nothing is a problem." Tom felt sick inside. He didn't want to think about how much time an infant would add to his trip downtown. It took an hour to get one strapped like a paratrooper into the car seat.

"But you have your big case today, don't you?"

"Don't worry, you take care of Ashley. I'm late. I have to go," Tom said. He off-loaded Ashley into Marie's lap and unhooked Brittany from her baby chair. Her head flopped to one side and her non-skid feet drooped in her fuzzy pink sleeper. He boosted her onto his shoulder and kissed his wife on the cheek. "Am I a hero or what?"

"Take the diaper bag."

"Heroes don't need diaper bags," Tom said, and hurried out of the kitchen with the baby, trying not to get slobber on his suit.

"Take my car!" Marie called after him. "The keys are on the hall table!"

"Gotcha!" Tom called back, and scurried into the hall, genuflecting to pick up his briefcase and Marie's keys. He bolted out the door into the sun, running in a cramped position so Brittany's head wouldn't bump around. Lucky it was spring, a warm morning, and Brittany was warm enough in her sleeper, the body bag for babies.

Tom dashed across the lawn to Marie's huge Ford Expedition, the only car larger than their home, chirped it unlocked, and threw his briefcase in ahead of him. Then he popped the baby off his shoulder and into her car seat, facing backward in the passenger seat. Her head bobbled slightly but her eyes didn't open as he fumbled with the woven straps, then ended up tying them in a knot. He didn't have time to get fancy.

Tom jumped in beside the baby, started the ignition, and roared out of the driveway, his hand on Brittany's tummy. Her minuscule chest rose and fell with a reassuring regularity. Her fleecy sleeper felt warm and soft. She smelled milky and sweet. She slept, well, like a baby.

Tom smiled. This was going to be a piece of cake.

"WWWWAAAAAAAHH!" Brittany wailed, and a thoroughly shaken Tom Moran skidded to a stop at the NO PARKING—TOW ZONE sign in front of the Office of the District Attorney. "WWWWAAAAAAAHH!" Shock waves of sound bounced around the Ford, reverberating off the windshield and walls. Tom thought his eardrums would explode.

"Shh, honey, don't cry, shhh," he said, struggling with the knot on the car seat. His fingers shook. His skull pounded. His brain hurt. "It's okay, quiet now, please be quiet." Tom couldn't hear himself speak, but he saw his lips moving in the rearview mirror.

"WWWAAAHHHH!" Brittany cried. She squeezed her eyes shut. Her face had gone dangerously red. Her mouth was a wet trumpet of sound, blasting like Gabriel's horn.

Tom broke into a sweat. He glanced at the car's digital clock. 8:21. He had to be in court by 9:00. He couldn't take her into the office hysterical. He didn't have time to wait. What's a lawyer to do?

"WWWAAAHHH!"

Tom looked frantically around the car. Wasn't there anything here to amuse her? Baby toys, plastic links, things that squeaked? Tom checked everywhere, covering his ears. Nothing. Damn! Marie was too damn neat. His gaze fell on the ignition. Keys! The babies loved their Fisher-Price keys. Tom yanked his keys out of the ignition and jingled them in front of Brittany's face like a mobile from Pep Boys. "Keys! Keys, Brit!" he yelped.

"WAAH!" The baby kept crying, and Tom jingled harder.

"Keys! Look, Brit! Keys! You love keys! These are the real thing! The others are knockoffs!"

"Waah!" Brittany cried, but her heart wasn't in it anymore. She was watching the keys, her eyes brimming with unspilled tears.

"Look! Genuine keys! Supply limited! Order now!" Tom bounced the keys around, and the baby finally made a kitten's swipe at them. "Yes!" Tom exclaimed and handed her the keys. Her lower lip buckled as she struggled to hold them, cross-eyed with absorption. Tom looped a baby finger through the keychain to hold them on, and her crying ceased as quickly as it had started. "Thank you, Jesus," Tom said.

He slipped Brittany from the car seat, grabbed his briefcase, and jumped out of the car. He didn't bother to lock it, he couldn't risk taking the keys from Brittany. Let the punks steal the car; let the cops tow it. He was only one man. Tom whirled through the revolving door, babe in arms, and got the hoped-for response from Luz Diaz, the knockout receptionist.

"A baby! You brought one of the babies!" she squealed, her lipsticked lips parting in delight. Luz had a black mane of oiled curls and a body that had never borne children, which was undoubtedly why she was so happy to see this one.

"Luz, this is Brittany! Say hello!" Tom hurried past the packed waiting area and thrust Brittany in the arms of a startled Luz. Possession was nine tenths of the law.

"Oooh, she's so pretty, so pretty." Luz smiled down at the pink bundle, then her face fell. "Tom, she's eating car keys."

"She loves car keys." Tom glanced at the big clock

on the wall. Its hand ticked onto 8:29. "Don't touch her car keys."

"But she's got them in her mouth," Luz said, horrified, and Tom looked down. Brittany was sucking on an ignition key. So what? When he was little, he ate worms.

"Listen, Luz, you gotta help me. I have to go to court and I need you to take Brittany, just for the day."

"What?" Luz looked at Tom like he was nuts. "I'm at the front desk. I can't do that."

"Then give her to somebody who can."

"Who?"

"Somebody you trust. One of the other secretaries. Just not Janine." Tom knew all about Janine. She kept sex toys in the drawer.

"I can't do that." Luz pushed Brittany back into Tom's arms. "I need this job. Ask one of the girls in your unit, upstairs."

"Okay, okay, fine. Thanks anyway." He hustled Brittany from the front desk and hurried down the corridor, flying past his colleagues who were going in the opposite direction. To court, childless.

"Moran, aren't you supposed to be trying *Ranelle?*" Stan Kullman asked, squeezing past him with two trial bags.

"I do it all," Tom called back, on his way to the staircase. He was running out of time. Maybe one of the girls in the Major Trials Unit could help. His secretary was on vacation this week, since he was on trial. Tom bounded up the stairs two-by-two, cradling Brittany's head. She was starting to whimper again. The jingling had vanished. God knew where the car keys were.

Tom reached the second floor and scurried past the secretaries' desks, which were empty. Everybody was in the coffee room, where he'd be if he didn't have a murder case to win and a baby to unload. Tom took a hard left into the tiny room, fragrant with the aromas of coffee and perfume. "It's a girl!" Tom said to the group, who flocked around Brittany, cooing.

"She's so little!" Rachel said.

"She's so cute!" Sandy said.

"She's so good!" Franca said.

"She's the best baby in the world," Tom said, smiling. "She's little and cute and sweet. She sleeps a lot. She loves keys. Can anybody baby-sit her today?"

The secretaries looked at Tom like he was nuts. "Tom, we *work* here," Rachel said. She was an older woman, and her tone was kind yet stern. "We can't just drop everything and baby-sit for the day."

"Maybe you could take turns, an hour for each of you? I'll pay, I swear. I'll pay anything. Each of you. Overtime."

Rachel shook her graying head. "She's an infant, Tom. She needs complete attention. I can't type with her on my lap, you know." Behind her, Sandy and Franca and Judy nodded in agreement, which panicked Tom. They were all turning against him.

"But it's an emergency. I need help, and she's no trouble. She sleeps all the time. Well, a lot, anyway."

"My boss is away," chirped a voice from the back, and Tom's heart leapt with hope.

"Who said that?" he asked, on tiptoe, and the crowd parted, revealing a black leather minidress and a pair of spike heels. Janine. Our Lady of the Handcuffs. Tom's mouth went dry. He looked from the black leather to the pink fleece. "Uh, no thanks, maybe I can handle this," he said, and fled the coffee room.

Brittany whined as Tom ran down the corridor, his mind working furiously. The wall clock was a blur. 8:42. Tom had to think of something fast. He ducked into his office, slammed his door closed with his heel, dropped his briefcase on the floor, and set Brittany down on a soft pile of correspondence, which was when he smelled it. Babypoop. No wonder Brittany was fussing. She was knee-deep in shit. Now she knew what it was like to be an assistant district attorney.

Tom unzipped her sleeper and took her feet out, exposing her Pampers diaper. The stench was assault and battery. The sight was cruel and unusual. Brittany would need a new diaper and new clothes. Tom reached for the diaper bag, but there was none. "God help me," he murmured, but he didn't have time to think, only to react.

Tom took off the soggy diaper and sleeper, ripped some legal paper from a pad to wipe the baby clean, and rolled the mess into a basketball and shot it into the wastebasket. Brittany, smooth as a cherub, kicked her feet and calmed instantly, which almost made her his new favorite.

But she was naked. How could Tom palm off a naked baby, still a little sticky? He needed a diaper. He'd have to make one. Go! He grabbed a suppression motion, good for nothing anyway, and ripped it into four strips, lengthwise. Then he took one of the strips and stuck it between the baby's legs like a loincloth. "Well, it's a brief, isn't it?" he said to Brittany, who smiled even though she'd heard that one.

But how to hold the diaper up? A rubber band was too small. Eureka! Tom grabbed his tape dispenser, yanked out an endless strip of Scotch tape, and wrapped it around Brittany's waist. She kicked happily all the while, then shivered visibly. "You cold?" Tom asked and frowned. There wasn't anything on the baby's legs.

Tom kicked off his shoes, tore off his black socks, and slipped one over Brittany's left leg and one over her right. Then he stapled the socks to the briefs and checked his desk clock. 8:47. The courthouse was fifteen minutes away. He sweated bullets, and Brittany wriggled on the correspondence, making her legal diaper crackle. Her tiny face squinched into a frown, and her mouth opened and closed like a puppy. Uh-oh. Tom knew what that meant. She was hungry.

Damn it! Some things couldn't be improvised. Nursing, for one, and maybe that was it in toto. Tom thought a minute. Brittany was too young for solid food. The only liquid around was Half-&-Half. That was no good. What did Marie give her when they were out of breast milk? Tea. Tom was a tea drinker, he had plenty of tea around.

He scooted behind his desk, splashed some water from a plastic pitcher into a Styrofoam cup, and plopped his immersion coil inside with a Lipton's teabag. Tom put on his shoes as the clock hand moved to 9:01. *Come on.* He tested the water with a fingertip. Not too hot, not too cold. Perfect! And he cooks, too!

Tom plucked the coil and teabag from the cup and scurried with the brew back to Brittany, whose bow-shaped lips were making sucking sounds. He scooped up the baby and raised the cup, then stopped stupidly in midair. What was he thinking? Tom had fed the twins enough times to know they weren't drinking from Styrofoam yet. Hmm. Another hurdle, but Tom had been quite a hurdler in his day.

"Got it!" he said. Tom grabbed a brown coffee stirrer from his desk, wiped it clean on his pants, and dipped it in the tea. He held his finger over the top until the skinny straw was full, then he brought the straw over to Brittany, cradled in the crook of his arm.

"Down the hatch, honey," Tom said. He removed his finger from the top of the straw and released the tea into her mouth. The baby's face contorted almost immediately and she looked about to cry, then her lips latched onto the coffee stirrer as easily as a nipple.

"That's my girl," Tom cooed, then went down for another strawful and let it trickle into the baby's mouth. She took it, sucking eagerly, and was on her third helping when the phone rang. Tom let it ring, then reconsidered. Maybe it was one of the secretaries, regretting her professionalism. He hit the speakerphone button.

"Moran, you there?" bellowed a man's powerful voice, and Tom jumped, leaking Lipton's all over Brittany's briefs. On the telephone was Bill Masterson, the district attorney himself. *Jesus, Mary, and Joseph.* Tom would have dropped to his knees but he had a baby to feed. "Moran, you there?" Masterson boomed.

"Yes, sire. I mean, sir."

"You there, Moran? You in your office, Moran?"

"I am, sir."

"What the fuck are you doing there? You're not supposed to be there. You're supposed to be in court. You, in your office? What the fuck, Moran?"

"I, uh, had to get some exhibits."

"I don't care. You think I care? I don't get it. You're trying the case but you're in your office. I'm at the courthouse. You're not here."

Gulp. *"You're* at the courthouse, sir?"

"I'm here but you're there. I'm at the courthouse but you're at the office. Why does this always happen with you, Moran?"

"I'll be leaving right away, sir."

"What the fuck are you doing in your office? You're supposed to be in court, not in your office. I'm not trying the case but I'm in court. You're trying the case but you're at the office. I don't get it, do you? Moran? Why?"

"I'll be right over, sir. I'm on my way."

"What the fuck, Moran?" Masterson said, without further elaboration, then hung up.

Tom punched the Off button in a panic. Masterson would be watching the trial today. Holy Shit. Tom had to get to court. Now. He looked helplessly at Brittany, nestled in a manger of correspondence, dressed in black socks and a losing brief. He couldn't leave her here. He couldn't park her with anybody. He was her father. She was gurgling happily, her tummy temporarily full.

There was only one choice.

Tom approached the reception area carrying his briefcase in one hand and a large black trial bag in the other. The lawyer's bag was as wide as a salesman's sample case, which wasn't a bad analogy, and stuffed with shredded exhibits had proved an ample crib for Brittany, who rested quietly on its flat bottom. A careful observer would have noticed the airholes punched in the top of the briefcase, but none of the people seated in the waiting room were careful observers. They were Commonwealth witnesses, after all. They saw what they were told to see.

"Tom, where's the baby?" Luz asked, as Tom walked by.

"All taken care of," he answered. He whirled out the revolving door and hit the pavement just in time to see Marie's Ford Expedition being towed down the street in traffic. Tom closed his eyes in prayer, then squared his shoulders. He'd lost the keys anyway. He hailed a cab.

"Yo!" Tom shouted, and a Yellow cab pulled up. Tom and his bags got in. "Criminal Justice Center," he said, closing the door.

"Weee," came a sound from the trial bag.

"What was 'at?" the cabbie asked. He was a squat

older man in need of a shave, with a soiled Phillies cap pulled low on his forehead.

"Nothing."

"I heard something. I heard like a squeak."

"It's my shoes, they're new," Tom said, but he knew it would happen again. Brittany would never last through the day in the trial bag. But Tom was an experienced father. He knew what to do. "Stop at that store and wait for me," he said, pointing, and the cab pulled up at the curbside.

Tom jumped out with the trial bag and burst into the store, squinting at his watch on the run. 9:11. Where was the goddamn aisle? Tom forced himself to think. It was a chain, and the layout was the same in every store. He ran to 4D, grabbed the package from the shelf, and hustled to the cashier, where he forked over a ten-dollar bill. "Keep the change," Tom said.

"Weee," said the bag. And they both fled the store.

Tom leapt back into the cab, set the trial bag on the floor, unlatched its brass locks, and plucked Brittany from its bottom. She emerged writhing, looking vaguely colicky. Tom was just in the nick of time.

"Your shoes, huh?" said the cabbie.

"It's not what it looks like."

"Sure it is."

"Drive."

The cab lurched off, and Tom set the baby on his lap. He grabbed his bag and reached inside for his purchase, then tore off the cellophane with his teeth and shoved a spare finger through the thin cardboard top. INFANTS' TYLENOL, read the pink pastel carton, and underneath, "Suspension Drops."

Tom ripped the safety seal off the bottle with his teeth, then did the same to the tiny plastic dropper. One dropper of Tylenol would buy him three hours of slumbering baby. Tom felt a pang of conscience, but it was a necessity. It wouldn't hurt her, it would just make her sleep. With one dose now and one at lunch, Brittany wouldn't wake up until the jury came back with a conviction.

"Where'd you get the baby?" asked the driver, a wary eye on the rearview.

"It's mine."

"What are you doin' with her in the suitcase?"

"None of your business."

"No man is an island, buddy."

"Talk to me when you have twins, professor." Tom took the dropper, plunged it into the bottle, and extracted a dropper of Day-Glo-pink sleeping potion. The fill line on the dropper read .8 milliliters, but Tom had no idea how much a milliliter was. He just knew it was what Marie gave them.

"So what'sa matter with the baby, she sick?" the cabbie asked.

"No, just sleepy."

"Baby don't look sleepy."

"Well, she is," Tom shot back, defensive. He squirted a dropperful of cherry-flavored syrup into the baby's mouth, and Brittany swallowed, apparently happily. "Good girl," Tom said. What a kid! He gave her a quick good-night kiss and stuck her back in the bag just as the cab pulled up in front of the Criminal Justice Center. Tom dug for a ten and handed it to the driver. "Keep the change," he said, but the cabbie turned and scowled at him.

"It's blood money," he snarled, so Tom threw the bill in the front seat, leapt out with the bags, and slammed the door behind him.

The sidewalk in front of the Criminal Justice Center was thick with cops in blue uniforms, talking and smoking, waiting to testify. Tom normally felt welcome among them, but things were different now that he'd become a borderline child abuser. One of the uniforms waved at him, and Tom acknowledged him with a jittery nod, then escaped inside the courthouse with his living luggage.

The lobby was jammed, with long lines leading to the metal detectors. The courthouse clock read 9:14. Oh, no. He was late. Tom barreled through the crowd as politely as possible. If he didn't get his ass upstairs, he'd be held in contempt. Fined. Fired.

He picked up his pace and hurried to the lawyers' entrance on the far side of the security desk. As a member of the bar, Tom could bypass the detectors and the security personnel, which was the only way he could smuggle his own offspring into a courtroom. No security officer had planned for that contingency, probably because no lawyer would be boneheaded enough to try it. Overestimating lawyers was not a smart thing to do.

Tom crossed the marble floor to the elevators. A throng of three-piece suits waited in front of the modern brass-lacquered doors, and Tom got bumped by a defense lawyer. "Hey, watch it," Tom said.

"It's not his fault," said the defense lawyer, and Tom turned away as the elevator doors opened. To protect his cargo, he let the others rush into the cab and stepped inside last. The doors closed almost on Tom's nose, so he got a good look at himself in the mirrored insides of the doors. A tall, lanky Irishman with rumpled dark hair and blue eyes as guilty as a felon's, carrying a briefcase of exhibits and a trial bag of baby. What kind of father was he? Stuffing his kid in a bag? Drugging her with cherry gunk? Having a favorite in the first place? Tom had a lot of confessing to do.

Ping! went the elevator, and Tom got off into an

even bigger mob. Second floor, the *Ranelle* case. Tom used to think of it as his "baby" until now. He wedged his way into the crowd of reporters, lawyers, witnesses, and spectators who didn't get a seat in the morning's lottery. On the far side of the throng was Masterson, standing above the crowd like the power forward he used to be at Bishop Neumann.

Tom's stomach churned. His hands sweated. He was going to lose, he was going to be disbarred, and his child would have memories of being locked in darkness. Also he'd lost Marie's car keys. Tom shuddered, then shook it off.

"Fashionably late, eh, Moran?" Masterson boomed, his hail-fellow manner disguising how furious he must be. Tom, for once grateful for Masterson's phoniness, made his way over to his boss as casually as if he were at a cocktail party.

"Shall we go?" Tom said, with ersatz confidence.

"Sure," the district attorney said, surprised, and Tom threaded his way to Courtroom 206, ducking reporters and their questions. He wasn't the grandstanding type, which meant he'd eventually wash out as an A.D.A. Tom was one of those guys who became a prosecutor because he wanted to do good. Several were still left. In the world.

"Any comment, Mr. Moran?" the reporters asked, notebooks at the ready. "What will you do today, Tom?" "What's your strategy for Hammer, Mr. Moran?" "Think you can get a conviction?"

"No comment," Tom said, holding his trial bag close to his side. None of the investigative reporters seemed to notice the airholes in the bag. Not a Geraldo among them.

"Of course he'll get a conviction, friends," Masterson boomed, spreading his arms as the reporters swarmed to him. "How can you doubt one of our best and brightest?"

Tom left them behind and entered the courtroom, where his trials were just beginning.

Tom hated every sterile inch of Courtroom 206, which looked just like all the other courtrooms in the new Criminal Justice Center. It was sleek, modern, and spacious, with muted gray fabric covering the walls, and a dais, jury box, and gallery pews of gleaming rosewood. Tom preferred the old courtrooms in City Hall, a creaky Victorian dowager of a building, with grimy brass sconces and dusty radiators that rattled. Tom liked things to stay the same. He wished they still held mass in Latin.

He shifted unhappily in his slippery chair at the prosecution table. His trial bag snoozed next to him, and Tom kept the toe of his wingtip protectively near the end with the baby's head. He had already determined he wouldn't travel far from the table during his cross, even if he had to sacrifice the theatrics. Brittany's cerebellum was more important. Tom had some priorities.

He tried to compose himself during the defense examination of the witness. In the morning's confusion, his careful preparation of the night before had flown from his head and he'd accidentally left his notes under Brittany in the trial bag. Tom sighed. At least the baby was asleep. He forced himself to forget about Brittany and focus on the direct examination by the defense.

"That's right, I work part-time in the rifle range," the witness was saying. The witness, Elwood "Elvis" Fahey, was a low-rent punk with a coke-white pallor and jet-black hair. He looked scrawny on the stand in a black windbreaker that said MEMBERS ONLY on the pocket. Tom wondered what club Elvis was a member of, and made a mental note not to join.

"What do you do in the rifle range, sir?" asked defense counsel Dan Harrison. Harrison was a trim forty, on the short side but natty in a tan Italian suit, no vent, that draped just right on the shoulders and broke on the instep. Lawyers who defended drug dealers always wore Italian. It was like MEMBERS ONLY with a law degree. MEMBERS OF THE BAR ONLY.

"At the shootin' range? I clean up, hand out the earphones, help out, stuff like that."

Harrison nodded. "This is a steady, gainful employment for you, sir?"

"Sure. For three years. Three days a week. Regular."

"And you met the decedent, Guillermo Juarez, at the rifle range, did you not?"

"Yeah. We got to be friends, me and Chicken Bill."

Harrison winced. "By 'Chicken Bill' are you referring to the decedent, Guillermo Juarez?"

"Yeah. Guillermo is the de-, the dece-, the dead guy," Elvis answered, laughing with a deep-throated *huh huh huh.*

The jurors didn't find this amusing, though their hearts weren't bleeding for the decedent either. A conscientious group of nine women and three men, the jury had already heard testimony that Chicken Bill had been a crack dealer. Nobody was crying over his demise, least of all the defendant, James Ranelle, who listened quietly, his sweet face covered with freckles and his cropped hair the color of barbecued potato chips. Ranelle looked more altar boy than drug dealer, but Tom wasn't fooled. He was a better Catholic than most.

"Now, sir," Harrison continued, "would you tell the jury, in your own words, what happened to Chicken

Bill on the night of August 12, at around eleven o'clock in the evening?"

"Well," Elvis began, and grabbed the microphone like his namesake. He had been in and out of prison, and his many court appearances had sharpened his skills as an entertainer. "I hear a gunshot downstairs, and I wake up and run down the stairs."

"Where were you at the time, sir?"

"In the bedroom, sleepin'. I hear the noise and I run downstairs and all hell's breaking loose. Everything's real bright. There's big flames everywhere. I see smoke. I smell gasoline. It's all orange and real hot. I know right off it's a fire."

Tom made a note. The genius club.

"And what were the other inhabitants of the house doing, sir?"

"They're shoutin', yellin', runnin' out the door." Elvis waved his hands, to add courtroom drama. "Sammy and his girl Raytel, then Jamal. They all get out in a hurry, so they don't get a hotfoot."

"When did you see Chicken Bill, sir?"

"Right when I come down. He was just lying on the floor. I went up to him to see if he was okay, but he was half dead."

"And what did you do, sir, when you found Chicken Bill dying on the floor?"

"I lifted him up, like, and held him in my arms. Like a cradle."

"And did you say anything to him, sir?"

"I sure did. I axed him, 'Who did this fire, Chicken? Did you see who did this fire?' "

"And did Chicken Bill answer you?"

Tom sprung to his wingtips. "Objection, hearsay, Your Honor," he said, and Harrison did a custom-tailored half-turn toward the bench.

"Your Honor," Harrison argued, "I believe this testimony falls within the dying-declaration exception to the hearsay rule. Chicken Bill—Mr. Juarez—was clearly in extremis at the time he made the statement."

A *dying declaration?* Tom couldn't believe his ears. He hadn't seen a case with a dying declaration since evidence class. You didn't have to be a member of anything to think up this whopper. It was so absurd, all Tom could say was, "A dying declaration. Your Honor?"

"A dying declaration, Mr. Harrison?" Judge Amelio Canova repeated, only slower. Canova was a short, sluggish sixty-five, and his smooth bald head stretched from his robe like a turtle's, craning over his papers on the dais.

"Yes, Your Honor," Harrison said. "Our experts yesterday testified as to his approximate time of death, if you recall. Mr. Juarez perished from third-degree burns at or about 11 P.M. Any statement he made to the witness falls squarely within this well-accepted exception to the hearsay rule."

Judge Canova blinked, heavy-lidded. "I'll permit it," he said wearily, and Tom sank into his chair.

Harrison turned back to his witness. "Now, sir, before the prosecutor interrupted you, you were about to tell the jury what Chicken Bill said, as he lay dying."

"Yes, I was." Elvis straightened at the microphone. "It's like this, Chicken can barely talk, his throat is all burned up, and he's, like, whispering. He says to me, 'Cowboy Ron did this to me, Elvis. Cowboy Ron did this fire.' "

The jurors reacted, shifting in their seats and sneaking glances at each other. They didn't like Elvis but Tom knew they'd find it difficult to completely discount his testimony later. Elvis was the only witness, and the defense had put up a chorus line of experts. Tom had seen expert witnesses seduce even the smartest juries. They were like hookers in lab coats.

It made Tom's blood boil. He knew the way the murder went down, he just had to prove it; Ranelle had torched a competing crackhouse, run by Chicken Bill. Chicken Bill got dead as desired, and everybody else got out alive, including Elvis, who instantly perceived that the murder of his friend was the opportunity of a lifetime. If Elvis helped Ranelle beat the murder rap, he'd have a new job with Ranelle's organization. One man's ceiling is another man's floor, even in crackhouses.

Harrison leaned on the witness box. "Did you know who Chicken Bill meant by Cowboy Ron, sir?"

"Yes, he meant the dude wore a cowboy hat, a brown cowboy hat. Lived a block away."

"And, to the best of your knowledge, is this Cowboy Ron known to be a drug dealer?"

"Yes, far as I know. Cowboy Ron competed with Chicken Bill."

"Is Cowboy Ron in the courtroom this morning, sir?"

Elvis's bedroom eyes swept the courtroom, for show. "No, sir."

"Is the defendant James Ranelle also known as Cowboy Ron?"

"No. The defendant ain't Cowboy Ron. Cowboy Ron is somebody else. Cowboy Ron ain't here today."

"I see." Harrison lingered with a frown before the jury box. He was pretending to think, but Tom knew he was only pausing to let the testimony sink in. Harrison hadn't had an unrehearsed moment in his life. It made him a superb defense lawyer. "I have no further questions," Harrison said. "Thank you, sir."

Tom rose quickly to his feet. "If I may cross-examine, Your Honor," he said, then stopped as the law clerk murmured in the judge's ear.

Judge Canova peered down from the dais, waving a wrinkled hand. "Not quite yet, Mr. Moran. Sit down, please."

Tom resettled in his chair and glanced over at Harrison, who looked pleased at the defense table. Any interruption would only give the testimony time to set, like concrete.

"Ladies and gentlemen of the jury," Judge Canova said, turning to them, "please excuse me for just a minute or two. I have a brief matter to attend to in chambers, and since I'll be gone but a minute, I won't put you to the trouble of dismissing you and bringing you back in again. Please stand by, as they say on the television." The jury smiled, and the judge shuffled from the dais and out the side door.

The jurors relaxed when Judge Canova left, but Tom didn't. As long as they were in the box, he was on show. Harrison turned to make fake-conversation with Ranelle, who stayed in character as a candidate for the priesthood. Tom struggled to remember his outline of the night before. He was grateful for the recess, but worried, too. He didn't have much time left on the Tylenol, did he? He snuck a peek at his watch. 10:15.

Tom told himself to relax. He wouldn't start to worry until 11:45. And that was a long way off.

But at 11:45, the judge was still out. The jury was dozing in the jury box. The bailiff was reading the sports page. The courtroom reporter was cleaning the black keys of her steno machine with a Q-tip. The gallery conversed quietly among themselves. The courtroom was in a state of suspended animation.

Except for Tom, who was in a state of panic. His

shirt was soaked under his jacket. His legal pad was full of scribbles. He crossed and uncrossed his legs. Suddenly he heard a rustling in the trial bag. Holy Christ. Was Brittany waking up?

Tom bent over and unlocked the trial bag as casually as possible. A square of fluorescent light fell on the baby's face. She squirmed in the sudden brightness and her blue eyes flared open. Tom snapped the lid closed. Oh, no. What was he going to do? Where was the judge?

Tom looked around in desperation. Masterson, sitting in the front row of the gallery, leaned over the bar of the court and handed him a note. Tom read it with a shaking hand:

WHAT THE FUCK IS THE MATTER WITH YOU, MORAN?

Tom shoved the note into his pocket and closed his eyes in pain. *Father, forgive me, for I have sinned. I lost my notes. I locked my baby in a briefcase. I don't know how much a milliliter is.* He opened his eyes just as Judge Canova entered the courtroom, his face etched with contrition.

"Ladies and gentlemen," the judge said, even before he reached his leather chair, "I must beg your forgiveness. I was detained on an emergency administrative matter and kept thinking it would be over in just five minutes. Well, you know how that is," he said, sitting down with a red face. The jurors smiled indulgently, and Judge Canova gestured to Tom. "Mr. Moran, please pick up where we left off. I'd like to get something accomplished before we dismiss for lunch, at twelve-thirty."

"Of course, Your Honor." Tom edged forward on his seat, unsteady. He had to come up with a killer cross-examination before Brittany exploded. "Now, uh,

Mr. Fahey, you were at the home of Chicken Bill on the night in question, is that right?"

"Yes."

"Did you live at that home?"

"No. I just visited."

"Why did you visit there?"

Elvis glanced at Harrison, who didn't object. "Just because."

"Because why?" Tom rose, finding his footing next to the trial bag, which rustled softly again. It must have been Brittany's briefs, crackling around her legs. His heart raced in his chest.

"I just kind of hung at Chicken Bill's."

"By 'hung,' you mean smoked crack, don't you?"

"Objection!" Harrison yelped, leaping to his Gucci loafers.

"Your Honor," Tom said, "defense counsel opened the door on this testimony yesterday. The witness is an admitted crack user, and the prosecution is entitled to impeach."

"Sustained," Judge Canova said. He banged his gavel half-heartedly, but the sound provoked more rustling from the trial bag and a quiet, though unmistakable, baby yawn. Tom glanced around nervously. No one seemed to notice the sound. He was the only one close enough to hear it. How long would his luck hold out? And his baby?

"Uh, Mr. Fahey," Tom said, wiping his forehead, "you said you ran down the stairs when you heard the gunshot, and you smelled gasoline."

"Yeah."

"Did you see where the gasoline came from?"

"No, it was all on the floor, on fire."

"Did you see anyone throw the gasoline in the house?"

"No."

"Did you see anyone shoot the gasoline to ignite it?"

"No."

"So the only way you know who the perpetrator of this crime is, is because Chicken Bill told you?"

"Yeah, he told me hisself."

"Weee," said the trial bag softly, and Tom gulped. Harrison looked over at the sound, and Tom coughed twice.

"Mr. Fahey," he continued, clearing his throat, "you testified that people were running out the door, isn't that right?"

"Yeah. They're runnin', screamin', crying."

"Weee," repeated the trial bag, and Tom started hacking away like he had tuberculosis.

Judge Canova stretched out his neck in concern. "Mr. Moran, perhaps you should pause for some water."

"No, sure, well," Tom stammered. "Actually, Your Honor, if we broke for lunch, I could compose myself."

Judge Canova shook his head slowly. "I'd rather not, counsel. Let's do as much as we can. Please proceed. Perhaps some water will help."

"Yes, Your Honor," Tom said, a sickening feeling at the pit of his stomach. He choked down his water and glanced at the trial bag, which began to wobble slightly on the carpet. Tom froze. Brittany was awake, squirming inside the bag. She was hungry. She was thirsty. She was wearing an evidentiary motion.

"Please proceed, Mr. Moran," Judge Canova repeated.

"Yes, sir," Tom said, setting down his glass. "Mr. Fahey, you were downstairs with the screaming and the crying, correct?"

"Yeah. Everybody was yellin', runnin' for their lives."

"Weee," insisted the bag, and Harrison looked over again, arching an eyebrow.

"Mr. Fahey," Tom said loudly, to mask the sound, "you ran down the stairs to Chicken Bill's side, is that correct?"

"Yeah, he's lying there, all messed up. All burnt up, yeah."

"Weee," said the bag, and Tom coughed again. Out of the corner of his eye, he could see the courtroom sketch artist stop her drawing. A reporter blinked, holding his steno pad. The front pew of the gallery was looking in the direction of the trial bag. Soon Masterson would hear. *Jesus, Mary, and Joseph.*

"And you asked Chicken Bill who started the fire?"

"Yeah."

"Weeaah," said the bag, slightly louder than before, and Tom watched helplessly as the court reporter startled at the sound. Two of the jurors in the front row exchanged puzzled looks. Tom's heart jumped to his throat. What was he going to do? His coughing fit didn't work. Maybe if he just ignored it. He walked away from the bag to distance himself from it.

"Mr. Fahey," Tom asked, standing before the witness, "is it your testimony that Chicken Bill named Cowboy Ron as the perpetrator?"

"Yeah. That's what he said. Cowboy Ron did the crime." Elvis nodded in the direction of his new employer, but Ranell was staring at the trial bag.

"Weeah, weeah," said the bag, but Tom pretended not to hear. Behind him, he glimpsed Masterson shifting angrily in his pew.

"And while he was telling you who set the fire, the others were yelling and screaming?"

"Yes."

"WeeAh, weeAHHH," said the bag, getting hungrier, and the bailiff cocked his head at the noise. Next to him, the law clerk giggled, and the jurors in the back row were looking around, their heads swiveling toward the fussing.

Tom plowed ahead, apparently oblivious. "And they were running out the door, Mr. Fahey?"

"Yeah."

"WeeeeeAHHH," the bag said, a decibel louder. The jury was completely distracted by the noise, and even Judge Canova was adjusting his hearing aid. Then Tom realized something. Everybody could hear Brittany but Elvis.

"How did you hear what Chicken Bill said, with all that noise?" Tom said quickly, following a hunch.

"I heard him just fine."

"You heard him just fine, despite the screaming and yelling?"

"Yeah."

"Over the noise of the fire? The panic? The confusion?"

"Yeah."

"Weeeaaahhhh," fussed the trial bag, and only Elvis didn't react.

"Even though Chicken Bill was injured, near death, and speaking in a whisper?"

"I heard him," Elvis insisted, though he didn't flinch at the wailing that set the entire jury looking from the trial bag to Elvis and back again. Judge Canova craned over the dais and signaled to the bailiff. Suddenly Tom knew what to do.

"Don't you work in a firing range, Mr. Fahey?" he asked.

"Yeah, for three years. I clean up."

"You work while gunshots are being fired, correct?"

"Sure." Elvis snickered. "That's why they call it a firin' range."

"You don't wear earphones when you clean up, do you, Mr. Fahey?"

"No way. Them things are for wussies." Elvis *huh huh huh*ed at the jury, but again, they weren't laughing. They were grave, beginning to understand. Tom was giving them a reason to reject Elvis's testimony and they were going to take it. The gallery murmured among themselves. Masterson broke into a grin.

"Objection!" Harrison said, loud enough for Elvis to hear, but Judge Canova waved the defense lawyer into his seat.

"Mr. Fahey, isn't it a fact that your hearing has been impaired from your job at the firing range, so much so that you couldn't hear what Chicken Bill was saying to you?"

"Whut?" Elvis said, and just then the trial bag broke into an earsplitting cry.

"I have no further questions," Tom said, and rushed to rescue his cocounsel.

Later, Tom and Marie dozed on the patchwork quilt over their bed, completely dressed. The babies had finally stopped fussing, and snuggled between them. Ashley snored slightly as she slept, her breathing still congested. Brittany slumbered quietly. A golden glow emanated from a porcelain lamp on the night table. The alarm clock read 2:13 A.M. It was so late. Tom wanted to turn off the light but he was too exhausted to do even that.

"You sure you won't get fired, hon?" Marie murmured, half asleep.

"Nah. I'm a hero."

"I knew that already," she said, and stretched her toe to touch his, still barefoot.

"Is this sex?" Tom asked.

"Yes."

"Funny. I remember it differently," Tom said, and Marie burst into laughter. Tom closed his eyes, listening to his wife laughing and his children snoring, and realized suddenly that heaven itself was only a slight variation on this scene, with somebody to turn out the light for you.

Then he fell soundly asleep.

Afterword

I've been asked to divulge what inspired "Carrying Concealed," and my only excuse is that I have a soft spot for men like Tom Moran. Tom first appeared as a minor character in my novel *Rough Justice*, and he has integrity, brio, and a warm heart. He's handy with a diaper. He's a better Catholic than I am. And he's not Superman: like all of us, he juggles home and career, with mixed results. Above all, he loves being a father.

Which is a wonderful thing.

This anthology is scheduled to be published just before Father's Day, and my story is dedicated to the triumvirate of wonderful fathers in my life, my father Frank, my father-in-law Carl, and my husband Peter, who are all such successful, and such loving, jugglers. Thank you for everything, gentlemen.

—LISA SCOTTOLINE

ABOUT THE AUTHORS

WILLIAM BERNHARDT

William Bernhardt made his debut as a novelist in 1992 with *Primary Justice,* a national bestseller that went through eight printings in its first three months. Since then, he has published seven more bestselling novels, which have sold millions of copies and have appeared on bestseller lists all across the nation. Called by the *Vancouver Sun* "the American equivalent of P. G. Wodehouse and John Mortimer," Bernhardt is best known for the *Justice* series of courtroom novels featuring attorney Ben Kincaid *(Blind Justice, Deadly Justice, Perfect Justice, Cruel Justice, Naked Justice),* which inspired *Library Journal* to name Bernhardt the "master of the courtroom drama." He is also the author of *Double Jeopardy,* a suspense-thriller described by the *Washington Post* as a "breathless page-turner," and *The Code of Buddyhood,* a college-days coming-of-age novel described by the *Oklahoma Daily* as "a powerful and sophisticated novel about the nature of friendship." His books have been translated and published in more than a dozen countries. For *Perfect Justice,* Bernhardt received the Oklahoma Book Award for Best Fiction. In 1997, he was inducted into the Oklahoma Writers Hall of Fame. His most recent novel is *Extreme Justice*.

JAY BRANDON

Jay Brandon has a master's degree in writing from Johns Hopkins University. His novel *Fade the Heat* was nominated for the Edgar Award for Best Mystery of 1990. Jay has served as an attorney with the district attorney's office in his hometown of San Antonio, and with the Court of Criminal Appeals, the highest criminal court in Texas. He was a staff attorney at the San Antonio Court of Appeals and still practices criminal and family law.

Jay's sixth novel, *Loose Among the Lambs*, was a Main Selection of The Literary Guild. His 1995 novel, *Local Rules*, was selected as a Reader's Digest Condensed Book. In 1996 his first nonfiction book appeared, a history of practicing law in San Antonio called *Law and Liberty*.

Jay's novels have been published in more than a dozen foreign countries, and movie rights have been optioned by Steven Spielberg, Bill Cosby, and Burt Reynolds, among others.

Jay lives in San Antonio with his wife and three children. His next novel, *Angel of Death*, will be published this fall.

PHILIP FRIEDMAN

Philip Friedman, author of the international bestsellers *Reasonable Doubt, Inadmissible Evidence,* and *Grand Jury,* was born in New York City and raised in the neighboring city of Yonkers. He studied mathematics in college and graduate school before going on to law school, where collaborating on a short film taught him the joys of telling stories and determined the future course of his life. Like the unnamed protagonist of "Roads," he's driven cross-country a number of times, but never to argue a death-penalty appeal.

JOHN GRISHAM

John Grisham lives with his family in Virginia and Mississippi. His previous novels are *A Time to Kill, The Firm, The Pelican Brief, The Client, The Chamber, The Rainmaker, The Runaway Jury, The Partner,* and *The Street Lawyer.*

JEREMIAH HEALY

Jeremiah Healy, a graduate of Rutgers College and Harvard Law School, was a professor at the New England School of Law for eighteen years. He is the creator of John Francis Cuddy, a Boston-based private investigator.

Healy's first novel, *Blunt Darts,* was selected by the *New York Times* as one of the seven best mysteries of

1984. His second work, *The Staked Goat*, received the Shamus award for the Best Private Eye Novel of 1986. Nominated for a Shamus a total of eleven times (six for books, five for short stories), Healy's later novels include *So Like Sleep, Swan Dive, Yesterday's News, Right to Die, Shallow Graves, Foursome, Act of God,* and *Rescue*. His last book, *Invasion of Privacy,* was a Shamus nominee for Best Novel of 1996, and his current novel, *The Only Good Lawyer,* appeared in February 1998.

MICHAEL A. KAHN

Michael A. Kahn is the author of *Sheer Gall* (Dutton, 1996), *Due Diligence* (Dutton, 1995), *Firm Ambitions* (Dutton, 1994), and two other suspense novels starring savvy St. Louis trial lawyer Rachel Gold, who has been described by *Bookends* magazine as "a heroine for the '90s."

Mr. Kahn is a trial lawyer and a partner at a leading St. Louis law firm. He is also an adjunct professor of media law at Webster University. His novels have been translated into many languages around the globe.

Publishers Weekly has praised Mr. Kahn's novels for their "intelligent, breezy dialogue and clever plotting," and describes his latest, *Sheer Gall,* as "an intricate, suspenseful story." The *Orlando Sentinel Tribune* declared that "*Sheer Gall* and Rachel Gold are a great combination of wit, intelligence and inventiveness." In its review of *Firm Ambitions,* the *St. Louis Post-Dispatch* observed that "this clever series just keeps getting better."

PHILLIP M. MARGOLIN

Phillip M. Margolin grew up in New York City and Levittown, New York. From 1972 until 1996, he was in private practice specializing in criminal defense at the trial and appellate levels. As an appellate attorney he has appeared before the United States Supreme Court, the United States Court of Appeals for the Ninth Circuit, the Oregon Supreme Court, and the Oregon Court of Appeals. As a trial attorney, he handled all sorts of criminal cases in state and federal court, and represented approximately thirty people charged with homicide, including several who have faced the death penalty. He was the first Oregon attorney to use the Battered Women's Syndrome to defend a battered woman accused of murdering her spouse.

Since 1996, Margolin has been writing full-time. He has written five novels, all *New York Times* bestsellers. *Heartstone,* his first novel, was nominated for an Edgar for best original paperback mystery of 1978 by the Mystery Writers of America. His second novel, *The Last Innocent Man,* was made into an HBO movie. *Gone, But Not Forgotten* has been sold to more than twenty-five foreign publishers. It was the Main Selection of The Literary Guild. *After Dark* was a Book-of-the-Month Club selection. *The Burning Man,* his fifth novel, published in August 1996, was the Main Selection of The Literary Guild and a Reader's Digest Condensed Book. In addition to his novels, he has published short stories and nonfiction articles in magazines and law journals.

STEVE MARTINI

A writer before he was an attorney, Steven Paul Martini has worked as a newspaper reporter in Los Angeles and a capitol correspondent at the statehouse in Sacramento. To date Martini has authored six novels: *The Simeon Chamber,* his first, was published by Donald I. Fine, Inc., in 1988. His second novel, *Compelling Evidence,* was published by G. P. Putnam's Sons, Inc., and the Putnam Berkley Group in 1992 and became a Main Selection of the Book-of-the-Month Club. His third novel, *Prime Witness,* was published in 1993, and again was a bestseller, spending three months on the *New York Times* bestseller list.

Undue Influence, Mr. Martini's fourth novel in the legal venue, published in 1994, was called "the courtroom novel of the year" *(Kirkus). Publishers Weekly* called this book "a gripping courtroom drama," and said of readers, "by the time the trial starts, [they] will have their fingers glued to the pages." That book became a CBS miniseries. His novel *The Judge* was on the *New York Times* bestseller list in hardcover for seven weeks. His most recent novel is *The List.*

RICHARD NORTH PATTERSON

Richard North Patterson graduated in 1968 from Ohio Wesleyan University, where he now serves on the board of trustees. He is also a 1971 graduate of the Case Western Reserve University's School of Law.

Mr. Patterson studied fiction writing with Jesse Hill Ford at the University of Alabama at Birmingham; his first short story was published in *The Atlantic Monthly;* and his first novel, *The Lasko Tangent,* won an Edgar Allan Poe Award in 1979. Between 1981 and 1985, he published *The Outside Man, Escape the Night,* and *Private Screening.* His first novel in eight years, *Degree of Guilt,* published in 1993, and *Eyes of a Child,* published in 1995, were combined into a miniseries by NBC-TV. Both were international bestsellers, and *Degree of Guilt* was awarded the French Grand Prix de Litterateur Policiere in 1995. *The Final Judgment,* also published in 1995, became his third consecutive international bestseller. *Silent Witness* appeared in January 1997, and became an immediate international bestseller.

Mr. Patterson's newest novel, *No Safe Place,* which deals with presidential politics and the abortion controversy, will be published in August 1998. His occasional articles on contemporary society have appeared in such journals as *The London Times, USA Today,* and the *Washington Post.*

LISA SCOTTOLINE

Lisa Scottoline practiced as a trial lawyer at a prestigious law firm in Philadelphia, and also served as a law clerk for judges of the Third Circuit Court of Appeals and the Superior Court of Pennsylvania. She is an honors graduate of the University of Pennsylvania and of its Law School, where she was associate editor of the Law Review.

Scottoline won the Edgar Award, the premier award in suspense fiction, for her second legal thriller, *Final Appeal;* her first, *Everywhere That Mary Went,* was nominated for the same honor. Subsequent novels, *Rough*

Justice, Legal Tender, and *Running from the Law* received starred reviews in *Kirkus* and *Publishers Weekly,* and her books have been translated into over twenty languages. A native Philadelphian, Scottoline lives with her family in the Philadelphia area and invites readers to visit her website and write to her at http://www.scottoline.com.

GRIF STOCKLEY

Grif Stockley has been a lawyer for the past twenty-five years at the Center for Arkansas Legal Services, a non-profit corporation that is funded by the federal government to provide legal services to indigents in civil cases. In the last decade he has been honored as Citizen of the Year by the Arkansas Social Workers Association, and received the Jim Miles Advocacy Award from the Arkansas Foster Parents Association. In 1994 the Pulaski County Bar Association, the largest county bar association in Arkansas, named him as its Lawyer-Citizen of the Year.

He is the author of *Expert Testimony, Probable Cause, Religious Conviction, Illegal Motion,* and *Blind Judgment.*

ACKNOWLEDGMENTS

"The Divorce" by Grif Stockley. Copyright © 1998 by Grif Stockley.

"Poetic Justice" by Steve Martini. Copyright © 1998 by Steve Martini.

"Stairwell Justice" by Jay Brandon. Copyright © 1998 by Jay Brandon.

"The Client" by Richard North Patterson. Copyright © 1979 by Richard North Patterson. Originally appeared in *The Atlantic Monthly*. Reprinted by permission of the author.

"What We're Here For" by William Bernhardt. Copyright ©1998 by William Bernhardt.

"Cook County Redemption" by Michael A. Kahn. Copyright © 1998 by Michael A. Kahn.

"The Jailhouse Lawyer" by Phillip M. Margolin. Copyright © 1998 by Phillip M. Margolin.

"Voir Dire" by Jeremiah Healy. Copyright © 1998 by Jeremiah Healy.

"The Birthday" by John Grisham. Copyright © 1994 by John Grisham. Originally appeared in *The Oxford American*. Reprinted by permission of the author.

"Roads" by Philip Friedman. Copyright © 1998 by Philip Friedman.

"Carrying Concealed" by Lisa Scottoline. Copyright © 1998 by Lisa Scottoline.